PETER RANSLEY has written extensively for television. His BBC adaptation of Sarah Waters' *Fingersmith* was a BAFTA nomination for best series. His book *The Hawk* was filmed with Helen Mirren and he is a winner of the Royal Television Society's Writer's Award. His first novel in the Tom Neave trilogy, *Plague Child*, was published in 2011. *The King's List* is the final instalment.

D0916609

PETER RANSLEY

THE KING'S LIST

Harper
Press

Harper*Press*
An imprint of HarperCollins*Publishers*
1 London Bridge Street
London SE1 9GF

www.harpercollins.co.uk

First published in Great Britain by Harper*Press* in 2015

1

A catalogue record for this book is
available from the British Library

ISBN 978-0-00-731242-9

Printed and bound in Great Britain by
Clays Ltd, St Ives plc

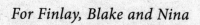

For Finlay, Blake and Nina

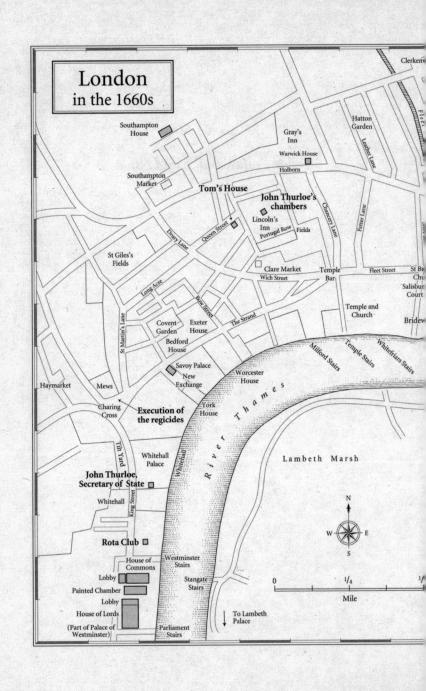

London
in the 1660s

Clerkenwell

Hatton
Garden

Southampton
House

Gray's
Inn

Warwick House

Holborn

Southampton
Market

Tom's House

**John Thurloe's
chambers**

Lincoln's
Inn
Portugal Row   Fields

Chancery Lane

Fetter Lane

Leather Lane

Fleet

Queen Street

Drury Lane

St Giles's
Fields

Clare Market

Wich Street

Temple
Bar

Fleet Street

St Br
Chu

Salisbur
Court

Long Acre

Bow Street

The Strand

Temple and
Church

Bridew

St Martin's Lane

Covent
Garden

Exeter
House

Milford Stairs

Temple Stairs

Whitefriars Stairs

Bedford
House

Savoy Palace
New
Exchange

Worcester
House

Haymarket

Mews

Charing
Cross

**Execution of
the regicides**

York
House

River Thames

Lambeth Marsh

Whitehall
Palace

Whitehall

Pall Mall

**John Thurloe,
Secretary of State**

Whitehall

King Street

Rota Club

House of
Commons

Westminster
Stairs

N
W   E
S

Lobby

Painted Chamber

Lobby

House of Lords

(Part of Palace of
Westminster)

Stangate
Stairs

Parliament
Stairs

→ To Lambeth
Palace

0   1/4   1/
Mile

Prologue

August 1659

On a bright, summer day I rode alone from London to Oxford, getting fresh horses by showing the ring that told the world I was Sir Thomas Stonehouse, Second Secretary of State and a mix of other titles and honours. These, not to put too fine a point on it, meant I was – or had been – Oliver Cromwell's spymaster.

Cromwell had been dead for eighteen months. His son Richard had succeeded him but had nowhere near the iron grip of his father on the country. Outside London, Oliver Cromwell's spectre still hung over the country. Some people could not believe he was dead. Others said his spirit had been seen at the great battlefields of Marston Moor and Naseby. Few wanted to rekindle that war except members of the Sealed Knot, Royalists who believed the executed King had died a martyr. They wanted revenge and the return of the King's son, who had done little for his country, except sire fifteen bastards at my spies' latest count. Some in the Sealed Knot were sincere. Most wanted their lands and power back.

My son, Luke, was sincere. When my steward, Scogman, told me Luke was a member of the Sealed Knot my first instinct was to confront him – not about being a Royalist, for he scarcely made that a secret, but about joining a hopeless, ramshackle conspiracy like the Knot. I dismissed this approach. Luke would not believe me. It would make things worse between us, and they were bad enough. I determined to let him find out for himself. The Knot leaked like a sieve. Simultaneous uprisings were planned in the north, the West Country and even in East Anglia, Cromwell's old heartland. Luke was part of a group planning to take over an armoury in Oxford. I could have told him who would let him down, the county gentlemen who would promise money which would not be paid, or troops who would not arrive. Instead I would let him find out for himself. He would be arrested. Scogman would see he was not charged or gaoled but brought straight back to me.

It would be a salutary lesson, better than any I could give him. He would be contrite, realising how false his friends were, how hopeless the Royalist cause was. England would never see a King on the throne again, least of all the self-proclaimed Charles II, who begged his way from one European court to another. I would be magnanimous. Because of the war I had rarely seen Luke as a child. This would bring us closer together, giving me the father–son relationship I had always wanted.

So I imagined until the rebellion grew closer and Scogman set out for Oxford. He wore bucket boots with a jump jacket of oiled leather, and carried an old-fashioned broadsword and a pistol. I not only felt a flood of nostalgia for the war, but the weapons brought me to my senses with a jolt. Years at my desk had given me the mind of a planner, not a soldier. I began to think like a soldier again and a soldier – unlike a politician – knew that nothing went according to plan. My intelligence might be wrong. It could be a full-scale rebellion. Luke might be killed.

When I reached Highpoint, my estate in Oxfordshire, I learned the intelligence was right. One of the leading Royalists in the county,

Sir Simon Barber, had been bought with land he had lost during the war. The others would not move a finger without him. From information Barber gave us some were arrested.

'Including Luke?' I said with relief.

Scogman shook his head. Luke had disappeared. From that moment the plan I had carefully constructed to bring my son to his senses, and the two of us closer together, fell to pieces.

Although the uprising was a dismal failure everywhere else, Sir George Booth, an excellent soldier and well-liked in his county, managed to raise 4,000 men and hold Cheshire and part of Lancashire for several weeks. This inspired Luke and a group of hotheads to try and take over an armoury. It was a foolhardy project; the sort Cromwell used to dismiss with contempt as going for glory, not results. Scarcely more than boys, they were too young to have fought in the war and were dying to distinguish themselves for their King. Two did. Several were wounded, including Luke. I made sure he was kept in a separate cell. I hired a coach and removed my ring so only the gaoler knew who I was and, with Scogman, went there late one evening.

It was hot and muggy. The stench of the gaol hit us through the windows of the coach. We clamped nosegays of herbs tightly to our faces.

'You'll need those, sir,' the gaoler said. 'Time of the year for gaol fever. Found one of them dead in his cell this morning.' He spat reflectively as he selected a key. 'Unless it was the plague.'

I silently cursed my stupidity. A fine lesson if Luke died from it! He had never been very well ever since he had suffered a bad burn to his face in the riots in London at the end of the war. Although she never said anything, I knew my wife Anne blamed me for not allowing them to shelter with her friend Lucy Hay, the Countess of Carlisle, because I suspected she was a Royalist.

'Hurry, man!' I said, almost snatching the key from the gaoler. Then, when he was about to insert it in the lock I stopped him, putting a finger to my lips.

Luke had a beautiful voice, which rang out like a church bell. What he was saying was the last thing I expected to hear.

> *'When Love with unconfinèd wings*
> *Hovers within my Gates;*
> *And my divine Sarah whispers*
> *At the prison Grates …'*

There was more. It was a poem by the Royalist poet Richard Lovelace, written in his cell. After lying 'entangled in Sarah's hair', the poet says, the very gods 'know no such Liberty'.

A hollow knocking came from the cell next door, and one of Luke's fellow prisoners joined in. His voice was much more feeble but its import just as determined as they chanted that when they sang about the glories of the King, 'the winds that curl the Floodes know no such liberty'.

I signalled to the gaoler. Far from stopping them, the sound of the key redoubled their defiant chanting of the final line. There was so little light from the barred window, I could see only a shape sprawled on a stone bench. As the gaoler opened the door further, the candles in a corridor sconce lit up his face. Few would have thought us father and son without the hook of the Stonehouse nose. There the resemblance ended. At seventeen, the fresh, tight curves of his good cheek held the lofty arrogance that only a privileged upbringing on an estate like Highpoint gives a man. The raw, rippled skin of his burned cheek, which at first had made him a withdrawn child, now only emphasised that absolute assurance, as he realised people often took it as a badge of the war he had never fought in.

Most people saw the same assurance in my face, but it was skin deep. Once I had believed in the republic as Luke believed in the King. I still did, but not with the enthusiasm of the child of the streets I had once been. Years of working with Cromwell, of looking for a form of government that would work without falling back on the army, had convinced me that power came first. If I looked in the mirror, which I seldom cared to, I saw a man who looked older than his thirty-five years, whose cheeks were rather too pink from sweet sack, and whose once fiery red hair was a dull copper streaked with grey.

The rush of relief when I saw that Luke was not only well, but apparently in rude health, was followed by anger both at his fool-hardiness and my weakness in not leaving him to take his punishment. At first, with the gaoler blocking his view of me and Scogman, he did not see us.

Luke gave the gaoler a long, languid look and raised a declamatory hand. 'When I think of my sweet King … a gaoler with his keys knows no such liberty!'

'Well said, Luke!' called the prisoner next door.

My anger was redoubled when the gaoler touched his forehead to Luke. 'Beg your pardon, sir –'

I pushed him to one side. Luke stared at me as if I was an apparition, before turning the good side of his face away. It was a habit of his when he was with me. The muscles were more rigid on his scarred side and made his expression difficult to read.

'Get up.'

Slowly he uncurled his legs and rose. He was an inch or two taller than me. I flung a nosegay at him. He caught it, then let it fall amongst the straw littering the floor.

'Did you have anything with you when you were taken?'

When he did not answer, the gaoler said, 'Packed and ready, sir. To be signed for. Thank you, sir!'

This when I tossed him a Cromwell, a half crown which he caught with the dexterity of a swift catching a fly, moving to bite it before his finger ran suspiciously over the edge to check its validity. It was the first coin to be milled at the edge against forgeries. It frustrated me beyond measure that from small innovations like this to large ones like the world's first professional army, Cromwell had transformed the country in a way that the gentlemanly but hopeless and untrustworthy King Charles had never done, yet my son and his friends called Cromwell a devil and Charles a saint.

The light caught Cromwell's head on the coin. Luke stared at it and found his voice. 'Where are you taking me? The Tower?'

I only just stopped myself from smiling. One moment Luke frustrated me, the next he touched my heart. He lived in a world of fancy. I was about to tell him we were going home but Scogman got in first.

'The axe is being sharpened at this very moment, Mr Luke.'

There was no love lost between them. Luke complained that Scogman was not a proper steward, for he could not write or add up, except in ways that suited him. In other words he was a thief. Not having served in the army, Luke did not realise that there were normal accounts and army accounts. I knew perfectly well what Scogman was doing. He did it out of habit, for the thrill of it, mostly for someone else, usually a woman he fancied. It was small stuff. At the same time he was ferociously loyal to me.

'I want the same treatment as everyone else,' Luke said.

'This is not a game!' I said. 'Come.'

He knew that tone, that manner. Automatically, he began to follow me, stumbling against the piss-bucket. He almost immediately righted himself, but Scogman made a move to grab him and save him. Luke must have misinterpreted that as an attempt to frogmarch him out of the cell. He lashed out at Scogman, winding him.

The bucket went over, spilling its contents over Scogman's boots. No one was more conscious of his status than Luke. Now, in a blind rage that a servant he despised would dare to lay a hand on him, he aimed another blow. Scogman caught Luke's flailing fist and twisted his arm behind his back.

'Easy, Mr Luke, sir, easy,' Scogman said.

This mixture of control and deference inflamed Luke even further. The more he struggled to get away, the more pain he inflicted on himself, but he would not give up.

'Enough!' I said. 'Release him.'

Scogman did so. Luke staggered into the gaoler before sprawling against the wall, rubbing his arm, tears of humiliation pricking his eyes. I was tempted to leave him there and be done with it, but Anne would never forgive me. My wife found an excuse for his every fault.

'Luke. Your mother is not well.' I hated saying it but it was the easiest option and it was partly true. Anne was sick with worry about him. There was no one he cared about more than his mother. I was convinced that was the problem. She alone had brought him up, eschewing nurses when he was a baby. Even after the war they lived in the country, which they loved, while my work with Cromwell kept me in town.

Luke's reaction was immediate. He forgot his humiliation in his concern for her, asking what was wrong. I would not answer, angry at both myself for my deception and at him that concern for his mother meant far more than any respect for me. But there was no more resistance, physical at least.

'God bless the King in heaven!' he shouted as we walked down the corridor.

'And the King across the water!' answered the man in the next cell.

Their cries were picked up by other prisoners. The shouts and the drumming on the cell doors could still be heard as our coach went off into the night.

PART ONE

The Perfect Marriage

Autumn 1659

The rebellion was soon put down. I brought Luke and Anne to London on the pretext that they would be safer with the guards I had there, but they saw it for what it was: a form of house arrest for Luke. I tried to make him see that there was no chance of the King returning. He could see what little support he had from the abject failure of the uprising. The army generals who were in control would eventually stop arguing and a new leader to replace Cromwell would be found. Then it would be business as usual.

He stood on the worn patch of the carpet in my study, where I had once stood as a rebellious bastard before Lord Stonehouse, and said nothing.

I tried reason. It was not his beliefs, I said. He was as entitled to them as I was to mine. If more people wanted a monarchy, it would return. But too many people had gained too much land during Cromwell's reign to want the King back. That was why all the Oxfordshire gentry who had made promises before the rebellion had not lifted a finger to help him and his friends when they were in prison.

He stood fidgeting in his bucket boots and floppy linen, staring straight in front of him, rigid in silence.

I tried diversion and flattery. He was mad about horses and had a very good eye for them. Would he go with the ostler to a horse fair and buy a pair?

His eyes gleamed for a moment, then he bit his lip and said nothing. Finally, I gave him an ultimatum. He could have his complete freedom and go into the City alone if he promised to have nothing more to do with the Sealed Knot and took no part in any further plots.

He stood rigidly to attention. He may even have clicked his heels. 'I am sorry, sir,' he said, in his beautiful, clipped voice, a real Stonehouse voice which Anne had made sure he acquired, unlike mine which slipped, sometimes intentionally, into the sound of the London streets where I was brought up. 'I am sorry. I cannot do that.'

I almost ordered Luke to dismiss, but that was part of the problem. He wanted to be a soldier. He had missed the war. Perhaps he believed that if he and his friends had fought, the Royalists would have won.

I sighed. 'Go away and think about it, Luke.'

'I suppose it's too late to beat the French dog,' said Scogman hopefully. He called him that because, in the manner of the man he declared to be his King, he dressed in French fashions: short doublets and increasingly wide-legged breeches which seemed about to fall from his hips. 'You could cut his allowance.'

I would not do that. Beatings and other punishments had never worked on me. Nor would I let him be cooped up, although I insisted that Scogman went with him into the City. Anne agreed with that, at least. She wanted no more trouble.

People believed we had a perfect marriage. It certainly was a perfect relationship, but only because we rarely saw one another. Love had gone. It went for me when I became convinced Anne was taking potions to prevent having another child.

The child might have been another little Liz, who had died in infancy. Or another son, giving me the chance to be a better father. Once or twice I even unlocked the left-hand bottom drawer of my desk, and took out the papers on my bastard son.

It had happened when I was a Leveller, struggling after the rebellion for rights for the people. I had broken up with Anne and lived with a girl called Ellie. But then I had returned to Anne, and it was only by chance, years later, that I discovered I'd had a son with Ellie. I paid to have him brought up at Half Moon Court, in the house where I was raised, and still owned. I gave him a rudimentary education. Nothing fancy. He had no idea of my existence, believing the man Ellie lived with, a candle-maker to whom he was apprenticed, was his father. The file I took out of my drawer was marked: *Samuel Reeves. Closed.* Payments had stopped when he was indentured. Each time I took it out with the intention of throwing it away. It was pointless, stupid to keep it. Anne had no idea of his existence. But each time I put it back.

Apart from Luke, Anne's child was Highpoint, our great estate in Oxfordshire. Estates were in decline. The extravagant years, when noblemen were expected to bankrupt themselves on the chance that the King might visit, went with his execution. The mood was, as one churchman put it, that 'a house had better be too little for a day than too great for a year'. Even so, Anne improved the classical facade and opened up the lofty hall to the great sweep of the imposing staircase. She had an eye for paintings which lived, as she put it, rather than just hung. Many were bought cheap at Parliament's 'Sale of the Late King's Goods', a chaotic affair in Somerset House where dusty masterpieces were crammed amongst tapestries and chipped statues. She spotted dirty Titians and neglected Van Dycks, and had them restored and reframed to their original beauty. Her gardens were marvelled at. I admired Highpoint, but could not live there. Its builders, staff, stables, brew houses, granaries and farms drained most of our money. While she spent it in the country, I economised in town. It suited us both.

It gave her the pleasure of creating it and me the power it emanated. We saw one another at glittering occasions there where I was Sir Thomas Stonehouse, charming to the county, most of whom were covert Royalists. Lady Stonehouse – I called her that at first, in a slightly mocking way, until, as the house gained in eminence, it became impossible to call her anything else – put on her sober dress and mien when she came to town to entertain Cromwell and the other old generals who ruled the country. Cromwell would call me Tom, but he would never dream of calling Anne anything other than Lady Stonehouse.

So we believed it would continue until the family grave at Highpoint (she had already planned it) bore not one of those stiff, heraldic memorials that were going out of fashion, but a personal portrait that recorded our enduring love and affection for one another.

2

Like a pebble in a pool, the summer rebellion made a small impact but caused wide ripples. There was unrest in the City. Mutterings that there would be a tax strike if a successor to Cromwell was not found soon. I had the usual vitriolic letter from my father, Richard Stonehouse, threatening what would happen to me when the King returned.

Cromwell had given me Richard's estates and made me Sir Thomas Stonehouse, in return for supporting him and signing the King's death warrant. I had done it for Anne, who had become so obsessed with the place she had fallen into an illness from which I was afraid she would die. It was also true that Richard's father, Lord Stonehouse, finally intended me to have it. He feared Richard's profligacy would destroy the estate, but had died before he could complete a new will. Richard saw it much more simply: I had seized Highpoint by signing away the King's life. The estate was blood money. To my father, I was what I had always been: Tom Neave, bastard, scurrilous pamphleteer, usurper and, worst of all, regicide – King killer.

At erratic intervals, from different parts of Europe, my father sent me such letters. Under Cromwell, who had built up a powerful navy as well as a full-time army, Britain had become the most feared nation in Europe. In those years I could afford to throw Richard's incoherent letters into the night soil without reading them. Now the armies – there was not one but several – were beginning to disintegrate. Soldiers had not been paid. Their generals quarrelled. Montague, who headed the navy, was suspected of being involved in the rebellion and there were moves to put him in the Tower. I read my father's letter with more than usual care.

He praised Luke for his courage and part in the rebellion. With all my father's old contacts in Oxfordshire, I wondered if he had deliberately involved Luke in it. In the same post was a letter for Anne from her old friend and mentor, Lucy, the Countess of Carlisle, who was in Brussels with the makeshift court of Charles Stuart. I had rescued her from the Tower, but Cromwell had exiled her for spying for the King. Now she was spying for me. Her letter was full of gossip about penniless dukes and duelling courtiers and – principally – about Mrs Palmer, Charles's new mistress.

'She has enslaved him,' Lucy wrote. 'When she is in the room he cannot take his eyes from her. She is planted of course, by the Villiers family – she was Barbara Villiers – for their benefit, if the King ever crosses the water. The whole place is alive with the feeling that it is going to happen but I am afraid we have all heard it so many times before & everyone is as poor as ever & the food just as vile.'

Anne, as usual, gave the letter to me for my amusement and, as usual, I took down my Bible to decode it. It made disturbing reading. Far from discouraging the Royalists, the failed rebellion had made them even more determined. Lucy gave figures for a large number of troops from Ireland. There was money from Europe and the West Country. Richard was heavily involved. He had played a major part in the summer rebellion.

It was late evening when I decoded the letter. I went from my study to return it to Anne. The door of Luke's room was open as was that of the anteroom of Anne's apartment. He often slipped in to see her, to agonise over the width of a pair of breeches, or the colour of a cloth. I could hear the murmur of her voice from the corridor and was raising my hand to knock when Luke spoke.

'When I have the estate I will have a proper steward, not that rogue Scogman.'

Her reply was inaudible but I could guess she agreed with the sentiment. She had her own house steward at Highpoint, a correct and punctilious man. I went into the anteroom. Unlike the rest of the house, which was dark and gloomy, she had, in a short space of time, made her rooms bright with fresh paper and a few of her favourite pictures. There was no sign of her maid and I raised my hand to knock again.

'Of course, Grandfather will have Highpoint first,' Luke said.

She loathed Richard much more wholeheartedly than I did and once would have had him killed by Cromwell if I had not interceded, but her reply was chiding, indulgent. 'Oh. Will he. Then what will happen to your father and me?'

'Oh … don't worry. I will protect you, Mother.'

It was banter. She did not take him seriously, but still I could not trust myself to speak. If I had gone in he would have thought I was spying on him, which, by that time, it was impossible to deny.

I returned to my study and picked up my father's letter. Luke's grandfather would have Highpoint first, would he? Again I wondered if my father was in contact with Luke, and picked up his letter.

Richard Stonehouse was a threat to the state. That was how John Thurloe, the Secretary of State, for whom I worked, regarded him. Throughout fifteen years of turmoil and change, whatever people thought of his methods, John Thurloe had kept a steady hand on the affairs of state. He had built an admired and feared network of contacts, spies and informers that made one ambassador say: 'He has the secrets of Princes in his pocket.' Not just princes. Nobles, gentlemen, politicians, merchants, lawyers, ministers: anyone of any consequence was recorded in papers at his offices in Whitehall. He was one of the few people with Cromwell when he died. Cromwell trusted him implicitly. So did I. I knew what he would say about my father – he had said it often enough.

'Write to Amsterdam.'

In other words, have him killed by our agent there. I had always recoiled from it. Thurloe thought it was a sign of weakness, but it was not just that he was my father. What was the point? He was a pathetic figure with no real hope of his King returning. But I could not stand the thought of him poisoning my son's mind.

I had much more to do but Luke's words and Anne's indulgence continued to irk me. I felt excluded in my own house. I had put Luke under house arrest but, in a curious way I did not fully understand, I felt I had imprisoned myself.

I flung down my pen and had a glass of sack while I shrugged into my shabby old Brandenburg coat. Anne would call a servant to put on a coat but I detested all that formality. A servant sprang up from the booth in reception, the gold embroidered falcon glittering on his cuffs. He was new – Anne had been dissatisfied with some of the staff – and for a moment I could not recall his name.

'I am going to the club. Would you be good enough to tell Lady Stonehouse that I shall not be in for supper?'

No, I did not want the coach; nor the ostler to get my horse. I went down the steps into Queen Street, turning surreptitiously to put two fingers up to the austere stone falcon over the entrance. With a feeling of release I breathed in the stink of the streets, walking my legs back to life through Covent Garden towards Parliament. There, swathed in the mists from the river was New Palace Yard, a huge open space full of eating houses, taverns and coffee houses. Coffee had taken London by storm, almost overnight, like pantaloons and feathers in hats. It was in the Turk's Head Coffee House that the Rota Club met.

It was a pretend Parliament. A republican debating society that anyone with eighteen pence could join and have a vote. Cromwell had purged Parliament, reducing it to a small number – the Rump – until even that had been dismissed. With historically a large Royalist majority he could never have governed. Yet he never reformed it. God would provide the answer. God never did, and there we were, crammed into the smoke-filled Turk's Head a few steps from Westminster, the republican Parliament that might have been.

The eighteen pence included coffee and pipes of tobacco. I found the coffee foul, boiled thick as soup and bitter, but many sniffed appreciatively and were very knowing about different Turkish blends. It certainly kept people sober and the debate fierce. As novel as the coffee was the Balloting Box. The motion was put and every member dropped his ball in the Aye or the Noe section. That evening the question was whether a Minister should serve a fixed term only and it was decided he should, to avoid consolidation of power.

We streamed into the night, flasks of Dutch brandy coming out to take away the taste of the coffee, and the real business began. William Clarke, whom I used to dub 'Mr Ink' in our republican days, took me to one side. He was now rather grand and staid, being secretary to the Committee of Safety, the hotchpotch of army officers that ran the country.

'Lambert won't fight,' he said, taking a pull from my flask. Lambert was the general who had put down the summer rebellion. He had gone north to subjugate another general, Monck, in charge of the Scottish army, who had refused to join the Committee of Safety, declaring it illegal. 'His troops are not paid. Some of them are without boots.'

He slipped me a paper, containing army movements and committee minutes. It was old, thin stuff, some of it rehashed from what I had seen before. He read the disappointment in my face and took another drink from my flask.

'What happened at the last meeting?'

He wiped the brandy from his lips. He looked ill and feverish. 'I wasn't there,' he said. 'I was excluded. How can I take the minutes of a meeting when I'm excluded?' He addressed me as if I was personally responsible, almost immediately muttering, 'I'm sorry, Tom. It used to be difficult to know who will be in charge tomorrow. Now I scarcely know who is in charge today.'

I laughed. 'Don't worry, Bill. This will be very useful.'

In other words, like Lucy, he would be paid. I ended the evening in a chop house with Sam Pepys.

We had both climbed out of the streets, his father having been a tailor. His patron, Lord Montague, was under suspicion of involvement in the summer rebellion and Pepys had lost his position as his secretary.

'So I have nothing to do, which is bad, and no money to do it with, which is worse, unless Lord Montague is reprieved …?'

He looked at me hopefully. I concentrated on my mutton chop in pomegranate jelly. Montague was able, if a little headstrong, and I had put a case for him but John Thurloe was adamant. Montague would go to the Tower. When the Secretary of State made a decision it was final. Montague was finished. I complimented Pepys on his choice of eating house. Only a good chef could turn a tough old piece of mutton into such a rare delicacy.

He made a face at me and sighed. 'Then I am done. I will have to while away my hours writing a diary.'

'A diary?'

'A record of each day. Big events. Plenty of those. There's a new government every day. Small ones – the sort of things you and I get up to.' He gave me a prodigious wink.

'How are you going to sell it?'

'Sell it?' He looked shocked. 'I'm writing it in shorthand. I could never sell it. My wife might read it.'

He roared with laughter and I ordered another bottle of claret to launch his new enterprise. By the time I stumbled out of the Hackney in Queen Street I was only too glad for James in reception – I remembered his name and used it several times – to help me out of my Brandenburg coat.

Two or three times a week I found my way to the offices of the Secretary of State in Whitehall. I say 'found' because the old palace in which Cromwell had installed government offices was a labyrinth in which even servants got lost. After going through the Elizabethan Great Gate, past buildings with crumbling timbered gables, I snaked through a warren of twisting corridors which seemed to get narrower and narrower, taking me past room after room of state papers before reaching John Thurloe's apartment overlooking the river.

He never wasted time and greeted me with no more than a nod. I gave him the figures Lucy had sent me.

'How sound are they?'

'I don't know. But Richard Stonehouse is at the heart of it.' In Thurloe's presence, I never referred to him as my father.

He shrugged. He had trained as a lawyer and counted his words. Words cost money. He had said all he had to say about my father, and the ball was in my court. Although I expected nothing, it was always worthwhile, when making a concession, seeking a quid pro quo.

'I wonder if it's wise to send Montague to the Tower?'

He stared at me coldly and I thought I had gone too far. With his dark eyes set rather too close together in a thin, cadaverous face, it was like being observed by a surgeon planning to operate. At last he spoke.

'As it happens, I've been reflecting on what you said. I'll send him to the country instead.'

'I'll write to Amsterdam about Richard Stonehouse.'

Another nod and he returned to the papers he was working on. The interview was over. I was surprised and gratified about Montague. I was almost out of the room when he spoke again.

'Tom.'

He never called me Tom. Perhaps Sir Thomas; usually he dispensed with names altogether. When I returned he was gazing out of the window at the hazy line of the river, watching the press of boats going under London Bridge. Two boats had collided and an argument had erupted.

'If you're going to do it, you'd better get on with it. I expect I shall be out of office next week. Or shortly after.'

I thought I had misheard him. He continued to stare down the river as if the accident absorbed all his attention. Oars were pushing the quarrelling boatmen to one side and the other boats resumed their steady flow.

'Out of the office?'

He turned his full gaze on me. There may even have been a hint of amusement on his face at my bewilderment. 'Out of office. The Committee of Safety is yesterday's story. They have caved in to General Monck. The Rump Parliament is to be assembled to er … run the country, led by Arthur Haselrig.' There was a wealth of dry scepticism in the hesitation. 'Arthur has been good enough to inform me that I will not be invited to join the State Council.'

I still did not take it in.

I could find nothing to say. If he was out of office, so was I. The boatmen had settled their difference and were steering back into the stream of traffic.

'I suspect we shall be wanted again,' he said. 'I suggest we meet once a week at my chambers in Lincoln's Inn.'

I stammered something, which he interrupted with a final nod before returning to his papers.

I got lost on the way out in the web of alleys that linked small courts and gardens, where the first piles of fallen leaves were being swept away. I had to be directed by the gardener to the Great Gate. It was a bright, unseasonal day. I walked aimlessly back to Queen Street. I badly needed a drink, but dare not. Everyone seemed busy but me, from hawkers crying to gentlemen in coaches on their way to the City. I did not have the heart to raise two fingers to the falcon over the door, but hurried up the steps, suddenly realising how much there was to do.

Everything that I had put off I did that day, coming to a decision on problems that had seemed intractable yesterday, dictating to my secretary, Mr Cole, until the servant came to light the candles. I left my father till last.

'There is one more.'

I had coded the letter a year ago, after a particularly vitriolic letter from my father when Cromwell died. The code was embedded in a letter ordering some diamonds from a jeweller in Amsterdam, one of our agents. As proof that the job had been done, I requested him to send Richard's ring. If Mr Cole did not know what it meant, he knew what it signified. He had done enough such letters for Richard's father, Lord Stonehouse, including one ingeniously condemning me as a plague child, which should have resulted in my death. His only reaction was to push back his long white hair and rub his wrist with a sigh of relief.

'Mr Thurloe has kept us busy today, sir.'

'He has indeed, Mr Cole.'

I said no more. He would know soon enough. I poured myself a large sack and raised it to the portrait of Lord Stonehouse over the flickering fire. Anne thought it dreadful – 'even worse than he looked in real life, if that were possible' – but, for me, it was an old companion. In the shifting light of the candles and the fire, my grandfather's smoke-blackened face with the beaked Stonehouse nose seemed to come alive. That evening I thought he looked disapproving. No Stonehouse had been out of office since before the reign of James the First.

I finished the sack. I considered going to the club but, with my sudden loss of influence, felt disinclined to, and found, for the first time in years, I had nothing more to do than go down to supper.

3

The first sign of unrest in the City is always when apprentices, egged on by their masters, begin to riot. They were roaming the streets, hunting down Quakers, a sectarian group which the City saw as a serious threat to order. Church ministers hated them because they were against tithes and interrupted services. I came across a group of them when I rode through Covent Garden on my way to my weekly meeting with John Thurloe.

It had been raining since early morning. Some of the Quakers had no outdoor coats and the feet of their children were bare, but their eyes shone exultantly as they chanted. A growing group of apprentices jeered at them, but their singing only grew louder. I tried to force my horse through. The apprentices tipped or drew off their hats at me.

'Remove your hats for the gentleman,' yelled an apprentice at the Quakers.

He was provoking them. They acknowledged no social betters and whatever tattered scraps they wore remained firmly on their heads. The rumble of an approaching carriage caused the apprentices to cry out in increased fervour.

'Off with their hats!'

One caught a woman a stinging blow on the head. Her bonnet flew off. The blow scarcely interrupted her singing but the child with her flinched and darted away, stopping when she saw the carriage. There was no danger. The coachman saw her, slowed and turned away the horses. But the occupant of the carriage, no doubt in a hurry, rapped loudly with his stick. The coachman jumped, lost the reins for a moment and the horses panicked, heading straight for the child. There was an innocence in her mud-stained face, a curiosity in her widening eyes as she stared towards the tossing heads, the shafts that were about to impale her.

There are some instincts that, however rusty, spring back into life. It was the cavalryman I had once been who drove his horse between the carriage and the child, diverting the horses towards the street posts and helping the coachman bring them back under control.

The apprentices had stopped shouting and the Quakers singing. The child had not moved. She still had that fixed look of curiosity on her face. I picked up her hat, which had been swept off in the draught from my horse, and gave it to her. She turned and ran, disappearing into the group of Quakers.

The door of the carriage scraped open, its occupant so corpulent he could extract himself only with the aid of the footman, whom he berated, before flinging abuse at the coachman.

I found my breath. 'You should leave your coachman to do the driving, sir.'

He moved to face me at the speed of a ship turning round. His fat cheeks narrowed his eyes into slits. 'You should leave the country, Sir Thomas, to those who know how to govern it.'

I had not seen Sir Lewis Challoner for years. Cromwell had thrown out Royalists like Sir Lewis, creating the Rump Parliament, which had now returned, giving the army some semblance of legitimacy. It was another sign of unrest that, in spite of his part in the rebellion, he was back.

'Go home, Sir Lewis. You are banned from the City.'

He smiled. Suddenly he was enjoying himself. 'You are forgetting yourself, sir. You are dislodged from office, are you not, Sir Thomas?'

The singing began again, this time on a triumphant, exalted note. A man was holding up the child I had saved. He was an odd figure in that crowd, dressed in sailor's slops, a coloured jumble of canvas doublet, breeches and linen shirt, tight-fitting to avoid being caught in the rigging of a ship. At his side stood a woman who would soon be in danger of wearing no clothes at all. She was flinging away her tattered skirt and beginning to remove her blouse, the singers round her chanting in ecstasy. The apprentices watched in a mixture of stunned disbelief and licentiousness. I had heard of this Quaker rite, but never seen it. The woman reached a state of euphoria where the innocence of Eden came upon her and compelled her to remove her clothes before God entered the garden, asking who told her of her nakedness.

In this attempt to return to a time before sin she had unpeeled her blouse, revealing breasts which, from bearing children, were as shrunk as old leather wine bottles. Perhaps the girl perched on the sailor's shoulders was her child. Far from feeling the cold and the driving rain, the woman embraced it, her skin glowing with effort, drawing superstitious awe from the watching crowd.

Except for Sir Lewis. What was innocence for her was the utmost depravity for him, a consequence of the religious licence Cromwell had given such pernicious sects.

As she dropped the blouse in a pool, spurning it with her dancing feet, Sir Lewis ordered his footman to seize the whore while the coachman went for a constable.

'If there still is anyone keeping order in this Sodom and Gomorrah,' he said.

'Leave her,' I said to the footman. 'I will deal with her.'

Sir Lewis lost all restraint. The brooding sourness built up during his enforced exile burst out of him. He looked the arrogant, despotic hanging magistrate I had first met years ago.

'You? You can do nothing! You are one of the creators of this evil!'

The woman, now naked, danced in a mounting frenzy, matched by the insistent rhythm of the Quakers' singing, accompanied by the apprentices, whose shocked outrage had been overwhelmed by prurience. They outdid one another in nudges and jokes, gazing lasciviously, their handclapping, which had begun with a mocking slowness, increasing in speed until it matched the ecstasy of the singers.

'Your master Thurloe has been sacked. You have no power. No position. It is you who should flee – if you can, regicide!' He spat the word out. 'There was a ballot to be on the jury of those who killed the King. I was lucky enough to win a place.'

When you have been in power for a decade you do not lose it overnight, whether it has substance or not. 'Get in your coach, Sir Lewis, or I will bring an action against you for endangering the life of that child.'

'That slattern –' he began, but saw the look on my face and turned to shout at his coachman to open the door.

I strode over to the crowd. The apprentices stopped clapping when they saw my expression. Disgust and outrage began to return to their faces at the sight of the naked woman.

'Stop her,' I said to the sailor.

'I cannot. She is with the Lord.'

I told an apprentice to fetch a constable. 'Name,' I said to the sailor.

'Stephen Butcher,' he said, with one of those beatific smiles that made me want to strike him across the face.

I knew of him. He was one of the followers of the Quaker preacher James Nayler who had re-enacted Christ's entry into Jerusalem by riding into Bristol on an ass. I had wanted Nayler to be dealt with quietly, but he had been charged with blasphemy, flogged, and his tongue bored. As I feared, his supporters had increased tenfold.

There was no sign of the constable. The apprentices were looking at me expectantly, itching to be told to lay their hands on the woman. Blood oozed in a muddy rivulet on one of her feet where she had cut herself on a stone, but she seemed unaware of it. I looked away but, in spite of myself, could not keep my eyes from her. Shrivelled as her breasts were, her gyrations and the look of ecstasy on her uplifted face smoothed out its lines, giving it a strange, mesmeric beauty, and leaving no doubt that the girl who had nearly been killed was her daughter.

Her dance not only took the years from her; it took them from me. Anne's body was a distant memory. When the urge came on me, Scogman found me a whore. Working for Cromwell late into every night had killed the desire even for that. I was not sorry. I thought of love, if I thought of it at all, as a false god, a spy within which robbed a man of his secrets and left him helpless, out of control. I had seen many men ruined by love; I had almost been destroyed by it myself. Had not my relationship with Anne become immeasurably better without love?

As I stared at the twist and turn of the woman's rump, I caught the sailor's smile, more knowing than saintly. I snatched up her clothes and thrust them angrily at him. 'Cover her.'

'Is that what your voice is telling you?'

I had had enough of the Quakers and their inner voices. I flung the clothes at him. 'Do it!'

Without the smile leaving his face, Stephen Butcher picked up the clothes. 'Martha,' he said. 'Martha.' He seemed to be calling her from a great distance, for at first she did not respond. But the mood was broken for most of the Quakers, whose singing gradually stuttered to a stop. That slowed the woman's dancing but did not stop it. Like a top, her whirling became a stagger until the sailor caught her by the arm. She gazed at him dizzily, as if she did not know him. He held her patiently until she regained her balance.

'Martha,' he said gently. 'He is here. The man who saved Hannah's life.'

She looked at him blankly, her breasts heaving as she drew in great gulps of air, and then at the clothes he was holding out to her. 'I heard the Lord coming. I heard him. I saw him!'

'Put them on,' I said.

Martha took a step towards me. The lines were folding back into her face. Stretch marks slackening her belly suggested several children. 'The sin is in your eyes, not in my clothes.'

Butcher dropped the blouse over her head and held out her underskirt. At least he was a pragmatist, I thought – he had seen the approaching constables. Automatically, Martha hooked the blouse to her skirt. Her body disappeared, except where the wet rags clung to it. Momentarily, perversely, before the constable came up to me, I felt I had destroyed something.

'Lewdness in a public place,' I said to the constable.

'Your name, sir?'

His colleague dug him in the ribs and pointed to the falcon ring on my finger. 'I beg your pardon, Sir Thomas.'

He seized Martha roughly, although she made no resistance. Some of the crowd bowed their heads; others began singing. Her daughter Hannah stood staring, thumb in mouth, before flinging herself at her mother. I suspected Martha was a recent convert, for the girl had absorbed none of her piety. When a constable pulled her off, she bit him, momentarily freeing her mother, yelling that they would escape to Spital, beyond the walls. Incensed, the constables began to drag them both away. Martha broke down and began to struggle, pleading with the constables that her daughter had the flux, and would die in gaol. This was a fine show for the apprentices, who liked nothing better than seeing the rewards of sin – unless they were committing the sins themselves – and began jeering and applauding.

I cannot say why I acted as I did next, for it was quite out of character. Perhaps the girl crying that they would escape to Spital, like her dancing mother, brought back to me the time of my life I preferred to forget.

'Leave them,' I said.

The constables stopped, staring at me uncomprehendingly. The girl half-wrenched away, screaming as a constable twisted her arm behind her back.

'Release them,' I snapped.

The girl immediately turned to run. Her mother stopped her, giving me a bewildered look which changed into one of gratitude, tinged with the piety that so aggravated me. The apprentices, robbed of their prey, began to mutter rebelliously.

'Arrest him,' I said, pointing at the sailor, Stephen Butcher.

'On what charge?' said the constable whose hand had been bitten.

'Incitement to lewdness.'

In Puritan England there was no distinction between sin and crime. Adultery had become a felony, and, just as Eve picked the apple, it was invariably the woman's fault. The apprentices moved threateningly towards me, but one of them, who from his superior clothes looked like a lawyer's clerk, cried: 'We have a Solomon amongst us. He has arrested the whoremaster, not the whore.'

The apprentices switched in a moment from threatening me to applauding me. 'The whoremaster not the whore,' they chanted.

Hannah stood puzzled, her thumb in her mouth again. She whispered to her mother, who pointed to me. Hannah darted over to me. She looked as if she was about to hug me but the thought of her flux, and the stench that came from her, made me draw away in disgust and she made a strange genuflection, somewhere between a bow and a curtsey, before fleeing back to her mother.

Stephen Butcher went without resistance, but stopped as he passed me. The constables attempted to jerk him away, but they might as well have tried to move one of the ships he sailed in. His muscles bulged under his linen shirt as he anchored himself in front of me. There was a livid scar on his neck and one of his ears was twisted out of shape. For a moment I thought the smile on his face was a feint and he was about to strike me, but in a voice as gentle as melted butter he had a much more cunning blow to land.

'Your voices are telling you different things. Listen to the right one.'

4

When Anne and Luke first came down from the country we had a variety of dinner guests, chosen to avoid politics: lawyers, doctors, City merchants and the like. Luke was perfectly mannered and scrupulously polite, but remained at a distance. At first Anne did her best. She sparkled and drew the best out of me. But whereas her table at Highpoint was the most sought after in the county, full of wit and life, this was hard work.

Everyone knew Luke was there under duress. It was impossible to ignore and equally impossible to talk about it without the risk of an explosion or a penetrating silence. Gradually Anne's sparkle died and she became as mechanical as Luke. I felt that, with her growing desire to return to Highpoint, tacitly she was taking his side, but would not give up. More and more guests found excuses not to come; others were reluctant to go out as the nights drew in and the disturbances increased.

Often the table was reduced to the three of us, as it was on the evening after the confrontation with Sir Lewis Challoner. Conversation ran out during the grouse soup, with stewed carp, ox tongues, fricassee of rabbits, lobsters, a choice lamprey pie, tarts and sweetmeats to come. I ate and drank well, both to cover the growing silences and because, although out of office, with Thurloe I was keeping my hand in, preparing – perhaps plotting would be a better word – for the next government. I had fallen into the bad habit of taking documents to the table, as I did when I lived alone. I finished my soup and began to glance through the documents.

Anne, who had scarcely had a mouthful of soup, dropped her spoon. A servant scuttled from the wall to give her another. She gripped it as if she was about to fling it at me. 'I cannot stand this place!'

She stared directly at me, as if she meant it was me she could not stand. The servants were as still as the hunters woven into the tapestry behind them. Luke gazed at the piece of lamprey pie embedded on his fork. It was so quiet I could hear a candle gutter, and the rustle of silk as her bodice rose and fell. Side ringlets of her hair, normally carefully arranged, were in disarray. Among them a bead of sweat gleamed. Disconcertingly, at that moment, I wanted her. It was extraordinary how familiarity had stopped me seeing how young she still looked. She had avoided the constant ravages of childbirth that aged most women at thirty. The guttering candle went out, snatching away the ringlets and the tightly laced bodice, sketching there the lines of the haughty, scornful, but in some strange way vulnerable, girl I had first met.

A servant sprang to replace the candle. With it came back the ringlets, the sumptuous dark green of her dress and the measured voice of Lady Stonehouse.

'I mean, sir, it is so dark and gloomy.'

I picked up her manner with relief, mingled with a lingering regret. 'We are not spending money on Highpoint, madam. Why not employ your talents here?'

She took a sip of soup. 'He would not approve.'

She indicated another portrait of Lord Stonehouse, which hung over our proceedings. When I dined alone, if I noticed him at all, I always saw him as a stern but comforting presence for, in spite of our differences, we were alike in one thing: we both hated extremes, and struggled to keep things together rather than let them fall apart.

'He is not here to stop you.'

'His ghost is.'

'Nonsense.'

'He haunts the place. He does not want us here. When his wife died he spent all his time here. As you do.'

She began calmly, almost flippantly, but again her voice shook and the implication of what she had said only seemed to strike her when she had spoken. She dabbed her lips, her hands trembling, said she was out of sorts and begged to be excused. Luke and I finished our meal in silence. I went up to her apartment to enquire after her. Her maid, Agnes, told me she was not well and had retired for the night. Agnes had come from Highpoint and I sensed her disapproval as she put away Anne's dress. The crackle and sheen of the silk, black then sharp green as it caught the light, aroused me again. I took a step towards her room. The maid turned to me enquiringly. I felt my cheeks burning like a schoolboy as I brought out some stilted phrase about wishing her ladyship a good night, and almost walked into a chair on the way out. Her ladyship! For the first time it struck me that what had kept us together had also kept us apart.

I tried to work. I had a report for Thurloe on the City I must finish. Together with the generals, money would decide the next government. Everything was in the balance. I knew the hidden vices of every alderman in the City: who might be bought, sold or persuaded. But every time I began writing, the crackle of the paper brought back the lustre and sheen of her dress. Her ladyship! She was a printer's daughter from Farringdon. I saw the rain gleam again on the twisting rump of the Quaker woman. That was how it had started. Of course. A good whore was all I needed. I had not been to Southwark for a long time.

The lantern clock in the hall showed midnight. Was it really that time? It was too late and too dangerous. And the servants would know. They knew, or sensed, everything. Somehow I could not bear it reaching her. The indecision raged around in my head. Normally I fell asleep as soon as my head touched the pillow, but that night I slept little.

Up late, stupefied from lack of sleep, I enquired after her again. She was still indisposed. Indisposed! Far from going away, my sudden, inexplicable desire for her had grown during the night. It was absurd, laughable, to have a wife and not have her if I chose. I pushed past the maid. As well as brightening the place, she had altered the layout of the rooms. I found myself in the changing room next to the bedroom. It was full of the smell of her, herbs which I fleetingly recognised, like lavender and sage, intensified by some aromatic oil. A shift of voluminous white linen lay ready to be stepped into. Crimson-faced, the maid snatched up a linen cloth. The sharp, acrid odour reached me before I caught sight of the blood staining it. The maid thrust it among the dirty washing.

It was the time of her flux, her flowers as the delicate put it. I turned away, muttering apologies, covering my nose. I did not, like the uneducated, believe that the woman's flux turned wine sour and sugar black; but, being nature's device to upset her humours, it might affect mine.

On the landing I saw Luke, who was going in to see her, and told him she was still not well. 'She is missing Highpoint, sir,' he said. 'As am I.'

For a moment I was tempted. Highpoint was probably safer than London. I longed for the even tenor of what had been virtually my bachelor life. I could concentrate my energies on trying to influence what the next government would be. But I saw the hope and expectation in Luke's face and dismissed the thought. He might get up to anything near Oxford with his Royalist friends. I told him curtly it was better if we stayed together.

He bowed his head. 'Then can I go out alone, sir?'

'If I have your assurance that you will have nothing more to do with the Sealed Knot.'

He tightened his lips stubbornly. 'Then can I have a guard other than Scogman?'

'He is not your guard. He is your companion.'

'He is not respectful, sir.'

'Enough! You will do as he says.'

Nevertheless, a day or two later, I told Scogman to be more respectful. He looked astonished and said no one could possibly give Luke more respect. 'Even when I'm insulted I turns the other cheek.'

'He insults you?'

'He calls me a bilker and a leather-mouthed prig.'

I was shocked that Luke knew such thieves' cant, let alone used it. Perhaps he picked it up in his short stay in prison. I took a guilty pleasure in enjoying the thought that Luke might be less of a gentleman than he appeared. The fact that there was some truth in Luke's allegation started to bring a smile to my lips, but Scogman was displaying such righteous indignation I bit my cheeks and looked at him sternly.

'A bilker. When was this?'

'At the Moor in Watling Street. He told me to wait outside, sir, while he had a coffee. When I told him I would follow him casual-like, as if we did not know one another, he said I was like a pair of frigging darbies round his ankles.'

This time I could not prevent a smile coming on my face. The Moor Coffee House was frequented not by Royalists but by shipping merchants and posted news of ships. There was a reason for Luke to go in there. The Highpoint estate owned part of a ship and Luke had shown an interest in it.

'Let him go in there.'

'Alone?'

'You are always telling me you cannot stand the coffee there.'

'Foul-smelling Turkish piss.'

'Wait for him in the alehouse next door then. They could do with some of the business they're losing to the coffee houses.'

As a scout in the army Scogman had sensed trouble like a rat smelling a ferret. He had that look now, his lips tightening belligerently. 'Very good, sir. But he's up to something.'

It was a little later when I asked Agnes about Anne's condition that the thought occurred to me. Curious that I had been so repelled by the sight of that bloodstained linen pad, it had never occurred to me. If she was still bleeding, she could bear a child.

5

I was determined to be as formal in my approach as she was. I even considered calling her into my study. After all, was not having a child a business like any other? A business at which I had singularly failed? Luke was weak, a milksop who ran to his mother, easily led by others. Scogman believed a good flogging was the solution but it had never worked for me. I believed with Thomas More that a whip should have the violence of a peacock's tail. In any case it was too late. When he was building the New Model Army Cromwell used to tell me that selection was more important than training. You could not train damaged goods.

I would have to start again. In the end I did not call her into my study. It would have been unheard of. To my knowledge no woman had ever been in that room, save the maid who cleaned it. Lord Stonehouse frowned from his picture above the fire at the thought of it. It was curious that, since she had remarked on it, I saw him everywhere: portraits in little-used rooms, one in the library I had never noticed before. There were no pictures of me. It was as though I was a temporary resident. She said so at one of our stilted dinners.

Strange, also, how dark the place had become since she had mentioned it. I noticed as never before how the tapestries smelt of soot and how grey the walls were in contrast to her apartments, where I had made an appointment to see her. It was as dark as evening in the corridors, but became afternoon in her drawing room. I had not seen her since she was indisposed, and was struck dumb at the sight of her.

She wore dark blue silk which was almost black, white lace and a single diamond in her hair. Her skin was translucent and paler than the lace. She had ordered tea unless I preferred coffee or chocolate? There was a selection of sweetmeats which I remembered from Highpoint, but which never appeared at Queen Street, including small sugar cakes of which I was inordinately fond. My hand went out to them but I withdrew it. Business first.

The words I had prepared flew out of my head. She seemed genuinely pleased to see me, saying it was kind of me to visit her. Or was there some kind of edge to it, as if I had just arrived from a distant town?

'Should a husband not visit his wife, madam?'

It was what I called Highpoint language, the sort of social glue that had kept us together for so long, as comfortable as slipping into an easy chair. I was sorely tempted to do so. After all, these things took time, like an angler catching a fish.

'Ah,' she smiled. 'But you have not been treating me like a wife, sir.'

She could only mean one thing, surely. I sat painfully upright, her words, accompanied by that smile, which was like a distant memory, giving me such an instant arousal I had not had for years. I shifted uncomfortably, seeing for the first time the virtue of Luke's fashionably wide new britches. I swallowed. I could not get rid of the wretchedly light Highpoint tone with its accompanied fixed smile.

'That, that is precisely what I have come to amend, madam.' The pain from my tight britches was so excruciating I had to walk about. 'I wish to visit you.'

She was picking up her bowl of tea. 'But you are visiting – oh. I see.' Tea spilled on her dress. I pulled out my handkerchief but Agnes appeared from nowhere with a cloth. When she had gone and fresh tea was poured Anne went to pick up her bowl, but did not trust her shaking hand. Her cheeks had coloured but when the blood retreated it only emphasised how pale she was. She looked at me directly, a thin blue vein at the side of her forehead pulsing.

'When I said treating me like a wife, I meant, sir, you have shown little concern for me while I have been ill.'

'I'm sorry. I did not realise you were so ill.'

'Were you not told?'

'Yes, yes, of course I was, but ...' What was the use? Why did I not say what I wanted, as other men did? Why did she always put me on the wrong foot? She always had from the very beginning! I wished I could go back and start again with that welcoming smile. No, no. That was contrived. She played this game far better than I ever could. All this, as I paced about on the pretext of looking at her pictures which she must have brought from Highpoint, for they were all from the King's Collection. Whereas the pictures in Queen Street were blurred with dust and dirt, these were as bright as if painted yesterday. One I could not take my eyes off was an enigmatic picture of a woman, fully clothed, while another, naked apart from a stole which had drifted over her sex, leaned over her. A puckish-faced child was absorbed in his own play on the stone bench between them.

'Naturally, I will prepare myself,' she said. 'You only have to tell me when.'

When? I could have taken her there and then. She was as calm and inscrutable as the clothed woman on the stone bench. That made her even more maddening. Her hand had stopped shaking and she was taking a sip of tea, as if we were discussing an alteration to the east front at Highpoint, which always troubled her. But was that not what I wanted, what I had planned? A business transaction? The object was not the treacherous will o' the wisp of desire, but the solid certainty of having a child, who would be different. My child, not hers.

I bowed. 'Thank you.'

The worst was over. The rest would happen at night. Agnes would be instructed, the door left open. Wait, wait, wait. I stared at the picture. The clothed woman seemed to have a mocking smile on her face. Prepare herself? What did she mean by that? I remembered when Highpoint had first taken over her life. We were still together then. We even talked about love. Did I really say something inane like I loved her when I first saw her, when I did not hate her for mocking my large, bare feet? She certainly said that she fell in love with me when she discovered I had greater prospects than putting boots on my ugly feet. She said it as a joke, but I began to believe it to be true when her body became as cold as the stone bench I was staring at. At the time of that first move to Highpoint I had wanted a child, a child brought up in peace, which I thought would bring us together. One never came. That was when she became wedded to Highpoint and I to the power I had just lost.

My throat was so dry the words came out with a hollow, parched ring. 'When you say prepare yourself –'

She must have signalled for Agnes, who, when I turned, was staring at me as if I was about to suggest some bestial act. Her mistress dismissed her with an agitated gesture. For the first time she looked at a loss.

'I want to have another child.'

'You do.'

Her maid must have been listening, they always were, but I no longer cared. This was what other men and women took for granted.

Scogman was astonished I felt I had to discuss it. Have her and be done with it, was his philosophy. The last thing he wanted was a child. If one appeared, he disappeared.

'Another child. Yes. So I would be grateful if you –' I strode across to a door which led to the bedroom and maid's room and pulled it open. Agnes was bent so close to the door she fell towards me, only just stopping herself. She gaped up at me open-mouthed before scurrying into her room and slamming the door. 'Grateful if you and your maid took no steps to prevent it.'

The blue vein in her forehead thudded as if to burst out of her skin. She tried to fish out a leaf floating in her tea. She kept missing it. It seemed the most important thing in the world to catch that leaf. When she had done so, she stared at it and said in a voice so low I had to bend to hear her: 'I am afraid it is not possible for me to have another child.'

'It is perfectly possible. You are still bleeding.'

She gave me a shocked look of fear and disgust. I was in the uncharted territory of *Secreta Mulierum* – women's secrets. I had become so obsessed with having another child that for the first time in years I had not worked from early morning to night. I had cancelled my appointments with the City aldermen I had promised to persuade or cajole. I had not even seen John Thurloe. Why should I? He was no longer First Secretary of State and I was no longer in power with him. The state would right itself without us. A general would shoulder his way through the pack to replace Cromwell. Then we would be needed. Instead I read every book on reproduction I could lay my hands on, from old texts which held women to be leaky vessels whose menstrual blood poisoned children and gave men leprosy when they had sex with them, to more modern texts which criticised the secret world of women delivering women where an impatient midwife in a slow labour might yank off a baby's hand or foot.

I interrupted my reading only when I realised that, from the number of days which had passed since the bleeding I had seen, my wife was, as one account put it, at the apex of her fertility.

She opened the door as if about to follow the maid, then slammed it shut, turning on me. 'No gentleman would speak of such things.'

'As you used to say often enough, I am no gentleman.' I almost retorted that she was no lady, but that was the problem. She was. She was far more of a lady than most women of aristocratic lineage. She was a lady from her exquisitely small feet to the sculptured bones of her face. She was accepted by Royalists as such without question, whereas I, who had aristocratic blood, was dismissed by them as an upstart.

She told me she could not bear having another child. At least that was how I heard it. Her old friend and mentor, Lucy, the Countess of Carlisle, who had no children, wrote pamphlets against late child-bearing, which, she declared, ruined a woman's figure and her health.

I was having no more of this. 'It is your duty to bear one,' I said.

She clenched her hands, colour flooding her cheeks. 'Don't you understand? I don't mean I don't want one. I can't have any more –'

Tears choked her words. We had been so far apart for so long that I thought it was an act. But only for a moment. She flung her hands over her face. She could not stand tears, her own least of all. She hated losing her composure but walked about as if she had lost her senses, knocking into a chair. I caught it and put my arm round her.

'Please don't touch me.'

She groped at her chair as if fearing it was insubstantial before sitting heavily, taking in air with great rasping gulps.

'I'll get the maid.'

She shook her head violently. A blue tint from her eyelids was smeared down one cheek. Apart from that, the colour had fled her face again and she was deathly pale.

'Doctor –' She began to cough.

'Get a doctor?'

'No!'

Nevertheless I determined to get one and picked up the bell to summon Agnes, but that seemed to distress her more. She pointed to the tea. I held out the bowl. Her hands were shaking so much she could not take it but breathed in the infusion. Gradually the gasping subsided and her breathing returned to normal. She took a sip, then a few more until her eyes began to close and the bowl tilted in her hands. I took it from her. The room was hot, the fire blazing, and I thought she was falling asleep. Then something between a sigh and a shudder ran through her body.

'Dr Latchford said I must not have any more children.'

'When did he say that?'

She jerked up in her chair and stared at me, as if I was a stranger who had just walked into the room. 'I am sorry, sir. I … have not been myself.' Her dress had ridden up, showing her ankle and crumpled shift. She smoothed them down and, apart from the blue smear on her cheek, looked as composed as ever.

I began to bridle again. Another ruse! 'When did Dr Latchford say you must not have any more children?'

'After our third child was born.'

'Third …?'

She nodded. I thought in spite of her matter-of-factness, the effect of the flux was still unbalancing her mind. The books I had been reading had spoken at length about the woman as a weaker vessel, whose unstable womb bred irrational fears.

'Anne,' I said gently. It was the first time I had used her name for months. 'We have only had two children.'

She jumped up, saying the room was suffocating. I opened a window, but in spite of the chill air beads of sweat formed on her forehead.

'There was a third child,' she said.

6

A strange calm came over her. Although the room rapidly became colder she would not have the window closed. A thin breeze drew the sound of a street crier, selling poor jack, crabs and eels. Traders' cries were growing longer and more persistent as indecision over who would take over the country went on. Trade was seizing up, jobs were scarce and there was less money for people to buy.

It was the year after the first war ended, she told me: 1647. 'You were away,' she said bitterly. 'As usual.'

'You mean the child was not mine?'

'Do you think I would bear a child who was not a Stonehouse?'

I believed that. Oh, I believed that. I envied other men whose wives were unfaithful with someone of flesh and blood whom I could kill. But what could I do when she was in love with stone pillars?

'But we did not sleep together.'

'Oh, we did, sir. We did.'

It flooded back to me as if it was yesterday. It was she who was desperate then to have another child. A male child to find favour with Lord Stonehouse and increase my chances to inherit. When Luke was born, Lord Stonehouse furnished the house he had given us. When the second child turned out to be the little girl I loved passionately, Lord Stonehouse barely gave us a grunt of acknowledgement.

Anne loved me then. She wanted me in her bed then, although she was thin, ill, and had been warned by Dr Latchford to wait until she recovered. Oh, I remembered. World Upside Down – she went on top of me like a whore. She was still Anne then, not Lady Stonehouse. We laughed, joked, we talked not bantered, we looked into each other's eyes. We were in love. Oh, I remembered that time.

She was quite still by the window. The fish crier had been joined by a fruit seller, a woman who called hot codlings with 'pears-and-lemoooooons!'

Again I wondered if it was a fantasy. I had been back briefly during that summer and seen no sign of her being pregnant. But it was impossible to tell with the stays which ballooned out the dresses. A terrible thought occurred to me. The child had been a girl, another girl like little Liz, and she had got rid of her.

'Another girl,' I said harshly. 'Is that what it was?'

She continued staring out of the window. Her voice was so soft I could scarcely hear her against the cries from the street.

'A boy.'

Her voice broke. The breeze strengthened, whipping a gust of smoke from the fire. It billowed around us. She began coughing and I shut the window and led her back to her chair. The tea was cold but she would not let me call the maid. She took tiny sips until her coughing abated, staring into the fire. Rather than warm her, it seemed to make her colder, for however close she crept to it she kept shivering.

'Was it the fire that caused it?' she said. 'The smoke? Or the riots? But there are always riots.'

She seemed to ask the question of the glowing, shifting coals, not me. For the first time it occurred to me that, as I had done, she had split herself into two halves. It was the Anne she had once been, a distant, remote figure whom Lady Stonehouse, in that impeccable voice, was questioning.

It was one of them, or all of them, she answered herself. The riots were the ones that broke up Parliament before Cromwell took over. I had been in the thick of it, while my own house was burning. She turned on me then. It was the old Anne, full of bitterness and contempt, but how I preferred that to Lady Stonehouse's icy indifference.

'You were never there,' she kept whispering, as if the incantation expressed our whole story.

She told me it was not only Luke's face that was damaged in the fire. She was seven months pregnant. Perhaps eight. She went into labour as she was trying to comfort Luke at her close friend Lucy's house – the house where she would have been when the fire happened, if I had not forbidden her to go there because I suspected her old friend and mentor Lucy, the Countess of Carlisle, of spying for the King.

Her face was flushed from the fire, but still she shivered. 'He was perfect.'

'A boy?'

'A boy.' Her voice was hollow, a mere wisp of sound.

'But how could I not have known?'

I shook my head as she turned, the answer coming to me. Arriving late – always too late – that burning afternoon and believing them to be in the house, I had made a futile attempt to rescue them, sustaining injuries from which it took me weeks to recover.

'He was perfect,' she repeated.

'Was he?'

She nodded, cradling her arms as if she was still holding him. The warmth of the fire enveloped us, shutting out the rest of the room. I bent over, picturing him as she described him. A mischievous smile crossed her face, a smile from years ago, young, eager, hopeful.

'He was not so much of a Stonehouse.'

'No?'

'Well, the nose, of course. But he had your red hair …'

'Not my terrible red hair!'

'I swear it. He was like you … I kept thinking his eyes would open –'

Her voice choked off. I held her. She was like a small bird I once held who could not fly, still but constantly trembling. Gradually, in fits and starts, she told me how she would not release the child, refusing to believe he was dead. Only when Dr Latchford and Lucy told her she might lose Luke as well did she let him go. He was buried with Liz. Mr Tooley said prayers over him and christened him.

'What did you call him?'

'Thomas.'

The servant lighting the candles knocked but I told him to return later. She rubbed her elbows as if they had just borne the weight of a child. The coals had burned down to a dull flickering crimson. One fell on to the tiles.

'Why did you not tell me any of this?'

She stared at the eddying shreds of smoke from the fallen coal. Only when I snatched it up and flung it into the fire did she answer. 'Do you think you would have kept it a secret?'

'A secret? Why should I keep it a secret?'

'Exactly!'

Just as it had been then, she went from an unexpected closeness to sudden acrimonious bitterness.

'You would never have kept it to yourself. When Lord Stonehouse heard, that would have been the end of it.'

Of course. With a burned child, frail as Luke was then, a stillbirth and no prospects, Lord Stonehouse would have written us off. A pity he didn't, I thought. Now she did not want any more children because she had what she wanted. She was about to call the maid to see to the fire and the candles, but I stopped her. I wanted the darkness to continue, the closeness to return. I kissed her, gently, tentatively. Her eyes closed and for a while she leaned against me.

'We could try again.'

'Again?'

She rose, looking around her as if she had just woken in a strange place. In a spurt of light from the fire she caught sight of a smear of coal dust on her cheek. She dabbed at it with a cloth. Like an actor slipping from one role to another, with each touch her reserve seemed to return.

'I am sorry, sir. I told you. I cannot, must not, have another child.'

I felt the stupid formality that had kept us apart for so long creeping back into my own voice. 'If that is true, madam, I will of course abide by it. See Dr Latchford again. That is all I ask.'

She put down the cloth. 'Very well.'

I found myself giving her a formal bow. Halfway through it I had a spurt of uncontrollable rage. She had Dr Latchford in her pocket. 'And I would like another opinion. From a doctor of my choice.'

She rounded on me. 'You have a son!'

'Luke?'

It came out then. All I had been brooding over since Luke and Anne had been in London that winter. The burning of his face, I said, his scars, his damaged childhood, that was my fault. I had always accepted that. I had done everything I could to make amends. He had had the best doctors, tutors and, when I discovered horses were his passion and would draw out those sickly humours, some of the best stables in the country. There was nothing I would not do for him. He stood for everything I despised. Well, that was common enough. The son rebelling against the father. I bore even that. He was entitled to his opinions, obnoxious though I thought they were. How did he repay me? By joining that rebellion. I warned him against it – not because it was Royalist but because I knew it would be a disaster.

'And you expected him to believe you?'

I retorted that she always took his side. She had made him into a milksop. I should have done what other fathers do and taken the whip to him.

That would have been better than ignoring him, she said acidly. Most of the time I was never there. When I was I had been cold, distant. What I had given him was money, when what he really wanted was a father.

And so on. I stopped listening, for it was at that precise moment the thought struck me. Why was I arguing when I had all the power I needed to do exactly what I wanted? No sooner were the words in my head than I spoke them. 'I intend to change my will so Luke will not inherit.'

7

I locked myself in my study and would not see anyone, even John Thurloe who wrote that the situation was getting critical. It was remote, but possible that the King might return. I scarcely finished Thurloe's letter. The situation was always critical.

What consumed me and kept me awake in the middle of the night was that bizarre outburst when I said I was going to change my will. At first it felt like an explosion of temper. A fit of pique. An empty threat. Anne certainly read it as such. She retorted I could not do it because the estate was entailed to the eldest son. But Cromwell had broken the entail. The estate was mine. I could dispose of it in any way I wished.

'Who would you leave it to?' she demanded.

'To whom would you leave it?' I corrected.

That was the end of the conversation. Her voice and manner were so impeccable, she loathed it when I corrected her grammar. But she was right. To whom would I leave it? A candle-maker?

It was she who had put the thought into my head. 'You have a son.'

Indeed I had. One she knew nothing about. The bastard that came when I left Anne to live with Ellie and became a Leveller.

Apart from me, only Scogman knew of his existence. I had met him only the once, when he was a boy, too young for him to remember. He believed the candle-maker who lived with Ellie and to whom he was apprenticed was his father. Ellie had been sworn to secrecy. I trusted her – but, just in case, had made it clear that if she broke that trust she would lose the house. I took the file out of my drawer. *Samuel Reeves. Closed.* As soon as I looked at Scogman's scrawl, noting that, through the years, at a cost of £109 8s 6d, he had been indentured, fed, clothed, educated so he could write and sign his name, add, subtract and multiply and progress from candles to candlesticks, the ludicrousness of the idea struck me. A candle-maker!

I shut the file in my drawer again, but could not shut it out of my mind. Deciding to scotch the idea once and for all and destroy the file, I rode to Farringdon.

It must have been early afternoon when I slowed my horse at the beginning of Cloth Fair but the low dark clouds gave it the pallor of evening. Spots of rain were falling. A figure came out of Half Moon Court. At first it was not the man I recognised, but his bag, the leather cracked and split so that the cupping instruments gleamed through. Dr Chapman used to come regularly to bleed Mr Black, the printer who had apprenticed me. I watched him go towards St Bartholomew's, a limp distorting his old, familiar bustle, feeling an unexpected pang of emotion. A voice called out after him and I gripped the reins in shock.

The youth who ran out of the court was myself. He ran for the joy of running, as much as to catch Dr Chapman and hand him some instrument he had forgotten. He was as polite with the old man as if he had forgotten the instrument himself, before striding back to the court, drops of rain gleaming in hair as red as fire. The hair was as brash and coarse as mine used to be. I tried to turn away as he saw me across the street and checked his stride. But it was merely to touch his forehead deferentially before vanishing into the court, whistling.

If I had thought for a second, I would not have done anything so stupid. But I was not thinking. Old forgotten feelings I thought had long gone rushed into me. I tethered my horse and, like one of the spies I employed, slipped through the entrance into the court. It was empty. The apple tree stood forlornly in the centre of the court, the last of its dead leaves hanging limply from it. I slipped behind it as I used to do as a child. There was no sign of the youth – Samuel. I had almost forgotten his name. A candle was burning in the room above the shop. Below the gable, where a half moon had swung when I was an apprentice printer, was the sign of a candlestick.

The rattling of a pail came from the coal shed. I was about to retreat from the shelter of the tree when I heard a woman's giggle, then the youth's voice.

'Mary, please don't distract me.'

'Dis –?'

'Stop me from working.'

'O, it is impossible to do that, sir. You are always working.' Her voice had a knowing pertness, followed by a deep sigh of regret.

The shed door creaked open, throwing light on the pair. The maid's apron was smeared with grease and her face marked with acne, but I could see how the tilt of her chin and the line of her breasts roused him. *What fools we are at that age*, I thought, with a growing sense of disappointment – *and not only at that age, perhaps.*

Now I was closer, I could see he was not like me at all. It was the hair more than anything. That and the Stonehouse nose. But it was the eyes that drew the attention, black, mild and enquiring; that, and his large roughened hands, tradesman-dexterous as they turned over a jagged piece of coal. My disenchantment deepened. Well, nothing fancy, I had told Scogman when he was planning his education, and nothing fancy was what I had got. Coarse and unkempt, he looked what he would always be: a candle-maker. I began to move back towards the entrance.

'These are the coals for the kiln, Mary. Not these. They have too much sulphur in them. You can see the difference.'

'Show me.'

She leaned forward, her dress dipping so he could see the curve of her breasts. I could feel the charge drawing them together like metal to a magnet. I turned away and had almost reached the entrance when out of the house came what sounded like the hollow beat of a drum. For a moment I was a boy again, running upstairs to my old master, who when he was ill, used to strike the floor with his stick.

'Go to my mother, Mary,' the youth said. 'The doctor has just cupped her.'

Mary came out of the shed with a flounce and saw me before I could reach the gloom of the entrance. She gave me a curtsey, followed by a look of curiosity. She was staring at my ring. In the dimness the glittering emerald eyes of the falcon seemed to produce their own light.

'Sam!' she called.

'See to my mother,' Sam ordered, emerging from the shed.

Hastily, clumsily, I pulled on my gloves. Sam brushed coal dust from his breeches. There was a smear of coal across his cheek. His nails were as engrained with filth and coal as mine used to be with ink.

'Were – were you looking for me, sir?' he said, with a slight stammer.

I was struck dumb by being such a fool as to come here. I clasped my hands behind my back as if afraid he could see the ring through the gloves. My initial warmth at seeing him was swept away by close sight of this gawky youth whose head seemed too big for his body, and the creaking old house, whose gable seemed about to topple into the courtyard. Was this really where I had come from? Where I had been brought up? Anne, who had a more pitilessly realistic memory than me, had been right never to come back here. It was little more than a hovel.

I was about to ask him directions to get to Holborn when he said: 'Are you the g-gentleman Mr H-Hooke said might call?'

'Mr Hooke?'

'Mr Boyle's laboratory assistant?'

I had not the slightest idea what he was talking about but there was something so eager, so hopeful in his manner, I began to relent a little from my summary dismissal of him. And curiosity bit me. Laboratory? What on earth was he getting involved in?

'I might be,' I grunted.

He must have taken my hesitation as a reaction against the squalor of the place, since he apologised for it, saying his father had recently died and he was only just putting the house to rights.

'He was a candle-maker,' I said.

He stared at me. He had the peering eyes of someone who does much close work. I pointed to the sign of the candle swinging from the gable.

'He made candles after the war,' he said, seeming ashamed of candles. 'When things were bad. P-people always need candles. He was trained as a glass-maker and he taught me. He was a w-wonderful –'

He turned away as his voice caught. I was both touched by this feeling for the man he thought his father and felt an obscure stab of pain for something I had lost, although how could I have lost something I never had? Mixed with it was a twinge of jealousy. Would Luke have anything like this reaction for me?

'I'm sorry, sir.' His eyes gleamed. 'Won't you come in?'

I could feel the heat from the kiln as we approached the house. From upstairs came a murmur of voices.

'Who? What sort of cove, Mary?' The voice, coming from upstairs, was weak and querulous but the strong Spitalfield accent came back to me as if it was yesterday. I stopped on the step. The last person I wanted to see was Ellie.

'He's a customer, Mrs Reeves.'

'That'll be the day!' Ellie laughed. 'I told him to stick to candles. Candles is secure, candles is.' She broke out coughing and could not stop.

Everything suggested that whatever had replaced candles was not secure. Half Moon Court had fallen on hard times. A window frame was rotting and the wall round it damp and mildewed. On the kitchen table was a piece of rye bread of the poorest quality.

Sam, hearing his mother's bitter comments, had gone as red as the mouth of the kiln.

'I do not want to disturb your mother,' I said.

'My – my mother is ill, sir. The maid is looking after her.' Sam rushed over and shut the door which led to the stairs, cutting off their voices. 'Please let me show you. I could equip you a whole laboratory, if that is your desire.'

He had the occasional odd choice of word or phrase, as if selecting what he thought a gentleman would like to hear.

'A whole laboratory,' I murmured, on edge at the thought of Ellie upstairs, but unable to overcome my curiosity.

We went into the shop. The stone kiln was where the printing machine had once stood, its flue going into the back wall. It used to be hot when we were printing. This was like stepping into an oven, although he apologised for the kiln being 'down', as he put it. The maid had put in the wrong coal and he had to let it cool and start it up again before he blew any more glass. Light from the still glowing coals fitfully lit up the room which seemed much larger. I could not work out why until I suddenly realised.

'This is where the office used to be!' I exclaimed, without thinking.

He stared at me. 'You have been here before?'

I cursed myself. I pointed to the ceiling in a shadowy corner. 'I can see the line of alteration.'

'You have sharp eyes, sir.' A compliment, or was there a trace of suspicion? 'This used to be a printing shop.' His nose wrinkled in distaste. 'A hotbed of radicalism.'

'Was it indeed!' I pretended to look shocked, intrigued and amused that, brought up in such modest surroundings, this youth should have such pretensions. 'You are a Royalist, sir?'

'A Royalist?' He laughed. For a moment I could see myself in him at his age, full of arrogant certainty, that the world was wrong, must be changed and he had the solution. 'A p-pox on both their houses! B-both the King and Cromwell destroyed this country!'

'They did?'

He crumpled suddenly, running his hand feverishly through his red hair. A flake of coal fell from the tangled mop. He might not have been on either side, but his change in manner, his body dipping in deference, told me he had abruptly remembered one should always be on the side of the patron. He gave a stumbled apology for what he called going beyond his station. Before he could continue, the stick thumped violently on the ceiling. He gave me an agitated, apologetic wring of the hands before running to the door at the bottom of the stairs and opening it.

Ellie might be ill, but her voice was as sharp and inquisitive as ever. 'How can I get to sleep when you make such a noise? Who are you talking to?'

'I'm s-sorry, Mother.'

'Who is it?'

'It's business, Mother.'

'Come here.' Her voice weakened and trembled into a wheedling tone which I did not remember, and which she must have fashioned during her trade as a whore.

Sam stood at the door for a moment, twisting and turning, before telling her he would be up in a minute, and hurrying back to me. I told him he should see to his mother and I would return later.

'She is –' His lips tightened in frustration. He never finished the sentence, rushing over to a long trestle table behind the kiln, on which were a number of drug bottles and cheap-looking tumblers, the glass thick and foggy. He drew back a cloth, almost tenderly, showing an array of tubing and flasks such as you might see at an alchemist's. The glass was thinner and clearer, albeit with a greenish tint.

'I can make you pipettes, sir, b-beakers and bottles of course. Chemicals do not rot glass as they do metal and l-leather –'

I saw that, in his eagerness, he was going to stumble. I knew the raised stone in that treacherous, uneven floor, having caught my foot in it many times, ruining work by dropping wet proofs or a forme. I moved almost before he tripped and, as the bottle slipped from his grasp, caught it, then caught him. He apologised profusely, floundering for support against me and the side of the kiln. Coals settled as he knocked against it, sending a bright flicker of light from the open kiln door which fell full on my face. I suppose it was the first time he had had a good look at me.

'You have red hair like – like me, sir.'

'Brown,' I snapped, taken off-guard. 'It looks red in certain lights.'

He stared at me, clearly puzzled by my vehemence at what had been an innocent remark. Sweat was coursing down my face from the heat of the kiln.

'Shall I take your cloak, sir?'

I began to unclip it, but then realised I would have to remove my gloves, exposing the ring which bulged through them. 'No, no. I am not staying.'

The cold air at the door revived me. He looked so wretched in his disappointment at losing me as a possible patron I tried to soften the blow by changing my tone. I was also intrigued. 'You declared a pox on both the radicals and the Royalists – what do you believe in?'

In a whirl of movement he grabbed upwards as if he was catching a fly. He brought his closed fist down before me, opening it slowly. His palm was empty.

'This, sir. This is what I believe in.'

I recoiled, thinking him mad.

'Air, sir.'

'Air?'

'People think it is one of the four prime elements, earth, fire, air and water.'

'So it is.'

'What you see in front of you is a fluid of massy particles resting on invisible springs.'

I stared at him, then at his cupped, blackened palm, convinced now he was ripe for Bedlam. 'I see nothing but your hand.'

'Exactly, sir. But Mr B-Boyle has proved that air is a substance, pressing down on my hand.'

I began to understand. Boyle was the son of an Irish peer, seeking to set up a society to promote natural philosophy. Sam must have mistaken me for one of his friends. 'This is the same Robert Boyle who has constructed – what is it? An air pump?'

His eyes lit up. 'The same! The apparatus was made by his assistant Robert Hooke and I had the honour of blowing the glass.'

'But ... but – what has this to do with radicals and Royalists?'

He looked at me triumphantly, subservience gone. 'They are the same.'

'The same? How can that be?'

'In that they both believe in argument. Arg-argument that goes nowhere. Then they fight. But what does that prove? Only that one is the better fighter.'

I began to warm to this strange youth again. 'Mr Boyle knows a better way, does he?'

'Indeed he does, sir, indeed he does,' he cried with fervour. 'Reason and experiment. Construct a theory, then prove it by an experiment others can repeat. People argued fr-fruitlessly whether air was essential to life. Mr Boyle put a bird in an air pump and drew out the air. The bird died. So did the argument.'

He put it beautifully, transformed by his belief, face flushed, eyes shining. Again, I saw myself standing there, pamphlets singing in my head. No, it was poetry at that age. I had forgotten every line of it, scarcely believed I could have wasted my time over it.

'Sadly,' I said, 'the world is not a laboratory.'

'It will be, sir,' he assured me, 'it will be.'

For a moment it was almost as if he was comforting me. He was talking nonsense, but it was infectious nonsense. We returned through the kitchen with its mildewed walls and scrap of rye bread. Out of the blue, in that tawdry room, with the acrid smell of burning coal drifting in from the shop, he became my son. Perhaps it was because the man he thought was his father had just died and I acutely felt his grief and need. Perhaps because I identified with his hopeless longings and dreams. Whatever the reason, what I had done for him before, I realised, had been out of guilt and duty. Now I felt such a tug of feeling for him I stopped abruptly. He was leading the way and turned to stare at me. I struggled to find the words to tell him, but they would not come.

He gave me a concerned look. 'What is it, sir?'

'Sam?' Ellie called. 'Is he still there?'

Ellie's voice pulled me back to my senses. I muttered something and hurried through into the living room. That scrap of rye bread brought back the memories of gnawing hunger, of trying to stave it by almost breaking my teeth on those indigestible, black husks. As he showed me to the door I wrestled to find a way to help him. I could hardly order a laboratory of glass to be delivered to Queen Street. I could not offer him money. He was too proud and Ellie would be suspicious. Then I saw it and had the idea. It came fully formed, all in that moment.

The one piece of furniture that had survived from more prosperous days was an old oak dresser. In the centre of it was a glass goblet, standing out against the dark wood.

'Did you make that?'

He dismissed it as a poor piece that was not worth selling. Once I picked it up I could see the flaws. The glass was misty and the base chipped. But the curved line was beautiful and a delicate design was engraved round the rim. I knew little about glass, but Anne did. For Highpoint she bought ruinously expensive Venetian glass as clear and sharp as this was dull. The Venetians kept the secret of the clarity of their glass as closely guarded as a miser keeps gold. Sam told me the goblet was one of a number of experiments from which he hoped to find the secret and break the Italian monopoly.

'What is going on down there?' Ellie cried. 'Help me up …' she muttered. There followed a series of creaks and sighs, then a heavy thump came from the ceiling above.

'Make me a goblet,' I said to Sam.

He blinked at me, then shook his head. 'I cannot. I will not sell such poor workmanship.'

'That is to your credit but you don't understand. I want you to experiment.'

'Experiment?'

'Isn't that what you believe in? Make me a goblet as clear as Venetian glass. Discover the secret.'

Sam seemed determined to be his own worst enemy. 'B-but if I fail?'

'You won't fail. I believe in you. I will make the investment.'

'Investment?'

He gave me a bewildered stare as if he had never heard of the word. There was the rasp of a door opening upstairs. Through the partly open door at the bottom of the stairs I glimpsed the wavering edge of a nightdress, the ferrule of a stick. Sam continued stubbornly to stare at me. The idea began to feel hopeless and risky. He was too ill-educated to understand it. Or was his look that of someone who knows there is something wrong somewhere, but can't quite put a finger on it?

'If you succeed I will take a share of the profits,' I said.

His face cleared. He understood that all right. His lips pursed and his expression became unexpectedly shrewd. There was a touch of the street child he was when I first met him, working in his mother's brothel. 'One th-third to you, t-two thirds to me.'

We were like two men betting at a cock pit. His face was flushed, his eyes standing out by his hooked nose. 'Sixty–forty,' I said. 'The majority to you.'

'Done.'

I clapped him on the back and drew out two sovereigns. 'My initial investment. There will be more when the contract is drawn up.'

He gaped at the coins, turning them over in his hands as if he could not believe they were real, dropping one and scurrying after it. I hurried away as I heard the steady thump of the stick on the stairs, followed by an expelled gasp of air as Ellie made her tortuous way downstairs.

'Wait! I do not know your name, sir.'

'Black. My solicitor at Lincoln's Inn will contact you.'

8

From the beginning, as soon as I recovered my senses in Queen Street, it seemed a hopeless project. The Venetians guarded their secrets well. I wrote to one of my spies in Venice, offering a reward for information on the process. For the first time the flow of money from Queen Street to Highpoint was reversed. I starved it of the income from the estate's London properties which were now substantial. After a fire at Half Moon Court and complaints from neighbours, I invested in a new kiln and laboratory in Clerkenwell.

There I could visit him without any risk of seeing Ellie. He was kept busy making flasks and bottles where the quality of the glass did not matter.

He made no progress at all that I could see on the project I had invested in. At first I did not care. I loved his eagerness, his hope, his despair, his determination, his belief. He was the return on my investment, not the project for a brilliantly clear glass which seemed like the search for the philosopher's stone.

Nevertheless, the more each firing failed, the more I was drawn into it. He tried different sands, different coals, higher and higher temperatures. Some days I got as excited as he did, sweating before the blistering heat of the kiln, waiting for the glass to form, spellbound as he blew and twirled the white-hot bubble, pacing up and down while waiting for it to cool. I was more optimistic than he was. It was better, I told him. I was sure it was clearer.

'Look!' I said.

'Compare,' he replied gloomily.

Compare it with the previous firings. Crucially, with the piece of Venetian glass he kept as a standard. I had to admit it was as foggy as ever.

'You see like a politician, sir,' he said sourly.

I reacted with some severity to his insolence, which he immediately apologised for; but I was secretly proud of him. Inside all that deference he was his own man. I had no inclination to acknowledge him as my son. It was too complicated. It might harm or even destroy our relationship; from birth I had had nothing but bitter experiences, both as son and as father. I enjoyed the secrecy. I had forgotten the pleasure of real work; of getting my hands dirty. I donned a smock in Clerkenwell and became Tom Neave; I hung it up, put on my cloak and rode back to Queen Street as Sir Thomas. My humours were perfectly in balance again.

I was affected in other ways. Living behind my desk or in meetings had removed me from the world where I had been brought up. Clerkenwell brought me back in touch with it. When the case came against the Quaker, Stephen Butcher, I went to see him in Newgate. I found that his main ambition was not to sing here, but in the New World. As a sailor, he was in a position to organise it. I withdrew my case against him and, with Highpoint money, funded his expedition, on the premise that it was both a more Christian and more effective way to clear the streets.

Mr Pepys not only bought me a large chop and a bottle of the best claret to thank me for Lord Montague vegetating in the country and not in the Tower. Knowing my inclinations, he offered to introduce me to a very pretty widow in straitened circumstances. To his surprise, and in a certain degree to mine, I refused, on the grounds that I was far too busy.

'I thought you were out of office, sir.'

'I have various projects.' I waved an airy hand, as if they were affairs of state.

'Are you, er … already accommodated?'

I shook my head and concentrated on my chop. He picked a shred of meat from his teeth, staring at me thoughtfully. 'I do believe you are in love, sir.'

I laughed, spluttering wine and almost choking on my chop. 'What absolute nonsense, Pepys!'

Obsession was the word I would have chosen. It was the third and most important of my projects. I wanted no diversion from the task in hand. I was determined to have Anne, and on my own terms. I made no more approaches. I was assiduous to her at supper. I took no more correspondence to table. I even took an interest in Luke's clothes, asking for his advice on the correct width of britches that season. He looked at me with deep suspicion of my motives, but was far too stiff and polite to question them.

It was when I sold land at Highpoint for Clerkenwell that Anne asked to see me in private. Because the transaction was done by my lawyer, Christopher Newton, she was convinced I had changed my will. I told her the truth. I needed the money. It was clear she did not believe me. Up to that moment I'd had no idea what I was doing, except that I was enjoying myself hugely: I had forgotten what enjoyment was.

It was during that cold, acrimonious conversation with her that it came to me. I would divide everything between my two sons. Not only would it be fair and equable, but it would divide up Highpoint. I would sell it piecemeal. It was a destructive, malign force. From the moment I was born it had nearly killed me. It had destroyed any chance of a relationship between me and my father, corroded that between me and my wife. I decided I would destroy it.

'I have a right to know if you change your will, sir.'

'The will is in my gift,' I said in my new, mild tone which infuriated her.

We met on neutral ground, in the reception room on the ground floor, where I sometimes took a glass of port or sack after supper. There were no prying servants from either side, only satyrs chasing nymphs endlessly round the oval ceiling. She was more than usually modestly dressed, her low neckline covered by a gorget, the opening in her long dress showing only a touch of underskirt. She wore no jewellery and, so far as I could discern, no perfume.

'In your gift to leave to Luke,' she said.

'He will be provided for.'

'Provided for? What does *that* mean? You are punishing him for his beliefs?'

'No. He can love his precious King to his heart's content. But when he lies to me and gets involved in plots behind my back, then I shall punish him.'

She would not give up. She said Luke had made no undertaking not to take part in the uprising and accused me of turning him into a Royalist because I had set myself against him from the beginning. I had ignored him – when I was ever there to see him – stopped him from becoming a soldier, which he dreamed of –

'To protect him. I know what soldiers are like. With his scarred face, his mannerisms –'

'You know what soldiers are like? Yes,' she cried bitterly. 'Do you know what *he* is like? You made him feel weak. Hopeless. *That* is why he became a Royalist. Because they would accept him as he is. As he wants to be.'

I was incredulous. '*I* turned him into a Royalist? If anyone did that it's you. You've become more a Royalist than anyone who was born one.'

'Do you think I want the King back? I want another Cromwell. Order. But if the King returns …'

'Long live the King? I don't have that option.'

It was odd. Very curious. We had never discussed it. I had never wanted Highpoint. In fact I had hated the very idea of it. But Anne's obsession for it had driven her to the point of madness. She would not eat and scarcely drank unless the liquid was forced down her. She was skin and bone that day twelve years ago when Cromwell's son-in-law, Ireton, called. He was desperate to get people of any stature to sign the King's death warrant. The staunchest Parliamentarians suddenly had urgent business in their country estates, or were too indisposed to pick up a pen. Ireton offered me the Stonehouse estate in return for signing the death warrant. It was almost as bald as that.

Anne had come in. It was the first time she had left her bed since her illness. I could see her thin, wasted figure, hear her cracked voice before she collapsed in my arms.

'Mr Ireton … it is good of you to come at last.'

I signed. That was the day I became Sir Thomas Stonehouse. Had I really been so much, so despairingly, in love with her?

For the first time, as we stared in silence at one another across the reception room, we acknowledged, without saying a word, that I might have signed my own death warrant.

In the hall there was the rattle of plates being taken from the dining room. I stared up at the ceiling where, in the candle-lit shadows, even the satyrs seemed to have stopped chasing the nymphs. The raised voice of the ostler passed, complaining to someone about the shortage of fodder for the horses. Everything was short and would get shorter until a new government was formed. If there was a tax strike, as the City threatened, everything would stop altogether.

'Could it happen?' she asked. 'The King?'

Somewhere a door banged, making both of us jump. 'I don't know.'

'What does Thurloe think?'

I did not answer, again because I did not know. She thought I was seeing him every week, or going to the City to sound out the aldermen who mattered. I resolved that the next day I would see Thurloe. The trouble was once I got involved, it would take over the whole of my life, every waking moment and half my sleep. I would have to do it, I thought. But not tomorrow. Tomorrow Sam had a new silica mix for the firing for which he had the highest hopes. Once I had not turned up and he thought I had abandoned the project. I remembered the look on his face. I could not bear that.

'If there is any way I can help …'

The words came out of her like drawn teeth. But she meant them. Thurloe distrusted her but recognised the value of her contacts and her political flair, and if I asked her to do so, in spite of the gulf between us, she would work tirelessly at it.

'Thank you.'

I could think of nothing more to say. We continued to sit there, exhausted by argument. It felt as though we had packed twelve years of differences, quarrels and bitter resentments into one short hour. Eventually she spoke.

'Suppose Luke does give you the undertaking not to have anything more to do with the Sealed Knot?'

She looked at the floor, twisting her hands nervously. There was no sign of that starched remoteness. She had come round. She must have talked to him. I felt a leap of gratitude. If he really had made that promise, she had done more than I ever could.

'I will be very glad to hear what Luke has to say,' I said warmly.

She touched the bell for the servant to clear away. As she rose, I stood up awkwardly with her. For a moment we were like two people who had never met before. She raised her head and gave me a half-smile. 'Thank you.'

I was wrong that she was not wearing perfume. There was the barest trace of it in the air as I followed her to the door. It was not the usual stronger scent she wore now, but the lighter, transient, barely discernible hint of rosemary and lavender she used when she was younger. A pad bearing it dropped from her bodice but she did not appear to notice. My heart beat painfully. When she had been desperate for a child she had not been averse to the old whore's trick of making such a signal.

At the door I touched her arm. As the servant's footsteps came towards the door, she turned and murmured hurriedly, 'I have seen Dr Latchford. It is as I feared, sir. He has warned me strongly against having another child.'

9

I took the pad from her bodice to my room, like a callow youth who keeps a flower his mistress has worn, long after the petals have paled and the leaves withered. The scent seemed to increase until it filled the room. My need was so great, so urgent, it overwhelmed a growing unease I could not put my finger on. I paced about until I heard the sliding of bolts and locking of doors and the house grew quiet, then slipped along the silent corridors, dim with night candles, and up the stairs towards her apartment.

I stopped. Suppose she was not expecting me? Of course she was! I knew the signs, I knew the rules of this particular game only too well.

The night porter's face swam in front of me, a mixture of deference and lewdness that almost, not quite, became a wink. 'Oh. Good night, sir.'

I grunted something and waited until he was out of sight. The door to her apartment was slightly open, a candle still burning in the anteroom. When I crept away, Agnes would snuff it out. I took a step and stopped as the source of my unease came to me. Of course. Only overwhelming desire had prevented me from seeing something so obvious.

She was doing what she had always done: a deal. Do not change your will. Leave everything to Luke and, in exchange, I give you my bed. Not her. Her bed. It was all there in the last words she said. 'It was as I feared, sir. Dr Latchford has warned me against having another child.' Was that true? I doubted it. She had Latchford in her pocket. This was a return to Lady Stonehouse, dutiful and submissive.

Well, why should I care? I had what I wanted. Another child. Sam. I could have her. Use her. Cheaper and much more convenient than the widow Mr Pepys offered me. I took another step. The door to the bedroom was open. I smelt the rosemary and lavender, intensified from the heat of her body.

I turned and went out of the apartment, leaning against the wall, shutting my eyes. I could not bear it. I wanted her, not her pretence. Puritans condemned pleasure in the act. They even expunged from the marriage service 'with my body I thee worship'. They averted their eyes from their wives' bodies. Perhaps that is why they said I was born of the Devil. I wanted to see her. I wanted her, body and soul, not this hasty coupling like a whore in a dark alley.

It came back to me so sharply I covered my face in my hands. That time when, whatever our differences, we were so much in love we were one flesh; the time of hope, the time of bearing children. Of course it was stupid to expect it to last; it had to cool and grow old, but with the long war it had been snatched away before its time, winter coming sharp into summer, with no gentle, preparatory autumn in between.

A light shone into my face. The night porter. There was no doubt now about the conspiratorial wink on his face, sharing what he must have thought was my satisfaction on the way back. 'Still up, sir?'

'You can see I'm still bloody well up, man! I can't sleep!'

But I did sleep, a strange restless sleep, disturbed with dreams in which there was a light shining in my face, which became the moon glimmering into the garret in Half Moon Court, where I was an apprentice searching for something I had lost. What made me even more frantic was that I had forgotten what I was looking for. It turned out to be the small pad, dipped in rosemary water, which Miss Black used to keep tucked in her bodice. Strange, that even in my dream, I could not call her Anne. I had found a pad on the stair one day and kept it under my pillow, in the hope that, if I found the right magic spell, she would fall in love with me. I awoke exhausted, my nightshirt wet, disgusted with myself. That had not happened since I was a callow youth.

I took no breakfast, determined to be out early and go to Clerkenwell. Sam would already have the bellows going on the kiln, which had slumbered overnight. My spirits revived. There was nothing like an early ride, breath steaming, beating together my frozen hands as the horse was saddled, stamping on the cobbles, eager to go.

Sam would have a meat pie kept hot by the kiln and a jug of small beer. A laboratory, I was discovering, was not like other worlds. Natural philosophers like Boyle worked with their servants among the glass tubing and air pumps. We were all slaves to the secrets of nature, of sand melting and fusing, turning into a shimmering glass which one day, Sam assured me, would be so clear when you looked through it, you would not know it was there.

I was riding out when Mr Cole shouted after me. I had forgotten to sign for a sale of more Highpoint property. While I was sealing the papers, Mr Cole told me that Mr Luke was waiting in the reception room in the hope of seeing me. I was incredulous, not so much that he wanted to see me, for surely his mother had put him up to this, but that he was out of bed. Luke scarcely ever showed his face before noon. I retorted that he would have to wait, then reined in my horse again. It was churlish of me not to see him for a few minutes. And she would make capital out of me if I did not.

I saw him in my study. As usual, he stood to attention like the soldier he wanted to be, toeing the line in the carpet that Stonehouse sons had toed before their fathers in memoriam. I hated that but it was what he expected, what he would subject his son to, if he ever had one.

I had thrown on yesterday's clothes. He bore the marks of Gilbert, the fastidious servant he had brought from Highpoint: barbered cheeks and fresh, clean linen. I could not help having the feeling that he should be sitting at the desk and I standing there. He was a Stonehouse from the tip of his elegantly coiffured crown, to his turned-down floppy boots. When he eventually spoke, his words were as polished as his boots.

'I wish to apologise, sir.'

That was all. I waited for more, but there appeared to be no more. 'Well, go on. Apologise for what? For being a Royalist?'

I cursed myself as soon as I had said it. Why did he always drive me the wrong way? He seemed to grow even taller. Or perhaps years at my desk had made me more bent. His nostrils flared; his voice was edged with contempt.

'I will never apologise for that.'

Oh, to hell with you, I thought, *the fuse has been lit*. And in a moment we would be in the middle of a full-blown argument that would leave us worse off than before. I jumped up. Better end it before we reached that explosive point. I calmed myself by thinking of the ride to the City.

'Look, Luke, you can see I'm on the point of going out. If you have something more to say, please say it.'

He spoke carefully, painfully slowly, as if I was a lawyer ready to seize on a faulty argument. 'This house belongs to you, sir …'

I paced up and down. The toes of his boots seemed glued to the line in the carpet.

'… as does Highpoint.'

'Yes, yes. Thank you. I'm aware of that.'

His nose flared again, a fine Stonehouse nose with a sharp, aquiline tip. Words suddenly rattled out of him.

'While I am living here or in Highpoint it was, is, not the act of a gentleman to join in a rebel force whose aim was, is, to remove you from power, even though you gained that power by killing that blessed saint, the King.'

He was like a pump which, after producing the barest trickle of water, suddenly produces a great gush of it. He ran dry again, bowing his head, trembling. I did not know where to put myself.

'Sit down, Luke.'

'I would rather stand, sir.'

'As you wish.'

I sat down, struggling to compose myself. I translated what he had said to mean that, whatever his feelings about me and my beliefs, while he was under my roof he would take no part in any further Royalist plots or rebellions. Is that what he meant, I asked? It was.

'Did your mother get you to say this?'

He flushed. For a moment I thought he was going to cross the line in the carpet towards me. 'She talked to me but those are my own words, sir.'

Again I cursed myself. When one of us took a step forward, the other seemed to take a step back. 'I'm sorry, Luke. We always seem to get on the wrong side of one another.'

He blinked at me suspiciously, as if there was some hidden motive in my apology. I got up, my geniality only partly forced, for this prickly meeting was almost over and Holborn would still be clear enough to give my horse a good gallop. I was almost eating that hot pie, washed down with small beer, as I told him I was glad to accept his assurance that he would be involved in no more plots. We had had our differences, but I hoped that was all over. Still he stuck to that line in the carpet like a limpet.

'May I make a request, sir?'

'Yes, yes. Go on.'

'I would like to go into the City alone without ...' He could scarcely bring the word out. '... Scogman.'

I tried to tell him Scogman was there to protect him but he had been well primed by his mother. He believed, correctly enough, Scogman was there to prevent him getting into another Royalist mess, which would compromise my chances of office with the next government. I told him it was more than that. He thought himself a soldier who knew London because he had learned a little prig's cant in prison. But in the clothes he affected he would bleed freely, as the prigs put it – he was an easy lay. Before he understood the meaning of 'bite the bill from the cull' they would have snatched his sword, taken all he had, including those fine britches, and left him for dead.

I offered him other guards. He saw them in the same light as Scogman: they would be there to report back to me. He was adamant he could take care of himself. Or he would have his own guard, his servant, Gilbert. I thought Gilbert a country hick who would be no match for the prigs either. He said with a passion that astonished me that he had finished with the Sealed Knot. He loved his King but he hated them. When the moment came, they were found wanting. He used language like that. Biblical language. He gave me his word he would have nothing more to do with them.

'Nor with any other Royalist plots?'

'I cannot say that, sir. The Royalist cause is in disarray but I cannot read the future. If it comes to that, I will tell you. I can promise you I will never again make such a move under your own roof.'

It was portentous. It bore the mark of Anne. But if he was accepting advice that showed more maturity. And it was not only well put, it was delivered with such fervour I was silenced. He knew I was weakening, and held the silence with difficulty, his lips quivering slightly. He flicked away a tiny bead of sweat forming on his brow. There was something he was not telling me, I was convinced.

I made him wait in reception and rang for Scogman, scribbling a note to Sam, apologising that I could not come but would be with him in the next day or so for the first blow. I felt a strange kind of thrill at using the jargon he spoke, as I had with that of printing. I addressed it to Samuel Reeves and signed it Thomas Black. It was the first letter I had ever written him. It was only as the servant was taking it through the door and Scogman was entering that I realised I had sealed it with the falcon ring. I had to run halfway down the stairs to call him back, during which I heard Luke in reception singing. Singing! It was the Royalist song about the divine Sarah whispering outside the bars of prison he had sung in Oxford gaol. It did not improve my temper. I tore up the letter to Sam and wrote another. Having no other seals, I closed it with a wafer.

Scogman watched this elaborate performance in silence. He knew me too well. 'Won you over, sir, has he?'

I was in such a state of confusion that for a moment I did not know which son he was talking about. I told him I was considering letting Luke go into the City with Gilbert.

'Gilbert?' He sniffed. That sniff spoke volumes. 'Very good, sir.'

'Is that all you have to say?'

'I am very glad to see father and son reconciled, sir.'

'Stop that nonsense,' I said wearily, 'and tell me what you think.'

He did. Wherever they went, Luke insisted on ending up at the Moor in Watling Street, however inconvenient, however disgusting the coffee was. There were few gentlemen there, mainly merchants waiting for news about ships to be chalked up on the board.

'I keeps myself discreet, as instructed, with an ale on the bench outside The Four Sailors. He spends a lot of time in the jakes there.'

'Going out round the back?'

Scogman shook his head. 'No back entrance. Blind alley.' He hesitated. 'Once he gave me the slip. I thought he was in the coffee house, but he comes back up the street, like the cat who's supped the cream.'

'Why didn't you tell me this before?'

'Waiting to catch Mr Luke at it. Sir. And I will.'

In short, Mr Luke was up to something. I slept on it. Or rather I didn't. It came to me in the middle of the night. Something quite obvious I had missed.

Luke was ready for me, as carefully dressed as before, toeing the line. His eagerness made me even more uneasy. A man's reputation depends largely on his judgement of people, and I could not bear the thought of him getting involved in something that would embarrass me a second time.

'This ballad you keep whistling … To Althea. Stone walls do not a prison make … nor iron bars a cage … By Richard Lovelace, isn't it?'

He said it was, alert now, stiffening at this unexpected approach. 'Odd man.'

He stepped over the line of the carpet, incredulous that I might have met this wandering poet who ended up in a pauper's grave. 'You knew him, sir?'

'Not quite the words I would use. I arrested him in forty-eight.' I winced at myself as I grunted them. Did I really sound like those old veterans who, over their claret, talked about forty-two or forty-nine and the battles of the Good Old Cause, obscuring the chances of finding a new cause which would get us out of the current stalemate?

He had never shown that much interest in anything I had done. I grew more and more aggrieved as he asked me what Lovelace was like, what his cell was like, did I provide him with pen and ink to write to Lucasta, who was some whore Lovelace immortalised when he wrote *I could not love thee, dear, so much … Loved I not honour more.*

Honour! How I loathed the word! Born aristocrats believed that those below the nobility and gentry had no idea what honour was. It was not necessary for a nobleman to sign a contract. His word was sufficient. *Dictum meum pactum.* My word is my bond. What nonsense. Some of the biggest rogues unhung were nobles. After shaking hands with some of them, Cromwell said, you counted your fingers.

'You wrote poetry, didn't you, sir?'

The question took me unawares. I stared at him suspiciously. Was he laughing at me? Nothing in this interview was going according to plan.

'Poetry?' I laughed. Or tried to. 'Where on earth did you get that idea from?'

'My mother.'

That disconcerted me even more. I got up as I felt the blood rising in my cheeks, muttering something about doggerel. The few that had been published I had searched out and destroyed along with the pamphlets, making a clean sweep of those early embarrassments. Better a good soldier, even a good politician, if there was such a thing, than a bad poet. I had written the poems for Anne in the first flush of our love. I was surprised she remembered them at all, let alone mentioned them. One or two of them might have had something. One, I recalled thinking rather good, even as I destroyed it, and if I had continued to write … Unexpectedly, I had a sharp sense of pain and loss. I dismissed it almost immediately. End up in a pauper's grave like Lovelace? That doggerel was probably what I had heard Luke and Anne laughing about in her apartment. I rounded on him.

'Who is Sarah?' Now the blood coursed into his face. 'Lovelace's poem was dedicated to Althea,' I said. 'He speaks of Althea whispering to him and he … er, being entangled in her hair. You sing of Sarah.'

He retreated behind the line of the carpet. He blustered and blundered but eventually admitted there was a lady called Sarah who had caught his eye.

'Eye or heart?'

He stared at the carpet.

'This is why you're so desperate to go out unhampered by Scogman?'

'Yes, sir.'

'Some buttock, some wench on the game –'

He stepped over the line again. 'She is a lady of good blood, sir, who has fallen on unfortunate circumstances. I cannot stop thinking of her, sir. It is not just that Scogman is a gaoler. He sullies my thoughts. He leers at the madams and their dollymops. He says he will find me a good frigate not a fireship that will give me pox. I can't stand him! I would rather stay in this prison than walk another step with him!'

There was more. I let him have his piece. He had never strung more than two or three awkward sentences to me since he was a small boy. Of course no one had experienced what he was going through. Of course she was of good stock and was in unfortunate circumstances. They all were. I stopped him in full flow.

'Does your mother know about this?'

The blood left his cheeks. 'She has no idea. Please don't tell her. She will put a stop to it immediately.'

'And I will not? Give me your sword.'

He stood rigidly to attention again, his lips clamped shut, trembling. For a gentleman to give up his sword was surrender. Humility.

'Come on, man,' I barked, holding out my hand. 'I have wasted another day on you.'

Slowly he unbuckled his sword. Even more slowly he took the rapier from its scabbard. I took it with distaste. I was used to receiving gentlemen's swords; after Naseby I took a whole spate of them. For its master to have survived that long in five years of bloody conflict the sword had to have been a killing machine, with a balanced weight and a slicing edge. This was a toy, designed to go with the ringlets and wide britches of its owner. When I dropped it on my desk it gave out a tinny rattle.

'Useless.'

'Rupert has killed men with a sword like that,' he said hotly.

Prince Rupert was Charles's cavalry commander, who at one stage might have won the war. 'Rupert lost,' I said.

'Only because the King got rid of him!' Luke spoke with fiery contempt. For a moment it looked as if he was going to snatch back his sword. 'I know the points in the circle, the movements, the *stoccata lunga* –'

I tossed the sword back to him. 'Kill me.'

He almost dropped it but instantly took guard with a correctness and alertness that surprised me. Clearly he had been having lessons somewhere. I stared down at the sword, the point inches from my breast. The furrowed skin of his ravaged cheek looked as if it was on fire.

'Go on. Kill me.'

His eyes narrowed. A tiny blob of saliva leaked from the corner of his mouth. The tip of the sword drifted downwards. Someone had taught him well. One lunge upwards would travel between bone and pierce the heart. It was so long since I had been in this position I had to force my eyes away from his and focus on his feet. When his left foot went back, anchoring his body, and his right knee bent forward, he was about to lunge. There was a blur of movement. He was fast and I was slow. Far too slow. The tip glittered and danced in front of my eyes, before he returned to the guard position. I felt the trickle of blood on the back of my hand after the prick his rapier had given me. It was only then I realised my shirt was drenched in sweat.

'I do not fight unarmed men, Father.'

Father! When had he last called me that? Was there mockery in it? Certainly there was mockery in the pinprick, an insult in his code of honour. I sucked at my bleeding hand, my temper rising.

'Very well.'

I went into the anteroom and unlocked a cupboard. From it came a stale, musty smell. Luke stared at the thick, leather jacket I had worn for war. A hundred times I had told the servants to get rid of it, and a hundred times I had changed my mind. Its chapped, stained surface was a map of all the battles I had fought in.

Once Luke had helped me on with that sword belt, but he would not remember that; he had still been in skirts. The sword felt as if it had never left my hand. It was a short German sword I had taken from a dead mercenary. I wiped the grease from it; there was scarcely a flake of rust. With it went a *main-gauche*, a left-handed dagger. Luke gazed at them with a mixture of awe and disbelief, as if they had been disinterred from some ancient grave.

'Again. Kill me.'

He stared at me as if he thought I was moonstruck. The German sword looked unwieldy but it was perfectly balanced. And, unlike

86

the rapier Luke was holding, it had a cutting edge as sharp as a razor. When I flicked it forward, merely brushing the back of his hand, it immediately drew blood. An insult for an insult. He stared for a moment at the oozing red globules.

He was fast. God in heaven he was fast. And in that moment I realised I was too old for this, old and stupid not to believe what the stiffening of my bones was telling me, not to register that slow, insidious weakening of the eye which makes all the difference between life and death.

He drove me back into the cupboard, his blade darting like a snake's tongue, at my throat, towards my heart. My helmet clattered to the floor with other clothes and books. His blood was up. He hated me. I was the man who had killed his King. Who had thrown him in prison. If the fight, for it became a real fight, had not been in a confined space he would have killed me. I have no doubt of it. The rapier always needed space. He knew that and tried to drive me into the study. I would not have it. I kicked the anteroom door closed. He had been trained well, but too well. He fought correctly, according to the rules, in which elegance was as important as the hit, but elegance demands movement between the points in what a swordsman calls the magic circle, and I starved him of that. In desperation he struck. Too cramped to put his body behind a lunge, I caught the blade in the hook of my dagger and twisted it away from his grip.

The door to the study was open and Scogman was staring at us. How long he had been standing there I do not know. Gripping his sword wrist, which he must have sprained when I wrenched the rapier from him, Luke panted, 'That is not fair! Gentlemen do not fight in cupboards.' He turned and saw Scogman. 'Nor do they have someone to step in if they're in trouble.'

'Leave us,' I said quietly. Scogman knew that mood of mine, although he had not seen it since the war. When he had gone I gave

Luke his rapier. 'On the London streets you will not be fighting gentlemen. This will be worse than useless.'

Prigs, I told him, would stalk him for the jewels in its guard. In a mob fight, London apprentices used cudgel and buckler. The less tassels on his boots, the safer he would be. It only gradually dawned on him I was giving him his freedom, and it was only when I said I took him at his word that on his trips to the City he would not be involved in any more Royalist plots, that he believed it.

Scogman had no doubt I was wrong. The fact that there was a woman involved made it worse. He trusted women even less than Royalists, declaring he would never marry one. They bred children whom, he knew from his experience of mine, were nothing but trouble. Released from his duties with Luke, he was buying a house in Shoreditch, where the only women would be a housekeeper and a maid.

Luke and I remained awkward with one another, but in a different way. I felt the respect he gave me was no longer feigned. One day, when he was going into the City with his servant Gilbert, Luke said he had lost his own dagger and asked if he could borrow mine. It had been with me since the early days of the war. Its heft was chipped and its blade scarred, but it came smoothly out of its scabbard, as sharp as ever. I told him he could keep it.

I felt a pang of loss as soon as I had said it, but the expression on his face was worth it. I never wanted him to be a soldier, but after that I felt a strange kind of peace. And a respect for him I had never had before. I had mistaken his foppish dress for his character. He was not a milksop. He was headstrong and arrogant but brave. Above all, he was in love. It was there in the way he checked the mirror before he left the house, whistled and did a little dance of pure happiness as he entered the stable yard. I watched him from the window as he rode from the house. Once he saw me and waved. I stiffened, but only for a moment, then waved back. It was our secret, the only one we'd ever had together, one which Anne had no knowledge of. Childish? Naive? Of course. But I had rediscovered something childish, but fundamental, which, in the long years of being Cromwell's spymaster, I had lost. Trust. I trusted him.

In all this, I forgot Sam. I did not see him for well over a week. When I did the kiln was cold. He was packing a box of candles. I apologised for not attending to the firing and my long absence. To my amazement he said it was of no consequence. The experiment was over.

'Over?'

'It was a failure.'

Laconically, he packed more candles and took them out to a waiting carter. I could not believe that he had dismissed our experiment without consulting me, and said so with some warmth. This broke through his lassitude and he humbly begged my pardon, but replied when I had not turned up he thought I was the one who had lost interest. Sponsors often did, he added, on a whim, without notice.

That cut me to the quick and I apologised again, saying I had needed to attend to other urgent business.

'What business are you in, sir?'

My heart beat more quickly. It was an innocent enough question, but he looked at me with a certain penetration and I wondered if he had discovered or suspected who I was. That might account for his strange moodiness. I told him brusquely I had a small estate and said he must do another firing.

It all poured out then. His mother was still ill and was constantly asking who I was and what I did. When I did not turn up it was Ellie who convinced him that I had given up on the whole idea. That is what the rich did, she told him. One moment you were the whole world, the next they forgot you. I could almost hear her saying it, in that flat, fatalistic Spitalfield voice. She had wanted me. She had thrown herself at me. She expected me to leave her. When I did she never reproached me. But I reproached myself at that moment. I felt it so sharply I had to turn away from Sam for fear of betraying myself. I had ruined her life. Odd as it may seem I had never put it in such terms before. When I met her, years later, in that Southwark brothel, I regarded it as one of life's little ironies. Had I not made amends for that? Given them a house? A business? But that was just money, a few strokes of the pen. That was not making amends.

'Are you all right, sir?'

'A little fatigued from the ride. It is growing colder. It may soon snow.'

'Yes. Yes. I had not noticed – but – but that's true. Very true … I am sorry, sir. I have not been very hospitable. I – I have these black humours …'

Like me, I thought. He raked out clinkers from the bottom of the kiln, and began laying another fire and preparing the silica. The firings resumed. And, after this, I made sure I went in once a week.

One day I received a letter from my agent in Venice, claiming to contain the secret of making clear glass. From what little I understood, I gathered Sam was on the right track: what mattered were the temperature range and the impurities in the coal. I went to Clerkenwell in high excitement and gave it to him without a word. He read only a line or two before he handed it back to me.

'I cannot read this.' I had forgotten it was in Latin, which he did not understand, and began to translate. He stopped me. 'I know enough Latin. I mean I *must* not read it.'

'Must not?' I laughed. 'Why? Do you think there is some curse on it?'

'Yes, sir. Exactly. Some curse. Where did you g-get it?'

'That's my business.'

'No, sir.' His stammer became more pronounced. 'It's m-m-my business also. Did you …' It took several seconds for him to get the words out. '… steal it?'

The kiln was roaring away and for a moment I could not believe I had heard the word. 'Are you accusing me of being a thief?'

His face became as red as the fire. 'N-no, but someone m-must have stolen it.'

'I obtained the information as part of a commercial transaction. Now let us get on. I have many more things to do.' I handed him the paper. 'If this is right you need an even higher temperature.'

He swallowed, apologised, and took the paper into the light of the kiln. He translated painfully slowly, his finger tracing to the end of the first line before he suddenly folded up the paper and shook his head violently. It really was as if he thought the paper was cursed. With many contortions and hesitations, he said he was sorry but he could not read it. He wanted to discover the secret for himself. It had been his father's dream to find the answer and he was doing it for him. And he wanted to be a natural philosopher. Such a philosopher did not steal secrets. Nature was not a commercial transaction. Nature was everybody's. A man approached it humbly or shared his work with others. He did not steal.

At first irritated, I was drawn in by the fervour of his belief, softened by his naivety, by his rose-tinted memory of the man he thought was his father, whom Scogman – I had never met him – described as an honest nonentity. A candle-maker.

I squeezed his shoulder. 'Come, Sam. That is all very well in a tale. Or a penny book. But it is not the way of the world. This would make your name in London.'

He gazed at me wonderingly. 'Would it?'

'If it is true, yes. And the man I deal with would not dare cheat me. You would be talked of in the same breath as Robert Boyle. And make more money.'

'Robert Boyle …?' His voice was full of awe, reverence even. His eyes shone, the dancing flames of the kiln reflected in his pupils. I clapped him on the shoulder, laughing at the awe on his face. He unfolded the paper, stared again at the first line, then crumpled it up in a ball and flung it into the fire. It bounced on some coals at the front which had not yet set alight. I stood in disbelief, gaping at the smoking ball, before plunging forward to rescue it. It burst into flames as I touched it. I fell back with a cry, sucking at my burned fingers, berating him.

'Idiot! Fool! That is my only copy! Was! Have you any idea how much I paid for it? How much this has cost me?'

Only the thought that I would have to give my real name stopped me from going out for the constable. I told him that people only got one chance in life and that was his. Did he really think an uneducated boy could discover what it had taken a whole city a century to find and perfect? Through all this tirade he stood silent, hands clasped, head bowed.

'Well? Have you nothing to say for yourself? Eh?'

His lips quivered before he spoke. 'I will repay the money you have given me, sir. Every p-p-penny of it.'

'What?' I gestured derisively towards a bench where he melted the wax for the mould. 'With candles?'

He stared back mutely at me, his only answer the stubborn look in his eyes that reminded me of that in the Quaker seaman Stephen Butcher's face, or my son Luke's, which I could only call belief, whether it was in God or the King, or natural philosophy, and which never failed to raise a stab of envy before I despised it, for all I had to remotely compare with it was fighting with

Cromwell, then the Levellers for the battered, discredited Good Old Cause.

'A pox on it!' I said as I walked out. 'I will write it off as a bad investment and there's an end to it.'

When I rode away he was doggedly working the bellows, pumping up the kiln to a white heat. I regretted not what I had said, only the way I had said it. I wished we could have parted on better terms, but mingled with regret was a sense of relief. He wanted to go his own way and, in truth, that suited me. Without him I would never have had the prospect of such harmony in Queen Street. But with his moods and the constant risk of him discovering who I was, which would destroy that harmony, he was becoming a liability. I kept his papers together, in a file marked *Samuel Reeves, Bread Lane, Clerkenwell*. With the amount I had spent on the kiln, materials and the spy in Venice, I considered he had done very well out of me. I closed the account and locked it securely in my desk in the drawer I kept for finished business.

My newfound trust in Luke seemed to run magically through the whole of that gloomy old house. The rattling of his boots on the stairs on his way out cured Anne of her indispositions. She begged for this area to be lit, for those dark pictures to be replaced by brighter ones. Dinners came alive again as we invited generals, City councillors and MPs. I tried with Thurloe to move on from the dictatorship to find a workable franchise which would lead to a more representative Parliament and carry the ideals of the Good Old Cause.

Lucy sent more gossip from Brussels, which I decoded. Money had been raised in Dublin, and an Irish force would link with a rising in the heavily Royalist south-west. Kent would follow. London was vulnerable because, apart from the City militia and a scatter of disorganised, quarrelling regiments, the only strong, viable force was George Monck's in Scotland, several weeks' march away. By the time Monck reached London any rebellion would be over. The City had never been more exposed. I would awake in the dark in a cold sweat, hearing the rattle of carts, convinced the Royalists had struck, then stumble to the window, only to see it was the shit wagons collecting the night soil. I would call myself a fool, thinking – or persuading myself – that the Royalists had learned their lesson that summer. They were too weak and disorganised to invade.

After years of being at the centre of affairs, the worst thing was not knowing. The centre had moved elsewhere – if there was one.

As the old year died in the shortest, darkest days of December, London, like a great ship when there is no wind, lay becalmed. Frost gripped the City, icing the shallows of the Thames. Everything seemed frozen. Stephen Butcher and his motley band of Quakers could not move from Poplar: the naval fleet lay in the river at Gravesend, sealing off London. Lawson, its commander, flew no flag. Like everyone else, he had no idea who was in charge of what.

In Queen Street, too, I felt our relationship was becalmed. Anne was still very much Lady Stonehouse, but gradually, very slowly, so slowly I dare not press it, a new intimacy began forming between us. We were like casual acquaintances who have known and been on friendly terms for years, and who suddenly discover there might be something more than that. I winced now and went hot with shame like a blundering youth at the crass demands I had made of her. It was as though I had picked up the disease from Luke; it was like those early days in love, before anything has been declared, and one grows more and more apprehensive of doing so, in case those looks, that smile, are nothing but imaginings, which one clumsy move might destroy.

PART TWO

The King's List

January–February 1660

11

Fourth of January and snowing hard. It was before the fires in the house were lit, but I had to be up early for I was meeting Thurloe and had papers to prepare. My breath hung in clouds above my head as I drew back the sheets. The water in my jug was iced over and fern leaves frosted the windows. In Queen Street a man with a courier's pack slung over his shoulder galloped silently over the carpet of snow. My clothes were stiff with cold. By the time I had hurried into them the horse's prints had disappeared.

In my study the maid, eyes still gummed with sleep, had barely finished stoking up the fire. Mr Cole, hands blue with cold, brought in the courier's message. It was coded and brief, even by Thurloe's standards.

'General Monck crossed the Scottish border on New Year's Day and is marching south. Get here as soon as possible. JT.'

General Monck? What on earth was he up to? I looked at his file. When he had objected to the army generals taking over completely and called for the Rump Parliament's return, he had told its leader, Haselrig, he would await Parliament's instructions. I sent an urgent message to Haselrig, asking what instructions had been given.

In the file were copies of the flattering letters I had sent to Monck, dangling out to him various inducements in lands and honours. His soldiers called Monck 'Honest George'. With his West Country burr he portrayed himself as a simple soldier, but he was shrewd and calculating. His only mistake was to marry his cook, a shrew who incensed the other generals. Unlike them he had acquired no titles or land. My letters had been designed to put that right.

'Did we ever get any replies?'

'No, Sir Thomas.'

I swallowed a small beer and a piece of turkey pie without tasting it while Mr Cole brought in the mail. Some of the letters were for Anne. Mr Cole put them to one side, handing me a packet, on which were instructions that only the addressee should open it. I had been sent all manner of unsavoury objects, including plague and leper dressings, and told Mr Cole to use the coal tongs. With them, and a pair of scissors, he teased the wrapping away. Normally inscrutable, even he was shocked. He had served my grandfather, Lord Stonehouse, whose casual brutality easily outdid mine. Perhaps Lord Stonehouse had been more successful in keeping these acts beyond his own front door; or perhaps Mr Cole, his scanty hair silver, his face crazed like old porcelain, had reached an age when his Maker felt closer than the man he served.

I could swear he turned away to cross himself, an unwise thing to do in Protestant England. His hand shook as he put the remains of a cut-off finger, with a ring embedded in it, on my desk. An insidious smell of decay rose from it.

I decoded the letter. The agent wrote as if he was sending me a specimen of the diamonds that were his trade, apologising for the state of the ring. It had been difficult to clean it properly before the boat left. Evidence of hurry, or revulsion in removing it from the finger, was embedded in the intricate, decorative twists and turns of the ring. The smell seemed to grow stronger, as if the air had released it. The Stonehouse falcon, raised from the surface of the ring, glared at me. I wore a similar ring. Like its partner, it had sunk into my flesh, becoming part of me over the years. Nausea brought the taste of the pie back into my throat. I put the decoding in my drawer and locked it. I gave Mr Cole the original letter, innocuous in itself, dismissed him, flung the packet and wrappings into the fire and forced myself to study the ring carefully.

There was no doubt about it. The ring was genuine, engraved on the inside with his initials *RAS* and the Stonehouse motto, *Ab Imo Pectore*: from the heart. It was a gift from his father, Lord Stonehouse, his inheritance, his whole life. He would never have parted from it willingly. That was why I had demanded it as proof of his death. It was an indication of how my mood had changed in the last few months that a wave of guilt overcame me before I put it with the agent's letter into the drawer for finished business and locked it. Gradually, mixed with the guilt was relief. It was necessary. Richard was not Prince Rupert, but without his organisation and leadership flair plans for a Royalist invasion would be seriously disrupted. I had bought us time, at least. Perhaps to assuage the guilt I went to tell Anne. I had no doubt what her reaction would be. She was leaving her rooms, on her way out too, wearing a heavily quilted cloak and a mask against the cold.

'How did he die?'

'A brawl in Amsterdam.'

'Typical.'

She tore the mask away. Not for years had I seen her act with such spontaneity. She hugged me. Her eyes sparkled. Her relief swept away the remains of my guilt. I only realised as we held one another that, although he had been in exile, not a day had passed without my feeling I had glimpsed him at the back of a crowd or in a shadow in the street.

She pulled away. 'You're sure? You have proof?'

'I have his ring.'

She gripped me so tightly her nails bit into my shoulders. 'We have a chance,' she said. 'Whatever happens, we have a chance.'

She was thinking of the estate, of course, but at that moment I did not care. I was about to draw her to me when at the door of his room I saw Luke. He was shivering in his nightshirt, half-dazed with sleep. He rubbed one frozen foot against another. How long he had been there I did not know.

He started to speak, coughed, and had to clear his throat before he continued. 'When did Grandfather die?'

'I don't know,' I said. 'I only got the letter from Amsterdam this morning.'

'I remember,' he said inconsequentially, 'he put me on a horse. He knew about horses. I must have been …'

'Eight,' I said. 'You were eight. He was on the run. You thought he was the new ostler while all the time …'

'All the time he was planning to kill your father,' Anne said.

Luke glanced from one of us to the other. He wore no wig and scratched his shaven head. 'Yes. Yes. I know. I know the story.' He drifted back into his room.

We looked at one another, wordlessly regretting that he had seen our jubilation at the death of someone who was not only my father but, to him, a Royalist hero. I went to follow him, but Anne stopped me.

'You go. I'll talk to him.'

12

I was riding down Queen Street when I saw Haselrig's courier. Thick flakes of snow clung to our faces and settled in the crevices of our cloaks as I fumbled open the message. I could see Haselrig's choleric face, the spittle that flecked the air when he spoke, as I read the scrawled words.

'Monck has received no instructions from Parliament. What does he want? Another civil war? General against general? Order him to return!'

On the one hand I was given no powers, on the other told to order him to return.

'No reply,' I said.

There were boxes of papers in Thurloe's chambers, stacked in the corridors and in his office. He was going through one box, marked *Not to be removed from Whitehall*. He was using his time out of office, he said, to write a history of Cromwell's rule. I told him my father was dead. He nodded, but because of the news from the north it did not make the impact I expected. He turned to a map on the wall.

'General Monck is here.' Thurloe pointed to York. 'Or here.' He pointed to a place so small it had been inked in on the map.

'Nun Appleton? Fairfax's seat?'

Fairfax was Cromwell's old commander, a conservative who had distanced himself from the King's trial but was revered by troops as a symbol of the Good Old Cause. Crippled with gout, he had to be lifted into a coach to travel anywhere. Thurloe told me that, following Fairfax's intervention, the small garrison in York had opened the gates to Monck. The only troops that stood between Monck and London were those of Lambert's republican army in the Midlands.

'How many troops has Monck?'

I consulted my dispatches. 'Seven thousand.'

'Lambert?'

'When he put down the uprising in the summer, twice as many. But they have not been paid. Perhaps a few thousand? Morale is poor.'

Thurloe gazed at the map, silent for a while. The only sound was the scraping of snow from the cobbles so a carter could get through. Snow shrouded the trees and the light reflected from the wide stretch of Lincoln's Inn Fields was blinding.

'What is Monck up to?'

'You're asking me?'

'You wrote to him.'

He had the prosecuting lawyer's trick of dropping his voice when he reached a key moment in his questioning, so one strained to hear, with the feeling that you were about to be found out – whether or not there was anything to find.

'He never replied.'

'Are you sure?'

'Of course I'm sure!'

'Were your letters intercepted?'

'Intercepted?'

There were shouts outside. The carters were making snowballs. One saw me watching and picked up his spade guiltily. The other, a boy, hurled his ball, hitting the carter full in the face and shrieking with laughter before he, too, saw me and scuttled to his spade.

'Was this one of them?' Thurloe took a letter from a file marked *Monck*.

My face must have looked as white as the landscape. There was Mr Cole's carefully chiselled Italian hand, my obsequious blandishments, with preferments between the lines, requesting that we might meet, in Edinburgh or London. From the furred folds and greasy fingermarks, it looked as though it had gone through a number of pockets. It was dated mid-December and must have been the second letter I sent to Monck.

'Where did you get this?'

'A courier was killed leaving London. Enfield. Eventually it found its way back to me.'

Not me. One of Thurloe's paid constables. In the past I would have put the letter in a secure coach, but being out of power I had no access to one. The system which for years I had taken for granted was falling apart. Normally, I would have checked. Persisted. But I had not been normal these past months – if you called normal becoming part of these boxes of paper as Thurloe was, not just during the day, but during sleep, so that you awoke in the middle of the night with the answer to a problem, fumbling to make a note for fear you might lose it, spilling ink, lighting a candle, then lying in the half-darkness unable to get back to sleep because the problem you had solved raised a host of others. I had committed the sin of falling in love and it was true that love and politics did not mix, even if it was love for your own wife. It was an odd moment to admit it. An odd place. I gazed out of the window, oblivious of Thurloe's stare, for the first time seeing how beautiful it was: snowflakes, as big as coins, whirling, dancing, whitening the hair of the carter's boy who had lost his cap, coming to rest on the bare branches of trees to form strange, bulbous shapes.

'Are you secure, Tom?'

'What?'

His voice never rose, never lost its even, steady monotone. 'It might have been a normal robbery, of course. But the constables don't think so. He had nothing of value except to the Royalists.'

Thurloe's eyes never left me. He was good at waiting. And he never repeated questions; the one he had asked hung in the air.

'There are no leaks from my end.'

'Are you sure?'

'Of course I'm not sure. How can one ever be sure?' His secretary had brought me a dish of coffee. Either it was getting better, or I was growing used to its sharp, bitter taste. It helped to steady me. 'You're thinking about Luke.'

'I didn't say that.'

There was a clattering of boots from the corridor. The carter was delivering more boxes. There followed a short argument between Thurloe's secretary and the carter who was expecting a signature. Thurloe sighed and went out to the corridor. I turned to put the letter back in the Monck file. On top was a note in Thurloe's neat hand. *Sir Richard Grenville. Letters to Edward Hyde*. There was a list of dates, one recent. Evidently it was not just history that Thurloe was writing. Hyde was Charles Stuart's chief adviser in Brussels.

'No signature,' Thurloe said in the corridor. The carter muttered that it was irregular, but there was a clink of coins, followed by the sound of his retreating boots. When Thurloe returned I was staring out of the window at the drifting snow.

'Luke has given me his word he will not consort with Royalists while he is living in my house,' I said.

The faintest of smiles crossed Thurloe's face. 'His word.'

'He is a gentleman,' I said. Was I really saying that? With all my contempt for gentlemen?

'Unlike you and me,' Thurloe said.

'Unlike us,' I said, with an echo of his faint smile, 'his word means something. I believe him. I'll write to Monck again and send it by a man I can trust.' That word again. 'What does Monck want?'

'I have no idea.'

'Who is Sir Richard Grenville?'

He was still. For Thurloe, a little too still. 'How do you know him?'

'I don't. I saw his name when I put the letter back.'

'A nonentity in Somerset. I try and keep an eye on everyone who writes to Brussels.' He closed the file. 'Monck told Fairfax he's coming to the City to get more pay for his soldiers. Do you believe that?'

'Honest George? He's there to get pay for himself. Or, more likely, power.'

'Or broker it.' Thurloe went back to his boxes.

Of course Thurloe intercepted the letters to Brussels, or tried to. The interesting thing was the reason for it being in the Monck file. Thurloe only ever told me what he believed it was essential for me to know. For survival, it helped to know that little bit more and I determined to get Mr Cole to check Sir Richard Grenville as soon as I returned. One thing was certain. Whatever game he was playing, Thurloe's first consideration was always his own skin. He knew that if Charles Stuart seized his crown, as Cromwell's closest confidant and Secretary of State Thurloe would be among the first to be put on trial for his life. If he really thought there was the remotest possibility of that he would not be drinking coffee and writing a history of Cromwell's rule in his comfortable chambers; he would be on his way to Geneva on the first available boat.

13

The snow had almost stopped when I returned to Queen Street. While the ostler took my horse I stared at the strange shape in a corner of the stables. At first I thought it was a beggar who had wandered in for shelter. Snow had swirled in to cover the hat pulled over his head and powder his shoulders. Only his snore identified him. It was a most irritating sound which I recognised from nights in the field during the war; a throbbing bass cut off in mid-note, which hung in the air before ending in a dying whistle. I put my finger to my lips to motion the ostler into silence and bellowed in best army fashion.

'Atten – shun!'

Scogman scrambled up, his hat falling off, bringing his hand half-way up in salute, almost falling before he grabbed at the stable door for support.

'What the hell are you doing there?'

'Been dismissed, sir,' he said thickly.

I grinned. He looked like the trooper he once was, straw clinging to his steward's dark britches, his linen crumpled and a smear of horse shit on his green doublet. 'You certainly deserve it but I don't recollect dismissing you, Scogman.'

'She did.'

'Who?'

'Lady Stonehouse.' He turned away and slung a pack over the saddle of his horse, then belted it into place.

'Now come on, Scogman. What is all this?'

He came out of the stable trembling with rage. 'How long have I served you, sir? How long? Spying on me! You tells me not to spy on him and I don't – even though I knows they were twisting you round their little fingers. And all the time, all the time, he's spying on me.'

'Calm down, Scoggy, and tell me what happened.'

'He happened! He did!' He pointed up at the house. From a window overlooking the yard Luke's pale face stared downward. Anne appeared, said something sharply to him, and Luke withdrew. Scogman spat out a piece of straw. 'That fine son of yours. The French dog. The Royalist trickster.'

'Keep a civil tongue in your head or you *will* be dismissed.'

I walked away, weary of his battles with Luke. My closer relationships with Anne and Luke had made me think it really was time to get rid of him and employ a proper steward whose hand I could read and whose numbers added up. I was scraping the snow from my boots on the doorstep irons when I heard him behind me.

'Permission to speak, sir.'

I didn't even have the heart to go through the charade of telling him to stand at ease. He had taken off his hat and was shuffling from one foot to another.

'What is it now, Scogman?'

'I never told him nothing about the boy, Sir Thomas.'

'Boy? What are you talking about?'

'Sam. I never breathed a word about him, nor Clerkenwell, the kiln, not to no one.' His cockiness had gone. I had not seen him so frightened for a long time.

I glanced around. Steam rose from my horse as the ostler flung a pail of water over her before rubbing her down. There was no sign of anyone else. The house felt unusually quiet. I motioned him towards the tack room and told him he had better tell me what had happened.

After I had gone out, Scogman had arrived to collect some letters from Mr Cole when he saw Mr Luke loitering with intent.

'How can he loiter with intent in his own house?'

'He was upstairs, wasn't he? I saw him from here through that window up there. He slipped into an alcove. Looked suspicious to me, but I told myself Sir Thomas has told me to trust him and trust him I will …' Scogman spoke with the injured relish of someone who has been right all along but not believed.

'Get on with it.'

He told me he heard a cry which sounded as if someone had been struck. He ran back inside where he found Mr Cole sprawled out on some chairs on the landing, his papers all over the place, with Luke standing over him.

'He hit Mr Cole? Is that what you're saying?'

'That's what it looked like to me, sir. He had picked up a file and was reading one of your letters. I grabbed him. He called me a thief and said I was the one who should be arrested for stealing money from the estate and salting it away in Clerkenwell.'

'The kiln?'

'Just so, sir.'

My mouth was so dry I had to swallow several times before I could speak. 'How did he find out about that?'

It turned out that Scogman had been followed. He was as indignant as a gamekeeper who finds he has been stalked by a poacher. Luke, in his newfound freedom, seemed to have followed Scogman when he made payments to Sam to fund the kiln. It was at this point that, according to Scogman, Lady Stonehouse dismissed him. I told Scogman to go back into the house and stay there until I called him.

'Does that mean I'm not dismissed, sir?'

'Let me talk to Lady Stonehouse.'

'I'd rather stay here, sir, until I know where I am.'

'As you wish.'

'He's talked to Sam, sir.'

'Luke?' It felt as though the chill of that day had entered my blood and frozen it. 'Does he know who Sam is?'

'I don't know. That was when Lady Stonehouse told me to go.'

Once there would have been a number of people waiting for me in reception. Now there was only Alderman Collins. I had to have the City's reaction to Monck, but he could wait. He was paid for it. I could hear Luke's voice on the landing and as I went up the stairs could see the swirl of Anne's skirts. They were so intent on one another and Luke so distraught, they did not hear me.

'I must see him. I will see him,' Luke said. He was holding a letter.

'Give it to me.' She held out her hand for the letter.

He shook his head. 'I got myself into this and I must deal with it myself, Mother,' he said.

'Don't be a fool. You'll only make matters worse. I'll handle your father.'

He shook his head stubbornly. For a moment it looked as though she was going to snatch the letter from him. Then she saw me.

'Go to your room, Luke,' she said.

He swivelled his terrified eyes towards me, hesitating. The letter he was holding was the one from the agent in Amsterdam. 'Luke wants to see me,' I said. 'And I certainly want to see him.'

'Please,' she said. 'Let me –'

'Handle it?'

She flushed, twisting her fingers together. 'I meant, sir, you always get the wrong ideas about one another –'

She looked past me down into the hall. James and the other servants were pretending not to see us. I held out my hand for the letter. Mutely, Luke gave it to me and followed me into my study.

14

I sent for Mr Cole but was told he was ill. Luke looked ill as well, feverish, breathing irregularly as if he had been running. I told him to sit down. He shook his head and stood vacantly, not even finding the customary line in the carpet. Only when I asked him if he had struck Mr Cole did he look at me with astonishment and come to furious life.

'Strike him? Is that what that thieving rogue Scogman told you?'

'Show some respect for him.'

Far from striking him, Luke protested, he had gone to help the old man, who appeared to have had some kind of fit. Luke had reached him as he began to collapse and helped him to a chair, where the papers slipped from his hand. After calling the servants, he picked up the fallen papers himself, for he knew they must be confidential. He stared at the letter on my desk. He had seen it came from Amsterdam and because he knew his grandfather had died there could not help reading it. He admitted that.

'Then the rogue –' He swallowed and controlled himself. 'Your steward, Mr Scogman, laid his hands on me.' He brushed his clothes with movements of disgust, as if Scogman had permanently soiled them. 'I am afraid I lost my temper, sir. I know he has served with you, but I am afraid you do not seem to see what is happening. He has taken money from the estate and bought a glass-works in Clerkenwell. It is not in the London accounts.'

'You study these accounts, do you?'

He shifted uncomfortably. 'My mother does.'

This must have been when we were in the middle of our bitter arguments, when she thought I had changed my will. 'She suggested you follow him?'

He stared past me, a look of what I could only call shame crossing his face. Following someone through the backstreets of Clerkenwell was not the act of a gentleman, but reduced him to Scogman's sordid level. 'She said you would not believe me unless you had proof.'

'And you have that proof?'

He had. He was convinced of it. When Scogman had gone he went into the glass-works, pretending to have an interest in the subject, and talked to the glass-blower.

'Did you indeed,' I said. I thought of Thurloe asking if I was secure and the letters to Monck that had been intercepted. Every time I believed I knew Luke, something happened to confound the picture. 'You are becoming quite an accomplished spy, Luke.'

'Is it spying to try and protect your own property?' he flashed, before correcting himself. 'The estate's property?'

'And what did you make of this glass-blower?'

'Another rogue, sir!' I went to the window and stared out, afraid my expression would betray me. My reaction encouraged him in his vilification of the half-brother he did not know existed. 'Uncouth. Hair the colour of Devil's blood. He told me the works were owned by a man called Black, obviously a name Scogman has assumed.'

I let him wait while I pretended to make some notes. I had not worked for Thurloe for years without watching him in cross-examination. Picking up some of the tricks. The mildness. The pauses. Above all, the simple, unexpected question.

'What were you doing there?'

'Where?' He gave me a startled look, like a deer who thinks he has heard a sound, but is uncertain whether to run or not.

'The way down to the vault. That's a servant's passage, isn't it?'

'I – I heard him cry out.'

'Scogman said he saw you hiding in an alcove and then following Mr Cole. Is that true?' He was breathing more quickly, rubbing at his chest as if it was sore. 'Luke?'

'Yes.' He spoke so low I could scarcely hear him. 'When you told Mother my grandfather was dead I wanted to know when he had died … what had happened …'

'Why?'

'Why? He is … was … my grandfather.'

His breathing took on the steady crackle that I remembered from his childhood illnesses. It crossed my mind that he used his illness, perhaps even faked it. Perhaps his professed feelings, along with the respect he had shown me in the last months, were faked too.

'Go on.'

'I … I touched Mr Cole on the shoulder. He was startled. He was not feeling well, I think. He dropped the papers. I helped him to a chair and when the servants came I picked up the papers. Then Scogman came and accused me of stealing them.'

'Were you?'

'What?'

'Stealing them?'

He gave me that old, superior look of contempt which had irked me so much when he was in prison. 'I will not even answer that, Father. I wanted to find out when … how my grandfather died.'

'He died in a brawl.'

He stared at the letter from Amsterdam on my desk, his rasping breath the only sound in the room. He could surely have got little from the letter. Even if he knew the code, he would have had no time to decode it. His eyes only left the letter to stare again at the map of the Highpoint estate, as if he was longing to be there in the pure air of the country. He mumbled something, more to the map than to me.

'I cannot hear you, Luke.'

'What does that say?' He pointed to the letter.

'It confirms the purchase of some jewellery.'

'I know what goes on in this room.' His voice became shrill. 'They use codes in the Sealed Knot.'

'Not very successfully.'

'No,' he said bitterly. 'No. That's true.'

'You followed Mr Cole, didn't you?'

His look became sullen, defiant. 'Yes.'

'Intending to read this letter?'

'Yes. I had to.'

'Had to?'

He almost spat out the words. 'For your sake.'

'My sake? Stop talking in riddles. Look at me. Have you read any more of my private correspondence?'

He gave me a look as if the question was not worth answering. 'No.' He glared at me directly. 'I am not like one of your spies.' His gaze never flinched; either he was very good, or he was telling the truth.

'Two months ago I wrote a letter to General Monck. It never arrived. Did you see that letter?' There was a tiny stiffening of his body, a checking of his breath. 'The letter never reached Monck. A courier was murdered ...'

'Oh, God,' he said.

'What is it, Luke?'

He was completely still. There was no sound except for the steady rasp of his breath and the flickering of the fire. I had been through many such moments during the war, when torture was a matter of course on both sides. I never used it. People would say anything to stop the pain. Far better to find a point of weakness and let a man torture himself. The art then was to be like, well, what I was. A father. To be gentle, caring, understanding, sympathetic; above all to stop questioning: he would do that himself. I could see the self-interrogation in the growing fear in his eyes, the increased tempo of his crackling breath, the dart of his tongue across his dry lips. I rang for a servant to bring in some cordial. At first he refused it, but when I put it back on my desk he almost grabbed it from me. Finally, when, lips shining with cordial, he began to talk, what he said was the last thing I expected.

'You must go, Father.'

'Go? Where?'

The cordial had soothed his throat and his voice came out more strongly, urgently. 'Europe. Anywhere. There is no time to lose. Go now. Before it is too late.' He twisted his hands together, speaking in the hackneyed phrases of a mystery play. 'There is an army you cannot defeat.'

'The King has raised another army?'

My heart sank. In spite of what I had said and the botch-ups and betrayals of the last rebellion, he was involved in the Sealed Knot again. At least he was telling me about it, instead of him being involved in another crazy enterprise.

'Where is this army? Ireland? The Netherlands?'

He seemed totally unaware of the scepticism in my voice. 'Have you heard of the King's List?'

The Puritans had closed the theatres, censored print and condemned bear baiting and cock fighting. But they could not put an end to betting. Somewhere most nights south of London Bridge there was always a pair of gamecocks fighting. And when people could not bet on the cocks there was always the public hanging. They would wager on whether a man would die game or piss in his britches. How long it would take him to die. Would he accept the preacher or curse him? Would the doctors seize his body or his relatives claim him for burial?

No one knew who started it. When London ground to a halt there was a lull even in public hangings. The King's List began to circulate in coffee houses where they took wagers on the King coming back. The list was a grisly adjunct to that: offering odds on the regicides; who would stay, taking his chance on the King's mercy; who would run and, of those who gambled and stayed, who would be caught and hanged, drawn and quartered.

'I believe I am number eleven on the list.'

'Number nine.'

'The odds must have shortened.'

'It is not a joke, Father.'

'Go on. Enlighten me.'

He was not talking about the gamblers' list, circulating round the taverns, he said. There was a real King's List, naming people who would be executed when the King landed. It was held by Edward Hyde, Charles's chief counsellor in Brussels. Luke claimed to have seen a copy of it.

An alehouse pamphleteer would have headed it with John Cooke, who prosecuted King Charles at his trial. Any fool could list the regicides. Of the sixty-nine who signed the death warrant, forty-one were still alive. It was a name, Cooke insisted, that was missing that marked it out as a forgery, a tawdry piece of Royalist propaganda. Although he had not signed the death warrant, any genuine list would have had, after Cooke, the man who had been closest to Cromwell.

'John Thurloe will be mortified to know he is not there.'

'He is not on the list.'

'It is nonsense, Luke. Claptrap. Whoever has shown you this is trying to get at me.'

His voice became low and quiet. 'It is true. I know you think I am a fool, Father, but I am not that much of a fool. Thurloe's name *was* there but it had been crossed out.'

A chill crept into me, like damp finding old wounds. I only realised the light was going when I could not see Luke's expression, lost in the deepening shadows. I remembered the meeting with Thurloe. Had there been a change in his attitude towards Charles Stuart? For the first time he had considered Charles as a possibility, albeit remote. I had never before heard him confess that he had no idea what was going on. No idea? I tried to remember the name of the man in the Monck file. I should have made a note of it.

I strode across the room and pulled open the door. 'Are there no candles left in this house?'

Servants scurried, colliding with one another as they removed stumps, trimmed old candles and put in new. The taper boy, flame cupped in his hand, rushed to light them as soon as they were in place. Luke blinked at the sudden light, reduced from a threatening shadow to a youth playing soldiers.

'Where did you get this nonsense from? The Sealed Knot?'

'It is not nonsense and it is not from the Sealed Knot. I told you I would leave them and I do not break my word.' He started to cough again.

'Then where did you see the list?'

He shook his head violently. The coughing had brought tears to his eyes and he brushed them away angrily. I was sure he was telling the truth. It would have been easier if he told me half-truths and lies, as most people did. Eventually they always tripped themselves up, but with this obdurate honesty the more I questioned him, the more he tightened his lips. Much as he exasperated me I could not help admiring him for it. In the leaping light of the candles I could see behind his belligerence the fear in his eyes, in the constant twist of his thin, beautiful fingers.

'Why are you telling me this?'

'Because you are my father.'

No subtlety was needed to interpret Luke's expression. The fear in his face was as vivid as a slash of Dutch oil paint. He would break soon. Perversely, in that instant, I didn't want him to. I wanted him to be better than that. His eyes stared, his lips quivered. I changed my tone, as the anglers have it, easing him through the pain so the line does not break.

'I am grateful. It sounds like a forgery. But if it is not, there are other people on the list I have a duty to warn. You do see that, Luke, don't you?'

He did. It was evident in his constant drawing of his tongue over his dry lips, his eyes staring anywhere but at me. He knew, or had met, a number of people on that list. Some he loathed, but some he respected, had even warmed to as a child before he knew what the word *regicide* meant. A number of them had been to Queen Street recently, and we had agreed to warn each other if we heard about the King's plans. A few, taking no chances, had already left the country. Outside a carriage approached, silent except for the cry of the driver.

'I don't know what to do,' he muttered.

There was a knock at the door. 'No,' I called, but the door was opened by James, on duty at reception in the front hall. 'I said no.' He shut the door immediately, muttering an apology. I struggled to hold on to the moment between me and Luke through the scuttering of James's feet across the marble hall, but my anger at his interruption found its way into my voice. From that moment I lost Luke. It would be more accurate to say I lost myself.

'If you do not tell me where you saw the list I will have you arrested.'

He stood up. This time he found the line in the carpet. He seemed more comfortable there. 'You are not in power now, Father. Nor will be.'

'I am not, but to the people who are, even talking of this list is seditious. You can tell me where you saw it, or you can tell them. It is your choice. Go to your room. You have an hour to think about it.'

He stood stiffly to attention. For a moment I thought he was going to salute me before he plunged away, stumbling, almost falling as he went up the stairs towards his rooms. In the hall I told James never to interrupt me in that way again. He stammered out another apology. He knew that normally I should not be interrupted, but Alderman Collins said he had been waiting an hour and could not wait any longer, and he thought that was important.

I ran into the street. The moon was coming up, its ghostly light glinting in footprints and the winding track of the carriage that had arrived for Alderman Collins when I was totally absorbed in Luke. Like an angry, petulant child, I kicked at the already freezing track, slipping and almost falling. James was staring at me from the top of the steps.

'You were quite right, James,' I said. 'It was important.'

A month ago, no matter how long I kept them waiting, nobody would have dared do that to me.

15

I would have questioned Gilbert, Luke's personal servant, but he was out, no one knew where. His absence alarmed me enough to think of putting a discreet guard at the reception in case Luke attempted to leave, but I dismissed it. It would be round the servants within minutes and I feared it would destroy what remained of the relationship between us. Already I was cursing myself for being too heavy-handed. I still could not believe he was a spy, but he had reacted with dismay when I told him the courier carrying the letter to Monck had been murdered. Because he had seen the letter and told someone? And where had he seen that list?

Instead of a guard I went to speak to the ostler, whose discretion I could rely on. But he had slipped on the ice and was suffering a bad sprain or fracture and was waiting for the doctor. I was reluctant to give Scogman the role because of the animosity between them but had no choice. He was only too ready to do it and was oddly comforting.

'He ain't a spy, sir. I can smell 'em and my nose says he ain't a spy.'

I was astonished. 'But you were convinced of it! You told me!'

He sniffed. 'You can be convinced of anything when a man treats you like shit. He thinks I'm rabble. Something that should be thrown out for the scavengers. That's why he spied on me. But you're a Stonehouse. He'd fight you, but he wouldn't cheat you or grass you. Ever since you fought that duel he's thought the world of you.'

'But you told me he followed Mr Cole! Knocked him over!'

'Well, it was confusing, sir. Dark in that corridor. Maybe I was over-anxious to be believed after her ladyship gave me the boot. Maybe Mr Cole had some kind of a fit and Mr Luke caught him.'

'But he read that letter?'

'Oh, he did that all right, sir. As soon as he had got Mr Cole comfortable and called the servants he grabbed the letter. He was shocked, sir. His face went as white as this snow.'

I was more confused than ever. What did he see in a list of jewellery? He knew what I did, guessed it was coded. But what did he see that shocked him?

When I returned to the house I found Anne had tried to speak to Luke but he had locked himself in his room. From it came the familiar, musky smell of the laudanum he took to ease his cough. It also made him feel drowsy and she had decided to let him sleep.

She came into my study and I told her what had happened. In her brightening of the house it was the only part she had not touched. She rarely came in here. While I spoke she stared at the carpet where Luke had stood. His foot must have caught in it, for there was a tear through which you could see the boards.

'I was wrong about him,' she said. 'I'm sorry.'

'No, no. You weren't wrong. Not entirely.'

'He lied to you. He's been working with the Royalists.' She now seemed more intent on condemning him than I did.

'It's more complicated than that.'

'What do you mean?'

'I don't know. I don't know what I mean, Anne.'

The coals shifted and several fell in the grate. I snatched them up and dropped them back in the fire. From the street came a faint crunching sound. I peered through the window but could see nothing.

'What is it?'

'I thought I heard someone.'

'So did I.'

She clutched at my arm. It was an animal reaction neither of us had felt for years, when you lived from day to day, hour to hour, not knowing what was happening, who was round the next corner, where you would lay your head that night, even if you would lay it anywhere at all.

'Is it happening?' Her voice was as sharp as ice cracking.

'What?'

'The King.'

'I don't know.'

'What does Thurloe think?'

'I don't know about Thurloe.'

'What do you mean – you don't know about Thurloe?'

'Anne – I don't know *why* I don't know about Thurloe!'

There was the same crunching noise, sharper now, at the same time as a metallic click which sounded like the dog lock of a pistol. I pulled Anne away from the window.

From the shadow of a tree a man emerged. I could not see much at first because of his wide-brimmed hat. There was a glint of metal in the moonlight. He put back the instrument he had dropped in the open bag he was carrying and crunched slowly over the snow towards the stables.

'The apothecary. Come to treat the ostler's leg.'

She pressed her head against my chest, shaking like me from relief as much as laughter.

* * *

After all the anticipation, the embellishments, the careful studying of women and their humours, the insidious dangers of their bloody flowers, the lover's agonising of wanting her soul as well as her body, I took her like a whore in an alleyway. Or she took me.

For so long I had satisfied my animal needs in such low company that I had forgot how well defended the respectable woman was. Even widows morally beyond reproach who wished to re-enter society with a man had to make their underskirts reasonably accessible. The front panel of Anne's skirt was an easy entrance, but I got lost and more and more frantic in the maze of petticoats, then, when I did get through, was completely blocked by the keep of her busk, as rock-stiff as I was, a solid wall from her belly to her honour.

To my amazement she thrust me to one side. I had forgot that before she was Lady Stonehouse she was Anne Black, with a calculation in these matters you would normally find only in a woman south of London Bridge. With short, crisp movements, she unlaced the busk. The sharp snaps of the lace sent me even further aloft. Her belly, save for the weal-like marks the busk left, was as smooth as a young girl in spite of the two children – or three if she was to be believed – who had passed through it. Her smell intoxicated me, the sweet clinging musk released by her clothes, cut by the unexpectedly rank odour of her sweat. Her look, as slippery as her bush, drove me into a frenzy of ineptness and impatience. It went from mockery, to hunger, to desperation, to love, to hate, to tenderness, to violence that one moment threw me into a daze, the next maddened me. Clumsy as a boy, I fumbled to enter her. Her hands moved to guide me, but at their touch I came. The seed that for months I had been determined to plant inside her pumped on my hand, the carpet, her petticoats – anywhere but in its intended target.

She began to laugh. I went to push her away. Still she laughed helplessly, pointing at my side. Embedded in the bare flesh was a cinder that had fallen from the fire when I kicked it. It must have been hot, for the skin round it was reddened, but I had not felt it. It clung like a limpet. In a sudden movement she unpicked it, flung it into the fire and kissed the burn, burying her lips deep into my skin. We held each other tightly, in a way I had thought would never happen again. Even the insidious thought that, under the guise of helping me, she had played the old whore's trick of making me come too soon did not disturb me. Trickery was part of her and if there was deception in her heart pulsing against mine, there was none in the feeling of utter peace that stole over us.

How long we lay there I do not know. The warmth of the fire was like a blanket over us. Her breathing became more and more shallow and mine began to rise and fall in tune with it. From time to time, as clouds drifted away from the moon, an opalescent light flickered slowly over the room, turning the furniture into strange, dancing shadows.

A short, sharp cry rang out. She jumped, an eye jerking open, her breathing checked. There was another cry, followed by a dying series of groans. We twisted our heads in unison. The sound came from the stables.

'The ostler having his leg re-set,' I said.

'Ah. The poor ostler.' She buried her face back into me. There was a silence, followed by sounds from the stables, comforting rather than disturbing: the clank of a pail, the scrape of a door. There was a protesting, penetrating neigh from one of the horses, which set another one off. A cavalryman in the field listens to his horses in his sleep, for if you lost your horse you lost your legs, and often enough your life. I tensed and felt her body tighten against me, but the horses settled and we began to slip back into our dream-like state.

There was a thud of doors bursting open, a snapping clatter of hooves. I scrambled up, falling against the desk as my britches fettered my ankles, yelling at the top of my voice, an almost scream I had not uttered for ten years.

'The horses! See to the horses.'

In the stable yard servants milled around in confusion. In the whirl of mashed-up snow it was impossible to see what horses had been taken. The rest had panicked and were rearing and neighing in their stalls. From the darkness inside came spasmodic groans of pain.

'Two of you! The rest check the street. Calm the horses. Bring a light.'

James brought a lantern, gaping at my half-buttoned shirt, clumsily hitched back on to my britches on the wrong hooks. The light glinted on specks of blood outside the stalls. Two were empty. Luke's horse had gone, along with Scogman's. Whoever had stolen them knew his horses. Unless it was Scogman himself. As things were slipping into chaos and anarchy, I could believe anything. Scogman was aggrieved enough and he might have taken Luke's horse to spite him.

The groaning came from the other end of the stables. Sprawled outside the door to the tack room was the ostler, face down in the snow. I summoned James. The ostler screamed and writhed as we lifted him. One leg was hanging uselessly. I could feel the movement of the broken bone as I gripped him. I shifted position. He screamed again and we almost dropped him before we managed to get him on a trestle bed in the tack room. Mercifully he passed out. Below a workbench where the ostler had been repairing a saddle, I saw a boot and the familiar black steward's britches Scogman wore. As I pulled him out from under the bench he aimed a blow at me. I caught his arm. He stared up at me, one eye blinking away blood trickling from a gash at the side of his head. He made a feeble attempt to get to his feet, his voice slurred.

'That ... country hick ... Gilbert ...'

Luke's servant. I left him to James and ran back into the house, almost colliding with Anne. She said something but I did not catch it. I could smell the laudanum halfway down the corridor. It grew worse as I approached his room. I had the dreadful fear he had killed himself. It was exactly the sort of thing the idiot would do. Another martyr for the cause of his beloved King, which another fool would write a poem about. I yelled his name, pushed servants to one side and flung myself at the door, swearing to God that he could have his wretched King if only he was still alive. Whether from the strength of fear or rage, or a combination of both, the lock snapped and I spun into the room.

At first I could see little. The sickly smell of laudanum almost overpowered me. A draught of cold air disturbed the heavy drawn curtains. A brief flash of moonlight lit up a still figure in the bed. On the table next to it was an empty bottle of the drug. That glimpse, before the curtains dropped back into darkness, held a lifetime of regret; regret that we had not come together sooner than we had over that duel; regret that I had pushed him too far; regret that, in the end, far from trusting him too much, I had perhaps not trusted him enough.

I went to the bed and touched not cold flesh but pillows stuffed under the counterpane. I pulled back the curtains. By this time servants had brought candles. They illuminated sheets knotted to the bed-head, passing through the open window. The makeshift rope had not been long enough, leaving a considerable drop to the roof of the stables, which depended on a steady nerve and sure feet. He was unlikely to have taken the laudanum. I found it poured into a saucer near the door, the thick odour seeping beneath it suggesting to anyone outside he was in a deep sleep. Perhaps, in the confrontation in my study, he had even faked his cough. Near the laudanum was a picture. It was one from the King's Collection which Anne had never put up; a Van Dyck of the King with Richard. Luke must have got it from the cellar. In a brief, uncontrollable flash of rage I kicked the saucer across the room. If Anne had not stopped me I would have put my boot through the picture.

16

The sword belt was old but the sword I buckled into it was new: Flemish steel with a simple shell guard; almost a rapier, but still with a cutting edge. Anne did not know the sword, but she knew the belt. It was an old baldrick, one part going over the shoulder, the other round the waist. Faint traces of a pattern in silver cord long gone were dotted in the dark, sweat-soaked leather. I had taken it from a dead Royalist at Marston Moor. Anne took one look at the belt and said nothing. She knew it was useless.

Although it froze the whole house, she insisted on having the windows of Luke's apartment wide open, as if she wanted not only to remove the thick cloying stench of laudanum, but Luke's whole presence. The draught blew out candles, and kept others dipping this way and that. When I mounted my horse the house looked like a ship rolling crazily in a storm at sea. Scogman, who was more mortified than hurt, insisted on coming with me.

'Women. Children,' he said. 'And you wonder why I never take a wife?'

I told Scogman to take me to Moor's Coffee House, in which Luke had shown an inordinate amount of interest. Part of me still believed, or wanted to believe him when he said he would have nothing more to do with the Royalists. Then I remembered his reaction when I told him about the murder of the courier I had sent to General Monck. Guilt had been written all over his face. A fresh surge of bitterness ran through me and I kicked my horse forward. The trampled snow down Fleet Street was turning to ice and she slipped and almost threw me. Scogman, who spent much more time in the saddle than I did, came to help me.

'I can manage.'

'Horse can't, sir. Beg your pardon, sir. Knows you're angry. Thinks it's with her.'

I let him talk softly to the horse. It was a kind of ballad, which some people thought came from the Devil, but which I knew came from his time as a horse thief. He not only quietened the horse, he calmed me. It was as if we were in the field again together.

'The Good Old Cause,' I said.

He flashed me a toothy grin, in which the moonlight caught a glint of silver wire. As a sign of his increased status, rather than for their chewing capacity, he had replaced his lost teeth with false ones. One of the strange trades that had grown was that in human teeth. After the war there was a plentiful supply.

'The Good Old Cause,' he said.

Without another word we rode together down Ludgate Hill, past St Paul's towering above us like a giant iced cake, catching the smell of the river as we turned into Watling Street.

The man running the Moor Coffee House smelt as if he had been boiled in his own coffee. His apron was stained with it and grains of it had found their way into his greying beard. While I gave a description of Luke he was constantly in movement, wiping the counter, putting chairs on top of a table, giving hopeful glances towards the last of his customers. There was a man on his own, going over a shipping table, and two merchants arguing heatedly. One, a young man, was for the King coming back. The other, an old man who looked like his father, spat on the floor.

'Never happen! Last one taxed everything in sight – soap, ships. Someone told me this one would tax having a piss. It's true!' he said in an aggrieved tone when the other laughed. 'A privy tax.'

The man behind the counter gave it another unnecessary wipe and said he had never seen anyone fitting Luke's description. Customers were mainly merchants and he knew most of them, he said, with another tired glance towards the old man, who looked a permanent fixture in his comfortable chair in a corner by the fire.

'He was a regular customer several months ago,' Scogman said with an encouraging smile. There was something of a threat in his display of unusually perfect teeth. The man stopped wiping the counter. The old man and his son ceased talking.

'French clothes? About eighteen? Ah, yes. I think I know the fellow you mean. But he hasn't been in for a long time.'

On our way out the old man drained his coffee, spitting the grounds on the floor. Scogman went to unhitch the horses. Next to the coffee house was a timber-framed house, one of a street of similar houses where craftsmen had lived and which merchants had extended upwards by building jetty after jetty dotted with windows which leaned perilously over into the street, as if they were about to fall into it. Out of one of these windows I thought I saw the red jowls of a familiar face – that of Sir Lewis Challoner, the man whose coach had almost run over the Quaker girl. The next moment the face had gone.

A servant passed one of the lower windows, dousing candles. I told Scogman what I had seen and tried the front door, just as the house steward, with his bunch of keys, was about to lock it. The force of the opening door almost made him drop the keys. He recovered quickly, clenching his fist round the keys, bringing them up as a weapon. Only my hand near my sword stopped him.

'I do beg your pardon, but I believe Sir Lewis Challoner is staying here.'

'You are mistaken, sir. There is no one here of that name. My master is at sea.' He tried to close the door but Scogman jammed his boot in it.

'Sir Lewis is wanted for questioning by Parliament,' I said.

The servant who had been dousing the candles hovered in the background, gripping a candlestick. 'Have you a warrant, sir?'

'This is my warrant.' I held out my hand. In the dimness of the hall the jewels on my ring seemed to produce their own light. Its power would not last much longer, but it was sufficient. The steward motioned the servant away and without another word, keys jingling at his belt, led me through that musty, creaking maze of a house, answering my questions civilly but tersely. His master was a navy captain. Mistress and daughter in the country. On the walls were what looked like every ship in the navy. We went from room to room, stumbling over uneven floors and ducking under beams. They were all empty except for one at the top of the house where there was a grumbling maid and her skivvy.

'I wouldn't mind,' I heard the maid say as we approached, 'but we'll have to do it all over again, mark my –'

She stood up stiffly from the bed she was making, curtseying awkwardly, and at a gesture from the steward the two of them fled. It was the last room to be visited, reached from a narrow flight of stairs into the jetty. A sweet smell of marjoram had been released from the sheets the maids had put on the bed. By this time Scogman was losing faith in the whole enterprise.

'House is as empty as my stomach, sir,' he said hopefully.

With simulated patience, the steward held up a candle so I could peer under the bed. There was nothing but a chamber pot. I took the candle from him and held it up. Against the wall was a chest of drawers, perhaps large enough for a man to crouch behind. The floor was so uneven here that I stumbled, catching the lid of the chest to save myself, wincing as hot wax dribbled over my hand. The chest contained nothing more than women's clothes, folded among layers of rose petals. Outside, the clank of a pail rang through the still air. The jetty overlooked the backyard of the coffee house. The owner was trudging back inside. A dark smear stained the snow where he had tipped away grounds.

As I gave the candle back to the steward, it caught a darker patch on the wall. 'What picture was there?'

The steward barely concealed a yawn. 'Another of the master's fleet, sir. Damp. The wall needs replastering.'

Scogman said nothing as he unhitched the horses, but his whispering to the horses suggested scepticism. 'I saw Challoner,' I snapped, sucking at my burned hand. 'I wasn't imagining things.'

Before Scogman could reply there was the sound of an argument outside the coffee house. The old merchant and his son were leaving. The merchant broke away from him, crying that he would salute old comrades in arms, slid on a patch of ice and was caught by his son, only to break away again, making a precarious passage towards us, holding out his stick.

'Trail your pike … Palm … Charge your pike!'

'Lord have mercy,' Scogman said. 'Drunk on coffee.'

The man's son began walking away. 'Come on, Father. Leave it. You'll only have another fall.'

The merchant was certainly drunk on something, perhaps memories of the war; if so they must be false memories, for he appeared far too old to fight. 'Know you,' he said, poking his wavering stick at my chest. 'Fought with you. Turnham Green.'

Turnham Green? I shook my head. I had not been there and in any case the Royalists had never got that near London. The son had turned, with the resigned, hopelessly confused look of a man who had to both obey his father and deal with the elderly child he had become. 'Your son is waiting.' I took him by the arm to guide him to his son, but he slipped and fell against me.

'All Hallows, Farringdon,' he said.

'Good Lord,' I said. 'The All Hallows Trained Band.'

'The very same.'

Now I remembered. Just before the war there was no army for Parliament. The City trained its own militia, mainly apprentices. The merchant must have been at least fifty. There was a battle of Turnham Green, or rather a skirmish. Prince Rupert had got as far as Brentford. The sacking of it so enraged the City it rose up, old as well as young, often with no more than sticks such as the old merchant was brandishing, but their numbers blackened the common that November day and Rupert retreated. The Royalists never got near London again.

'You had red hair. Carrot red.'

'So I did.'

Suddenly he gripped me tightly by the shoulder band of my belt. He stank of coffee and what remained of his teeth were stained with it. I thought he had had some kind of a fit, but his voice suddenly became sharp and urgent as he whispered in my ear. 'The young man you're looking for was in there tonight. Mr Purge.'

'Mr Purge?'

'That's what we call him. Spends more time in the privy than drinking coffee. You might find him still on the pot. I ain't seen him leave.'

'Come on, Father.' The young man gripped the merchant's arm and the old merchant did a capricious little slide across the snow, dropping his stick. 'Sorry about that,' the young man said. 'He thinks he knows everyone.' They were still arguing as they made their wavy journey down the street. The son gripped him by the arm, refusing to give his father back his stick, rather as he might keep a toy when a child has thrown it once too often.

'The Good Old Cause!' the old man cried, twisting a bent head and raising a crooked arm.

'The Good Old Cause!' I returned, raising my sword.

17

The coffee shop was locked, but the gate at the side leading to the yard at the back was open. The owner was filling a coal scuttle to damp down the fire for the night.

'I have urgent need of the privy,' I said.

He lifted the coal scuttle, blocking the way, and replied that I should use the street like everybody else. Scogman professed shock and said as a freeman of the City he would not soil his own streets. The owner looked at him sourly, eyed his sword, stood to one side and said that as a freeman he was welcome to the experience.

I could smell what he meant several feet from it. They talked in the Rota Club endlessly about great political issues of religion and speech but ultimately the fate of a government, whether it was ruled by a Crown or Parliament, turned on the price of bread and the state of the privies. The City was only threatening a tax strike, but scavengers had not been paid and in some parishes shit wagons had not rolled for several weeks. When I pushed open the rotting, creaking door the stench was overwhelming, even for London. The hole was filthy and encrusted. The door swung to and I was in darkness. I slipped on a slimy patch and retched, kicking the door back open. A weak patch of moonlight revealed someone had a bad case of worms.

It was capacious, for a privy. Driven into the back wall was a nail, from which hung torn scraps of old shipping reports. A crumpled used one stuck to the toe of my boot. I kicked at the wall to release it. There was a hollow sound. I rapped round it.

'Scogman.'

'After you, sir.'

When I began kicking at the wall he entered, clasping a handkerchief over his nose. The keyhole had been crudely concealed with a plaster-coloured piece of paper, but nothing more was needed for no one in his senses would visit that place for longer than strictly necessary.

We kicked in turn. The lock was new but the wood, like most in that rambling Elizabethan house, was rotten and soon splintered. There was a short passage, at the end of which was a steep winding flight of stairs. At that point what little light there was ended. I swore as my head hit the ceiling. Plaster pattered round us. I felt my way as the stairway curved. Backs bent, we inched our way upwards, the sewer-stink of the privy giving way to the damp smell of mildew and decay. Abruptly we were in a wider space. Groping around in the blackness there was what felt like a truckle bed. I knocked something over.

Scogman seemed able to see like a cat in the dark. 'A candlestick,' he whispered. 'Nothing to light it.'

I gripped his arm at the sound of voices and footsteps on a stair, followed by a door closing.

'I know where we are, sir,' Scogman said.

By this time I was shivering cold, my boots smelt vile and I feared another dead end. Luke was not here, if he had ever been. 'How can you possibly know that?' I said, with great irritation.

'There was a time when my neck depended on it. We have gone thirty-five steps and in a house built in Elizabeth's time that's about four flights. We started west but twisted back a half circle. I reckon we are in that jetty above the shop and … ah, yes. Look up, sir.'

I saw nothing, but he took my hand and drew my fingers over an uneven line in what I took to be the ceiling above us. We pushed upwards but the ceiling was as solid as a rock.

He bent his neck, flexed his shoulders, and while I pushed he heaved. A chink of light appeared at the edges of a trapdoor, illuminating his bulging neck and the throbbing pulse in his forehead. There was a small sliding noise above us, then Scogman's legs started to buckle. Frantically, I got both hands on it and heaved. There was a crash which seemed to bring the whole crumbling house down and the trapdoor flew backwards, releasing a cloud of dust. Somewhere there was a scream, then silence.

Scogman coughed as the motes of dust eddied round him. 'Well done, sir. You'll be a prig yet.' He heaved himself into the room above and pulled me after him. We were, as he had predicted, in the room above the coffee house. The thin moonlight shone on top of the oak chest we had dislodged. The rest of the house was dark, apart from a wavering glimmer of light at the top of yet another twisting staircase which led to the attic. The skivvy, a shred of a girl, screamed in terror and hid in the maid's arms, convinced we were evil spirits.

Scogman, whose voice was never gentler than when he talked to a woman, particularly as pretty as the girl was, said if she was not convinced they were flesh, at least she could give them credit for having blood. He tapped the stained bandage on his head and grinned. It was the grin more than the bandage that reassured her and, while the maid remained mute, the girl, whose name was Amy, told us that the steward had gone. They had been warned never to go into that room and the rooms near it. Well, they didn't need no warning, it was a blessing, weren't it, not to clean anything in this rambling old tub of a place. By this time she had gone from childlike terror to a pert, knowing cockiness.

That morning, the whole house had been turned upside down.

'What time was this?' I asked.

She told me she thought it was a hundred.

'A hundred?'

She marked the hours by the number of flights she climbed, by which method she was hoping some day to learn her numbers table. By this process she hazarded it to be ten of the morning. A cart came and took away books and pictures. What they were she did not know. They were told to clean the forbidden part of the house. They were terrified but forced to do it. Worst thing was cleaning the floors, muddy as a street. And shifting that heavy chest. Amy lit us both candles and followed us, at a distance, terror returning as abruptly as it had gone as she gaped from the corridor towards the open trapdoor.

A cold draught almost blew out our candles. Shielding them, we squeezed down into a small chamber which had the musty smell of the river. As well as the truckle bed there was a small wickerwork chair. Propped up against it was a picture which had presumably come from the wall of the room above. It was of Charles I portrayed as a Christian martyr. A beam from the clouds above him carried the words *Clarior e tenebris*: brighter through the darkness. The plaster wall behind the bed was scrawled with names and dates, going back to Elizabeth's time. Some of the names ended with the initials *SJ*.

'What is it?' Amy peered down at us, curiosity overcoming fear.

'A priest's hole,' I said. 'SJ is the Society of Jesus. Catholics used to hide in here.'

She gave a little scream, and vanished. For her, Catholics and evil spirits were one and the same. Up and down the country, from the time when Elizabeth persecuted the Catholics, there was a network of such cramped hiding places, by which priests could administer Mass throughout the land. This, however, had served a more recent political purpose. Stacked at the foot of the bed were crates of a book, *Eikon Basilike* or *Royal Portrait*, which claimed to be Charles's diary in the months before his execution. I leafed through a copy. If I had done anything for Parliament, it was to help start the war of words, which, with pamphlets, had opened the eyes and ears of the common people about how they were ruled, or more often misruled. The Royalists had learned late, but they had surpassed us. This was their masterpiece. I doubt Charles had written a word of it. It portrayed him as a forthright King, appointed by God, who confessed his weaknesses in striving to do his best for his people, and accepted his fate, as Jesus accepted the cross. Milton produced a lofty argument rebutting it, but it was the King's diary that people read. What they wanted was not theology, but tears.

I lifted the candle. If I needed any more evidence Luke had been here it was scrawled waveringly on the crumbling plaster.

I could not love thee, dear, so much … Loved I not honour more.
LS SM

The initials of their names were intertwined in a love knot, fashionable on rings. The King and a woman. A martyr and love. I threw the book down. The draught extinguished the candle. I felt not the rage that had consumed me earlier, but a deep sadness. I had lost him.

18

Anne still had the windows open in Luke's apartment. Her teeth were chattering, but at first she would not let me close the shutters, swearing she could still smell the laudanum. When I told her what I had seen in the priest's hole she began pulling open drawers, searching in Luke's clothing. She found what she sought between the leaves of a book: a scrap of poetry, hasty scribbled lines about meeting, trivial, but the sort that a lover can never bear to throw away. *Four of the Clocke … I shall be there. S.* It was dated November.

'This must have started months ago,' she said.

'I know. He told me.'

'He told *you*?'

She could scarcely get the words out. There must be no parents on earth, however much they love each other and their children, who do not have special bonds with one child or another. He told her everything. That he had told me, of all people, seemed at that moment almost as bad a defection as going over to the King.

'Why didn't you tell me?'

'We were scarcely speaking.'

147

She was shivering uncontrollably and, afraid she would catch a chill, I guided her back to her room, sat her in front of the fire and told Agnes to bring her a hot posset.

'You *let* him walk into the Royalists?'

She spoke as if I had planned it, part of the plot, perhaps, when I told her I was changing my will. 'Do you honestly think I would do that? He swore, on his honour, he would have nothing more to do with the Royalists while he was in our house.'

Her eyes shone with a sharp brilliance that made me wonder if the laudanum in Luke's room had affected her, or if she had taken some. 'Then he would abide by that. I'm sure.'

'The whole place deified Charles! The room where he met this woman was full of books justifying what he did. I think he's been looking at my correspondence.'

'Spying?' She stared into space, the cup slipping from her fingers. I took it from her. 'You must find him.'

'I will.'

Abruptly, she dipped her head into her hands. I put my arms round her. She held on to me for a moment, then pushed me away. 'I'm all right. You will find him?'

'I will. Don't worry.'

She caught the edge in my voice, her head jerking up. 'What will you do?'

I said nothing to that, telling her she must get some sleep. I rang Agnes and, before her maid arrived, her eyes were already closing.

People who were expecting ice on the Thames were disappointed, for the next day the wind changed and the snow was melting to a dirty slush as I made my regular journey down Holborn towards Lincoln's Inn. It was comfortingly normal. An ass was being milked, fish criers were shouting that mackerel were particularly good that day, and smelts and flounders and mussels had the tang of the sea, and there were pudding pies and hot bread. The bitter sharpness of yesterday's wind had mellowed and a lemon-yellow winter sun brought fresh vigour to the cries, and fresh heart to me. It was impossible to believe that London was in crisis. The criers must sell and the great belly of London must be filled. Like the wind, fortune would change.

Among this brightness was a thin black cloud. It came from Thurloe's chambers. The chimney was on fire. Clarkson, Thurloe's clerk, was struggling with a servant to fix a hose to a nearby water pipe. Under London's main street ran a network of elm pipes. Sometimes, in a hot summer, aled-up apprentices bored a hole in the pipe, to create a cooling fountain.

This, or something like it, seemed to have happened here; the pressure in the pipe quickly dropped, the flow from the hose reduced to a mere trickle. Sometimes the wonders of what my Spitalfield son Sam called the new philosophy got in the way of the obvious. The panic-stricken Clarkson and the servant seemed to think the only solution was to find the damaged pavement, which would lead to the hole in the pipe.

'Use snow,' I shouted. 'Is Mr Thurloe in there?'

'No, sir.'

'Thank the Lord for that.'

By the time we carried in buckets of snow, what was an everyday hazard of London life, the smouldering chimney, had spread to the panels round the fireplace in Thurloe's room and was charring the floorboards. It took bucket after bucket and the bootboy clambering up to the roof to tip more melting snow down the chimney, before we managed to put it out.

The servant brought hot Dutch gin, which we drank outside, while the windows were opened to clear away the acrid, damp smell. I asked how the fire had started.

'It was all those papers,' said the bootboy.

Clarkson looked uneasy and sharply told the boy to go and clear up the place.

'Where is Mr Thurloe?' I asked.

Clarkson looked even more uncomfortable. 'In the country, sir. He left at first light this morning.' He excused himself and went back inside. Through the window I saw him go into Thurloe's room, carrying a sack. He bent down over the fireplace. Puzzled that he was doing such a menial task which would normally have been given to the servants, I finished the gin and went inside. He was so absorbed in his task he did not look up as I squelched in a puddle in the doorway. He was not clearing the fireplace but picking out any half-burned scraps of paper, crushing and tearing at them with an obsessional persistence to make not a line readable.

Behind Clarkson, like a drift of dead leaves blown by the draught from the open window, were a number of blackened pieces. I recognised them as the state papers Thurloe had said he was consulting in order to write a history of Cromwell. It was clear from a scrap I picked up that there was another, rather more urgent purpose for writing, or rather rewriting, history. The fragment was dated January 1650, a year after the King's execution. His son, from his makeshift court in Europe, had declared himself Charles II. The stained words outlined an elaborate plot to poison him, guaranteeing that the symptoms would replicate those of the plague. I remembered it. It was from a time when all Europe recoiled in horror from England for, as they saw it, murdering its divinely appointed monarch. It was one of a number of such schemes put forward in the first heady but panic-stricken year of the Protectorate.

Cromwell had dismissed them all with contempt. The last thing he had wanted was for Charles Stuart – he never referred to him as King – to die. If he actually died of the plague, Cromwell said,

Europe's crowned heads would blame him. Let them. Cromwell, as always, was sure God was on his side. Charles Stuart was a fly, he said. Open the window and he would disappear. Unfortunately, Cromwell had disappeared, but not the fly. Thurloe, I recalled, had agreed with Cromwell, but might find it difficult to convince Charles Stuart of this, should he ever cross the Channel.

I coughed. 'You've missed these, Mr Clarkson.'

Clarkson shot up, dropping blackened bits of paper and scooping them up again. His face was drained of colour. 'Th-thank you.'

As he moved to take them, I withdrew them. 'Is Mr Thurloe in the country? Or has he left it?'

He gaped at me, his linen, damp from the snow, clinging to his shaking frame. He eased his wet collar away from his throat, as if he feared the noose could tighten round his own neck. 'I – I beg your pardon, Sir Thomas.'

'I think you heard what I said.'

He swallowed. 'In the country.'

'Where?'

His eyes were fixed on the charred documents. He swallowed. 'I don't know.' I moved to pocket the documents. 'He made me swear not to tell anyone!'

'I am not anyone, Mr Clarkson, and if I made these public, both you and he might be wise to leave the country.'

'He has gone to a cousin's. Mr Grayson. Radlett. Hertfordshire.'

'Thank you.' I crushed and tore up the pieces of paper, displaying some of his obsession to make certain nothing was legible. 'If these were found, they might not bode well for me either. Be sure you make a better job of it.'

When I rode away Clarkson was cramming the remaining papers in a brazier in the courtyard. Turning into Holborn, I could see those fragments of history disappearing in a rising plume of smoke.

19

'He was your closest friend,' Anne said, when I returned. She had slept very little, and was searching Luke's room, but had found no more indications where he might have gone from the house next to the Moor.

'Friend? I never saw Thurloe as a friend. We worked closely together. If he was, he would be the first to say there is a limit to any friendship.'

'Do you believe that?'

'It is why we have broken every rising of the Sealed Knot with scarcely a fight. Every European conspiracy. Every person believes he is different, but everyone lies, or at most withholds the truth. Everyone breaks. Everyone has a limit. Or a price.'

'You have not solved this conspiracy.'

I shrugged. 'They got rid of us.'

She stared out of the window from which Luke had made his escape. The tied sheets had been removed and the bed made. 'Everyone lies, you say … You did not talk like that when I first met you.'

'I was a young fool. In love.'

She turned to me directly. 'And you're not now?'

'Not young, no.' I smiled, but she did not return it.

'Have you ever lied to me?'

'I may not have told you the whole truth when something did not concern you. Or might hurt you.'

'I mean lied about something that did concern me, something that might hurt me if I knew?'

I laughed. 'What is all this? Truth or Die?'

She searched through the pockets of a suit of Luke's she had been through several times before. 'Last night ... did you mean it?'

'Yes. Did you?'

'I want to.' She put the suit away. 'I told Luke to spy on you. It was when you changed your will. When you were selling Highpoint.'

'A patch of land. On the fringes. Scarcely Highpoint.'

She stopped pretending to search and came up to me. She was very calm. Only a pulse, a thin blue vein at the side of her forehead, beat more quickly. 'Luke thought it was Scogman but I knew that even he would not sell land. You sold it for a kiln. Trade.' She spoke the word with distaste. Buying property was one thing, trade quite another. 'Glass?'

'Natural philosophy.'

'Is that what this ... red-haired boy was doing when Luke saw him at the kiln?'

She knew. It was there in her level gaze, in the slight dwelling on the colour of Sam's hair, that fiery red that had given me away as a child in a rioting mob, or a forbidden alehouse. 'Exactly,' I said, echoing my son Sam's words. 'Experiment is at the heart of the new philosophy.'

'Who is he? A boy, a prentis, Luke said, younger than he is?'

For a second – it felt an hour – I could not speak. Her question was as bald and direct as her confession about Luke's spying had been. I had wanted her back, and by God I had her back as she was at first in our turbulent relationship, remote and distant one moment, the next raw and bleeding, all her feelings trembling on the surface.

I was on the brink of telling her, of having no secrets, of sharing everything, of complete trust. Then – what was it? That I had trusted Luke, and look what had happened? The suspicion that whatever her feelings for me or Luke it was Highpoint she wanted? Or was it, simply, that dishonesty had become my business?

'His name is Sam,' I said coldly. 'You have been frank with me and I will be just as frank with you. When you refused to have another child –'

The pulse in her forehead looked about to break through her skin. 'I cannot have more children! Dr Latchford –'

'Latchford! If I doubled his fee he would tell me the opposite. When you would not go to a doctor of my choice I decided to adopt.'

'Adopt?' For the first time she looked uncertain, confused, her clenched hands slackening, plucking at her dress. One day, by chance, I told her, I saw this youth. Sam had violently red hair, just as mine used to be. It was when, I told Anne, we were tearing each other apart, Luke and I scarcely spoke and I had to face that I would have no more children. Sam was bright, full of hope, of a new form of thinking, as clear as the crystal glass he hoped to make. I had not told Anne a story like this since we were children, full of fervour, but laced with a kind of sourness, which she liked, and I was good at telling.

When she rejected me, I said, I took solace in Sam. But our partnership was over. We had parted, and not on good terms. I would never see Sam again. That, at least, was absolutely true. It must have struck her as such, for she flung herself at me with an abandonment she had not shown since the early days of our marriage. It was the kind of release that followed agonised partings and quarrels – I had forgotten the sheer, leaping joy of it. Half a dozen times she tried to speak but tears or laughter stopped her.

At last she got the words out. 'Oh, Tom! I have been such a fool. I have been driven half crazy by it! I thought … I thought he was your son.'

The next day she rose early and went out. No one knew where. All her maid Agnes could tell me was that she wore a cloak and a velvet mask. She did not take the carriage. I thought everything; she had gone to the City to search for Luke, a dangerous place for a woman alone in the increasing unrest, or to Clerkenwell to see Sam for herself. I became so convinced that was true I was on my horse to ride there when a Hackney came into Queen Street.

She would say nothing until we were alone in her rooms. At first she would not even take off her mask. It was not the ugly full mask, but a very pretty deep-green half-mask which emphasised the curve of her lips, trembling bewitchingly, as she told me to my astonishment that she had been to an even more dangerous place than the City, Spitalfields Without.

She had been to see my old army friend Ben who, to the fury of City doctors like Latchford, practised medicine outside the walls, where the City had no jurisdiction. Doctors called him a quack because he was an apothecary. Anne did not tell him who she was. She asked him if he thought she could have another child. She expected, as was the case with doctors, charm and a high fee. She got neither. She was horrified when he said he would examine her and almost walked out. Latchford would not dream of touching her *there* – his midwife did that.

Ben shrugged and told her it was always the shepherd that delivered the lambs. The shepherd never interfered unless he had to, and when he did, lore handed from father to son told him how to right the position of the lamb in the womb. There were more human babies lost than lambs. Lambs were money. Food. Children were just another mouth to feed. Would she rather have a shepherd, or a midwife?

She let Ben examine her. It was a risk, he said, a higher than normal risk, but it was possible. Taking the risk depended on how much she wanted another child.

20

There was no word from Luke. However much I searched and enquired, I drew a blank everywhere. I expected renewed grief from Anne. Instead she seemed to dismiss him from her mind whereas I, in the middle of the night, awoke to wonder if I had misjudged him. He could have got away when Scogman had challenged him. But he had stayed to warn me, putting himself in jeopardy.

Anne had his rooms cleared, and the boots and doublets he loved sold to the carter who collected from houses where someone had died. Gradually it became apparent that she wanted the room to be a new nursery.

Perversely it was Anne who now craved another child while I drew back. It was the worst of times to bring a child into the world. Lambert's army, the only one between Monck and London, had collapsed. Still no one knew which side Monck was on. I found out from Ben that the risks for her having a child were even greater than she had told me.

'She is driven by the estate, by Highpoint,' he said. 'I don't know if she wants a child, or an heir.'

I tried to reason with her but it was swept away by her energy, her sense of purpose, of direction where everyone else seemed adrift.

She even breathed life into the Good Old Cause. It was the only way in which she could keep Highpoint. For the first time for years we were together, in hearts and minds. By the time Monck had reached Barnet, half a day's ride from London, we had put together a list of seats which would expand the Rump to a full Parliament, with places open for both republicans and Royalists. The only proviso – our safeguard – was that candidates would swear an oath renouncing the King and the House of Lords. To our delight, Parliament's leader Haselrig said he would put it to the vote.

The riots grew worse. Apprentices, who hated the Rump, thrust their arses at constables and shouted, 'Kiss my Parliament!' Others cried for a free Parliament, which, if brought back under the old franchise, would vote for the return of the King.

General Monck marched into London in February. He reduced the riots to sullen pockets after the alehouses had closed. He had talks with both the Rump Parliament and the City. Still no one knew what his intentions were. On the one hand, he obeyed Haselrig and the Rump by destroying City gates in retaliation to the City Council's tax strike. On the other, he refused to swear an oath renouncing the King.

London went quiet again. Anne's energy seemed to leave her. She was sometimes sick in the mornings and I had hopes she was with child, but she dismissed it. There were no letters from Lucy in Brussels. At the Rota Club it was decided that the Roman Senate had never had a steady form of government. I had my usual chop with Mr Pepys. His only news was that he had had a violent argument with his wife, threatening to throw her dog out if it pissed on the floor again.

Returning to Queen Street that night, I could not believe what I saw was real. I had not seen Lucy's carriage, with the familiar coat of arms of the Countess of Carlisle, since she had been exiled by

Cromwell. She was stretched out on a chaise longue in Anne's rooms, sipping hot chocolate. She was one of those women who go silver, rather than white. It gave her an imposing grandeur and she had kept the lines of her famous beauty, albeit only – as she said herself when I complimented her – by painting over the cracks. I told her she took a risk in coming to London.

'Cromwell is dead. They cannot make up their minds who is in charge, let alone arrest me. And I grew so tired of Brussels.'

'What is happening there?'

I had not heard from her since she sent me details of a Sealed Knot rebellion planned for Ireland and the West Country, before my father's death. 'The most important news in Brussels –' she finished her chocolate before continuing – 'is that Mrs Palmer's wasp-like waist really is achieved without lacing.'

Anne laughed at my expression. I had forgotten how Lucy loved to prepare her audience. She never came without some revelation, some bombshell; but she liked to drop it in her own good time. And we had time. Anne wanted to hear about the waist of the King's mistress, what people were wearing and saying in Brussels and Paris. We both needed and sank into idle comforting chatter in which we could pretend everything was normal. The claret I had drunk with Mr Pepys made me feel sleepy and to keep awake I drifted over to the window.

The moon was up, glinting on the church spires of the City, quiet as a graveyard. The streets were empty, not a church bell rang. Once I would have known what was going on there. Now I was as ignorant as the poorest beggar.

There were the flickering lights of a fire from the City. At first it seemed to be a house fire, but as it grew higher it looked to be in an open space, perhaps Artillery Ground. It might be Monck's soldiers, burning wood from one of the broken gates to keep warm. Or it might be a beacon. Anne and Lucy joined me at the window.

There was the crack of a musket followed by several others, the sounds echoing in the still night air. I could see two more fires burning, one in the direction of St Paul's Churchyard, the other, a much larger one, in the area of Smithfield. From Holborn came the clatter of horses. It sounded like a troop of soldiers.

'Well, well. This is exciting,' Lucy said. Where Anne, ever since Luke had been burned, became nervous at the sight of fires, Lucy's eyes gleamed and she craned to see more. It was as if she had organised it; this was her bombshell.

'What's going on?' I said.

'How do I know? Look. There's another fire. Just by London Bridge.'

Anne was now agitated, as much by Lucy's manner as by the fires. 'Tell us what is happening. Please.' When she did not answer, Anne gripped her arm. 'Tom saved your neck.'

Lucy turned on her. 'I *don't know* what is happening. I *don't know* anything any more.'

She spoke so bluntly, nakedly, it rang true. All the same she was lying. There was something feverish about her reactions. She knew more than she was saying; she always did. It was no coincidence she had returned to London after all this time. She clapped her hands at the sight of the next fire, like a child at a surprise party.

'Why did you leave Brussels?'

'Because the King left.'

'To come here?'

'Don't be ridiculous. He wants to be asked. Begged. He has gone to Breda.'

'Where on earth is that?'

'Some God-forsaken place in the Netherlands. His sister Mary's court. He left in a great hurry. I have never seen him more excited, except for a new woman, of course. Hyde, his chief adviser, was calming him down. Charles listens, you see, unlike his father, who only listened to God. Charles Stuart has been a beggar half his life and has had to listen to other people. Much more dangerous. Something's going on. But that little bitch, Mrs Palmer, would tell me nothing. *Nothing!* After all I've done for her.'

There was another hail of gunfire. More fires had begun to appear along the curve of the river. At the nearest, Milford or Temple Stairs, a large crowd was assembling.

'This must be the rising you wrote about.' I turned from the window back to Lucy. Her outburst and our questioning had exhausted her, quite apart from travelling in the coach from Dover the previous day. She leaned against the wall, her eyes closing. I shook her. 'How many troops have the Royalists? Five? Six thousand?'

'Plus the Irish ... don't forget the Irish ... ten thousand on their way from Cork.' Her voice was slurred with tiredness. 'Oh, Tom ... I'm sorry. I am afraid I have not been entirely accurate.'

'What do you mean?'

'Like you, I have been somewhat out of favour ... when not ... forgotten.' She had a stunned look, as if she was admitting it to herself for the first time. Her lips quivered and she walked across the room in a burst of anger. 'I was never in the court at Brussels. If I saw the King it was through my window in the hovel I rented opposite. Twenty guilders it cost me. For a glimpse of the King.' Bitterness laced her voice. 'I was thrown crumbs, titbits from that nineteen-year-old whore. I taught her everything. Like I taught you, my dear.'

She swivelled round on Anne. She not only looked old now but ugly, her low décolletage exposing fretted skin mottled like rust. 'Everything. How to defer to a man's superiority while establishing your own. How to look, how to stand, be modest, be a virgin – men like to believe they are the first. How to be immodest – a man likes to believe he is the only one who can unlock hidden passions – how to talk, how to seduce while the man believes he is doing the enticing, how to promise the apple, while never quite giving it to him to bite.'

It was so much a description of the torture Anne had put me through it was her turn to move into the shadows. Lucy lifted the folds of her skirt from the Louis heel of her pointed shoes with a coquettish froth of the underskirt, lowering her head in a perfect, if slightly unsteady bow, as if being received for the first time at the Caroline court of the executed King. There she had drawn all eyes and, if a fraction of the stories were to be believed, had seduced – or been seduced by – both Royalists and Parliamentarians, according to who was in power.

I lost my patience. 'How many men do the Royalists have?'

She was in the middle of a low bow in which, perhaps, she imagined the King was receiving her. She stopped abruptly, staring for a moment as if she did not recognise me. The heel of her shoe went over and she would have lost her balance if I had not caught her. She sat down heavily on the chaise longue, staring at me in bewilderment.

'How many … There were plans. Before your father was killed in some stupid brawl he had plans for a great army. A final thrust!' She gave a sweeping gesture, mirroring Richard Stonehouse's grandiose manner. 'But the little bitch told me Edward Hyde squashed them. The King wanted no more defeats. Richard found himself as out of favour as the rest of us. I was told that was why he got drunk one night and fell into some stupid quarrel where he was killed.'

My father, who had revered his King, out of office! Out of favour. Eventually out of touch. Had I really been as out of touch as my father that I had believed his pretentious plans for a great rising? Or did I just use it as an excuse to kill him because of the threat to me and my estate? Either way his murder now seemed pointless, like so many other decisions made in a welter of others across that torn, leather-topped desk.

It had gone quiet again. Slivers of moonlight broke through the thick cloud and a number of carts, which might have been part of an army baggage train, came from the direction of Smithfield. The fires had settled from the first bright blazes to dull glows, whose reflections were broken up in the river. I was reminded of so many times during the war, of that uneasy calm before battle when men had what might be their last meal, and were praying, or drinking, or in a stupor, having no idea what was in front of them. It was a lifetime since I had been in that position, knowing no more than the common soldier.

The little charade of her first appearance at court had exhausted Lucy, who lay slumped back against the chaise longue.

'What were the figures you sent me?'

'Richard's figures that the King rejected. They were phantom armies, Tom. Paper soldiers. I had to send you something. Live on something. I thought … You didn't really believe me, did you, Tom? I thought Thurloe at least would –'

'Thurloe has gone. Defected.'

'Thurloe?' Lucy sat up. At least it was a change to drop the bombshell on her. 'John Thurloe? Joined the King?'

'I believe so. I don't know. I'm beginning to realise how little I do know. If the figures you sent me were false where have all these men come from?'

Lucy shook her head helplessly.

Anne peered through the window. 'Where is Monck's army?'

'The City,' I said. 'They will protect the City. Money. A pity they burned down the gates.'

There was an explosion and a flash. Near the river, just out of range of a fire, a group of men appeared to be setting up a battery.

'A cannon,' I said. I did not need to see what other men were carrying up to the battery. Soon there would be the acrid smell of powder, the whistle of a ball, a moment's silence, then the scream of dying soldiers. Never in ten years of war had the Royalists penetrated into the heart of London. I told them to get away from the window. I ordered Scogman and two servants who had been in the war to prime pistols I had obtained for such an emergency and to lock and guard the stables. I told others to snuff out candles to reduce being a target.

'She said they did not need an army,' Lucy muttered.

'Who?'

'The King's bitch. She came to see me before they left for Breda. Out of pity. She left me dresses they had no room to take. She said they would soon have plenty of dresses. Plenty of money. They were going home. The King had had a letter which simply told him to go to Breda. He and Hyde got so excited and the King immediately told her to pack. She did not know who sent the letter but she had overheard Hyde say to the King the man was so obscure, buried in some dreadful place like Cornwall, or Somerset, where London would never dream of intercepting his mail.'

'Somerset.' It meant something to me. Something in a conversation just as trivial as the one Lucy had had with the King's mistress: so inconsequential I could not remember it. I paced about the room, struggling to recall it. Once Lord Stonehouse had said to me that only the small things were true. It was the large picture built up from them that distorted the truth: the bigger the picture, the bigger the lies. Sitting at that leather desk I had lost my edge: Lucy had sent me what I wanted to read.

'Thurloe,' I said. 'Just before he left, Thurloe asked me if I knew a gentleman from Somerset. Sir Richard Grenton ... Grenson ... Does it mean anything to you?'

Lucy became alive. The names of everyone in the courts of the executed King ran in her blood. 'Somerset? Grenton? … Grenson …' She shook her head. 'Are you sure you've got the right name?'

'Brenton? … Brenville …'

An explosion and a flash of light through the room, followed by a crackle of firing, made us duck instinctively. There were more explosions before a great burst of cheering. Slowly we raised our heads. A bang shook the windows, lighting up the sky over London with coloured stars, rising and drifting over St Paul's before winking out one by one.

Anne clutched at my arm. In that bemused and bewildered moment we were like children, half enchanted by the sight, half fearful that London, frozen so long in gloomy dissension, had, as Quakers and other sects long predicted, met its end and that God's wrath was about to descend on it, as it had on Sodom and Gomorrah.

'Look! A dragon,' Lucy cried.

She laughed wildly. It was not the Great Beast of the Apocalypse but a raft of light wood propelled by fireworks. As rocket after rocket set each other off in sequence, it whipped and dipped and twisted like a demented kite. What I had convinced myself was a cannon being set up to fire balls at the City was a battery filling the sky with exploding colour. Puritan London had not seen such a sight for twenty years. Lucy knew them all from old court extravaganzas. In the dark room, lit in flashes from bursting cascades, she had the verve and energy I was in awe of when I first met her.

'Firedrakes … Tumbling balls … Petards … Oh, I remember them … what do you call them …? Dolphins!'

She pointed to a group of what looked like brilliantly coloured fish, darting and skipping over the water, before they fizzed and sank, only to be followed by another shoal. The last one hissed and plunged into the river, the last brightly coloured star winked out in the sky. There was an astonished silence in which, for a moment, London returned to its grey, huddled grimness. It was followed by a great roar. Fires were blazing up higher and higher and in their light we could see crowds swelling, people shaking hands with Monck's soldiers.

'Not Grenston, Grenville,' Lucy said. 'Not Richard, but John.'

I stared at her blankly, numbed by the sight, my ears still ringing from the explosions.

'The obscure gentleman in Somerset.'

I snapped my fingers. 'That's it. That's the name Thurloe dropped to me. Sir John Grenville.'

What I once thought was dead lived on as brightly as the fireworks, in Lucy's head. No one knew better than she did the peerage of the pre-Protectorate court, with its complex network of kinship and marriage. Her livelihood had depended on it.

'Sir John Grenville, third son of Sir Bevil, sometime Gentleman of the Bedchamber to Charles Stuart when he was Prince, gave the living of Kilkhampton Church to a certain cleric Nicholas Monck, brother of George Monck, and George Monck is cousin – no, not quite right – *second* cousin to Sir John Grenville. Charles Stuart has been in correspondence with George Monck all along.'

Somewhere in the City church bells began ringing. I sat down heavily on the chaise longue. 'Oh, Lucy, dear, dear Lucy, you are sharp as ever. Would you had sent that to me instead of all the make-believe. Thurloe knew. He was working with them all the time. He couldn't risk jeopardising his own safety by warning a regicide directly. He could deny he ever told me anything. He dropped me a hint. He told me what was going on. I missed it. I was too busy on other things. There were no soldiers. They didn't need any. It's not a rebellion. It's a coup. From the moment George Monck rode over the border.'

PART THREE

The Burning of the Rump

February–April 1660

21

What began it was a mystery only London could answer. After being paralysed in indecision for month after frozen month, as if winter had not only chilled people's fingers but numbed their thoughts and stopped their tongues, London, in an hour or two – it could not have been more – made up its mind. Impossible to describe it in any other way. People lost their individuality in the crowds that gathered round bonfires burning in every other street. No one was immune. With scarcely a word, we put on coats against the night air to get into Lucy's coach. Only Scogman retained any sense.

'Not the ring, sir.'

He was right. Even so, I did not take it off immediately. The ring had become as much a part of me as my fingers, the staring jewelled eyes of the falcon a symbol of my power. It was not only my power that finally slipped away that evening, but the last vestiges of the Protectorate itself. The word spread, as quickly as the fires. Scogman picked it up from the crowd as he rode down Holborn ahead of us. Monck had done a deal. What deal he had done was unclear, except for one thing. He had cut himself off from the hated Rump Parliament. You could smell it. People were burning the Rump, not in effigy, but in meat.

The normal London stench, made worse by scavengers not clearing the streets, was overwhelmed by another smell. Roast meat.

At the old maypole in the Strand butchers rang a peal with their knives. They turned spitting and sizzling joints, roasted steaks on hastily rigged-up spits, or sliced off bleeding chunks, skewering them and searing them over the open fires. Hawkers who had done little business for months yelled themselves hoarse as they sold the charred steaks. 'Eat your Rump and vote for a Free Parliament!'

On Cheapside the heat was so intense it blistered the paintwork on the coach and I ordered the coachman to wait with Lucy and Anne near the Guildhall, guarded by Monck's soldiers, where there was some semblance of order. I pressed on with Scogman to the Royal Exchange, where the crowd was thickest. Everyone was celebrating, whether or not they knew what they were celebrating. We cheered with the rest when a juggler tossed cubes of meat in the air, catching and swallowing them.

Before a turning spit I saw the familiar, rotund shape of Sam Pepys, with other people from the Rota Club. As well as butchers, prigs were busy that night. One was dipping Sam's cloak. I yelled a warning, but he was slow to react and the thief wriggled through the crowd towards Cornhill.

He was remarkably sanguine about his loss. 'He will find very little in it. This morning I felt poor in purse and office but now I feel rich in both.' He beamed at me and embraced me, his cheeks shining with grease from the lump of meat he was clutching. 'General Monck has come out for the City. The Rump is finished. The empty seats in Parliament are to be filled. My patron, Montague, will be back.' He saw my expression. 'I am sorry, Tom. This is not good news for you. I'll get you some meat. You'll take it rare?'

'Very rare,' I said.

Earlier the Rota Club had been debating the form of government for a republic. Now, most that I saw were toasting the return of the King. Only William Clarke looked how I felt. He stood dazed like a soldier when a ball has exploded near him. Smuts from a brazier smeared his cheeks and his cuffs. He looked very like his former self, Mr Ink, as I had thought of him then, who had smuggled speeches for me to print to depose the old King. And, in his immaculate shorthand, he had recorded every twist and turn of government ever since.

He drew me to one side, his voice wounded, accusing. 'You knew what was going on, didn't you, Tom?'

He refused to believe me when I told him I had no idea. Why else had I saved Lord Montague from the Tower? Of course. That was why Thurloe had followed my suggestion. Not because he accepted my reasoning, but to save his own skin. I tried to change the subject by tapping into his intricate knowledge of politics.

'Where is Breda? The King has moved there.'

'Breda ... Dutch Netherlands ... Ah. Yes. That bears the mark of the King's adviser, Edward Hyde. Breda is in the Dutch Republic, while Brussels is in the Spanish Netherlands.'

'No King wanting to be invited back would stay in a country with whom we are at war.'

'Exactly.' More fireworks went off. He stared as they coloured the sky and the crowd gasped and cheered. 'Edward Hyde hates me. You might put in a word with Montague.'

He was still convinced I was involved, in some way, in the coup and had influence. Just like me, he believed what he wanted to believe.

Outside the Guildhall Monck's soldiers trod reassuringly, keeping order. Scogman spotted the coach on the corner of Milk Street.

Only when Ralph, the coachman, was pulling down the steps did I realise Anne was not there. Lucy was dozing in a corner.

'I thought she was with you, sir,' Ralph said. 'Her ladyship was worried – I could not stop her going to look for you.'

Lucy's eyes jerked open. 'She's on the Guildhall steps. She said she would not move beyond the soldiers.'

There was a large crowd before the Guildhall, waiting for Monck to appear with the Mayor. Soldiers from Monck's Life Guard held them back.

'Lady with a red cloak, sir? She was here.'

Another soldier said he saw her going down Coleman Street towards Moorfields. I went a little way down but could see no sign of her. Nor had she returned to the coach. Increasingly anxious, I went further up Coleman Street as far as St Stephen's Church. Most women would never go unaccompanied in a crowd like this, but Anne was not most women. Two butchers, bare-chested before a roaring fire, were spearing a huge joint on a spit.

'Tom! Tom!'

I could hear her but not see her. I fought to get through the heaving, solid mass of bodies. Men eager for their meat turned angrily as they believed I was trying to take their places at the spit. Grease from the fatty side of the turning meat dripped on the fire, hissing and throwing up splashes of light. One of them lit up Anne's red cloak. A man was clutching at it, offering her a drink from a flask. She pulled away. He staggered backwards, red wine splashing over his doublet, before lurching after her angrily. The turning meat reached the lean side and I lost sight of her in the dark of the street.

'My wife. I must get through to my wife.'

As well try to get through a stone wall. I was wedged against a heaving mass of bodies stinking of sweat, wine and meat, trapped so I could not move arm or leg. People were struggling to get through to the spit, others trying to get away with their meat. A woman was crying out for a lost child.

'Has anyone seen her? Her name is –'

The rotating meat sent up another flare, catching a flicker of red disappearing round the corner. I stamped on a foot, kneed, kicked, elbowed, clawed, butted: all the vicious in-fighting I thought I had forgotten since I was an apprentice in a brawl, until I broke through and rounded the corner to see Anne in the grip of a man, and in the same burst of frenzy dragged him off and found myself staring at Luke.

22

Impossible. She was impossible to understand. She had renounced him. Cleared his room, removed every trace of him from the house, but the moment she had seen him from the Guildhall steps she had fought her way through the milling chaos of Coleman Street to embrace him.

Impossible? Was I not the same? The prodigal son. Had I not been a prodigal son myself, running away and returning to my old master? The words poured out of him. He could not get them out fast enough. It began to seem that he had told me the truth that day. It had the ring of it, in the sense of its mixture of the unexpected and the obvious and, above all, muddle and misunderstanding.

He had met Sarah in his Sealed Knot days. He had nothing to do with the Royalist books in the priest's hole, he said. He was only interested in one thing. He saw his mother's expression and avoided her eyes, but, I think, she was too happy to see him and said nothing. Sarah's room was the one above the priest's hole. She would leave him a message in the coffee shop, telling him when her father, a widower, was out and it was safe.

One day he had picked up such a message. The chest was withdrawn from the trapdoor – she had the help of the maid I had met

– but her room was empty. He waited. He opened the door and listened. The house was silent. He crept downstairs to the next floor. A floor or two below he could hear a faint murmur of voices. He reached a room where the door was open. Flung on the bed was a travelling bag. From it had been taken some papers and night-clothes. He saw the seal of the King's court on one but it was another he picked up. It was a scrawled copy of the King's List with my name on it and John Thurloe's deleted.

A door had opened downstairs and he heard the sound of two men arguing. As he fled down the corridor he caught sight of one of them. It was a blur from above and he was wearing a wig, but he thought he had seen him before. The panic-stricken maid ran up the stairs and told him to go. Sarah's father had returned with an unex-pected visitor. She had tried to change the message but had been too late.

Luke was breathing heavily as if it had just happened. Anne put her hand out to him but stopped short of touching him. We were sitting on tree stumps near what, in the open space of Moorfields, must have been one of the biggest fires in London. Two butchers and their boys, sweat running down their bare chests in the heat, were, as fast as they could slice it, selling a whole roast pig, killed that night.

I wanted to take him home but hesitated to interrupt him. And there was no sign of Lucy's carriage or Scogman. He knew we had gone in the direction of Moorfields, and I hoped he would search for us. I bought small beer and a hot cordial for Anne from enter-prising hawkers, who picked up the cheap pewter and chipped pots littering the common on their return to a tavern. Luke drank his beer almost in one draught.

'I must go on, or I won't finish.'

The unexpected visitor and Luke's hurried exit had happened, he said, two or three days before he came across us talking about the death of my father. As soon as he heard his grandfather's name it came to him that he was the unexpected visitor. He dismissed it as nonsense. He was upset. He had scarcely met his grandfather and that was when he was a child. He had caught only a brief glimpse of the visitor. But he could not get it out of his head. He went down to the basement and brought out the one picture his mother would never hang: the Van Dyck of Charles I with Richard Stonehouse. His grandfather was the visitor. He had no doubt of it. That was why he'd had to intercept Mr Cole and look at the letter from Amsterdam. Not to read it … not to spy …

'But to check the date,' I said.

He nodded. 'I saw him in Watling Street. Three days after the letter was sent saying he was dead.'

He stared into the shadows beyond the fire into which more and more people were disappearing. The pig had been carved until the ribs shone in the firelight. The butchers and their boys were squatting to have their own meal. A coach passed, but it was not Lucy's.

The letter from Amsterdam was make-believe, like Lucy's figures. I could see my father enjoying that. Cutting off the finger of the man sent to kill him and – the final touch – putting his ring on it.

'I didn't know what to do,' Luke said. He uttered a curious sound, half laugh, half mockery. 'Betray my father. Or my grandfather.'

Anne put out her hand to him. He pulled away. 'Can't you stop it?' he burst out. 'Hating one another? Can't you stop? Can't you …'

He stood up, knocking over his empty tankard, staring again towards Moorgate.

'What did you do?' she said. 'Where did you go?'

'To Watling Street.'

'To Sarah,' I said.

'To Richard,' he said, with a kind of triumph.

I dropped my face in my hands. He had demanded to see Richard. Demanded! I could not speak. Neither could Anne. Was that not exactly the sort of stupid, unpredictable thing I did at his age? No wonder the house was empty when Scogman and I arrived.

But he did not, it seemed, go to warn him. Faced with the choice of betraying his father or his grandfather, Luke did neither.

Ever since he could remember, he said, he had lived not in one family but two. Or perhaps three. There was his mother. His father, who came in from one battle and, before the mud had been brushed from his boots, left for another. His grandfather, whom he never saw. Even when there was peace, there was no peace. Not in this family. If you could call it a family.

He reduced us to an uncomfortable silence. No doubt if he had talked to Richard in that way he had also rendered my father speechless. 'Luke … I'm afraid my father is nothing like the man you describe.'

'He – he admires you!'

'So much he wants him hanged,' Anne said.

'Why won't you listen? *He* listened. He said he had committed the first wrong, for which he was profoundly sorry. He said you may have come from the streets but you are more of a gentleman than most of the King's officers. And you are his *son*. He does not want the Stonehouse name drawn through the mud by some foul cart –'

'Luke.' Anne shivered and got up. 'Let us go home and talk about it there.'

I had not realised how deserted the common had become. The butchers were damping down the fire and putting on their shirts. There was still no sign of the coach, but we might be lucky enough to get a Hackney in Moorgate. I wrapped Anne's cloak around her. 'Come, Luke.'

He stared round the common for a moment before reluctantly following us. It was when we were just beyond the light of the fire that I saw him. My father. At first I recognised the way he rode, rather than the rider. He sat a horse better than any man I knew, effortlessly, as though they were part of one another. The horse felt his complete control and seemed to glide soundlessly across the grass. Unexpectedly, my first reaction was relief. I had not realised until that moment how much I had buried the guilt I felt at, as I had believed, killing my father. He wore a weathered Dutch jump jacket, brightened by the froth of a linen cravat. Red. Trust him. It was like going back to the war, when the Royalists sported red favours. Only his slackening jowls betrayed his age. The thinning hair I remembered was covered by a wig of fine curls descending to his shoulders.

'Tom,' he called, 'I am so glad you could come to the party. And your good lady.' He inclined his head courteously towards Anne.

I smiled. I could not help it. I always forgot how charming he was. 'You are looking well, Father.'

'Still in one piece, Tom.' He held up his left, ringless hand. 'Still in one piece. I've come to collect my ring.'

Luke stared up at him as if he was some kind of spirit who had materialised from the drifting smoke of the fire. 'You came.'

'Of course I came, Luke,' he said genially. 'Wouldn't have missed this. You have brought up a fine son here, Tom. With all your qualities I would not have believed you could have raised such a gentleman. More than that – a Stonehouse.'

Luke moved up to us, his eyes shining, gazing up at Richard and then towards me. Was he really that naive? Was I, to have come here? Or was it really an olive branch? After all, now he had Highpoint – for if the King landed that was certain – he must see the fruitlessness of the feud that had torn generations apart. The most that we could hope for was our lives. I had some cards: the parts of the estate I had divided up and concealed. If he was prepared to settle now, he might avoid the endless complications and arguments from competing claims by returning Royalists.

'You are prepared to intercede on my behalf,' I said.

His horse strained to reach at a patch of grass. He allowed it to do so, never taking his eyes from me. 'At a price, Tom, at a price.'

'Highpoint.'

Richard inclined his head.

'You do not want it.' Luke broke in. 'You are never there.'

'A mediator, a diplomat,' murmured Richard. He looked nonplussed, as if events had taken an unexpected turn. Perhaps they had. I only saw my father after long absences, during which time he wrote those long, insane letters. Now he looked level-headed and all too sane.

'There's the coach,' Anne said.

It was going slowly down Moorgate. She pulled off her muff, dropping it as she waved frantically. Ralph reined in the horses, signalling back.

'I appreciate your concern, sir,' Anne said to Richard. 'But it is late. We can pursue this some other time.'

She bent to pick up her muff. In a blur of movement Richard was riding towards her, rapier in his hand. Even though it was useless I drew my knife. I had forgotten, also, how fast he was, how his expression could change from sleepy benevolence to the naked intensity of battle. She stared rigidly as the horse was expertly reined to a stop in front of her. He scooped up the muff with the sword and held it out to her.

'It is a cold night, my lady.'

She took the muff without a tremor. 'I am most grateful, sir.'

Richard saw my dagger and raised an eyebrow. I sheathed the weapon. Luke was so entranced for a moment I thought he was going to applaud. Anne set out towards the coach but caught my warning glance. A little distance away were two men on horseback. Both had swords. One was sucking meat from a pork rib. They might have just been celebrating, but I did not think so. They looked like the sort of mercenaries Richard employed.

'No time like the present, my lady,' Richard said. 'Luke tells me how well you have looked after Highpoint.'

He spoke as if she was a caretaker, a temporary tenant. Her voice shook. 'How well? How well, sir?'

The butchers scattered scraps of fat on the embers, which flared up, etching the fine lines of her face against the night. The last time Richard had seen her she was a printer's daughter. But transforming Highpoint had transformed her. Even in that situation it was as if she was receiving Richard in court, not the other way round. 'Looked after? Looked after, sir? I have made Highpoint the finest seat in England.'

There was a movement near the coach, a sketchy outline of a horse and rider. Scogman. At least I hoped it was Scogman. Richard followed my glance but he would see nothing. Scogman was wearing his black steward's uniform.

'Will the King listen to you?' I said.

'I can promise nothing –'

'If you did it would be worth nothing,' Anne said bitterly. I told her to be quiet. Whatever slim chance there was of a settlement, she seemed determined to ruin it. Somewhat to my surprise she was not only immediately silent, but flustered, and contrite, dropping her muff again, then hurriedly scrambling it up as if she feared another display of the rapier. All of this Richard watched with some amusement.

'Your reputation reached the King's court, madam. I was told you wore the britches.'

She was trembling, her face flushed. She looked towards the mercenaries, one of whom flung the pork rib in the dying fire. The butchers had gone. She apologised to me before going over to Richard. 'I – I have a temper, sir. Sometimes I – I scarcely know myself. I apologise.'

One thing I had not forgotten was Richard's eye for a woman. He stared down at her as if he had never seen her before, as indeed he had not. When he had seen her last she had been, in his imagination at least, a woman of the streets, a fighting harridan. Now, as well as looking regal and flushed and very beautiful, she appeared the epitome of what he believed a woman should be: subservient, with a dash of spirit to arouse the interest.

Richard doffed his hat. 'Your reputation included your beauty, but it does not do it anywhere near justice.'

She dipped her head modestly, and stared down at her muff.

The romantic tableau they presented – the gallant knight submissive to women (providing they were submissive first) – was claptrap. But the myth lived on, certainly in Luke's head, where his mother's modesty and Richard's gallant reaction must have resonated with all the tales of chivalry he loved. His eyes shone.

'Grandfather has begun drafting a letter to the King. I – I have been helping him.'

Grandfather! The word had a curious effect on Richard. His voice lost some of its certainty. 'Well, well, I was never one for words …' He looked down at me. 'As you know. And you have quite a scholar there, Tom … quite a scholar.'

Luke beamed.

Richard had been a liar, a cheat and a dissembler all his life. He had tried to murder me. But was that because he felt cheated? He had lost his King, his inheritance by which, according to the strict letter of the law, Highpoint belonged to the eldest son. Now both were in his grasp. He could afford to be magnanimous. Had Luke, with his naivety and trust, worked a miracle in bringing us together? I would never know.

One moment Anne was standing quietly, submissively, near Richard. The next she slipped her hands out of her muff. In them was a stone. She must have concealed it when she dropped the muff and picked it up with apparent clumsiness. Richard stared at the stone, at such odds with her submissive behaviour perhaps he did not believe it. She flung it.

How did she know? Perhaps she had seen it in the war, or I had told her or it was pure instinct. She flung it not at Richard, but at his horse. Richard clung on as the horse reared, boots thrashing for the stirrups, then found them but lost the reins. Anne stood transfixed as he fell.

'Run!' I grabbed her. I threw my knife at one of the mercenaries riding down on us. It missed but the horse veered. The other mercenary was closing in on me when Scogman came out of nowhere, slashing at his horse with a whip. I heard Luke running after us. The coachman had the door open. Anne stumbled in, falling against Lucy. I pushed Luke towards the coach. He wrenched away.

'You've killed him!'

'Get in.'

'He meant what he said.'

'It would be the first time,' I said.

'Don't argue!' Anne cried. 'Pull him in.'

'Get into the coach.'

He stumbled in. Silhouetted against the fire was the tall figure of Richard, testing one foot, then the other. He gave a short cry and fell. Someone was bringing over his horse. I rapped on the roof. Ralph cracked his whip. Luke stared through the window at Richard being helped up. He pushed open the door and jumped out of the moving coach, staggered, found his feet and disappeared into the darkness.

'Luke,' Anne screamed. 'He will kill you!'

'Go on,' I shouted to Ralph, hammering at the coach. 'Go on.'

As the coach turned into London Wall, Luke reappeared in the light of the fire, running towards Richard. He never looked back.

23

For no reason that I knew, General Monck sent two soldiers to secure – as he put it in a brief letter – our house in Queen Street, saying it was to prevent disturbances. I thought at first this was a euphemism for house arrest but I found I could come and go as I wished. The soldiers treated us with utmost courtesy. I wrote to Monck to thank him, and try and divine a reason, but received no reply. This was of a piece with the way he governed London in the next two months. He opened up Parliament to members whom Cromwell had prevented from attending. Most were Royalists, which suggested he was leaning towards the King; but at the same time he declared he was for the Commonwealth.

I was grateful for the respite. What I had suspected a month earlier was true: Anne had conceived. She had not wanted to tell me until she was more certain. The day after the burning of the Rump, Anne had a miscarriage. The scarcely formed baby was not more than three months old. I blamed myself bitterly for pressing her to have another child.

I stayed with her day and night, except when I went to my study to go over my correspondence with Mr Cole.

'There is one from Mr Luke, sir.' His voice was neutral, comfortable, as if nothing had happened. He recognised it from Luke's fine Italian hand.

The letter was as vitriolic as his writing was beautiful. He blamed me for poisoning his mother's mind. Somehow – he never specified how – I had slipped the stone into his mother's hand. His grandfather was very ill with a high fever. His arm was broken. The writing lost some of its clarity and some splashes of ink marred the page as he scribbled that he had struggled all his life not to believe it but he was sure now I was the Devil's child. How else had I escaped death when I had been thrown in the plague cart –

There was more. I could not read it. I handed it to Mr Cole. 'Burn it. Say nothing about it to Lady Stonehouse.'

'Very good, sir.'

The letter Mr Cole brought me had a Parliamentary seal and was from John Thurloe, who begged me to attend him at a chambers in Gray's Inn at noon sharp. He signed himself Secretary of State. Thurloe back in power? Did that mean that Monck was for the republic after all? Was that why the soldiers were guarding my house? Did that mean I had my job back? Why else had John Thurloe sent for me? I chose a skimpy doublet that would show off my ruffled shirtsleeves. Only when I picked up my sugar loaf hat did I feel a pang of regret. My marriage may be fraught, not the stilted perfect marriage it once had been. But it was a real marriage. Did I really want to return to a world of paper, which would drain the life from it again? Well, I chided myself as I set my hat at a rakish angle: better, surely, to be offered it and turn it down, than not be offered it at all.

24

I suppose I should have known from the fact that the address Thurloe had given me was Gray's Inn, not his own chambers at Lincoln's Inn. It was a cold April day with a bitter easterly wind, which added to the feeling of desolation. Few people were about. The one or two I saw kept their heads down and veered away from people, as they did during a plague, although it was far too early in the year for that. The first surprise was that the chambers were labelled as those of John Cooke, who had prosecuted King Charles and signed the death warrant. The second was that there was a Parliamentary notice on the door forbidding entry.

Through a chink in the door an eye was staring at me. My hand went to my empty belt. I cursed the blind stupidity of hope that led me to spend time choosing the sugar loaf hat, yet forgetting my dagger. A bolt went and the door opened. It was Clarkson, John Thurloe's clerk.

'Did anyone follow you, sir?'

'Not that I could see.'

He directed me to the first floor. The air had the stale, sour smell of rooms that had been unoccupied for some time. I stepped over a pile of legal files in a corridor. The door was open on an office which

I could see, from the citation on the wall giving him the right to practise, was John Cooke's. A damp cold gripped the room. By the dead fire, a scuttle of coals was grey with dust. Sitting at the desk, still in his overcoat, checking some papers and writing a note, was Thurloe. He motioned me to sit, then rubbed his white fingers and resumed writing. For once he had forgotten his train of thought and the quill remained poised over the paper. I could stand the silence no longer and congratulated him on his appointment. He looked up, startled, saw the sugar loaf hat and the fine ruffled linen of my shirt, and gave me a dry, rather bleak look. The hat and the shirt told him everything: I was hoping for office. His manner gave me the answer: I would not get it.

A blob of ink had fallen on the paper. He snatched it up, crumpled it into a ball and threw it on the clinkers in the grate.

'Cooke has been taken.'

'Taken?'

'Imprisoned.'

Thurloe told me that Justice Cooke, architect of the King's trial and execution, was working in Ireland where he was invited to a meeting with Sir Charles Coote, whom he knew as a virulent opponent of the Royalists. Cooke found the meeting was with a troop of Coote's cavalry. They seized him and threw him into Dublin gaol.

'On what charge?'

'Regicide.'

'King killing?' I laughed. 'We are still a commonwealth. There is no King yet. And I know Sir Charles. He has never been a Royalist. He hanged a number of Royalist commanders.'

'That is why he needs Justice Cooke. For his royal pardon. Excuse me. I must finish this. We cannot stay here long.'

He glanced out of the window, took a fresh piece of paper and began writing again. I stared out through the dirty glass, tattered with the skeletons of cobwebs. The grounds were empty, apart from Thurloe's clerk, pacing restlessly, eyes never leaving the entrance. Gradually the words sank in. Royal pardon. Coote was saving his skin. Even if you did not have to take such extreme measures, the empty courtyard was an eloquent testimony to people rewriting their own histories before the King's return. The lawyers and clerks of Gray's Inn had seen the notice on Cooke's door and Thurloe's visit, and made themselves scarce. Cooke's presence had helped the chambers to flourish in Cromwell's time, but now no one wanted to be associated with the man who had prosecuted the King.

Thurloe finished the note. 'The Irish. The fools jumped the gun when they seized Cooke.'

In that stale room I could almost smell the stink of prison. I might have been there now. Like Cooke, I had been enticed to Moorfields that night. I began to tell Thurloe, but he cut me short irritably.

'Your father is another of those fools who jumped the gun. They had to be reined in.'

I had taken nothing that morning except bread and small beer. The taste of it came back into my throat. I groped for a chair at the side of his desk.

'You were part of the coup all the time.'

He put the note in his pocket and replaced the file he had taken it from. There was no change in his expression or his tone of voice. 'I was asked by General Monck for my advice and I gave it. That is all.'

'That is why I have two soldiers at my door. I must thank you for that, at least,' I said bitterly.

Thurloe shrugged as if to dismiss any idea of sentiment. 'The King could never even step on board a ship let alone cross the Channel if there were acts of blood beforehand. Edward Hyde, who is advising him in the Netherlands, knows that. Monck needed someone on this side of the Channel who knows what he's doing, who knows London is crying out not for blood, but maypoles. So the King invaded the country, if I can put it that way, not with troops, but maypoles. The blood will come later.'

From force of habit he began to tidy the desk, levelling the edges of some papers to leave them in a neat pile, closing the lid of the inkhorn. Maypoles, not blood. Of course. The fireworks. The fires. What I thought had been spontaneous, what Sam Pepys had marvelled at for 'its greatness and suddenness', had been carefully orchestrated. To rule England, you had to rule London. And to rule London you had to first rule the London crowd.

'Later,' I said.

'What?'

'You said the blood will come later.'

'There is a list –'

'The King's List. I have seen it.' I thought of his name, scored through. 'And I noticed it is possible to have one's name struck off …'

He returned my stare levelly. Not a muscle in his face moved before he answered with his usual care. 'I would not work under that assumption, Sir Thomas. Richard is clumsy, but he has been fiercely loyal to the King and he has his ear. He wants you on the scaffold as much as he wants Highpoint.' A measure of irritation crept into his voice. 'I was surprised to find you still here when I returned to London.'

'How long have we got?'

'A month or two at the most. Perhaps less. You will have to travel under a false name. Monck will protect you here, but Richard and other Royalists who want their estates back are watching the ports.'

Somewhere there was the rattle of a carriage, the shout of a coach-man. He rose and began buttoning his overcoat. I stood up and clutched at the desk. My legs felt as weak as water. I had not expected it to happen so quickly. Thurloe gave a little grunt of annoyance. He had put the buttons in the wrong holes. With fumbling fingers he began rebuttoning it, turning away to do so, as if he hated to admit even such a trivial mistake. That, and a glance through the window, were his only signs of nervousness. He would not want to be seen with a regicide.

I jumped as the door went and there was a creak on the stairs. I felt a sudden dart of suspicion. For Thurloe to tell me this so directly, instead of through one of his oblique signals, was completely out of character. It was not a risk he would take – unless it was another trap.

There was a knock at the door. My hand went fruitlessly to my empty belt again.

'Your carriage, sir,' the clerk said.

'Tell him to wait.'

Thurloe saw my hand at my belt and gave me a dry smile. He patted the last button on his coat into place. He coughed and cleared his throat.

'Sir Thomas … while I was in the country, my clerk burned some papers which were of no further use to me. When I returned a neighbour, a lawyer of some discretion, told me there had been a chimney fire. He gave me some half-burned letters which came into his possession and, in the present circumstances, might prove embarrassing. You were there, I believe?'

When I nodded, he said his clerk had confessed I returned another such letter. Had I, by any chance, come across any other letters on the way to my horse? It was delicately put. He was now openly anxious, although few except me, who knew him so well, would have noticed it. His tongue continually slipped over his lips. He had put himself in my shoes. Angry and disconcerted that his colleague had deserted him, he would have kept some of the letters. He could not afford to take such a chance. That was why he was helping me now: for his own safety. I found that oddly comforting. And his awkward, unexpected anxiety oddly warming.

'As a matter of fact I did come across one or two more,' I lied. 'Shall I return them to you?'

He blanched. 'No, no. The post is not secure. Nothing is. Burn them. And anything else you find that might be … misinterpreted.'

We went down the stairs. The clerk locked the door and put a Parliamentary seal on it forbidding entry. I saw Thurloe to his coach. There was some life, a brighter green in the muddy grass. The fat buds of an oak tree were still tightly furled, but in its shadow were groups of purple and yellow crocus. I was seeing an English spring, of which I would not see the summer. He shifted from one foot to another, anxious to see me go. I did not know then and I do not know now how much he had been involved in the coup. I felt no resentment. In his own words, in the face of all the rhetoric and grandiose plans, London needed someone who knew what he was doing.

'I don't expect we will see each other again,' I said.

He looked relieved, but at the same time took off his glove and shook my hand with an unexpected warmth. 'Safe voyage,' he said.

25

I suppose it was the sugar loaf hat and the ruffled linen that did it – that and Anne ordering stewed carp and ox tongues and roasted pigeons and a special sugar cake for just the two of us, together with the deep-pointed dark-blue velvet bodice she wore, which gave her pale skin the lustre of ivory. All this told the servants I was in office again. They expected it. The Stonehouses were always in office. The last six months were an aberration. The soldiers at the door looked less like guards and more like a symbol of honour as they crisply saluted. The servants had a spring in their step as they served the meal. Only when they had served the meal and I took the unprecedented step of dismissing them did I feel the mood of the house change.

When I told her she listened in silence, drinking wine and eating carp. She was particularly fond of its strong flavour and urged me to eat, but I could not touch a morsel until I had told her everything.

She dipped a piece of carp in caper sauce. 'No chance of office?'

'None.'

'Well, that is a relief,' she said, eating the carp and finishing her wine.

'A relief?' I feared that her illness had unhinged her.

'We would have lost each other again.'

It was part bravado, part the wine, part that it had not sunk in yet. The servants had set us at the correct formal distance and she moved her place next to me. She raised her glass. Bemused, I raised mine and we clinked them together.

'Now eat,' she commanded.

I was suddenly hungry. The carp was good, strong and meaty. The sugar cake burst in our mouths with flavour. The wine went to our heads. We ate and drank as we used to during the war when we never knew where the next meal was coming from, laughing as we remembered things we thought we had long forgotten. The serving men, who had stationed themselves outside the room, must have been totally confused. Only when they came to clear away and we took coffee in the drawing room did reality seem to strike her.

'A month?'

'Better say three weeks.'

'I must go to Highpoint tomorrow.'

'Richard will have thought of that. It's too dangerous.'

She stared into space. 'Everything I have done there … my pictures,' she said. 'I shall be sorry not to see them again.' She gazed at one of the few paintings she had brought with her, of Luke on his favourite horse and Highpoint in the background. 'Nothing from Luke?'

Three days before there had been a letter from Luke to her. Mr Cole had given it to me and I locked it in my drawer with the others. I could not bear the thought of her reading a letter like the one he had sent to me. I shook my head.

'Well, he made his choice,' she said. 'But I thought he would have written to me at least.'

* * *

That night she did something she had never done before. She came to my bed. It must have been well after midnight. She said she could not sleep and it was driving her mad. Gradually I quietened her and in the darkness I painted a rosy picture of where we would go, where Matthew, the cunning man who had brought me up, had promised me I would sail to one day, where the sun shone and there were strange fantastic animals and everyone was equal and there was peace, for there was nothing to quarrel about.

'Why, Tom,' she murmured sleepily, 'that is one of those stupid stories you used to tell me when you came to my father as an apprentice, with the biggest feet I had ever seen.'

'They were not big,' I protested. 'They stood out because I had no boots. Look –'

But she was fast asleep. She slept in my arms like a child.

We told the servants we were going to the country. They assumed we meant Highpoint. I felt certain that would reach Richard. Only Agnes and Scogman, who would travel with us, knew the truth, and they did not know where we were going because we did not know ourselves. At first Scogman was reluctant to go.

'I haven't been on no water, sir, except the Thames,' Scogman said. 'Bit wider than the Thames, I reckon?'

He was remarkably ignorant about what was no use to him. When I told him we might be days or even months without seeing land he looked seasick at the thought of it. Even worse was the thought of leaving London for ever.

'What about my properties?'

'Properties?' I said innocently.

'The little savings I scraped together I put into a few hovels Shoreditch way.'

'Put them into gold.'

'Gold?' His eyes lit up. 'I never stole gold. Too heavy.'

The gold did it. The Stonehouses had always had an account with goldsmiths in Amsterdam. When Cromwell died and the future began to look problematic, I had sold land at Highpoint and London properties and transferred the proceeds to Amsterdam in the name of Thomas Black. The thought of a gold account in Amsterdam confirmed to Scogman that he was on his way to being a gentleman and banished all fear of the water. We fixed on going to Geneva; a free city and a republic. The problem was how to get across the Channel. Knowing that various members of the Rota Club were in the same position, I went there. It was closed. A notice read: *The Rota Club will be closed until further notice. J. Harrington. 13th March 1660.*

A dirty grey cloth was draped over the debating table. The floor was littered with the remains of broken clay pipes and coffee grounds. Next to a pile of pamphlets, *The Rota, or Model of a Free State*, was the overturned ballot box. I jumped as a hand touched my shoulder. It was Mr Pepys.

Being Mr Pepys, he confessed that when he had seen me, he had been tempted to creep away. But, being Mr Pepys, he felt he owed me a last chop. His patron, Lord Montague, had been appointed to run the navy and he was his Secretary.

As soon as we had broached the first bottle and ordered our chops, I told him I needed a berth across the Channel. His manner changed. He was sober in a second. He glanced round at the nearby stalls, lowering his voice so I could scarcely hear him above the yells, laughter and clattering of pewter plates.

'I am scarce warm in the seat.'

It was a measure of the desperation I was beginning to feel that I could not stop the request becoming a plea. 'A safe port will do.'

To escape attention I was wearing my oldest clothes. For the first time he took in the tear in my grease-stained jump jacket, my cap with a round crown and flap brim which was losing some of its fur, while I registered his silver hatband and cravat of finest Venetian lace. They were probably gifts. People on the rise were showered with them.

A hard edge entered his voice. 'I am sorry, Tom. I cannot help you.'

I recognised the tone. I had used it often enough myself. In a society oiled by patronage anyone in office was bombarded with requests for favours. I was not surprised he had become impervious; only that he had reached it so soon.

He looked round and lowered his voice. 'No port is safe.'

Things were moving quickly, he said. Customs officers, some in the pay of Royalists, were active in Gravesend, making the journey down river hazardous. Any regicide was worth a price as the unfortunate Cooke had found out in Dublin. Harwich? That was where Richard was expecting me. The Kentish ports were, if anything, worse. They were a hive of activity. He was in charge of it there re-equipping a ship to carry the King. No agreement had yet been reached with him – Monck was still seeking assurances from Edward Hyde. But Lord Montague did not want to be caught with his britches down. The Royalist flag was made, but not yet run up.

Mr Pepys finally had his position. I watched him go with a pang, bustling out, worried that he had said too much; that apprehension, however, rapidly giving way to pleasure as people made way respectfully for the silver hatband and the lace cravat.

The only hope now was to find a route used by less reputable traders who sailed to the edge of the law and beyond. It was a sellers' market. People who feared the King's return were being charged up to eighteen pounds a head to cross the Atlantic, whereas normally it cost five or six. From the look of the traders it was impossible to tell whether we would get there, or if they would cut our throats or sell us on to make even more money. Scogman saw them at a tavern. There was one particularly disreputable trader who gave his name as Ferryman. Scogman said he was the most disrespectful cur who ever lived. He had crossed him off immediately, for he charged only three pounds and a few shillings, suspiciously low, but he would not go away, he said, until he saw me.

He was curled up like a bundle of rags on the steps of the tavern. The Quaker Stephen Butcher's sailor's slops looked a little more worn and torn, but he wore his flat seaman's cap at as rakish an angle as ever.

Scogman kicked him. 'Up! You may not take your hat off to me, but by God you will doff it to Sir Thomas.'

'Leave him,' I said. I turned to Stephen Butcher. 'I thought you had gone to the New World.'

He told me one boat had left in February, but there had been such demand he was fitting out another.

'I am to take you on it,' Butcher said.

'Take me? Where?'

'The New World.'

I laughed at him. 'I wish to go to Geneva.'

He shook his head. 'You will go to the New World. With the Quakers.'

Nothing is more irritating than a man who believes you need to be saved and who will not listen to you when you say you prefer to go to hell in your own way. I was at the end of my tether and had had enough of men making money out of people fleeing the country. Using it to capture their souls was even worse.

'Knock his hat off,' I said to Scogman. 'It might knock some sense in him.'

Scogman duly obliged, but when I came to leave he was still sitting on the step, his hat firmly back on his head. Patiently, he rose to his feet, a little unsteadily, but his voice was as even as ever.

'I said with the Quakers. Not one of them.'

26

The more I thought of it, the more it made sense. Governments may have changed but the regulations for emigration, both to Europe and New England, changed little. It gave too many jobs to petty officials and yielded too much tax from Customs. Would-be émigrés took their papers to Haberdasher's Hall for scrutiny. There were searchers and customs men at Gravesend and more at Deal to extract their fees. Among these the Royalists would certainly have planted men on the lookout for me. But while they would use all kinds of pretexts to stop regicides boarding, they could not wait to see Quakers, loathed as radical disturbers of the peace, leave the country.

It was the perfect cover.

To my astonishment, Anne preferred New England to Geneva. Mostly it was because she preferred country to city, but it was also partly the name, partly the language, and partly that she had an even vaguer idea of distance and size than I had.

'It is two or three times bigger than this country?'

'Nobody knows the end of it.'

She sat in silent amazement at the enormity of what we were doing. But there was too much to do in too little time to dwell on it.

She got Agnes to dress her in black with a falling white collar and a large hat over a coif. Old Mr Tooley, who had married us, came over to sign our papers for Haberdasher's Hall. He disapproved of what we were doing, but his disapproval of the King's return was even greater. He was able to salve his conscience by giving her back her maiden name.

She sat staring at the documents before I locked them away in my case. They were for two émigrés, Thomas Black, Master Printer, and his wife, Anne, of an address in Shoreditch, which was one of Scogman's houses. I chose the name because it was that of the gold account in Amsterdam from sales of Highpoint land.

Three days before we were due to leave, Mr Cole told me that the soldiers guarding the door had arrested a man who was behaving suspiciously. He wanted to see Mr Black, and when the soldiers said there was no Mr Black at the house, insisted that there was. There was a struggle. They took his knife and locked him in the cloakroom.

It had been too quiet. Too easy. We had become too complacent. Richard, or one of his agents, must have tracked down our new identity. I told Anne to stay in her rooms and hurried downstairs.

The man was a sorry sight, huddled in a corner, head bleeding from a cut on his forehead. That was all I could see at first as the soldier opened the door. There were no windows in the cloakroom, which was used to store baggage as well as outdoor coats. Our chest was there, fortunately labelled *Highpoint*, so the spy could have learned nothing from that. The man was crammed up against it, head in his hands.

'Up!' The soldier prodded him with his stave.

The man shot up, banging his head against a low beam which immediately knocked him down again. The soldier dragged him up.

Somehow the man had managed to keep his hat, which was dislodged over his face.

'Doff your hat!'

I pushed the door open further so light fell on the man as he took off his hat. I had that moment of confusion when you see someone in a totally unexpected place and are thrown completely off balance. It was Sam. A trickle of blood ran down his cheek as he stared at me, twisting his hat between his hands.

'I will see to him,' I said.

'He is violent, sir,' the soldier protested.

Nothing looked less violent than Sam as he backed away from the soldier, almost banging his head against the beam again. His red hair was tousled, his cravat torn, his stammer as pronounced as it was when I first met him. 'I'm s-sorry – Mr Black –'

'Sir Thomas!' roared the soldier.

Sam gave him a bewildered, frightened look. I ordered the soldier away and as he reluctantly backed into the hall, stave at the ready, I beckoned Sam into the hall. Sam stood staring with awe round the checkerboard tiled hall, the statues of Mars and Venus, the sweep of pictures up the staircase.

'I'm sorry, sir … but I didn't know. She said but I didn't think … she's dying, sir. My mother. Ellie. She wanted to see you … before … before …'

I guided him towards the reception room. As we passed the foot of the stairs he looked up to see Anne staring down at him. In that moment his hair seemed redder than ever, burning like a beacon. My only thought was to get him out of sight. I pushed him towards the reception room. He almost collided with a statue, stumbled and went in.

'It's all right, Anne.'

'Who is that?' Her knuckles gripping the banisters looked carved there, bleached white.

'The intruder. I will deal with him. Please.'

She turned and went slowly back upstairs. There was a crash from the reception room and a stifled cry. I hurried in to see Sam bent over pieces of a porcelain vase.

'The edge of my coat ... I am always so c-careful. I'm so ... sorry, Mr Black. I never break things ...'

The words poured out of him in a never-ending stream. James talked over him as if he was not there, saying he would send for the maid. I glimpsed Anne, staring down into the room, before James closed the door.

'Leave it to the maid.' He stood paralysed, not knowing what to do with the pieces he had picked up. 'How did you find out my address?'

'She ... Ellie. She told me. I'm sorry. I knew I shouldn't come here but ...' He put the pieces on a table. One of his fingers was bleeding. 'I – I was just outside and the ... s-soldier grabbed me –'

'Go home, Sam. I'll come and see her when I can.'

'She's dying! Don't you under ... I promised her I would – would ask you to come and see her.'

'You had no right to do that!'

'I know ... I know ...' He plunged towards the door, stopping abruptly when he saw a glass goblet. Even at that moment his obsession claimed him. His hands were quite steady as he reverently picked it up, holding it up to the light. 'Venetian. Look at the engraving. You see ... Clear. How do they get it so clear?'

'You had better give me that.'

He did so and put his hand on the doorknob. His voice was so low at first I could hardly hear him. 'She told me ... I thought she was raving ... that you and she ...' He turned to face me. His voice strengthened. It must have been a pure act of will, for he overcame his stammer in a burst. 'I didn't believe her. I thought it was nonsense, but she kept on about it and on and on, and so I thought I would come and see and tell her it was nonsense, and then I saw the house and the soldier ... then you –'

'Sit down, Sam.'

He sat down again and looked at me in the way he had gazed at the goblet and the satyrs, as if I might break, or turn into a statue. Ellie had had a fall, he said, then a fever. The doctor could do nothing. She had told Sam I was his father. It was so muddled with the ramblings that came and went as the fever slackened, then burned afresh, that he did not know whether to believe her or not. But there were various things he remembered. What had meant little when it happened began to fall into place. My slip over the Half Moon, knowing it had been a printing shop. The fading glints of red in my hair.

'It used to be as red as yours,' I said.

He tousled his hair, in a furious movement of embarrassment. 'I hate it.'

'So did I. It goes. It will go soon enough.'

'It is true then?'

Even then it took an effort, like the last burst to reach the top of a steep hill. 'Yes.'

He stared at me, at the goblet, the broken pieces, the satyrs, before jumping up. 'I must go. I must be with her when ...'

He hurried to the door and opened it. The maid was waiting with her pan and brush. First he almost collided with her, then blundered the wrong way before half-running to the street door. Anne was still standing on the stairs, motionless.

'Is his mother the whore I once saw?'

'Don't call her that!'

Sam twisted round. 'I'm sorry ... I'm –'

I rounded on him. 'For God's sake stop saying you're sorry.'

He ran past James at the reception desk, between the two bewildered soldiers and, by the time I reached the bottom of the steps to shout after him, was at the corner of Queen Street, disappearing towards Holborn.

27

The Hackney dropped me at the entrance to Half Moon Court. I told him to wait, for it did not seem as if I would be long; in fact it looked as if I was too late. The curtains were drawn in the bedroom and the house was dark and silent. I went in through the shop. It was in a much better state than when I last saw it. A window frame had been repaired and the walls painted white. There were wooden crates containing cheap pottery for market stalls, laboratory flasks and pipettes. A basket contained rejected goblets.

In the dining room, in front of a mirror with an engraved frame which looked like Sam's work, was the maid Mary, reddening her cheeks with Spanish paper. She saw me in the mirror and jumped, smearing some of the cochineal on to her chin. She gave me a deep flustered curtsey. Her breasts dipped in the low line of her bodice, showing a tiny network of blue veins. By the mirror was a blue crayon with which she had probably touched them in.

'Sam here?'

'No, sir. I thought he'd be with you.'

'Is there a nurse with Mrs –' I could not remember the married name Ellie went under. 'Your mistress?'

'Nurse? She don't need no nurse, sir, when she's got me to look after her.'

I pulled open the door at the bottom of the stairs and went up two at a time. Even at that moment my feet did not forget which stairs sagged and could not be trusted. The smell hit me halfway up, a mixture of urine, blood-letting and sweat, cooked in an overheated room. The maid followed me up.

'Sam didn't want to go. I told him he must. I was right, weren't I, sir?'

Ellie had thrown off most of the bedclothes in the stifling room. I stopped at the door. I did not recognise the twisted old woman whose arm, with its emaciated muscles, was flung upon the pillow as if to ward off some evil. Her hand was as cold as ice.

The maid entered. 'Drifted off, has she.'

'You should have been with her. She's gone.'

She forgot her obsequiousness and pushed me to one side. 'If you think she's dead, you ain't never seen no corpse.'

As if she was pulling a doll into shape, she yanked the arm down and lifted the woman on to pillows. There was a sudden explosion of sound, a rapid gasping, which sounded as if she was about to expire, but, very gradually, she began to take slow, ragged breaths.

'Here. Have some of the elixir of life.'

The maid held a flask to Ellie's lips. More of the liquid dribbled down her cheeks and into her nightdress than her mouth, but it seemed to revive her. An odour of Dutch gin joined the other smells in the room and brought back the memory of the last time I had seen her, in a Southwark brothel, where I first met Sam.

'The gentleman's here,' the maid said.

More than the gin, the words jerked Ellie into life. 'Am I decent?'

In the dim light she could not see me. The maid gave me an outrageous wink and now seemed determined to show what a good and caring nurse she was. She brushed what was left of Ellie's old woman's hair. With another wink at me, the maid applied paste to whiten Ellie's cheeks and fill in the craters of smallpox. She looked more like a doll than ever, but one that resembled Ellie, and I realised she was not old. She was younger than me. She had been fourteen or fifteen when I met her – she was never quite sure. She could not be more than thirty. It was the life she led that had shrunk and wasted her, a life I had carelessly dropped her into and, just as carelessly, pulled her out of, believing it atoned for what I did. It did not. Nothing could. I could not look at her.

'Do I smell all right?' Ellie asked anxiously.

'Like a Southwark virgin,' the maid replied.

Ellie began laughing and could not stop. It turned into violent coughing. I could stand the charade no longer, dismissed the maid and sat by the bed, wiping Ellie's face with a cloth and giving her a sip of cordial until she sank back on the pillows exhausted, eyes closed.

'Sam …' she began.

'I'm here, Mother,' he said. He was standing by the door, still twisting his hat between his fingers.

She opened her eyes, astonished, and saw me. Her smile cracked the paste that had dried on her face, but somehow, among the flakes of it and the shrivelled skin, the ghost of the smile I remembered was still there.

'Tom? Is that you?'

'It's me.'

'You came.'

'I came. I'm sorry.'

She gripped my hand and fell into a doze. I told Sam to open the window. When he protested that the doctor had warned him to keep her warm, I said she needed air. Wasn't that what he, or Boyle, called it? A bird in a glass chamber died when air was pumped out. Wasn't that what he had told me? Silently, he drew the curtains and opened the window. A breeze ruffled her hair. She gave a tiny sigh. A house martin, which nested every year in the jutting gable, dipped and flew towards the apple tree I had planted to replace the one lost in the war.

'Sorry?' Her eyes jerked open. 'Lord love you, you were always the odd one. Sorry for coming?'

'No. For what I did to you.'

'Did to me?' She looked amazed. 'I knew what I was doing – better than you did. I'll tell you that for a plate of cockles.' Her head sank back against the pillows. 'You told me what would happen. You were honest. He's the most honest person in the world, Sam.'

Sam looked at the floor and twisted his hat.

'No, no,' I muttered. 'At least not now. Far from it.' The memory of Anne's expression as she stared down at Sam filled my head. The stink of the room, which I had begun to get used to, was suddenly overpowering. I had no idea how long I had been there and struggled to think of a way of leaving.

'Not now? Not with her ladyship, you mean?'

I had forgotten how acute she was. Ellie's eyes danced. Whatever else was dying, her eyes were alive. She was never malicious. Just open. I had forgotten that too.

'D'you still like herrings?'

The question came out of the blue. Sam shook his head, looking embarrassed, believing, I suppose, she was rambling again. I told her, unthinkingly, I never ate them. In Queen Street herrings were what cook called poor man's fish. They would never be served; it would be pike or lampreys, or carp. The light instantly went out of her eyes. Quickly, and with Stonehouse glibness, I said I had never been able to find anyone who could grill them as she did.

And somewhere, somehow, Tom Neave got in and the compliment became sincere. I could see her worming the largest, plumpest herrings from the hawker for a groat and a kiss and toasting her hands with them over the fire in the printing shop in Spitalfields, see the dripping oil send up little spurts of flame, feel the rich smoked taste on my tongue. I swear that the stink of the room disappeared. All I could smell was the kipper and the printing ink as we talked and remembered, and I realised, with an acute stab of pain, what I had lost. Tom Neave, that was what I had lost. Myself. She was right. She knew what she was doing, knew it would not last, knew, perhaps, that we both remembered it as wonderful because we just had the magic bit, not the reality afterwards. But those few months held so much more. Words that were not only going to change the world, but did. Soldiers who had lost half their colleagues in the war crammed into the church at Putney to tell Cromwell and his grandees they wanted their say.

Say?

I could hear the voice of Colonel Rainsborough ringing round that church: 'I do believe that the poorest he in England hath a life to live as the greatest he … if a man is to be governed, he should have a say in who is to govern him.'

I must have been speaking out loud.

'Dear Tom,' she whispered. 'You really cared about a better world then.'

She began to doze. Birds were making their evening calls. A red kite swooped on its way to Smithfield for its evening meal. I could tell exactly from the shadow of the gable across the courtyard what time it was. Had I really been there three hours?

I rose abruptly, miming to Sam that I had to go. He nodded. The door creaked as he opened it. It had always creaked but that evening the creak was like the crack of a musket. Ellie's eyes shot open, staring blankly.

'Sam? … Tom? … Why, you've come!'

'Tom … he … Mr Black's been, Mother.'

She gazed at him uncomprehendingly. 'Been?' She frowned, then her face cleared and she spoke to him as if he was a simpleton. 'Been? Of course he's been. Herrings …'

'Herrings,' I smiled and got a foot out of the door.

'Herrings? What did we talk about herrings for? I forgot why I asked you to come. Please, Tom.' She indicated the chair at the side of the bed. 'No. Not you, Sam. Leave us. Please.' When he had gone she said: 'Jewellery box.'

It was a chipped wooden box with a design long faded, which had once carried trinkets. In it she had stored mostly money, silver pence and Cromwell half crowns.

'Take it.'

'I can't do that.'

She gripped my arm with a sudden ferocity. She told me to get rid of the maid Mary. Pay her off. She would ruin Sam. Once, as Ellie put it, she had hopped it, Mary would get her claws in Sam, get pregnant, and the fool would marry her. He thought he knew every-thing but he didn't. He was very dependent. He was as stubborn as a mule and never listened to a word she said, but when the doctor said she had not long on God's earth he went to pieces. That was why she had broken her promise never to tell him I was his father.

'Does her ladyship know about him?'

'She does now.'

'Oh God, Tom, I'm sorry.'

'Don't you start saying that. I should have told her. Told him. I should have – well. I should have done lots of things. Look. I must go. I really must go.' But still I stood there. 'He's all right. Sam.'

Her face brightened. 'He ain't half bad, is he?'

'Stubborn as a mule but …'

She smiled as if it was the best tribute I could possibly give him. When I said I would pay off Mary but did not need the money, she told me to take it. 'Then,' she added, with some of her old street asperity, 'I'll know you'll do it.'

I took the half crowns, uncovering what looked like the remains of a broken white comb. It was a fish bone, part of a spine with a few smaller bones clinging to it. It came back to me, as vivid as if it had happened yesterday, when, after eating herrings in front of the fire, we had first tried to make love on the printing-shop floor. She had cried out and rolled away in pain. Sticking to her arse was a herring bone she had picked clean. We had laughed then. She was laughing now.

'Oh, Lord,' she said. 'I'd forgotten that was there.' Whatever blood was left in her pinked her cheeks.

I kissed her.

'Dear, dear Tom,' she said. 'You're too good for your own boots. You did care for me a little, didn't you?'

'Rather more than a little,' I said.

'You liar,' she said. But she turned away on the pillows, eyes closing, breath rising and falling more regularly.

Downstairs I told Sam she was sleeping more peacefully. Mary went to sit with her, and Sam stammered his thanks in his awkward stilted way, hoping that he had not caused me too much inconvenience.

Inconvenience! I became as awkward as he was and said he was right and I should have – and, well – I stuck out my hand, and he looked at it as if he did not know what to do with it, so I had to practically force his hand into mine and pump it. Then he took my hand in a grip that practically broke my fingers.

I embraced him and from being desperate to go found that for a second time I could not leave. I apologised for breaking off from him and he – it took him a full two minutes for he was punctilious in what he was sorry for and what he was not – for throwing the letter on the fire, but not for refusing the secrets, for that was against his beliefs. This took us as far as the door.

There the enormity of it struck me: I had found him again, but would lose him for ever when I left the country But I could not find the words, not at that moment, and decided to tell him the next day, when I came to fulfil my promise about Mary. Instead I stumbled out some politeness about his work and he confessed, with equal formality, that he had made little progress on glass, but, through Mr Boyle's laboratory assistant Mr Hooke, had had much work on the stretching and breaking of materials. I congratulated him on that and in this manner we parted.

This time I got as far as the apple tree.

'Mr Black …'

He wrung his hands. His fingers were twisted together so tightly I thought he might never unknot them. He understood I was his father, he said, but he could not *see* me as that. His father was the man who had brought him up. He was Samuel Reeves. He felt that the man he still thought of as his father would turn in his grave if he changed his name.

I stood thinking of the chain of events that had begun when Matthew Neave had heard what he thought was a dead baby cry out in his plague cart. It was as twisted and knotted as Sam's fingers. What would he change his name to? Black? Neave? Stonehouse? The last thing I wanted him to be was a Stonehouse. At least it was something to say to Anne. He was making no claim on us. She knew everything. It would be in a past which, in a few days, would be on the other side of the world. I pumped Sam's hand again and assured him I knew exactly how he was feeling.

28

When the Hackney dropped me back at Queen Street it was almost dark. The candles were lit. It was very quiet. I took a deep breath – several deep breaths – and went up the steps. The soldiers saluted. The falcon looked down disdainfully. James rose from reception and I asked him if Lady Stonehouse was in her rooms.

'She has gone to collect you in the carriage, sir.'

'Carriage? Collect me? Where?'

He did not know. Nor did anyone else. I discovered her trunk had gone and Agnes had left with her. Mr Cole understood we had decided to leave for Highpoint early. She told him something had happened and Sir Thomas had asked her to collect papers he urgently needed from his study.

'Papers?'

Poor Mr Cole. His mouth opened and closed several times before he could find his voice. He drew his hand over his silver hair as if to make sure it was still there.

She told him to unlock the drawers to which only he and I had keys. He thought it somewhat untoward – those were his words – but in these uncertain times …

I asked him how she was. Was she angry? Disturbed? No, no. She was very calm. She told him she did not wish to trouble him at this time in the evening, but to give her the keys which she would return later. She was her normal, thoughtful self. Thoughtful about the servants, he meant.

She would be. The perfect lady.

All this while we went upstairs to my study. He looked as if his world had collapsed.

'This was not your request, sir?'

'It was not. But, as you say, Mr Cole, these are uncertain times. It is not your fault. Please do not distress yourself and go and rest.'

The perfect gentleman.

Once inside my study with the door locked I was less than perfect. Much less. It looked as though nothing had been disturbed, but then she was always fastidiously neat. We knew each other's minds and habits so well I instinctively went to what I knew she would look for. Money. Property. Anything relating to Sam. I found it immediately – or rather did not. The draft will I had scribbled when I had been in such a dark mood with her and Luke that I had cut him out of the London properties and substituted Sam's name was missing. I could see myself writing, with brooding relish, in my best Italianate hand: *To Samuel Reeves of Half Moon Court, in the parish of Farringdon, the monies and properties here-enunder listed.* I had not even discussed it with my lawyer, let alone enacted it. Stupid to keep it.

I looked feverishly into the same files over and over again, in the hope that I was mistaken. I was not. She had taken Sam's file. Not only that. She had taken the documents for the gold I had deposited in Amsterdam. They were no use to her without my seal and signature. Very calm, Mr Cole had said. Inside that perfect exterior she must have been boiling with rage.

In a glass cabinet Lord Stonehouse had kept a very old brandy, so old that it had become a decoration that I never thought of drinking. I could not find the key. I smashed the glass and, sucking a cut in my hand, took a deep draught. It made my eyes water and my head sing, but it knocked a little sense into me. I had not changed a clause in my will. Once I found her, a session with the lawyer would clear up the misunderstanding.

Almost at the same time as that comforting thought, I saw the letter. It was underneath my seal, partly hidden by the inkwell. I had missed it because I had been so fixated by the drawers. I did not imagine things could possibly get any worse until I moved the seal and saw that underneath Anne's letter was another I had forgotten. It was the letter Luke had sent to Anne. I had kept it from her to protect her from more of the foul utterances he had flung at me, yet, in the guilt of concealing it, had been reluctant to destroy it and had locked it in the drawer without ever opening it. She had torn open Luke's letter, in such a hurry – or a rage – that, in breaking the seal, she had torn the paper.

I could scarcely bear to read Luke's letter to her. How could I have been so wrong! So stupid! The letter had contained no foul utterances. It was a cry for help. It was hastily scribbled, the ink blotched and the words scarcely readable.

Forgive me, Mother. I have been a fool and a bad son. I dare not write to Father after the letter I sent him but perhaps you would –

A passage was crossed out but I picked out *Sarah* and *love of my life but* and *found them in bed together* and – I could almost hear the disbelief and outrage in the smeared capitals – *HE IS AN OLD MAN!*

I poured myself another brandy. The letter was dated about a week after the one he sent to me, in which, compared to me, Richard was a man of unimpeachable honour and probity. A lot could happen in a week. After the deleted passage Luke wrote, in an increasingly incoherent scrawl:

I discovered Sarah was Richard's mistress and declared it my intention to leave. They stopped me. I do not know what they are going to do with me or what is going to happen. Am at Stavely Manor, Epping. Please –

There was another crossed-out passage before it ended.

There is a maid here who has been kind to me and has promised to deliver this. Must finish –
Your Loving son
Luke.

I sat with my head in my hands, staring at Luke's slashed deletions and chaotic scrawl, the end of his belief in love and honour being like a penny-book story, before I could bring myself to pick up Anne's letter to me.

When she had taken over Highpoint Anne had been determined to improve her hand. I had been flattered that she had chosen my Italianate script as a model. Her writing had become so like mine that when I began reading her letter it was almost as if I was accusing myself.

Of all the things you have done, this is unforgivable, she wrote.

That I could accept, but the rest was so wrong, so unbelievably wrong that I laughed out loud when I first read it. She could not believe this of me, not when we had come together again, lain together, miraculously, as we were when we first fell in love.

You never cared for Luke. If you had, you would never have let him
go into the City to see that woman. Either you were as naive as he
was or you knew what would happen.

In other words, I planned it. Again I laughed. Could she not see,
remember how happy, how close Luke and I had become in that
short period of time, when I had yielded to his desire to be a swordsman? When I had encouraged his infatuation because falling in love
and then into despair was what a man did?

Why else would you keep this letter from me? Richard will kill him, if
he has not done so already. If he does, his blood will be on your
hands.

A slow chill crept through me. There was a madness in this I had
seen before when she was driven to the edge, but it was a madness
with its own terrible logic.

Why else would you cut Luke out of your will to give to that bastard
whom you swore did not exist? Whom you planned to adopt?

Adopt? She really had gone over the edge. Adopt? I picked up the
brandy and put it down again. If she was mad, then I had colluded
with it. I remembered when she confessed she had got Luke to spy
on me at the kiln, when she had asked about the youth with red hair.
That was when we had come together, with my glib answer that I
had thought of adopting him because she refused to have another
child. I could hear her laughing at herself, with relief and
abandonment.

'Oh, Tom! I have been such a fool. I have been driven half crazy by
it! I thought … I thought he was your son.'

Impossible to tell her now that I had finished with Sam, we had quarrelled and it was over and done with. Over and done with? I had been glib with that too. Glib all my life. Dividing myself up, thinking I could live one life here, another there, committing not only the unpardonable sin of lying to her, but the stupid one of lying to myself.

Well, he will not benefit from Highpoint. Nobody will.

She ended the letter there. There was no closure, as there was no greeting. It gave the letter a blunt, uncompromising sense of purpose. Whatever she had decided to do, sane or insane, she would do, unless I stopped her.

I could have caught that boat. Taken Sam with me. New world, new opportunities. He would have jumped at the chance. I never thought about it. Not for a second. I was like an animal driven by old instincts. I put on my old torn army jerkin. In an inside pocket I put Anne and Luke's letters. I took my broadsword and a pistol in my saddle bag.

One of Monck's soldiers was asleep in the porch. He awoke with a start. It was a moment before he recognised me in my old jerkin. He stared at the torn leather, not knowing whether to salute or grin. In the end he did both.

'Ain't seen one of those for years, sir.'

It was a measure of my love, or my obsession if you prefer it, that, as soon as I was in the saddle I went west towards Highpoint where I was sure she had gone, like an iron filing dragged towards a loadstone. Yet I knew perfectly well what I had to do and where I was going. I dragged my horse round clumsily and forced myself to stay still and quieten her.

'I'm sorry. It's this way, I'm afraid.'

The horse had smelt the fields and the orchards. The moon was up, the stars glittered in a clear sky, and she neighed restlessly at the prospect of going into the stink of the City. An overwhelming tiredness crept over me. Only growing apprehension at what I had to do kept me awake. A distant watchman called the hour of eleven. My mouth was dry and all I wanted was to finish the bottle of brandy and find oblivion. I clicked the horse into motion and turned east into the City.

29

As Scogman had an office in Queen Street, where he sometimes slept, I never visited him at what he disparagingly called his hovel in Shoreditch. If I thought about it at all, I considered it slightly odd that he should choose that area, where murders and prostitution were commonplace, when, with his increased status, he could choose a little better. I supposed it was his nostalgia for his dubious past.

How wrong I was. It was years since I had been outside the walls on this side of the City. I found that Crooked Billet Yard – did he choose the name, or did it choose him? – was a new development, brick, not ramshackle wood, close enough to the walls to be under some jurisdiction from the City. There was a well and a patch for growing herbs, which looked most unlike Scogman.

Another surprise was that Scogman was up. In the light of one of the ornate brass candelabras a shop in the Exchange sold for 'Men Rising in the World' he was packing a trunk. He put some clothes in, then took them out. He picked up some papers, hesitated, then must have heard the horse for, shading his eyes against the light, he stared out in astonishment.

The door seemed to have several locks and bolts. He left a chain on it before opening it fully. 'It is you, sir. What is it? Has there been a change of sailing?'

The little hall was dark and gloomy but the room where he was packing was bright and cheerful. On top of an oak chest was a vase containing some of the herbs and a bunch of forget-me-nots. A fire smouldered before a fine walnut chair with cresting rail and well-turned finials, which I suspected I had seen at Highpoint. Opposite it was a stool, beside which was a basket containing bobbins of wool and needles.

He stared at my torn leather jerkin and broadsword. 'What's happened?'

What had begun as apprehension in Queen Street was now that familiar mixture of fatalism, fear and jauntiness I always felt before battle. 'So this is your hovel.'

He saw me looking at the chair and colour crept up his neck to tinge his cheeks. 'Wrong side of the walls, sir. Bad area … never get back what I paid for it …'

'Very fine chair,' I said, running my fingers over the cresting. 'We have one almost as good at Highpoint.'

His cheeks were red as fire. 'Lady Stonehouse never liked it. Did her a favour by getting rid of it.'

By now he was convinced that this unprecedented midnight visit was to expose his thefts, but abruptly I tired of the game and drew out Luke's letter. He went to the walnut chair, recollected his position, drew it out for me and sat on the stool. He read slowly, with complete concentration, his tongue running over his lips, his finger jerking over every word. The stubby nailbitten finger was hypnotic. I must have dropped off, for I came to with a start, not knowing where I was for a moment or what I was doing there. He was standing over me, waving the letter.

'It's a trap.'

'Of course it is.'

'The dog! The French –'

'Not him.'

'What?'

The heat of the fire was like a warm blanket. I struggled to put words together, let alone speak them. 'Luke is a prisoner. He's unaware he's part of a trap.'

He brandished the letter with derision. 'A maid here who has been kind to me? Promise to deliver … That's horse shit.'

'I know. He doesn't.'

His voice was incredulous. 'He's fallen for another one? Being used again? Is that it? You can't believe that.'

'I believe that he found Richard in bed with the girl he thought was the love of his life. I believe that. It follows that this could be a cry for help. It doesn't matter whether it's true or not. I've got to believe it.'

'Got to? Got to? Beg pardon, sir, but you ain't making any kind of sense.'

I was scarcely making sense to myself. But, in the end, instincts are what matter, not sense. And I had spent what felt like a lifetime poring over letters containing all manner of lies and half-truths to know that you could never trust words, but there was a truth in the anguish of the collapse of his normally perfect writing, in the savage deletions, one of which went through the paper. I knew my son now, I believed. It was probably too late, but I knew him.

I got up and held out my hand for the letter. It had suddenly become very precious. I folded it carefully, put it in my inside pocket and buttoned it.

'What d'you expect me to do, sir?' he protested. 'Break in? Rescue him? I've done with that. I'm an honest man.' He looked at the chair. 'Well, more or less.'

I turned to leave. 'I'm sorry. I shouldn't have come.'

I tried to get past him but he blocked my way to the hall. 'We sail the day after tomorrow. The first tide.'

'Your passage is booked. Everything is in order.'

His voice rose as I pushed him to one side. 'You ain't coming? What are you going to do?'

Before I could answer a shrill voice rang out. 'Oliver! Ain't you never coming to bed?'

If his face was red when I saw the chair, it was now scarlet. For a moment I could not see where the voice had come from. Then, when it repeated the question, I saw a pert little face, topped by a flowered nightcap, with a snub nose and a mass of ringlets dangling from under the cap. She gave a shriek when she saw me, and disappeared. Scogman did not know where to look. His discomfort spread to me and I did not know what to say.

'Is your name really Oliver?' I said at last.

'*She* calls me it,' he said savagely. 'I keep telling her not to, having always been Scoggers, or Mr Scogman, when I am acting as your steward.'

I looked from the stool, with the basket of wool bobbins and needles, to the brass candelabra, to the vase of herbs and forget-me-nots. 'Is she …' I did not know how to put it, 'the lady of the house?'

He flushed, clenched his fists, and was saved from answering by the lady in question hurrying down the stairs. She had removed her nightcap and looked even prettier with the ringlets bobbing around her cheeks. A flowered mantua was wrapped around her with a sash at the waist.

'I'm sorry,' I said, 'to intrude on you at this time of night, Mrs Scogman.'

She looked very pleased to be addressed as such, but Scogman bridled and shifted even more uncomfortably. I suppose from the dimly lit stairs she had taken in my torn jerkin and thought I was one of Scogman's more dubious acquaintances. Then, when she saw my face, she said: 'You ain't –' She dug Scogman fiercely in the ribs and said, 'He ain't –' When she found out I was, she bobbed a confused curtsey, began to rush back upstairs, then stopped.

'Have you offered the gentleman anything, Oliver?'

It was no use my refusing, or Scogman ordering her to go back to bed. She lit a candle and went towards the kitchen. On the way she saw a bleary-eyed head peering through the banisters. The boy must have been about five. His straw-coloured hair, sticking out at all angles, and air of urban knowingness were reminiscent of Scogman when I first met him.

'Bed,' she cried, adding, when he only reluctantly withdrew his head, 'now.'

She poured small beer and rapidly sliced bread. When Scogman advised her to kick the maid out of bed to do it and she refused – 'I bin a maid. Poor bitch needs her sleep' – I warmed to her. When she added, 'And she wouldn't cut the bread right,' I warmed to her even more. Upstairs a baby broke into an explosion of cries, followed by another. I stared at Scogman, who was now looking anywhere in the room but at me.

'Dick does that deliberate,' she said grimly. 'Takes it out on the little ones. Like you,' she added to Scogman.

She gave us the bread, lightly toasted so it had already absorbed the butter she spread on it, curtseyed again, excused herself and, after locking up, was gone. Scogman winced as if he was about to be struck when her voice rang out telling Dick to look direct at her hand and not look away or he'd get worse. There was a resounding slap and a snivelling cry. Only when I began to eat did I realise how hungry I was. The bread was coarse but freshly baked, the butter good and soaked into every pore of it. Gradually it became silent upstairs. I looked at the trunk.

'You're leaving?'

'Like a bloody shot,' he said. 'Before she can breed any more brats.'

The beer had a nutty flavour, and was well-hopped. I pointed upstairs. 'What about them?'

'They'll cope. I told them I'd be away for a bit.' He saw my expression and looked away. 'What about you, sir? What did you mean when you said "*Your* passage is booked"? You really ain't coming?'

It was my turn to look away. The whispers of the dying fire, the cry of a child and the murmur of the woman quietening him, the taste of the bread and the beer on my tongue, all were weakening my resolve. So I told him. Then it would become reality. Then I would have to do it.

He shifted his stool away from me, as a man does when he fears his companion has a disease. 'You can't do that, sir! Worse than a break-in is that. At least with a blag you have a chance.'

'Get on with your packing. They'll come for your trunk tomorrow.'

I refused the offer of his bed. With some cushions, and the warmth from the fire, the chair was comfortable and capacious enough. I heard him go over to the trunk then return.

'You're not yourself, sir.'

'Let me get some sleep, will you.'

I was surprisingly calm. It was like that moment before battle when the positions had been decided and decisions, right or wrong, taken. There was nothing more to do except wait. And sleep if you could. Vaguely I heard him move about, then the scrape of the stool.

'I picked her up one night, sir …'

This, too, was common before a battle: the urge to talk about something one has comfortably put off, which now becomes overwhelmingly important.

He meant to boot her out the next morning, but she could brew and bake and he had just bought the place and needed someone to look after it … Then …

I was not quite asleep and not quite awake. A layer of ash had formed in the grate. With the poker he drew in it the crude outline of a child's face with a turned-up nose and strands of hair sticking out of his head. I nodded. I understood that all right.

'But she drives me mad sometimes. She pretends to know her place but she don't. Sometimes I don't feel like my own man any more. When you told me you were leaving and said "You haven't no ties, Scogman, have you?" we'd had a row. I'd belted her one. Made no difference. So I thought: right, my girl. You just walked in here. Never talked about it. Just happened. I'll just walk out. But …'

The word hung in the air. He drew a few more hairs sticking out from the child's head. When I nodded, he said, 'Beer's not bad either.'

'Exceptionally good,' I said.

He brightened. 'D'you think so?'

'So is the bread.'

'Does a bit for the baker. Uses his oven. Now we're not going I'll maybe let it drift on a bit.'

'I wouldn't do that. You might lose her.'

'Lose her? Fat chance.'

'Make her Mrs Scogman.'

'Mrs – You're joking, sir.'

Suddenly I couldn't trust my voice. I couldn't bear to look at him. Or the crude drawing of a child grinning at me. Or the herbs and flowers neatly arranged in the pewter tankard. I got up. The chair went over. I went one way, then another, before plunging into the tiny hall. I undid a chain but the door was locked and bolted.

Scogman came up behind me. 'What is it, sir?'

'Open the door, Scogman.'

There were no keys in the hall. He said it was one of her faults, mislaying keys. Keeping them in a safe place was how she described it. While he searched, or pretended to, he said, 'You aren't really planning to go through with this crazy idea, are you, sir?'

'It's the only way I can save him and get her back.'

He sighed. 'What exactly do you want me to do, sir?'

30

We meant to leave at first light but life got in the way. Life in the form of crying children, the baby of which Mrs Scogman – as Scogman now called her, with heavy irony – suckled on the move, as she told the straw-haired boy Dick to get bread and another to draw water and beer. Life leaping into her eyes when Scogman said he wasn't going on a long trip after all. Just a short one.

'Got you under my feet for a bit longer, 'ave I,' she said.

Life in the hawkers' cries as they poured into London as we left, in the barking dogs protecting their farms, in the stiff, protesting creak of winter-closed windows at Stavely Manor as its occupants responded to what promised to be a warm day.

Life everywhere except in the letter I had managed to scratch out with a blunt quill at Scogman's, and which I drew out of my pocket as we stopped our horses on a slight rise overlooking the manor house. Not one of my better efforts, I thought, as I read through its cold, flat phrases, but it would serve its purpose. It might even be deemed appropriate.

Scogman stared down at the house. Since he had become a man of property he had built up a critical vocabulary of the houses he used to rob. He sniffed. 'Late Tudor. Built on the cheap. All porch and columns. Open court. Kitchens there. Look.'

Trudging from the court at the back was a milkmaid, empty pails swinging. 'They're probably keeping Luke there. In one of the store-rooms.' From his saddle holster Scogman pulled out the spyglass he used as a steward. 'Nice skin. The maid. I could use my charm on her.'

'I thought you were done with that.'

'I mean to gather intelligence, sir,' he said, with injured innocence.

'Put your glass on that.' I pointed to a patch of cropped grass in a fallow field before a copse.

Scogman reluctantly swung it from the maid, then grew still. 'Six horses. Mercenaries. German, going by the Dresden wheel-lock one of them has. Richard must be spending money he don't have.'

I could guess where it came from. The goldsmiths, with whom I had deposited funds, were lending them to Royalists in the expecta-tion of them regaining their lands on the return of the King. Whoever won, it was the goldsmiths who counted the profits.

'They're expecting us,' I said.

Up to that moment I had the lingering hope that I could free Luke with deception or force. I was no longer young and stupid enough to take such a chance. It had to be done the way I first planned it. I took his glass. There was a field towards one side of the house, in which cows grazed peacefully. It was well away from the mercenar-ies, with cover from a barn. I discussed the terrain with Scogman and he agreed it would do.

'This is the sort of thing gentlemen do, innit, sir,' Scogman said.

I agreed it was.

'He may be a gentleman, sir, your father, but he's a liar and a cheat –'

'He won't cheat on this. It's a matter of honour.'

'Honour!' He spat.

I drew out the letter I had written. He put out his hand, then pulled it back again. 'Permission to speak, sir.'

'Go on.'

'When we met you saved me from that hanging magistrate, Sir Lewis. You said it was a military matter and flogged me. I still got the scars. You saved my life but … you went on flogging me until someone took the whip away. You got that look on your face now. You … you're not yourself, sir …'

'Do you want to do this or not?'

He swallowed and without another word took the letter. He had no handkerchief – he had the disgusting habit of drawing his nose over his inside cuff – so I gave him mine. I kept his spyglass. We rode together, fording a small stream before reaching the road that led to the manor. A pair of swallows dipped and whirred before disappearing under the eaves. I put the glass to my eye.

'They've seen us. Give me your sword.'

He went to wipe his nose on his sleeve, remembered himself and blew it on my handkerchief. 'He don't see me as a gentleman, sir. The rules don't apply to scum like me and –'

'Don't argue. Give it to me slowly. Make a bit of a ceremony of it. Try and be a gentleman for once.'

'Ceremony. Hocus pocus rubbish that's all it –'

He saw my expression, silently handed over his sword, turned his horse and checked it. Beyond the porch, Richard was standing, shielding his eyes against the glare of the sun. He must have recovered from his injury, for he moved his arm quite freely. He looked as if he had just got up, for his shaven head was bare and he wore only knee britches and a shirt. Scogman glanced back at me. I gave him an impatient gesture forward. He rode towards the house but stopped almost immediately. Beside Richard stood a mercenary with the wheel-lock pistol in his belt. Clumsily, Scogman pulled out my white handkerchief and held it above his head as he rode on, the soft, hypnotic thud of the hooves turning to a sharp clatter as he passed under the porch and into the courtyard.

The mercenary pointed the pistol at Scogman and made him dismount before he would take the letter. I watched Richard read it. I had written it as I thought it, with no hesitations, no changes.

You have my son. I am willing to exchange myself for him but you must do exactly what I say. Your men, apart from your second, must remain within the grounds of the house. I will hand my sword over to your second as Scogman is given safe custody of Luke. Luke will leave with Scogman without hindrance from you or your men. I will return to the house with you. You must say nothing to Luke whatsoever except that we have reached an agreement together. I will accept your word to Scogman that you agree to the terms of this letter.

Was it a coincidence that, as with Anne's letter to me, there was no salutation and no signature? It was as if I had become a non-person. Richard had never acknowledged me as a son, certainly not as a Stonehouse. Richard read the letter, looked up and read it again. The swallows flew out of the eaves in search of more insects.

Sweat trickled down my back. I unbuttoned my jerkin and took off my cravat. Scogman pointed to the mercenary's pistol. The man looked at him suspiciously, then showed him the operation of the dog lock. My grip tightened on Scogman's sword. I was sure he was going to ruin everything by grabbing the pistol, but then Richard called the mercenary to one side. Normally he was good with men, assessing situations quickly, reacting incisively. Now, however, he looked uncertain, glancing continually towards me as the mercenary talked. Finally, in one angry outburst, he brought the discussion to a close and Scogman rode back. I was convinced then my father would not do it. I could not help a feeling of relief stealing over me. The swallows darting, the rattle of the hooves on stone and their measured thud on grass as Scogman approached suddenly seemed wonderful, precious things.

'He'll do it.'

He told me the mercenary was convinced it was a trick. '*Very English*' were the words he used, sir, and he didn't mean it as no compliment. Knows what he's doing, even though his pistol ain't up to much. Probably misfire,' he added hopefully. 'They argued. Couldn't hear anything except one thing your father said.'

'What was that?'

'He's a Stonehouse.'

I stared across at the house. My father was going inside. The mercenary leaned against a wall. He chewed a nail as he watched us.

First I had been nothing, something thrown to die in a plague cart. Then a nuisance, taken in to be made a Stonehouse, a folly of his father's. Then a threat that must be got rid of. Then a child of the Devil, who must be hanged and chopped into small pieces so they could not be put back together again. Only now, in a kind of ritual beloved by medieval knights, although it was legend rather than reality even then and had certainly finally died with the Civil War, did he consider me worthy of the Stonehouse name.

'My father said that?'

I must have smiled for he grinned back at me. 'Bollocks, sir, innit. I mean, he's as tricky as they come and you have your moments but one thing you ain't is a –'

He stopped abruptly and swallowed when I gave him a freezing look. It was acceptable for me to deride it, not him. Perhaps, in spite of all my efforts to be something else, to save the world, or however else you might like to describe it, in the deep centre of my heart that is what I was. A Stonehouse.

The field I had chosen was perfect for the purpose. Scogman tethered our two horses near the barn. It was, I judged, about three-quarters of a mile from the house. The ground was flat and open, with no cover for Richard's mercenaries. Yet behind the barn it dipped and skirted the beginnings of Epping Forest. Scogman knew it from when our regiment had been based in Essex. He and Luke would have a head start and a good chance of evading any pursuit.

'Where do I take him?'

'To the Countess. She will know where Lady Stonehouse is. They are to take the ship. Luke will use my assumed name. They will never be safe here.'

He looked about to speak but thought better of it.

'Oh. One more thing. Marry Mrs Scogman.'

He grinned. 'Is that an order, sir?'

There was a movement in the trees where the mercenaries were sheltering. One of them was taking something from his saddle holster. The air was so still and clear that even at such a distance I heard a rattle that sounded like the loading of a musket ball. Scogman went to his horse and drew out his flintlock pistol. I put the glass on them, catching a hand in the air shaking something, then the rattle. They were doing what all mercenaries do when they are not killing. Playing pass dice.

Scogman wafted away a fly. 'She ain't the sort of person you marry, sir.'

'Isn't she?'

'She's bread and beer. I was thinking of, well, more of a lady. Someone with … what would you call it …? Finer feelings.'

'To go with the firedogs and the walnut chair?'

'That's it, sir. Exactly.' He became suddenly still.

The bearded mercenary was crossing the court. Keys swung from his belt, catching the sun. He was carrying a linen shirt and disappeared down a corridor leading to the back of the house. As it grew warmer the cows, which had lumbered away on our approach, came back, seeking whatever shade they could find. They brought the flies with them, which became more and more irritating.

'Finer feelings.' I almost spat the words out. 'D'you think she didn't *know* you were leaving when she saw you loading that bloody great trunk? Did you not see the joy on her face when you said you weren't going?' He gave me a bewildered look, shifting from one foot to the other. 'I'm sorry. I'm sorry. I … I don't care what you do but tell her the things that matter. Secrets are poison. Open secrets, where the other suspects but does not know are the worst.'

I turned away, flailing at a fly, which veered and buzzed round me the more I struck out at it. He gripped my arm tightly, pointing. Luke was coming out of the passage into the open court, shading his eyes from the sun. I watched him through the glass. He was wearing the white linen the mercenary had been carrying, but it was too large and only emphasised how bedraggled he was. His britches were soiled. A button was hanging from his short doublet and another was missing. There could not have been a greater contrast between the rebellious youth I had removed from Oxford prison the previous summer and this one. Then his position, or mine, protected him. It had been all show and bravado. Now his face bore the look I had seen too many times during the war ever to forget, the look of suppressed terror borne by a prisoner dragged from his cell, fearing he was going to be shot or tortured. I could not bear to look but was afraid to take my eyes away.

Another door to the court opened. He jumped at the sound. Fear made him rigid. Then he underwent an extraordinary change. His fists clenched. Mixed with the fear was revulsion. Walking towards him across the court was Richard. Luke would have flung himself at him if the mercenary had not grabbed his arm and twisted it behind his back. I could see but not hear the cry of pain. Blindly, scarcely realising it, I was halfway to the gates of the house before Scogman seized my arm.

'Easy, sir, easy.'

Such was the force of Luke's reaction that Richard momentarily backed away. Nothing could illustrate more the innocence, the truth, of Luke's letter. I could picture him discovering Richard in bed with his divine Sarah – love and belief destroyed in one frozen moment.

Richard recovered in an instant. Even at that distance I could feel his charm – see it working like a soothing ointment over Luke's fear. Richard pointed towards me. I laughed with joy at the changes in Luke's expression. He was staring in the sun. He peered, blinked, looked again as if he was uncertain whether I was some kind of mirage, then jumped up and down, waving frantically. I waved back. Richard beamed in an avuncular fashion before speaking long and seriously. At first Luke responded with distrust, with several glances towards me, but gradually he appeared to be drawn in by the atmosphere of ritual, by his grandfather's grave manner and by my similar stance. At that moment the letter I had sent Richard seemed the most ridiculous thing I had written in my life. Scogman was right. Why should I trust him? I had told him to say nothing but that we had reached an agreement. He might say anything. Do anything. Take us both. I had no sword. Nothing but the absurdity of the concept of honour, which I had always despised but put on because Richard professed it.

Richard had a new assurance, perhaps coming from the feeling he had Highpoint in his grasp. He was soberly dressed, except for a flamboyant cravat, embroidered in red and gold, the Stonehouse colours. His tightly curled wig was tied in a queue at the back, military style. The jewelled pommel of his Italian rapier caught sparks of light from the sun. Hypnotised by this, I only gradually became aware of a fly crawling across my forehead. When I brushed it away the bearded mercenary's hand instantly went to his pistol.

'I could take him,' murmured Scogman.

'Don't be a fool.'

From behind the trees where the mercenaries were playing dice came a shout of protest, followed by jeers and laughter, disturbing a flock of wood pigeons. Richard called sharply for the men to be quiet and turned smartly to leave the court, Luke and the mercenary falling into step with him. The wood pigeons drifted in lazy circles over their heads before settling, one by one.

The sun was at its height. Their feet kicked up small puffs of dust from worn patches as they walked towards us. It should not have worked, but it did. I felt its power, like that of some religious ceremony which you may not understand, or even believe in, but which nevertheless overawes you. I had committed a cardinal sin for which there was no redemption. No matter that Richard saw it as the murder of the King while I saw it as the murder of love; that he saw my name on the King's death warrant while I saw Anne's letter: *Of all the things you have done this is unforgivable.* It was the same thing, for different reasons.

What neither of us bargained for was that love will out even when – or perhaps particularly when – it is too late.

Luke broke from Richard. 'Father, Father.' He flung himself at me in a confusion of words and movement. Over the blur I saw Richard standing stock still, the mercenary drawing his pistol, Richard stopping him with a warning gesture but keeping his hand hovering near the pommel of his sword. Luke felt even slighter. They might have given him fresh linen, but they could not remove the stink. My hands tightened round him when I saw a bruise on his forehead.

'Have they hurt you?'

I could feel the bones in his body as he trembled against me. 'I was not a good prisoner,' he said dismissively, with an attempt at his old bravado, but his voice caught. 'Is it true what he said?' He looked towards Richard with a shudder. 'You have reached an agreement?'

'Yes.'

Inner voice, or inner spirit, whatever it was, seemed to knit the scarred side of his face with the other in one harmonious whole. 'God be praised! He has answered my prayers. I prayed for you both to be brought back together.'

I held him for a moment longer. 'Go with Scogman.'

For the first time he seemed to take in the silent, ritual stances of the other three men. 'Why? What are you going to do?'

'Have a few words with my father.'

Before he could reply I went towards Richard. He gave me his long, easy-going, affable smile. If the dice had fallen differently we might have at least respected, perhaps even liked, one another. So it must have seemed to Luke, for some of the tension left his face and I saw him go to Scogman as I approached Richard, who ordered the mercenary to keep back.

'Hello, Father.'

'Hello, Tom.'

'That wig suits you.'

He stroked the tight curls. He had always been vain. 'D'you think so? Worst thing was having all my own hair shaved off.' He glanced past me and I followed his gaze. Luke was talking excitedly to Scogman. Richard dropped his voice. 'You will be imprisoned and go on trial. There is nothing I could do about that, even if I wanted to.' I nodded and smiled, as if he had passed some pleasantry. He stared at me nonplussed, never taking his eyes off me, distrust, I felt, gradually giving way to a grudging admiration.

'Let's get on.'

I began to walk towards the house. I cared not a jot for his distrust or his admiration. All I wanted was to keep up the friendly charade until we were beyond the gates where Luke could not see us. Although the mercenary had been told to keep back, as the gates grew nearer he was practically on our heels. From his darting glances about him and the changing rhythm of his steps, I knew what he was thinking: *if he's going to try anything it will be here*. Still far enough from the other mercenaries but with the cover of the gates, the small lodge house. I tried to reassure him with inane chat to Richard about the weather, but this only made him increasingly edgy.

It was the fly. Probably it was a different fly, but one always feels that it is the same fly that has marked you out, attracted by the texture of your sweat, your particular odour. It suddenly buzzed, loud and piercing, right in my ear. Automatically I struck out at it. The mercenary grabbed me on one side and Richard on the other. I began to reassure them but the mercenary was taking no chances and twisted my arm behind my back.

'Father,' Luke screamed.

It was like a dream in which you fear something dreadful is going to happen but are powerless to move. Luke grabbed Scogman's sword and ran towards us. In one swift movement the mercenary released me, drew his pistol and clubbed me to the ground. He levelled the pistol at Luke. I tried to grab his leg but got a boot in my face. The explosion deafened me. I could hear nothing, see little through blood coursing from the blow to my forehead. There was a smell of powder. The blur of the mercenary's boots. He was coming for me again. I rolled away, aiming a blow at his face. There was no face. A sightless eye, almost slipping from its socket, was staring at me. The other side of his face was smashed blood and bone. Sound rushed back with the cry of birds wheeling above me and the clash of swords. I got to my feet. Scogman was lowering the pistol he had fired.

Richard was parrying with his rapier a lunge from Luke. Luke had come to my aid, but it had become personal. It was in the set of his lips, the narrowing of his eyes, the ferocity of his attack, his sideways stance, arm held high and straight, point aimed unerringly at Richard's face. It was no longer a question of escape, but one of honour; not the fake honour I had put on to free him, but the honour of a gentleman, for whom the loss of it meant life was not worth living. Richard had made a fool of him with the girl he loved. He had borne that, but when Richard had tricked me – as he wrongly saw it – nothing else mattered but this. He meant to kill him.

The mercenaries emerged from behind the trees. One was tossing the dice from hand to hand. At first the ritual power of the duel cast a spell that kept them at a distance. They watched, as I did, hypnotised by the flashing swords, the weave of the men's bodies and dart of their feet. Then the mercenary with the dice stopped shaking them. He was staring at the dead mercenary at my feet, glancing at a colleague. I picked up the dead mercenary's pistol and pointed it at them. I could see from the looks on the men's faces that no one would be the first to move. They knew the odds. They were paid to kill, not to be killed.

I heard the drop of the ball as Scogman reloaded, the click of the dog lock as he covered them, giving me a chance to intervene. There are advantages in not being a gentleman or, at least, only a fake one. I was not bound by their ridiculous games. Cromwell, only half a gentleman himself, hated duellists. One of the reasons why the Royalists lost, he used to say, was because they killed one another.

I moved closer. I brought up my pistol and took aim. For a split second I had a sight on Richard. I was about to fire when Luke lunged in front of him. I lowered the unfamiliar, heavy pistol, my hand trembling. I was soaked in sweat. My eyes were blurred with it and the flash of the swords in the sun. The duel was much more evenly matched than I would ever have imagined. Richard was by far the better swordsman but his reactions had slowed. Luke's youth and energy made up for his lack of skill. Both men kept the sword points high, parrying thrusts with upward or downward flicks of the guard, each waiting for the opening to turn a parry into a riposte. Luke found it. His sword struck like the dart of a snake's tongue. Richard fell back. It was my opportunity. I raised the pistol again. I could not do it. Not my father. Not in cold blood. At the click of the safety catch, Luke looked round. Did I shout a warning? If I did, the words scarcely left my mouth before Richard lunged. Luke never uttered a cry. There was a look of surprise on his face. I ran forward, kicking Richard's sword from his hand as he fell. I started leading Luke away before he began to stumble.

'See to him,' I snapped to the mercenaries, two of whom ran to Richard while I carried Luke to the horses.

At first he did not seem to realise he was hurt. His face was flushed and his eyes bright. 'I hit him. It was a good strike, was it not, Father?'

'Yes, yes. Now you must be quiet, Luke.'

The mercenaries must have thought the whole business a curiously English affair. None came after us until Richard sat up, cursing and gesturing violently in our direction. Scogman fired, aiming towards the horses which the mercenaries were untethering. They panicked and scattered. I took off my shirt, ripped off the sleeves, wadded the body, and used the sleeves to knot it tightly into place. Only then did Luke seem to realise how badly he was wounded;

even then he stared wonderingly at his bloodsoaked shirt as if it belonged to someone else. I hated moving him but I had no option. The mercenaries were rounding up their horses and Richard was getting to his feet. Scogman took Luke while I mounted.

'You saw, Scoggy, you saw?' Luke said.

Luke had never called him Scoggy in his life.

'It was a good strike. You fought brave, sir.'

Luke smiled. To my knowledge Scogman had never called him 'sir', always the patronising 'Mr Luke'. He lifted him up and I cradled him against me on my saddle. The mercenaries fired two or three shots. The range was too great, but a ball from the musket ricocheted, clipping my shoulder. It hampered me, rather than anything else, as I tried to keep Luke as still as possible. We had a good start on them and it was old territory for Scogman. It was not far from where our regiment had been billeted, for which he used to 'requisition' a chicken, or even a pig. He knew of a small town where we might find a doctor.

Bright bursts of sun flickered intermittently with gloom as we plunged into Epping Forest, branches snapping against us.

Luke stirred, his eyes opening. 'Where are we?' His voice was a little slurred, slower and weaker.

'Nearly home. Not far.'

'Will Mother be there?'

'Yes.'

I told Scogman we had to stop and rest, but he insisted we went on a little further through a colder, deeper part of the forest where no plants grew except white fungus clinging to trees. We ploughed through wet dank leaves, finally emerging into a clearing where the sun was a shock of bright light. Scogman listened and nodded. We laid down the saddle blankets and put Luke on them. Scogman said he would ride for the doctor but I shook my head. Luke was breathing more quickly. He gripped my arm, seeming to have some consciousness of how badly he was hurt.

'Will you tell Mother I was brave?'

'Yes. You must rest, Luke.'

'Promise?'

'I promise.'

An unexpected smile crossed his face. 'You came, Father, you came.'

'Yes. I –'

I almost said bitterly I wished with all my heart I hadn't, but he smiled again and I kept repeating that of course I came, of course, and I held him and kissed him. Scogman took off his hat. With Richard's men looking for us, we had no option but to bury him there. Only Scogman could have found a spade in that God-forsaken spot. I waited with Luke until the sun disappeared beyond the clearing and the birds began their evening song. Scogman returned with a spade he had 'come across' and some kitchen towels. The wound on my shoulder, which I had been scarcely aware of, was worse than I thought and kept breaking open. I found some yarrow leaves to staunch the blood and Scogman bandaged it with a towel.

The soil was soft and loamy but giddiness kept overcoming me and Scogman had to do most of the digging. It was growing dark by the time we were done. Up and down the country there are many graves of unknown soldiers. At least the soldiers burying them had the soldiers' Bible to read from, which Cromwell insisted on everyone in the New Model carrying. We did not even have that, and had to be content with an Our Father, and, as the words choked in my throat, Scogman, just as he had done most of the digging, had to mumble most of them.

PART FOUR

The Good Old Cause

April–October 1660

31

Scogman convinced me I was too weak to continue riding to Highpoint, though in truth I needed little persuasion. The fever had gripped me and I could barely stand, let alone sit in the saddle. Somehow, for I have no memory of the journey, he got me safely back to London.

By the time the fever had abated, three days later, I found myself in a bed of clean sheets smelling of lavender and hops. A pert face surrounded by bouncing ringlets bent over me. 'You've been dreadful ill, sir. Oliver 'ad the doctor 'ere. Didn't you, Oliver?'

I was so confused I scarcely remembered that Oliver was Scogman's first name. I asked him why had he not taken me to Queen Street? The servants would have attended to all my needs. What Scogman told me left me in no doubt my old life had ended.

Anne was not at Queen Street. Nor could she return there. Monck's soldiers had gone and with them my protection. Scogman had somehow persuaded Mr Cole to hand over my papers and had brought them to his house for safety. It was Ben, my old army doctor, who had attended me during the fever and cleaned my wound, and Mrs Scogman (as I thought of her) who had looked after me.

The house in Queen Street was no longer mine. Soon Mr Cole would be welcoming Richard, who would be dictating letters from the leather-topped desk in preparation for the new monarchy. Eventually his son, by his French wife, Geraldine, would stand to attention at the worn line in the carpet before the desk, as I had done and all the Stonehouses before me.

It wasn't safe to stay at Scogman's, but it was another day before I was strong enough to move around, so I sat teaching his son Dick his letters. He learned quickly and we almost reached the end of the alphabet.

I sent Scogman to pay off the avaricious maid Mary, as I had promised Ellie. He did so, installing in her place a widow, Mrs Bridges, whose face, he said, would be no threat to anyone's morality. He explained why I had not come, telling Sam about Luke's death in my arms and that I was still in mourning for him. I was not surprised when Scogman told me how grief-stricken Sam was about the half-brother he had never known.

The wound on my shoulder was healing well, though I had been weakened by the fever. But I could not rest until I found Anne. I had to find her, tell her about Luke, what he said before he died, and fulfil the promise I made to him.

So despite Ben's advice to build my strength up first, I was soon on the streets as much as I had ever been as a runaway child. The Countess was still at home to me in Bedford Square, but only just. She pressed a nosegay to her face with barely concealed distaste and said she had not seen Lady Stonehouse, if indeed she was still entitled to that name.

The next day I dressed in the old torn jerkin, thanked Mrs Scogman for her care and saddled my horse. 'You ain't goin', sir, I ain't learned ev'ryfink yet,' protested young Dick. He yelled for his father and Scogman put his hand on the reins, telling Dick to fetch his horse. I told him I wanted to ride alone, but he insisted on following me.

We took the old drove road to Highpoint where there were only a few sheep for company, and, even on the brightest days, always a thin, bitter wind, which I greeted like an old friend. I say 'we', for I kept ordering Scogman to go back, but at the end of the day he was always there, like a dog, some distance behind me. At first I was irritated, then furious, yelling at him to go home.

'You have a wife and children! Leave me.'

'I ain't with you. Roads still belong to the people, so far as I know. Ain't been enclosed yet. I'm going to see to my property near Highpoint.'

'Property you stole from me.'

'You ain't yourself, sir.'

It was true.

The first sign there was something wrong was on the edge of the great forest. Coming down from the hills, out of that thin, constant wind and with a bed of leaves for a mattress, I slept heavily. Even the shot did not at first awaken me. Drugged with sleep, it became part of a dream about when I first came here during the war. The shot was still reverberating in my head when Scogman shook me awake.

There was a violent snapping of branches ahead of us, a thunder of hooves, growing slower and slower, before they suddenly subsided. It was barely light. We moved cautiously in the direction of the sound. It grew darker where the trees were more huddled together. Scogman signalled frantically, pointing to the ground. I could just see the dull metallic gleam of a trap, not for animals but poachers. As I skirted it, Scogman frowned. The trap had been disabled, sprung with a piece of wood. A little further on I saw on some nettles a dark stain of blood. A trail of it led us to a path. We collided into one another as we heard someone ahead of us.

We looked at each other. The man was not only unaware of us, but seemed unconcerned who heard him. He was whistling an old ballad, 'The Diggers' Song', that property belonged to everybody, and people could dig where they liked. Scogman had once whistled it himself, but it was no longer a song he cared for.

He drew his pistol. The man must have heard the click for he plunged away through some bushes. Scogman gave chase but came back panting, shaking his head, holding the fowling piece the poacher had dropped. Eventually the spots of blood took us to a dead deer.

'I have an idea who he is,' Scogman muttered. 'I'll have him. Stealing my game.'

'My game,' I said mildly.

'Beg pardon, sir. The game what I look after for you.'

We looked at the deer and then at one another. We had eaten little more than bread and cheese since leaving London. It would take us two or three hours to get to Highpoint. We were so hungry we ate the first slices half raw, watching in silence as the fat bubbled and the meat darkened before we cut more.

'Richard's game now, I suppose,' I said, wiping the grease from my mouth. With that thought as sauce, the venison tasted even better.

On the way back to the horses, we found another disabled trap. Then, as he was putting the fowling piece in the saddle holster, Scogman frowned and pointed to the stock. There was an imprint, in lighter wood, of a metal crest bearing the Stonehouse falcon. I recognised the piece. It had come from the Highpoint gunroom, which was always securely locked.

'What's going on?' Scogman muttered.

We skirted round the edge of the forest, seeing nothing else untoward. The wind freshened, driving dark clouds from the west. You could always see the weather before it arrived at Highpoint and we wrapped our cloaks tightly around us. We rode on without incident until gone noon when we reached Isaac's Corner. Who Isaac was nobody knew, but there had always been a woodman here, who leased the rights of this part of the forest from Highpoint.

The forest was thinning and the wind grew stronger. Scogman's horse reared as something flapped across the clearing, coiling around the horse. It was a piece of oilcloth. Across the clearing there was normally a huge pile of logs, which the oilcloth had covered, and another of kindling wood. Both were gone. The ground was littered with splinters of wood. The wheels of a cart and a dropped log or two marked where they had gone – in the direction of the common land, high in the hills, too poor for any landlord to want to buy. Lord Stonehouse had been strict about forest rights. He would have treated the hunted deer and the stolen wood as hanging offences. I was much more lenient, letting commoners have the dead wood and rabbits, even turning a blind eye to small game. But this was too much. I forgot that I had ever hated Highpoint. Forgot that my grasp on it was, at most, tenuous, and rode through the last of the forest and up the rise that led to the house.

'There he is!' yelled Scogman, shouting abuse fruitlessly across the valley to the toy-like cart crawling up the hill road towards Shadwell. I told him sharply to be quiet, and dismounted. Half-buried among the long grass was a cooking pot. Near it were the tracks of a number of carts. Scogman checked the fowling piece was loaded and gave it to me, putting his pistol in his belt. The wind increased as we approached the top of the ridge. Scogman urged caution but I galloped on, fearing that something dreadful had happened to Anne. Scogman almost collided with me as I stopped abruptly.

Highpoint was dark and silent. As big as a small town, with its stables, brewery, bakery and kitchens, at any time of the year the great house was always full of life. There was not a movement, a servant, a candle in a window, or a sound, but for the wind as we descended slowly, fording the stream and approaching the driveway. The lodge door was open. Papers were scattered on the floor and it smelt of urine.

The fountains were not playing, green slime beginning to creep over the surface of their pools. The mouth of a cherub, which normally spouted water, was stuffed with dead flowers. The overgrown lawn was scarred with cart tracks. From the east wing a thin plume of smoke ascended. Windows had been smashed to gain entry to the kitchens, which had been looted. Our feet kicked against empty wine bottles. We doused the fire, which was in wooden cladding in a room near the kitchens. It looked as though it was the smouldering remains of a larger fire that had been put out, whipped into life again by the wind. There was a scampering sound in the corridor. Scogman lifted his pistol, jumping backwards as a dog burst through past us, a squealing rat in its jaws.

We walked through silent corridors into the main house, where our boots echoed through empty room after empty room. Odd pieces of furniture littered the place but anything of value had gone. The long gallery was stripped of its paintings, its Rubens, Titians and Van Dycks; the library of its most precious books. Gone were the earliest printed books I most treasured: Ovid's *Works* printed in Venice in 1474, Thomas More's *Utopia*, Ptolemy's *Geography*. Gaps on the wall marked where priceless Flemish tapestries had hung. Wherever I expected to see a rare, familiar object – a silver-mounted ebony table, a Ruckers harpsichord, a Japanese lacquer cabinet – there was an empty place. Whoever had pillaged Highpoint knew exactly what to take. Everything that Anne had carefully chosen and put together to create the magnificence that made Highpoint the finest seat in England had gone.

32

After this, it was almost as much of a shock to see Mr Travers, the minister of Shadwell, up in the hill country treat the matter so casually. He seemed to think we knew about it. He certainly knew we were without lodging for the night and, fat and jovial as ever, offered us supper and a bed.

We were only too glad to accept as the dark clouds had brought persistent rain. It dripped from the trees as I went to pay my usual respects to my mother's grave. When I first came to Highpoint I had found her in an unmarked spot. I had put up a stone, and expected it to be as neglected as usual. To my surprise fresh flowers were laid on it and there were bunches of sweet-smelling herbs: thyme, marjoram and basil.

The grass was cut and the moss carefully scraped from the wildcat's paw in the Pearce coat of arms, where it always gathered.

MARGARET PEARCE

1601–1625

Tantum Teneo

Only persist. My mother would have liked that. 'I will have one of them,' she had said, in her determination to marry one of the Stonehouses and take over their estate, as they had swallowed up her father's, causing, she believed, his death. *Tantum Teneo*. Only persist.

'Parsons are the biggest rogues!' Scogman exploded. He was pointing across the graveyard. At the back of the parsonage was a neatly stacked pile of freshly cut logs, covered by a piece of oilcloth similar to the one we had seen in the forest.

The careful tending of the grave had softened me and I said I was sure that, if the logs were stolen, the parson was unaware of it.

When I thanked the parson for looking after the grave he replied, 'Ah, not my doing I am afraid, sir, but that of my outer flock. They have gone from thinking your mother a malign spirit to benign. Some of them – although, of course, I counsel them severely against it – even believe her divine.'

He chuckled. His laughter, in which his eyes creased and his whole body shook, was as rich as his stews. He went no further for we were called in to supper. The mutton stew was as good as I remembered it; even more enjoyable since it was accompanied by gusts of wind throwing rain against the windows and flames from the logs, stolen or not, crackling cheerfully up the chimney. Scogman, however, seemed to have indigestion. When the parson left to get another bottle of wine he pointed indignantly to a pair of silver candlesticks on the dresser, which I remembered came from the dining room at Highpoint. I told him to be quiet and I would deal with it later, but when Travers returned, opening a bottle of claret with the Highpoint crest on it, Scogman could contain himself no longer.

'I see you have a very good vintage there, sir.'

The parson beamed. 'Thanks to the generosity of your master, sir. To me and the church.' He indicated the candlesticks. 'Sadly, in these times they are not secure in the church, but they take pride of place in every service.'

He poured the wine with reverence. It was a good vintage, which Lord Stonehouse had laid down for special occasions. Its aroma filled the room, mingling with the sweet herbs of the stew and the scent of the burning logs.

'*My* generosity,' I said.

He laughed. The table trembled and glasses shivered as his stomach quivered against it. 'You are too modest, sir. You have always moved in mysterious ways.'

'What mysterious ways? What happened at Highpoint?'

He laughed again. 'I was hoping you would tell me, sir. You do not recall sending me this?' He produced a letter from a drawer in the dresser.

Dear Reverend Travers,

Due to the changing circumstances, I very much regret having to leave Highpoint. As a measure of my appreciation for your services to the people of Shadwell and the estate, I would like you to accept these candlesticks for the church and this crate of good wine for yourself.

I remain, sir, your humble servant,

Thomas Stonehouse

It was clearly written by a professional scrivener, but the signature was mine. I did not remember dictating it or signing it, but I dictated so many, often barely remembering them when I did sign them. I had to look closely at it before I picked up the hesitation in the loop between the two words, and one or two other things which only I would notice. During this perusal, Travers stopped laughing, swallowing his wine nervously and pouring another glass, as if afraid I might take it back.

'Is it not correct, sir? You did not sign this?'

'I think you had better tell me what happened, Mr Travers.'

He told me that one day a carter had turned up with the letter and the crate containing the wine and the candlesticks. His cart was full, with deliveries he had to make as far afield as Oxford. Riding with the carter was a gentleman he did not know, who gave him the gifts. Beyond that, Travers knew nothing, saying there were several versions I could choose from. I replied that we had all night, and were in need of good stories.

He stoked up the fire, had cheese served with another bottle and told me what the outer flock believed. He called them the outer flock because they lived in scattered hill farms and hamlets on the fringes of the straggling parish. They were also on the fringes of religion, believing as much in magic as in the teachings of the Church. Horseborne, where my mother, Margaret Pearce, had died giving birth to me, was such a hamlet. To this day, Travers said, older people would not go near Horseborne in September when the nights drew in, for fear of meeting the plague cart into which, believing me to be dead, the carter Matthew Neave had flung my body. In spite of the heat of the fire a shiver passed through me. It brought back the worst of my boyhood, when people believed if I had survived the plague, I must have consorted with the Devil. Even Scogman began looking nervously at me, jumping and spilling his wine when a pail, blown by the wind, clattered across the yard outside.

'What nonsense!' I said.

Travers nodded. 'Exactly what I told them, sir. It made no difference. If a cow would not give milk, Margaret Pearce had cursed it. If a child misbehaved, he was told the plague cart would come.'

I stared into my glass, which reflected the leaping flames of the fire. As usual, the truth was unimportant. What mattered was what people believed. For years, until I had rescued it, my mother's grave had been desecrated with red plague crosses from the dye that shepherds used to mark their sheep. I went to the window. The wind blew clouds from the moon and, across the graveyard, I could see my mother's gravestone, gleaming from the rain and piled with herbs, the wildcat's clenched paw raised in what seemed to be a gesture of triumph. Travers stood at my elbow.

'They claim to have seen her. In the flesh. She talked to them. She said they had certain rights that the Stonehouses had unlawfully taken from them generations ago. The rights of common land at Lower Reaches.' Travers threw a log on the fire, a flicker of a smile across his face. 'Forest rights up to and including the old hill road. Fishing rights upstream from Stone Cross –'

Scogman spat derisively in the fire. 'Those are my rights.' He looked at me. 'I paid good money for those, did I not, sir?'

'They have proof, which they showed me,' Travers said. 'A letter signed by Thomas Stonehouse –'

'As he signed the letter for the candlesticks –' Scogman began.

I told him sharply to be quiet. 'This spirit, Mr Travers ... They saw her?'

'Dysart did.'

'Dysart.' Scogman spat again into the fire.

Dysart was the gamekeeper whose traps had been sprung. He came from the hill country and for years he had been talking of retiring there to live with his daughter near Horseborne. He was convinced (or had convinced the credulous) that he had seen Margaret Pearce but he told Travers a different story, which Travers corroborated with some other servants at Highpoint.

Late one afternoon a coach was seen approaching the Highpoint lodge gates. The lodge-keeper put his glass to his eye, identified the falcon crest and sent his boy running to the house. The servants, who had daily been expecting Richard Stonehouse, quickly assembled outside, marshalled by the house steward and housekeeper. To their surprise, Lady Anne Stonehouse stepped out of the carriage. Travers emphasised her Christian name for, I suppose, the servants were expecting another Lady Stonehouse to alight.

'How was she?' I said eagerly.

From all accounts, he replied, they had never seen her better, never seen her more dignified, beautiful, stately, in complete command of herself and, paradoxically, Highpoint. Although she was leaving it, she said, Highpoint was not the land, the bricks, stone and wood it was built from, but what they clothed it with. What were the lawns, the fountain gardens or the wilderness walk without the gardeners? What were the great oak dining table, the oak panelling of the long gallery, the carvings of the grand staircase, without the joiners, carpenters who made them and the servants who cared for them and polished them every day? What were the seasonal feasts, looked forward to by the whole county and beyond, without the cook and kitchen staff? She thanked each one of them, personally, by name. Long before she reached the smallest bootboy there was not a man who was not blowing his nose or a woman not dabbing her apron to her eyes.

I could picture it. Even I, who hated Highpoint, loved it at that time in the evening when the shadows lengthened and the sun glittered in the fountains and sparkled on the windows of the east wing. For a moment, the servants had told Travers, Lady Stonehouse stopped. It looked as if she was going to break down herself. Then she went on. They would shortly have a new master, she said. Some would remember him as a young man at Highpoint.

I could imagine their faces when she said that. If Richard, with his whoring and his gambling, had been the despair of Lord

Stonehouse, with his arrogance and demands he had been hated by the servants.

Travers looked into the fire, then at my torn jerkin and growth of beard, as if he regarded me as an eccentric philanthropist. He seemed suddenly convinced again that, just as I had helped the hill farmers before, I must be behind it, being as diffident and modest about it as I had been about those transactions.

'But you know what happened next, sir. You must do. You must have planned it – a, a masterstroke, if I may say so.'

'Go on, Mr Travers,' I said evenly. 'Just tell me what you heard.'

Lady Stonehouse told the servants that the furniture and other rare pieces were being distributed to those personal friends in the county who had always admired them, and who would cherish and appreciate them. Just as these treasures were esteemed, she said, so were they: she had chosen them with just as much care. Who in the county had not tasted Mrs Crosby's venison and raisin pie, savoured her sugar cakes? Who had not admired Mr Jeffrey's knot garden, or walked through his masterpiece, the Orangery? She had places and characters for all of them if they wished to go. They all did. With one voice.

My head was in a whirl. I did not know whether to laugh or to cry. What a coup! I only wished I had thought of it. She had been determined to have Highpoint, which she had turned, brick by brick, picture by picture, into the pre-eminent seat in the county. Now she was determined Richard would not have it. She had ripped the soul from it, leaving only its decaying body. It would never recover. Richard had neither the talent nor the inclination. On the other hand, it was my property. She had forged my signature. I would be seen as duped by my own wife and would be the laughing stock of the county. If I had ever cared for the county, I gave not a fig for it now. Worse, much worse, was that she would be branded as a thief. I could not bear that.

When Travers reached the end of his story, saying yet again with that look of incredulity stealing over his face, that I must have known about it, I gave him a modest smile. 'Mr Travers, it is better to give than receive.'

Scogman opened his mouth, but at a warning look from me said nothing.

Travers gave a great shout of laughter, shaking like a jelly, toasting me, his candlesticks and what was left of his crate of good wine. 'You had me there, Sir Thomas, you had me rather worried there for a moment, I confess it, sir.' He wiped his eyes, spluttering. 'I was beginning to think you knew nothing about it. Acts 20: 35. Better to give than receive. I will use it as my sermon on Sunday. We will remember you in our prayers, sir. You are a great joker as well as a great benefactor.'

33

When we left the next day, there were more flowers on my mother's grave. Riding through the village, people doffed their hats. One ran up and said, 'Bless you, sir.' Another, whose fingers had been mangled in a rock fall, begged me to touch his hand. When I told him it would do him no good, he retorted, 'Won't do me no harm, sir, will it?' I pressed his crushed fingers. They looked exactly the same to me but he claimed he felt a warmth, a movement that was not there before.

Scogman sniffed and said nothing. When we had staggered upstairs the night before he would not stop talking about the wretched candlesticks, the wine and his precious fishing rights. My head pounded and all I wanted was sleep. He had his own room but would not go away.

'What did you say that to Travers for, sir? Better to give than receive? She's a forger! If I did that I would be hanged.'

I jumped out of bed, stumbling, grabbing at the bed-head to keep my balance. 'Get out. If I ever catch you saying that again about Lady Stonehouse *you* will be hanged.'

I was almost asleep when I heard him at the door. 'Permission to speak, sir.' His voice sounded as if he was at the end of a tunnel. 'I know you're awake, sir.' I buried my head deeper into the pillow. 'You were as shocked as I was when you found the house was empty.' His voice grew even more incredulous. 'You mean you gave all that stuff away, sir?'

Again I leapt out of bed, this time pushing him out of the room. 'Yes! I signed those letters. Shut up and let me get some sleep.'

We climbed the hills from the village. I remembered that, before Sam's ill-fated visit, Anne had been preparing a number of bequests of chosen pieces to give to friends before we left for me to sign. There was a clause which retained them as our property, should we ever return or wish to sell them. Had she not merely carried out what we had already agreed?

We were approaching near where I was born and my mother died. I fancied I heard her laughter mingling with the wind, thinning the scudding clouds and bringing out the sun. Down there was the road where Matthew, after rescuing me from the plague cart, had fled from the Stonehouses to London, bringing me up until Lord Stonehouse had discovered me and decided I should wear boots and learn letters. Nothing more! Ever since then Highpoint had been like a millstone around my neck. I felt a great lift of the spirits.

'Look down there, Scoggy.'

The sun lit up the lower slopes and the valley, spread out like a map below us. It showed what generation after generation of Stonehouses had done, encroaching on the forest here, common grazing land there, higher land where the river rose, giving control of water, gradually taking the liveable heart from an area where hill farmers had scratched a living for centuries. Now, after what my mother had started and I had continued, with Anne's final gesture the enclosures had been demolished. Life was already pulsing back. Fences had been taken down from a common where cattle were grazing. A woman with a bundle of kindling on her back emerged from the forest. Even the river seemed to run more freely. A man and a group of children were fishing. They clapped and cheered as there was a flash of silver in the air and the man reeled the fish in. Scogman gazed at them sourly. I squeezed his shoulder.

'Come, Scoggy. You used to fight for the rights of the common man.'

He sniffed. 'That's when I had nothing, sir.'

'You can still fish there. It's free. There's enough for everyone. Enough land. Enough game. Enough water. Most of the food on the Stonehouses' table was thrown away. It was display. To show they were better than anyone else. Now –' I gestured again at the scene below – 'is it not better to give than receive?'

He groaned. 'But the house, sir. All those treasures. The furniture ... the paintings ... the, the ...' He seemed to take it as a personal loss. Perhaps it was. He must have had an eye on various pieces, like the walnut chair I had seen at his house. 'Better to give than ... I had no idea Lady Stonehouse was that way inclined, sir.'

'No idea? Look at her charity work in the county. What she did for the servants. They loved her.'

'Yes, but Lord Beacon ain't in need of no charity ...'

Lord Beacon was one of the recipients of the bequests I had discussed with Anne. I was almost certain the Mortlake tapestries, which his lordship had always admired, would have found a safe lodging there, but, unfortunately, Lord Beacon was not at home.

We pressed on to Catton Hall where Lady Geoffrey Wallace, a widow and one of Anne's closest friends, had always coveted the Japanese lacquer cabinet. She also was not at home, although Scogman thought he saw her briefly at one of the upper windows. I told him he must be mistaken, for although she was a fervent Royalist, she had always had a soft spot for me.

We rode on in silence for a while. 'I will say one thing for you, sir,' Scogman said eventually. 'You always think the best of people.'

By this time I was more than a little ruffled and beginning to lose faith in my theory. 'What's that supposed to mean?' I said irritably. 'Isn't it better than thinking the worst?'

It was late afternoon by the time we reached Watlington, on the edge of the Chilterns. I had no doubt Anne would have chosen the library at Seaton Manor for my Highpoint library. Andrew Seaton had fought with me at Naseby. It was he who had exposed the Sealed Knot rebellion the previous summer, and warned me about Luke's involvement. He was a great bibliophile and I could think of no one better to care for my books.

Andrew was not only in; he was in the library cataloguing my books.

'There you are, Scogman,' I said triumphantly.

Andrew welcomed us, wrapping his left arm round me, the other having been lost at Naseby.

'Tom, you old regicide! Scogman, you rogue!'

He had beer and ham brought to us in the library. I could not eat a morsel until I asked him if he had seen Anne. He shook his head. I told him things had been difficult between us and he nodded. He had heard about Luke's death and said how sorry he was. I took a sup of beer and tried to eat, looking towards one of my books he had laid out on his desk. The protective wrapping had been removed. From the exquisitely printed map of the mythical country, I could see it was More's *Utopia*.

'Anne must have contacted you about taking care of my books,' I said.

He shook his head. 'My books now, Tom.' Not only was there no thanks for the bequest, but there was an edge, more than a hint of the triumph of one collector over another in his voice.

'You must at least have had a letter from my lawyer about the bequest.'

'Bequest? What are you talking about? That shark of an agent of yours sold them to me.'

The ham caught in my throat and I could not stop coughing. Half-masticated bread was suspended in Scogman's open mouth. I remembered Travers saying the carter had a gentleman with him he did not know.

'Agent?'

'Richard Symonds.'

He was the antiquarian Anne had used when she was first furnishing Highpoint and buying the pictures from the Royal Collection. 'I know him,' I said faintly.

'Know him? I should think you bloody well do know him with the money he screwed out of me.'

When I told him he had no right to sell them, that Anne and I had talked only of making bequests, he snatched a letter from his desk drawer. 'Are you saying this is not your signature, sir?'

There it was. On Stonehouse paper with the falcon seal, written by the same impeccable scrivener, with the same telltale hesitation in my signature. Scogman stared from the letter, to the books to me with awe. I suppose it dwarfed all his petty rogueries as Highpoint had towered over the other seats in the country. It all came out then. I told Andrew everything. He had the beer taken away and Dutch brandy brought in.

After the Sealed Knot rebellion, Andrew had known all the arguments Anne and I had about Luke. He had been present at some of them. He poured more brandy, the evening light catching it as he set the glass down. He moved as quickly, as dexterously, with one arm as most people did with two.

'I understand you killed him?'

'Who?'

'Luke.'

Somewhere a fly buzzed, stopped, then started up again. Or was I imagining it? It brought back that hot afternoon, the moment when they seized me, when Luke realised I was being taken away and ran towards me. What was I trying to do that afternoon? Be a hero? Win Anne back? Was it guilt at keeping the letter back from her? Love for him? Her? A muddle of all these things? I did not know. All I could remember was what happened. That was all that mattered. All that ever mattered was what happened. I could see his blood, his face, hear his voice.

'You came, Father, you came.'

If I had not, he might be alive. That was all that mattered. That was what had happened. Intentions were buried with him.

Andrew was still waiting for an answer to his half statement, half question, his hand hesitating, as if to squeeze my shoulder.

'Killed him? Yes. I suppose I did.'

Andrew withdrew his hand, recoiling, even while he was struggling to bring out the usual excuse for it.

'That bloody war! Will it never stop? Father against son … Brother against …' He swallowed his brandy.

Scogman came to life. He had been shifting, staring from one to another. Now he stood up, heels coming together as if he was on parade. 'Permission to speak, sir. That's bollocks, sir. Double bollocks. Kill him? Sir Thomas went to give himself up for him. I ain't one for being noble, or honour or any of that shit, and when I realised I thought it the most stupid thing in the world until …' He turned away. I had never seen Scogman cry and he did not cry then, but he came close. 'He died game, sir. As he wanted to. Like a soldier.'

Andrew got up and looked at me with a puzzled frown. 'Like a soldier? What are you talking about? I thought Sir Thomas killed Luke in a duel –'

Scogman sprang at him. 'If you had two arms, sir, I'd fight you myself.'

I sprang up. 'You forget your station, Scogman.'

'Sorry, sir. I don't know what came over me. Maybe I'm getting a touch of the gentleman myself. Sorry, sir.' This to Andrew, whose brandy he had spilled over his cuff.

'At ease, Scogman.' Andrew shook his sleeve and finished the remaining brandy. 'We're not in the army now.'

'Feel as if I've never left it, sir,' Scogman said.

'Not Cromwell's army, no,' Andrew said. 'You never leave that.'

'Who told you I killed my son in a duel?' I said quietly.

'Who told the world, you mean.' Andrew saw the expression on my face. 'You mean it's not true?' It was as though a weight was lifted from him. 'God damn it! I knew it wasn't true, but all the same …' He went to his desk, opening one drawer, then another, before pulling out a pamphlet. 'You mean you haven't seen this?'

'I haven't seen anything. I was ill, then we went to Highpoint along the drove road.'

It was a Royalist pamphlet, *The Weekly Discoverer*. The headline was *A perfect relation of how the son of Lord Stonehouse was barborously kill'd by his own father. And several terrible circumstances of the fact.* I read it in a curiously detached way, with even some admiration at the way in which the lies had been skilfully sewn together to look a seamless truth. I was the evil demon, of course. Richard was the hero. I had tried to kill him because he was claiming his rightful inheritance. My son Luke, a committed Royalist who loved his King, had come to the aid of his ailing grandfather.

Ailing grandfather was a bit rich, but never mind. I turned over the fold to read the rest of the story and went very still. I took the paper to the window, not so much for the light, for the candles were now lit, but to be away from the others.

Tom Neave, as he shoulde properly be called, for he usurped the title
from his father, with his accomplice Scogmanne, hid the body in the
depths of a forest. Sir Richard Stonehouse recovered it, ensuring that
the Royalist hero was buried with all due ceremony in the family
grave at St Paul's. In a remarkable display of Christian charity &
forgiveness that brought tears to many eyes, Sir Richard allowed
Luke's mother Anne to attend the ceremony. In her griefe and
gratitude to Sir Richard, she is believed to be expressing penitence for
the foule acts of the regicide Neave, and it is said she won the hearts
of many of the mourners at the funeral. Neave has not been seen since
the murder, but is believed to be in hiding in London.

Andrew came up to me. 'You hid the body?'

'Buried,' I said. 'Buried. We buried him. Of course we did. What else could we do? As we did in the war. Like a soldier. As he would have wanted. We buried him.'

I turned away, feeling the earth on my fingers, smelling the leaf mould. I told Andrew I had intended to take Anne there, for she would have wanted a Christian burial, but I am not sure I would. Luke loved the forest at Highpoint where he hunted and I felt he would have wanted to stay there. At the very last, at least, he was my son. *You came, Father, you came.* For the first time since it had happened grief overwhelmed me. I sat on a window seat, looking out at the darkening beech trees which leaned over the house. Andrew offered me things and said things, but I took none of it in until I heard him say: 'Anne.'

I sprang up, blinking, from my dark corner, dazzled by the bright lights of the candles swaying in the draught from the open door. Anne was standing there, dressed in black. I could tell her everything. She would understand. She would believe me. She might never forgive me but that seemed no longer as important as telling her exactly what happened, what Luke had said. We would at least be together in that. In my hurry to get across the room I knocked over a chair.

'Anne –'

As she moved from the dark shadows of the door Anne shrank away, like the will o' the wisps I used to see as a child, flickering tantalisingly over the marsh. She turned into the maid, in the act of picking up a tray, staring at me in bewilderment.

'All right, Anne,' Andrew said to the maid, steering me to a chair. He pressed into my hand the brandy I had scarcely tasted. I took a swallow and spat it out.

'There's a fly.'

'Where?'

'Can't you hear it?'

They exchanged glances and Scogman said something to Andrew I did not catch. I could not stand the taste of brandy on my tongue and Andrew brought me some beer. I found I had a raging thirst and drank one tankard then another, reading the *Weekly Discoverer* until I could have repeated the story word by word. I knew now why Lord Beacon and Lady Wallace had not been at home. That was trivial compared with the desecration of Luke's grave. My grief was gradually displaced by mounting anger. I could not bear the thought of Richard's men digging up Luke's grave, laying their hands on him.

'I can understand now why she …' Andrew was waving the letter on which Anne had written my signature. At first I scarcely listened. The treasures, too, were trivial compared with what had happened to Luke. But by this time Andrew had taken several brandies and kept returning to the letter and the books.

'Had to sell land for 'em. God damn it! Nearly broke up my own marriage. Women. It's the war. At least my wife came to heel. You were always too free with Anne, Tom, got to say that. Too free. Much too free. Even so, I can't believe she'd go the length of …' He picked up the letter with the signature and went over to the books, lovingly turning the pages of More's *Utopia*, listening to the crisp crackle of paper, shaking his head in admiration at the workmanship of the map. He closed the book, his voice heavy with regret.

'Of course, I can't keep 'em.'

It was a moment before his words registered. 'Of course you must keep them, you idiot. You paid for them.'

He turned away from the books. He was almost in tears. 'No, no, no, old friend. Even if I wasn't a gentleman I couldn't do it. They were not hers to sell.'

Scogman, who had been drifting into a doze, sat up. His eyes gleamed: hope, no doubt, being rekindled for the fishing rights. 'Stolen goods, sir.'

'Exactly, Scoggers.' He turned to me. 'You must take action against her, Tom.'

I dismissed the idea. Court cases were at a standstill between governments. Andrew declared he would do it when the new government was in place. All he needed was my testimony that I had not signed the document. I stared at the books. At Highpoint I would turn to passages I knew almost by heart. Thomas More, Ovid and Caesar were like old friends with whom I had a chat from time to time. Again I felt the loss and anger when I had walked through the pillaged library. Again I looked at the signature on the document, uncannily like mine, but not mine. Andrew put pen and paper in front of me. He had trained as a lawyer and dictated what I was to write.

'*I, Sir Thomas Stonehouse, do affirm and attest …*'

I moved to sign it. My hand, which had been flowing fast and easily over the paper, was suddenly cramped and awkward. I rubbed it, moved to dash off the signature, but again came to a stop, acutely aware of the different parts, the ascenders and descenders, loops and curves that made up what I had done without thinking many thousands of times before. I even looked at the forged signature for guidance. I dipped the quill in the horn to make a fresh start, then scribbled over what I had written and flung down the pen. I pointed to the document giving Richard Symonds permission to sell.

'I signed that. I forgot.'

'Forgot?' Andrew and Scogman exchanged glances. Scogman looked about to speak but changed his mind when he saw my expression.

'That's right.'

I would not do this to her. I could not. I picked up the *Discoverer* and read the passage again. Of course she would go to Luke's funeral. But would she believe Richard's story? I had been drawn in, captivated by my father's lies, but she never had. She had wanted him turned over to Cromwell and hanged.

'... *in her griefe and gratitude she is believed to be expressing penitence for the foule acts of the regicide Neave ...*'

What garbage! She would never acknowledge me as Tom Neave. I was a Stonehouse. A gentleman. That was why she had married me. It was through me that she had her name and title. Sometimes, when the will o' the wisp's light flickered, I believed she loved me. But when the light went out, I accepted that I loved her and she loved Highpoint. That was the deal. The wholesale clearance of Highpoint was not a vindictive act against me as Andrew believed, but against Richard. Highpoint was hers, not mine, not Richard's. It was her creation and would remain in people's memories as such. She was determined neither Richard, nor I, for that matter, would sully it.

I said as much to Andrew and Scogman. Andrew was silent for a while. It was now quite dark outside, the only sound the rustle of the trees. Andrew picked up his glass, then put it down again without drinking.

'Tom, old friend, we've been in some tight situations together.'

'We have, Andrew, we have.'

'But this is as tight for you as any I can recall. Richard isn't waiting for the King. He's put a price on your head. There are bounty hunters everywhere. One came here. It isn't just the hanging, Tom, it's the drawing and quartering.'

'I'm aware of that.'

'Are you? Seen one?'

'No.'

'I have. Executioner's not just a hangman, he's a butcher. Specially chosen. Artist in his own way. Condemned man is cut down half-strangled. Aware enough to watch – made to watch, that's the point – his guts slowly cut out, very slow and lingering they do it, to please the audience. Then, as a finale, he will cut off your prick and balls and hold them up to the crowd.'

Scogman turned away, leaving his brandy untasted.

'When you came to the door, Tom, I was surprised. Surprised? Shocked. Thought you'd left the country. Leave now, Tom. Leave while you still have a chance. I'll do all I can for you if you need help.'

'Not until I find her.'

'Thought you might say that.'

'Not until I tell her the truth about Luke's death.'

He looked towards the books, the document she had signed. 'In spite of all this you still want her back?'

I stood over him. 'Back? What do you mean? We are together. Man and wife.'

'Till death us do part.'

'Till death us do part,' I said.

I went to the window and stared out. The wind was growing stronger, whipping at the branches of the beech tree, some of which tapped and scratched at the windows. Anne had probably returned to London by now. Dark as it was, I felt the urge to be back on the road. It would be safer at night. But I had the nagging feeling there was something here I had missed, something obvious. I struggled to think, but my head ached and Andrew began to recount some rambling story about the house. He pointed out a long crack in the wall, which had been plastered over several times. It was caused by the trees being too close to the house. Every winter he swore he must cut them down but every spring, when the new leaf came, he postponed it. He drew his finger down the crack, catching a small piece of plaster as it fell away and holding it in his hand. He sighed and said he knew he must do it, or it would bring the whole place down.

In the field I had sat round many a camp fire with him, listening to such stories which always had a moral or an aphorism, and were always a mixture of warmth, entertainment and irritation. 'What are you trying to say, Andrew?'

'Leave her, Tom. Before she brings you down. She's duped you.' He pointed to the document. 'God damn it, man, she's a forger –'

I went up to him, struggling to keep my voice steady. 'I told you, Andrew. I signed that document. If you ever repeat what you have said, our friendship is over.'

He swallowed. A trickle of plaster pattered to the floor as he crushed in his hand the piece he had taken from the wall. In the silence, I realised what I had missed. I searched the books Andrew had bought.

'Where's my Caesar? My Ovid?'

'They were not offered to me.' He breathed more quickly, his eyebrows lifting in astonishment. They were among the rarest books in Europe, what booksellers called the *incunabula*, the first books ever printed. My Ovid, printed in Venice in 1474, was once owned by Lorenzo de Medici, and bore his signature. 'They were for sale?' Andrew said.

'No. No. She would not have sold those,' I said. I was almost happy at the thought. It was a sign. Whatever she was up to, she had kept them back for me. Andrew said perhaps they had gone to another buyer with more money than him, but I shook my head.

'She knew how much they meant to me.'

He sighed and looked at Scogman, and paced about the room. He examined the crack in the wall. Listened to the wind. Studied the crack again and turned to me.

'Tom, old friend … Tom … she's gone over to the Royalists.'

It was as if the trees had finally brought the house down and I had been struck by part of it. When my senses began to return Andrew was saying she had always been something of a Royalist. I must have been aware of that. Look at Highpoint. It was never a place to live, but a place for the King to stay. Did I never realise that was why I hated it? I must have done. Surely! Why had Luke become such a Royalist? Scogman was nodding. It seemed that everyone knew what had been happening in my house, except me.

'Best you hear everything, from me, rather than anyone else, Tom … There's a rumour going round the county that there's another man. Some people are even saying that …'

34

I could not stand any more. They say that when disaster strikes you need your friends more than ever, but I could not bear any more friendship. Of course, it was obvious. Why was I the last person to see it? At Anne's great parties at Highpoint there had always been men round her. And I had gloried in it! I may not have been sleeping with her, but no one else could. She was mine by legal contract, just as the land, the house and all the treasures in it were mine. Whatever curdled mixture of love, hate and position kept us together, I had believed we would always be together. Till death us do part. I had lost my position and she had dropped me. It was as simple as that. She was a thief. I had refused to believe it. She had robbed me of everything, including, with the use of my signature, myself. And I had protected her! What an idiot. What a fool. I walked out into the wind, which was the only companion I wanted. It bent trees, tore clouds from the moon, but it could not cool my burning head.

They thought I was mad when I saddled my horse. Taking the road to London at this time of night? Did I not realise there was a price of fifty crowns on my head? I did not care. All I wanted was to kill him, whoever he was, kill her and then myself. Scogman's

279

protestations were blown away by the wind and I was on the road before he could stop me. It was much worse than the green road, pitted and rutted, the horse stumbling into muddy pools. But it had a Roman straightness. A fitful, gibbous moon lit my way. Most of the time the howling wind was with me, and I was over the Chilterns long before first light. Not even thieves cared to be out that night. The only sign of life showed in the eyes of a fox staring from a wood; the only sound apart from the wind the scream of an animal he had caught.

I must have slept. I was half-slipping from the saddle, my horse lapping from a pool at the side of the road. A weak, hesitant sun was up and there was an eerie stillness. The wind had dropped. Birds were deafening. No sooner was I back on the road when I realised my horse was lame. I asked a passing labourer where I was. He looked at me with a mixture of curiosity and fear, hurrying away as he answered.

'Hounslow.'

He probably thought I was a prig who preyed on the coaches crossing the heath. It was a bad place to stop but I had no option. At least The Bull With One Horn looked a respectable coaching inn where I could get a fresh horse. The ostler tried to fob me off with a poor nag. I told him the one I wanted and he began to laugh with derision until he saw the look on my face. Perhaps he too, I thought, took me for a prig. At any rate, he transferred my saddle without another word while I went into the inn, drawn there by the smell of that morning's bread.

I meant to slip in, grab a loaf and leave. But however dead the mind is, the stomach will make its own demands and, once I broke the warm bread and my tongue tasted the butter, I was lost. I had to have another portion with cheese and small beer. I chose a dark corner. A coaching party, preparing to leave for London, was taking up all the attention, and I was congratulating myself on being unseen when I saw the ostler whispering to the innkeeper, who had a copy of the *Weekly Discoverer*. It was my red hair that gave me away, as it had when I was a boy, only this time it was my tangled, shabby, week's growth of beard.

You never lose that fear. Not when it is bred into you as a child. It pulled me to a stop at the door to the yard. *No wonder the ostler let you have the horse so easily*, the boy inside me muttered with contempt. Lounging near it, instructing a stable boy to polish the already gleaming brasses on their horses, were two men – one very handsome, until he laughed, showing a row of black, decaying teeth. The other had the face and build of a bulldog, but dressed very sharply, with rings that served as weapons and a bright red neck cloth stuck with a pin, openly proclaiming him to be a prig, a highwayman or, as I believe they called them on Hounslow Heath, a collector.

They had come to collect me. Their bounty. Fifty crowns split between them, with payoffs to the innkeeper and his ostler. No wonder the man with bad teeth was laughing. It was easy money. And it was legal! The man like a bulldog looked towards the door. He had eyes as pale as water. His rings glinted in the sun. I might take one of them on but not two. If I went through the front, the innkeeper and the ostler would pick me up. And how would I get to London without a horse?

'Last call for London, gentlemen! Leaving now!' the coachman yelled.

I darted down the corridor. Just inside the bar, an old man was struggling with a bag.

'Can I help you with that, sir?'

'Why, that's very kind of you.'

The innkeeper was staring from the bar but a man banged his glass down, demanding service, and in the moment he moved away

I slipped through with the case among the press of passengers, chatting manically to the old man, giving his case to the boot man. Only then did I see a constable riding on the back of the coach, pistol at his belt. He did not see me because he was staring towards the stable yard where the two collectors were standing.

'All aboard?' yelled the coachman to the boot man, followed by an incomprehensible cry to his horses to get them in line. As he drew back his whip, I ran up.

'Wait! A Cromwell to take me to London.'

He stared down at me with a look that said: *I know you from somewhere* … The horses, still responding to his last command, jerked forward. He dragged at the reins with another strangled cry, snatched at the coin and bit it.

'Might not be legal next week.'

'Another when we get there.'

'Jump in.'

There were mutterings and grumbles but the old man kept on saying, 'Gentleman obliged me and I will oblige him,' and somehow I squeezed in. I had a moment of intense exhilaration. It lasted for perhaps a minute. Squashed against the side of that boneshaker, whose rattling, squeaking door threatened to burst open any moment, I craned out to see the two collectors riding after us. They had no visible weapons, but then they did not need them. A short discussion with the constable was all that was needed.

'You have a regicide … a murderer in the coach …'

I leaned against the leather headrest which smelt of stale tobacco. I had left in such a hurry I had no weapon but my dagger. I could scarcely breathe, let alone move, sweating profusely in my cloak and jerkin while the old man rambled on about how obliging I was. Obliging indeed! Far from escaping, I had put myself neatly, obligingly, into a trap.

We left the heath and rumbled through Isleworth, the children running out cheering, as they did at every coach. Their bare feet reminded me of when I was a child and had wriggled out of everything. But then I just acted. I never thought. Thinking was fatal: it took too long.

At Brentford I leaned out again. The collectors were riding at an easy trot. I expected them to catch up with the coach and speak to the constable, but they remained some distance away. The handsome one gave me his gappy smile and raised his hand. Of course. He would not approach the constable. In fact it was the last thing he would do. They would have to share the bounty with him – or, if he effected the arrest, he might claim it all for himself.

Lack of sleep, the bread and cheese, the swaying of the carriage: all combined to make sleep, deep, delicious, betraying sleep steal over me. I was vaguely aware of the orchards of Chiswick, but awoke to a shouting, a clattering, a screaming and jerking of wheels over cobbles, a yelling of voices crying hot codlings and poor jack, and a stink that made me fight not to breathe, with an old man telling me he would be obliged if I released him. I heard the echo of the scream after I had made it and took away my hand gripping his arm, muttering an apology thick with sleep. The other passengers shrank away apprehensively.

They were still following me, with the same expressions, at the same remorseless pace. I recognised the metallic stink in the air as tannin, from the leather works that emptied its grey, clogging waste into the Fleet River. We were going along Ludgate, approaching the hill, the driver shouting encouragement to the horses and cracking his whip. I opened the door and leapt, staggering, falling, hitting and rolling over the cobbles, as the coachman yanked the horses to a stop. There was a shot. A stabbing pain in my shoulder. Someone was screaming and went on screaming. Dust choked me. The acrid smell of cordite cut across the stench of the river. I felt my shoulder. There was no blood. I had struck a street post. The man built like a bulldog was screaming, holding his shattered hand. The other was struggling to control his rearing horse while the constable, who had fired from the back of the carriage, was reloading his pistol.

I scrambled up and ran. I was in Farringdon Street before I heard the other collector riding after me. I had no chance there. He would run me down. I twisted into a series of alleys, my haven as a child. My legs were old and stiff but they had the memory, the cunning of that child. Snow Court. Cock Lane. An alley so narrow that his horse would never get through it. He would never abandon his horse. Or so I told myself.

The sound of the hooves died away. I leaned against the wall, slowly sliding down it, taking in great gulps of air. I could run no further. When he turned the corner his black-toothed grin was even wider – perhaps because there was one less to share the bounty with. I stared at him with a curious indifference. All I wanted to do was rest. Only when he was almost on me and I smelt his carious breath did an overwhelming rage sweep over me. If I did not fight, I would never be able to kill the man who had taken Anne from me. It was a blind, fruitless rage. He was much younger and fitter and easily knocked my knife from me. But I would not give up. I had found the energy of hatred. I clawed my nails at his face. It was his weakness, his vanity. In the instant he flung up his hands to ward me off and protect his face, I grabbed the knife and brought it up into him, again and again.

Most of the blood went on the cloak, which I abandoned in the alley. Even so, there was blood on my hands and face, which drew the odd look but no more than that, which I could not understand, until I saw a pile of offal dumped in the street with people fighting over it and birds wheeling and squawking round them. The birds were so bold I had to duck from one of them swooping down. Perhaps he sensed the blood on me. It was a red kite. I began to laugh uncontrollably. Smithfield. The butchers had just finished their morning killing.

Blood seemed to be everywhere. Staining the people carrying offal away, on the beak of a screeching bird, splashed on the cobbles, hanging in the air, fresh and potent. I had to kill the man who had taken Anne away from me. Then I must kill her. Cut her white throat. Silence the voice that gave me such torment. That mocking voice. Then I would be at peace. It would be over.

It was my boots that took me there. Sometimes, very oddly, there were no boots. My feet were bare, innocent feet, closer to the ground, testing every stone. It was the boy's feet that took me there. Long Lane, Cloth Fair – there was a market, so it must be Thursday – the sudden quiet and dimness of Half Moon Court, the gable of the house where it all began, tilting at an even crazier angle than I remembered, on the verge of toppling over on to the apple tree which, miraculously, was in full blossom. She would be hiding there as she always was.

'Can't find me!'

That voice. That throat. I felt for my dagger. She was not behind the tree. So it must be the coal cellar, or the paper store.

'Cold … colder … freezing!'

That laughter, that mocking laughter, as clear as hill water and as cold as ice. There was a strange woman at the door I had never seen before, a very ugly woman with a wart at the side of her nose. She began screaming. I had to silence her otherwise she would give the game away and I would never find Anne.

She backed into the house, yelling, 'Sam! Sam!'

Sam? The house swayed, the gable lurching even further over me.

'You have nothing to-to fear, Mrs Bridges,' he said. 'He is my f-father.'

Father?

Before I struck the cobbles he caught me in his arms. I had forgotten how gentle he was.

35

How long I was there I do not know. The fever I had suffered when I tried to rescue Luke returned. From time to time the woman with a wart brought me some herb soup, after which I would instantly fall asleep again. I must have told Sam about my old army doctor, for Ben came. He gave me something that smelt of the marshes where I used to collect feverfew and wild basil for the cunning man. I drowned in sleep, surfacing to hear them whispering together. Ben was saying I had had it before. It was partly the war. Some act of violence had brought it back. And it was partly some sickness of the mind or heart, which was beyond his herbs.

Beyond his herbs? What nonsense! She was not beyond them. Early one morning, when the light was just filtering through the window, I awoke to find myself in a strange nightdress. Tom Neave was sitting opposite me in a chair by the window, that cheeky smile on his face, the smile I used to have. She had stolen even that from me. She had left me locked inside that aristocratic wretch, Thomas Stonehouse. I shut my eyes and vanished into the marsh of sleep. When I surfaced again the sun was so bright it hurt my eyes. On the back of the chair was my hat. Draped on it were my linen, my britches and the jerkin. The stains were visible, but they smelt of wrinkled hands, beatings and fresh air. I dressed as quickly, as surreptitiously, as if they might be taken from me again.

The woman with the wart was sweeping the yard. The blossom had begun to fall from the tree and I could almost smell the apples to come. There was a buzzing sound, like a persistent bee. It stopped, then resumed as I crept downstairs. It came from the print shop. No, that wasn't right. The light dazzled me. It was a miracle. Everything came back to me as I stared at the clear glass goblet. He was so absorbed in his work he did not see me enter. He was working on something like a spinning wheel, which he operated with his feet on a treadle. It drove the engraving tool he was using to create an intricate pattern on a similar goblet.

'You did it, Sam! You did it!' I cried.

The point of the engraving tool jumped and he almost dropped the goblet. 'You should not be up. You are not well, Father.'

'I am perfectly well. Particularly when I see this.' I picked up the glass goblet, turning it towards the light, rotating it, marvelling at the clarity of the glass, with no milkiness or crazing, and the exquisite intricacy of the engraving.

'Please, sir.' He was twisting about in agony. 'It is not mine.'

'Then, as your major shareholder, it is mine.'

'The pair is for a customer.'

'Customer?'

'Lady Stonehouse.'

The glass slipped from my fingers. Sam dived forward, caught it, juggled with it and almost lost it, before holding it tightly to him as if it was a baby and putting it tenderly back on its shelf.

'Did you not know, sir?'

'No, no. I did not know. You mean Anne?' He did not even know her first name. 'My wife?' He nodded, as if it was the least remarkable thing in the world. 'She was *here*?'

It was the very last place I expected her to come. She hated it. It was beneath her. She wanted to expunge any idea that she had ever been a printer's daughter. The thought of her coming to Half Moon Court to see Sam, of all people, dazed me. I was not as well as I thought I was and the rest of the story came out in fits and starts during that long day in which Mrs Bridges, who was as kind as she was ugly, administered me Dutch brandy possets, laced with honey. They were the very best cure, she asserted, for the moonstruck and, after several, I was not one to disagree with her.

It must have been shortly after Scogman and I set out for Highpoint. Anne had arrived in a coach. It was so heavily laden with cases and packets, the boot was almost scraping on the cobbles. There was a woman with her who stayed in the coach.

'No man?'

'No.'

'Go on.'

He could not go on. He sat down, trembling, wringing his hands. Eventually, he said that at first he did not know who she was. She was masked. But he recognised her voice from when he had come to Queen Street that afternoon. She refused to take anything or even sit, looking at a drink he offered her as if it was poisoned, at a chair as if she might catch some disease. She treated him like a servant – no, worse than a servant, like a criminal, questioning him as if he was in a court of law, picking up a chemical flask or pipette from his workbench as if they were evidence of a crime. How much did that cost? What did you pay for that? Poor Sam had the worst head for money of anyone I knew. When he stammered that he did not know, she thought he was lying.

Was it anger, grief at Luke's death, that had driven her there? Anger that Sam was alive and Luke dead? She asked him endless questions about money. What I had paid him. What I had promised him. Proof of my crime. My crime against Luke. In those moods she sickened and disgusted me. She was like a Dutch usurer. She would have gone through the books, if there had been books. Worst of all, she had poured scorn on Sam's goblet, the nearest he had come to clear glass. Clear, she said? It was as clear as a London fog. Sam came out of his stammering awe. She could insult him, or me, but not his glass. He apologised for coming to Queen Street that afternoon when his mother was dying. He knew he should never have gone there. All the more so because we had quarrelled and our relationship was over.

'You told her that?' I said. 'What did she say?'

'N-nothing. She sat down. For the first time she said *n-othing*.'

He was trembling. He spoke the word with vehemence. I could imagine the scene: Sam switching abruptly, without warning, from deference to that stubborn, even arrogant, certainty when he felt he was right about something.

Outside there was the cry of the coal merchant and the rattle of his cart. Sam sent Mrs Bridges out to deal with him and drew me into the back room where I could not be seen. People were looking for me – there were notices everywhere, he said.

He went on with his story. He had read the *Discoverer* and told Lady Stonehouse what Scogman had told him – that Richard had killed Luke and I had tried to save him, how Luke talked of his love for his mother, and how Scogman and I had buried him.

No physic, no herb, could bring the life surging back into me more than the knowledge that she had been told the truth. Now Sam wanted to know more. What had happened that afternoon had been buried with Luke's body, and for the first time I began to speak freely about it while Sam listened, his hands knotted together, his head bowed. I had not shed a tear, but I did so then as Luke was buried again, the loamy soil falling until his smile had disappeared and I was exhausted with weeping. It was done. I felt I had told Anne. At least Sam had. It was done. She had been told. I could do no more.

'What did she say?'

He gnawed a nail. It was as filthy and cracked as mine used to be when I worked here. 'Nothing.'

'Nothing? She did not cry, or say a word?' He shook his head. This was inscrutable behaviour indeed, even for Anne. 'Did she believe you?'

'I don't know, sir. I – I do not understand her at all, sir.'

'No. Well. It has taken me a lifetime and I am no nearer. Nothing at all?'

All he could tell me was that she went back to the lady in the coach. From his description she sounded like Lucy. They had a long conversation, after which Lady Stonehouse –

His continual use of her title, with a kind of awestruck genuflection in the middle, began to irritate me. 'For God's sake, Sam, call her Anne.'

'A – A –'

'She is, after all, your stepmother.'

'My …? Lady …?' He swallowed. His eyes bulged. 'A –?' He could not say her name. In the end he settled for the pronoun. 'She – she came back, took off her mask and …' He bit the nail, then hid it in his other hand in a way that made me absolutely certain Anne had commented on it. The gesture brought back her disdain at the ink engrained in my hands when I was an apprentice, her amazed laughter at the size of my feet.

'She took off her mask and …' He stopped again and stared into space. 'She is very beautiful, sir.'

For some reason this irritated me even more than his inability, or his refusal, to stop using her title. 'Get on with it.'

There was a basket of rejects from the kiln near Sam's workbench, which he sold to cheap markets for a penny or two. He picked out one, somewhat better than the rest. It was of a similar quality, he said, to the one he was working on when she visited. At that time he believed he had reached a reasonable form of clarity, and he thought it might be sold in a higher class of shop at the Exchange.

She studied the goblet without saying a word. She tapped it, and turned it, and held it up to the light. Sam put the nail to his mouth and pulled it away again as he relived the misery of that long silence, punctuated only by the ring of her fingers against the glass. I knew those silences. I squeezed his shoulder in sympathy.

'She has a most eloquent way of saying nothing, Sam.'

'Indeed, sir,' he said. 'She threw it in the basket and broke it.'

Again uncontrollable anger rose in me at the thought of her in those focused, uncompromising moods, when she would say exactly what was in her mind, however brutal, whatever the consequences. She told him not to take such work anywhere near the Exchange. Far from making his reputation, as he hoped, it would stifle it at birth. She picked up her mask and wished him good day. She reached the door and paused. He remembered his manners – as he put it – sprang to the door and opened it. She continued to stand there.

'It might work,' she said.

'What might work?' I asked.

'I don't know,' Sam said. 'She seemed to be talking to herself.'

I knew those moods too, that strange vacancy in her face when an idea occurred to her and she pursued it relentlessly. I could hear the rustle of her dress as she returned to the basket of rejects, see her ringed fingers as they picked up one of the broken pieces. A tiny bubble of blood welled from a pricked finger. He rushed to produce a cloth to wrap round it but she waved him away irritably, sucking her finger while she scrutinised the glass again.

'Do you know Christopher Merrett?' she said at last.

Of course he didn't. Sam knew no one except the natural philosophers he consorted with, mostly as poor and obscure as himself. Only someone who lived in the enclosed, arcane world of magnificence like Anne would have bothered to ask the question. But, she went on with increasing impatience, he must be aware of Neri's *L'Arte Vetraria*? Abjectly, he had to confess he had never heard of it. Murano glass?

With the last question, she met Sam's own arrogance. Of course he knew Murano, the centre of Venetian glass-making for centuries. Their art was a closely guarded secret, so important to Venice the glass-makers were never allowed to leave the island.

'But this book did,' she responded. '*L'Arte Vetraria*.'

It revealed many of the secrets of Venetian glass-making and was published in 1621. 'Art,' she said, with that faint disgust I was also familiar with, 'travels from Italy across Europe but, when it reaches the English Channel, disappears without trace.' Only now was the book being translated by Christopher Merrett and was not yet published. She had seen an early proof.

All this time he had been holding the door open for her. She said she would have a proof sent to him and, should his work be satisfactory, commission a pair of goblets. The goblet he was engraving was one of them.

Sam went to a sack, plunged in his hand, and brought it out as if he was an alchemist who has discovered how to make gold. I blinked at the grey, dusty lump of rock he was holding.

'Galena. Common in Europe. We mine it in Derbyshire.' He pointed to a faint sheen in places. 'Lead ore. Lead is the secret.'

It took many hours after that, but all the work he had done before had not been wasted. Far from it. Lead was the last piece to fall into place. It brought down the temperature of the firing and increased the malleability of the glass when he worked it. Swept up as I was by his enthusiasm, I felt increasingly irked at him refusing to accept the secret I had bought for him at a considerable price – no doubt simply copied from the book, which increased my resentment – but accepting it from Anne. What was the difference?

He became defensive. Soon it would be public knowledge. He had to use the work he had done to stay ahead. Sam had certainly lost his previous stiff, purist approach. He said, 'All artists and philosophers, Father, build on each other's work. They never call it theft.'

'That sounds like my wife,' I said tartly.

He flushed brick red from his neck to the roots of his hair. Good God, he had fallen for her, fallen for her claptrap about art, for her poisonous mixture of devastating charm and brutal honesty. My anger at her walking in here and treating him like dirt was replaced by fury that she was manipulating him. I plied him with questions. What did she mean – it might work? What might work? He swore he had no idea, so passionately, I believed him. On other matters he was more evasive. Who were the goblets for? At first he said they were for her. Then he admitted he thought they were a gift. I felt a sharp stab of jealousy. A gift? For whom? He did not know! He was adamant. I could get no more out of him. He denied knowing where she was.

'Then how do you know where to deliver the goblets?'

'She said she would have them collected. L-Lady Stonehouse is travelling.'

'Is she. Is she indeed.' I paced about the room. 'I have to remind you, Sam, that we are a company. I set you up. I bought the kiln. Without it, none of this would have happened.'

He moved to bite his nail but pulled back his hand halfway. It riled me even more that it was her silent voice that stopped him. 'I will for – for ever be grateful for that, Father,' he replied. 'Apart from my father – I – I mean the person I thought was my father – you are the first person who ever had faith in me.'

'Good,' I said, somewhat mollified. 'Then, as the first fruits of the enterprise, those goblets belong to me.'

He bit his nail then. He bit it clean through and half swallowed the fragment, coughing violently until he managed to dislodge it. He straightened up. He was shaking like a sapling in a high wind. 'I – I have to remind you, Father, that I – I am the majority share-holder. You – you ended our agreement. You said you wanted noth-ing more to do with me.' He began coughing again.

'Have you quite finished?' I said coldly.

'Not – not quite, sir. Lady Stonehouse commissioned those goblets. She paid me. In advance.'

If I had stayed a moment longer I would have struck him. I went up to my room and lay on the bed. What was she up to? She cared not a jot for him. When he had turned up at Queen Street, to tell me Ellie was dying, she was furious. She had walked out. She hated him. What was she doing commissioning him, giving him money? My love child, my bastard? She blamed me for Luke's death and so was stealing Sam from me. That was what she was doing. Sam had told her what happened when I had gone to rescue Luke and what had she said? Nothing. What other explanation was there? She was steal-ing Sam from me. The thoughts ran endlessly round and round my head, as if driven by Sam's drill engraving the goblets in the shop below, until the door slammed and the drill abruptly stopped.

It sounded like Mrs Bridges returning from some errand or other. There was a scurry of whispered voices, followed by Sam coming up the stairs two at a time. He entered without ceremony.

'You must go, Father.'

Mrs Bridges had been to Smithfield to buy meat. A hawker had been selling pamphlets about a vicious murder near Shoe Lane by the regicide Tom Neave. Without thinking she had ordered more than her usual amount of meat.

'Got a visitor, Mrs Bridges?' the butcher said as he chopped the beef.

It was probably nothing more than a casual remark, but the butcher had a copy of the pamphlet near him and she grew increasingly flustered when she heard someone else say Tom Neave used to live at Half Moon Court.

At first, our argument still rankling, there was nothing more I wanted than to leave that place. Sam gave me a dusty workman's pack in which he carried things to the kiln. In it I put a change of linen, a flask of small beer and some bread. It was little more than I had when I came here all those years ago, but at least, I thought, I had boots on my feet.

I got as far as the door. It was market day. I could hear from the cries of the hawkers that the streets were crowded. I put the pack down and told them it would be safer to slip away at first light the next morning. But the truth was I could not face leaving Sam without trying to repair matters between us. When I saw his concern – where would I go, what would I do, how could they tell such lies about me? – I felt I had been churlish and petty. But my anger about Anne blocked me from finding words and we ate the excellent beef Mrs Bridges cooked largely in silence. By the time we went to bed we were reduced to muttered monosyllables.

'Night, Sam.'

'Night, Father.'

I could not sleep. Where would I go? Scogman's house? That was the first place they would look. And I would be a danger to him, as I was to Sam. I could not think. I could not stop thinking. Did that make sense? No. Nothing made sense any more. I jumped at every sound. The clatter of a late Hackney coming down Long Lane. The bang of a privy door across the court. The strangest sound of all, which made my skin crawl and my heart quicken: a hiss, followed by a thump, then a sigh. I shot up in bed. The house was silent except for the occasional crack of the old timber. The sound I had heard was that of the old printing machine. I must have dropped off and dreamed it. All the same, I crept downstairs, my feet remembering every stair, avoiding the cracks and groans.

I did not need a candle. The moon was the colour of skimmed milk, filling the workroom with a wash of pale, ethereal light. It glinted on the diamond tip of Sam's engraving tool, placed exactly in its groove. He was as neat a worker as I used to be. The goblets were small moons of lights, seeming to float in the air. I stared at the image he was engraving on one of them. I half expected it to be the Stonehouse falcon, but it was not. It felt strangely familiar, but I could not make out what it was. The soft, bluish light splintered into a rainbow on the shards of broken glass in the basket of rejects. I stared from the chaos of colours to the clear, dazzling perfection of the goblets. In that moment I saw.

Saw what to do. Where to go. Where I had been going all my life. Saw the printing machine, exactly where it had been, from the cracks in the tiles that had never been repaired. Smelt the oil. Felt the aching of my muscles as I brought the press down on the platens, saw the gleam of the wet ink as I pulled the paper from the type. One by one. Pamphlet after pamphlet. All gone. Forgotten. Waste. Trash. Or so I had thought. But it was not so. They had inspired people to fight. Not in the war, although they had done that, but in the much more difficult business of finding a better way to live. They were still there, those pamphlets, lodged in a few people's minds. Even speeches were never entirely forgotten.

I could still hear the Levellers in that Putney church telling Cromwell that the King must not return, hear Colonel Rainsborough's ringing voice: 'I do believe that the poorest he in England should have his say just as the richest he.' I picked up a goblet from the basket. It was crazed and milky. The poorest he. Have his say. What a ridiculous idea. After all, was not the King returning?

'What are you doing, Father?'

Sam, blinking, bleary-eyed in his nightshirt. Beyond the gable across the court, the first glimmers of light showed in the sky. A cart rumbled towards Smithfield. Soon there would be the drumming of the first cattle being driven down St John's to be slaughtered. I dropped the rejected goblet back in the basket.

'I must go.'

'Where?'

I did not answer; easier for him if they came to question him. I apologised for my boorishness. He was right. I had given up on him. Sadly, it was part of my nature. But perhaps it was not too late to improve on it, as he had worked on the goblets, for firing after firing. Of course he must finish them for Lady Stonehouse. They were wonderful.

'Do – do you think so? Every time I engrave them I see another flaw.'

'Nothing is ever perfect, Sam. You taught me that.'

'Did I? What do you mean?'

I refused to say any more, dressed and picked up my pack. He found it as difficult to let me go as I did to set off.

'You are leaving the country, Father?'

'Perhaps. There are things I must do first.'

'She says you must go abroad.'

'Lady Stonehouse?'

My heart hammered painfully. It would take a while but, sooner or later, I would stop reacting like that. I had done it before. No, it was not true, but with Sam's mother, Ellie, I had spent a whole afternoon, perhaps as much as a day, without thinking about her.

'Go abroad? Did she indeed. Was it concern, do you think, or was she trying to get rid of me?'

He was shocked. He did not know what to say. At that moment he looked even more like me at that age with his shock of violent red hair, his earnestness, his belief in himself. No. He was better than me, with his stubborn, dogged persistence, his refusal to be diverted, as I had been, by love and power. There was no Stonehouse in him. I had done that for him, at least. I was suddenly overwhelmed by a rush of feeling for him. If I did not go now, I felt I never would. His eyes were beginning to shine.

'If you go abroad, Father, I may never see you again.'

'Come, come, Sam. I have a terrible habit of turning up on this doorstep like a bad penny.' I was beginning to lose control of my voice and embraced him abruptly. 'Bless you, my boy. Be true to yourself.'

And before he could say another word I plunged across the court, touching the apple tree for good fortune, as I always used to do, and, following another habit, took the road east.

36

I deliberately got into a drunken brawl in which my nose, my fine patrician Stonehouse nose, was smashed. At a second-hand clothing stall where they asked no questions I sold my rich leather jerkin, my boots and my linen for long-legged breeches that stank of the privy and a torn dorneck shirt. Peering at myself in a scrap of mirror through the eye that was not swollen, I recoiled. I was no longer a Stonehouse.

They were clearing the City in preparation for the King, throwing out beggars, prigs, unlicensed hawkers, whores and Quakers. Richard had guards looking for me at all the gates. I walked out under their eyes, chanting with a group of Quakers. My feet were bare and, when I dropped a piece of bread, I stopped and crooked my toes to pick it up, as I used to do when I first arrived at the Half Moon printing shop and refused to wear boots. Seeing that, Anne had called me monkey, after one she saw on a gentlewoman's shoulders. I could hear her laughing. The chanting had stopped. People behind me were colliding into me. From the gatehouse came Sir Lewis Challoner, cold eyes staring. I felt he was rebuilding my pulped nose, opening my blackened, closed eye. I still could not move. A guard shouted. Another gave me a violent shove in the back. I stumbled, half-fell, and, as the chanting resumed, was carried by the press of the others out of the City.

I asked a Quaker to take me to Stephen Butcher but the man told me the sailor had left for the New World. But Stephen Butcher had a brother, Adam, also a sailor, the Quaker told me. Could he be of help instead? Adam Butcher lived in Spitalfields, near where I used to live with Ellie. He was not only a sailor like his brother, but a Quaker too. He and the other Quakers who remained had not wanted to leave their homes, so had not joined Stephen's band of travellers to the New World. I showed him a money order, payable at my goldsmiths' in Amsterdam, and told him I wanted a ship to the New World.

'A passage?'

'No. A ship.'

I told him I would do a deal with him. The Quakers, who had been given freedom to worship by Cromwell, were being thrown out of the City. They would be persecuted by the new King. They could freely cross the sea, along with my passengers.

'And who might they be?'

'Parliament.'

With my battered face and stinking clothes, he thought at first I was mad. But the money order looked very sane. And when I told him I wanted to make a Parliament that might have been, he began to listen. I told him about the day the Levellers had met Cromwell in that Putney church. We thought the world had changed, but we were wrong. It was like the glass goblet, foggy and crazed, fit only for the reject basket. But we were right, also. There could be another mix, another firing. We would learn from our failures. My passengers would be other regicides and people I trusted, who would not only travel to the New World, but try and build one. It would fail, but we would try again and, when that failed, again.

So I struck a common cause with the Quakers. Adam Butcher chose a ship with a legitimate trade, taking wool and various cloths from Europe and bringing back furs from Boston. Early in May the ship would leave Gravesend and divert from its usual route to stand off the coast near Deal. A two-masted brigantine, much favoured by smugglers, would ferry passengers out to the ship.

I rather liked my new nose, squashed and bent to one side of my face. In sober black, with my hair cropped short like a tradesman, I scarcely recognised myself. I slipped in and out of the City to see regicides and republicans. Some were only too eager to seize the opportunity. Others could not bear to leave their families and were persuaded – or persuaded themselves – that the King would pardon them. Some, like the regicide Major-General Thomas Harrison, were insulted.

'Run away?' he barked. 'D'you think I'm afraid of meeting my Maker? Eh? Eh?' At the door he softened and held out his hand. 'The Good Old Cause,' he said. He gripped my hand for a moment. 'I tell thee, Tom, there's only one thing I'm afraid of, and that's this leg of mine. It will tremble, damn it. Shot to pieces at Marston Moor. If it does happen, and I shake a bit, tell 'em it's this damned leg of mine, not me.'

My only real disappointment was that I could not persuade William Clarke to come. Although we had drifted apart, I still saw him as the Mr Ink who had once smuggled speeches out of Parliament, and he knew more about it than anyone else. John Thurloe's return had given him the hope that, after all, he might obtain a position in the new government. An even greater disappointment was that he could not let me have a copy of the Putney papers. They were in the hands of the army.

There was no news of Anne, only rumours from sympathetic friends. It was common knowledge now that she had become a

Royalist, out of sympathy with our dead son. The worst thing was that no one was surprised. People who had once described us as a perfect couple now said they had always known it would happen.

It was the talk of the Exchange. How Sir Thomas had been duped, his great house stripped. I had been forced to laugh at it, in order not to give myself away. Many of the treasures had been sold but the best of them, like my early books, had vanished. I checked rigorously, because through them I might find her. There was not a trace of them. In my worst moments it seemed obvious what had happened. Andrew had told me she had another man. They were in his house. She was waiting for the King to return and me to leave the country before she moved in with him not, perhaps, to build a new life, but to build another Highpoint.

And yet.

Why did she go to Sam, of all people? Yes, she was vindictive. Yes, she wanted to find out what money I had given him. Yes, when Sam had rounded on her and told her the truth about Luke's death she had said nothing. But what did her silence mean? I was wary of hope, that great deceiver, but I could not help it stealing back into me. I could picture her so clearly, so sharply, in her black dress, hands clasped, head bowed. No one looked better in black than she did. She wore grief with a kind of bitter resentment, her eyes less likely to film with tears than smoulder with anger.

Why had she helped him, commissioned the goblets? To spite me, of course. That was typical. What was not typical was that it meant recognising my bastard. Sam had heard her mutter to herself it might work. What might work?

Tortured by these unanswered questions, I went back to Half Moon Court, determined to ask Sam what he was engraving on those goblets. Foolish, maybe, but I thought it safe enough with my new disguise. He was away, Mrs Bridges said, she did not know where. The shelf, on which he had constructed two stands to keep the goblets safe, was empty. The kiln at Clerkenwell was cold.

It was the beginning of May. Our ship was due to sail in a week's time. I had chosen the date to coincide with the arrival of the King. There would be so much attention on his landing that we could slip away more easily. Already, only the most vigilant bounty hunters, most of whom I now knew by sight, were on the lookout for me. London had begun celebrating early. In the Strand apprentices jeered at Puritans as a huge maypole was erected, so large that sailors had to secure it with ropes, like a mast. At night fires burned and church bells rang. It is miserable being on your own while the whole world is celebrating. It was too dangerous to meet with fellow regicides, and I was glad to join Scogman to witness his wedding. For security, nobody knew I was going to be there until the last minute.

Being Scogman, he was married by a rogue clergyman with me as a witness, a child at his bride's breast and others round her skirt. If she was disappointed at this furtive, clandestine affair outside church, with the clergyman taking the fee as soon as the vows were exchanged, she never showed it; but a look of joy leapt on her face when she heard the deep sound of Shoreditch church bells and thought they were for her, and nobody had the heart to tell her they were practising for the King.

While people went down on their knees on the streets to toast the King's health, I raised my glass to the happy couple. For, I said, whether the country was Royalist or republican, or whatever muddle you chose, all depended on them raising their children. Children were the beating heart of the country. I did not say I had lost mine, for I did not believe I had. With Scogman's children around my feet, I celebrated the laughter of little Liz before she died, Luke's courage, Sam's stubborn persistence. Children were the chances we took; they were the future.

There was much applause at this from the friends present, most of whom had served with Cromwell. Some were old Levellers from my Spitalfields days. I doubt whether there was a warmer celebration for the new King than there was that night in Shoreditch for the Good Old Cause.

Scogman was still in bed when I left first thing in the morning, but he came stumbling after me in his nightshirt with Dick tottering after him, carrying a letter with an air of great importance. Scogman apologised. With all the excitement he had forgotten to give me it. The letter was creased, with small fingermarks all over it, the seal crumbling so it was unrecognisable, but the paper was good and it was addressed to me in a meticulous scribe's hand, and had followed me, in my peripatetic existence, from friend to friend, until it had finally reached Scogman. Up till that moment I was in a good state. I had applied Sam's natural philosophy to Anne. There was a limit for everything, I reasoned, even love. If she felt anything for me she would have written by now. I had not thought of the simplest obstacle. How could she write without an address?

My hand shook a little and I dropped the letter, almost scrambling over the child as I went to retrieve it before he did it more damage.

I broke open what remained of the seal. The first page was in shorthand. I read the second page.

'Bad news, sir?'

'No, no,' I said. 'It's the very best of news. Mr Clarke has managed to get the Putney papers from the army.'

I stared at the page of shorthand as if it was from one of my rare books. It looked like a copy, but even that was rarer than any of the books. One or two words were too much for Clarke's shorthand, and from them I realised it was the first page of *An Agreement of the*

People. It proposed sovereignty for the people, giving votes to a majority of men. It was the people's Magna Carta.

Scogman said he would collect the papers, but when I told him Clarke would only give them to me he was immediately suspicious. 'It's a trap.'

'Maybe.'

There had been similar approaches. I ignored them all even when I had known the person for years. I only ever worked through an intermediary. It was the best way to be safe. But I wanted those papers.

37

I left London as I had first entered it as a boy, by boat, carried by my old waterman, Jack. The Royalists might now rule the City, but they could never rule the water. With its complex currents and tides, it took years to know the river in its different moods and the watermen jealously guarded their trade. The previous day I had written to Clarke, telling him to meet me at Alderman's Stairs. I would not be there, but a boatman would be. If all looked safe, he would be taken downstream to meet me.

It was early, before most trade began, and watermen fought for space. Wisps of cloud were clearing and the still low sun flashed on water dripping from the oars. There was still a chill in the air and I huddled in my jerkin, watching the tip of St Paul's disappear, the grey walls of the Tower glide past. There was an unearthly quiet. The bell ringers had practised themselves into exhaustion.

Jack spoke no cant. He said he was glad the King was returning.

'Then why are you helping me?'

He rested the oars for a moment. 'Because you might come back, sir.' He gave a throaty laugh and spat into the river. 'Governments. Watermen have their own government and that's bad enough.'

The wind picked up as the City gave way to wharves where dockers weaved about with shouts and the thud of boots as goods were unloaded. Among the smoke and oily stink of the river I briefly caught the rich smell of spices. With some sense of irony, I had told the waterman who picked up Clarke to take him to King Henry's Stairs at Wapping. There he was, clutching a small case under his arm, cloak flapping from his dark, waisted jacket. The boat he had travelled in was moored, waiting to take him back to London. He glanced towards my boat, then paced away without any sign of recognition. Only when I shouted did he turn towards us. In his smart, square-heeled shoes he slipped on the muddy bank, almost falling before he righted himself at the top of the stairs.

'You have led me a merry dance, Thomas,' he said. 'Don't you trust me?'

'No. I trust no one.'

'Quite right,' he said, with unexpected savagery. 'You can trust no one. Not in these times.' The outburst caused him to slip again. I caught him, and for the first time he saw me close. 'What has happened to your face?' he muttered. 'From the bank I didn't recognise you.'

'That's the idea.'

'Yes. You were always good at that.' He hesitated, then with a sudden movement, thrust the case at me, walking away immediately, glancing guiltily around. There were only some children squabbling over a bottle washed up by the tide and two men on the opposite bank, fishing.

From the case I took a packet, sealed and wrapped in oiled paper. The top sheet was foggy, but transparent enough for me to pick out written words where Clarke's shorthand was inadequate. *Sovereignty* was one. *Sovereignty of the People*, the whole phrase would be. *Bedfordshire* was another word he had written in full – Clarke had been unable to catch the names of speakers, simply identifying them as *Bedfordshire Man* or *Suffolk Trooper*. For a week, these largely unknown men had crammed into a small church on the other side of the river to propose England's only written Constitution. I thought it had been lost. I might never see it enacted – I was thinking of Sam's doggedness – but I determined to plant the seed of it, even if it was in another country, as unknown as those who had proposed it.

I looked round, dizzy at the thought. There was no sign of Clarke on the riverbank. I thought he had gone, not wishing to be seen with me, or to find a constable. Then I saw him sitting further down the steps, hunched up moodily, the water lapping almost up to his shoes, watching Jack unwrap a wad of tobacco. From a chain at his waistcoat hung a small knife with which, for as long as I could remember, he had sharpened quills. It was the only sign of his previous trade of scrivener. His cuffs were flecked with mud and for an instant I saw him as I did the first time, in the lobby at Parliament, cuffs splashed with ink, writing tray wobbling, dipping down to me with a smuggled speech against the King, urging me to run to the printer with words that would change the world.

'Thank you, Mr Ink. God bless you.'

Normally he disliked me using the nickname, just as Anne dismissed Half Moon Court. He scrambled up awkwardly, looked moved to say something, but in the end simply raised a hand. I thought he was going to his boat on the other side of the stairs but when I was in mine he was still standing there, shifting from one foot to another. He did not look penniless, but he had no office and was too proud to go back to being a scrivener.

'I should pay you for this.'

'Money?' He flung the word at me in a tone of disgust. 'I don't need money. A passage, yes.'

'A passage?'

'There is nothing for me here,' he said bitterly. 'I have served the country for fifteen years but all positions will come through court favours. Everything will be closed to me.' He fingered the knife at his waistcoat. 'You are sailing today?'

'Soon. When the tide favours us,' I said evasively.

'I have my papers with me.' He showed me letters of introduction and credit. 'My servant will send on my chest.' His pride crumbled and he became haggard, pleading.

'I'm sorry. The ship is full.'

'Well. Bon voyage, Tom.'

I raised my hand as he returned to his boat, which would take him another merry dance. If he was part of a trap, by the time he reached London I would be miles away. I watched him clutch the waterman for support before lowering his ungainly, slightly stooped figure into the boat. I had known him as long as I had known Anne. He had taught me everything I knew about Parliament. We had drifted apart only since Cromwell's death. I glanced up and down. The anglers were still as statues. The children snatching at the bottle had lost it in the water and were blaming one another. There were no signs anyone had followed him. I did, in fact, have a place. A cabin I had kept for Anne. Just in case.

I told him not to expect creature comforts. Nor would I tell him where we were heading. We continued downstream, past the marshlands where I had grown up as a child, past the docks where I had been a pitch boy, past the gaunt skeletons of half-built ships, becalmed for the past year but already coming back to life at the prospect of a new government, with hammering and sawing and pitch fires burning, the smoke from them hazing the air as the boat cut through coal scum and bits of wood and rope, weaving past buoys and rusting hawsers. I touched the scar on my arm left by one of those pitch fires. I could almost hear myself screaming, see Lord Stonehouse picking me up, at the point when the whole story began. Then the river was clearing and widening and there were meadows and villages, and birds found their voices.

All this time we were silent, hunched up with our own thoughts, except once when I began to open the packet and he stopped me, like a father protecting his child, saying the oiled paper protected it against the water, and I reassured him I would contain my impatience until we were on board.

We crossed the river at Deptford, where he was somewhat disgruntled to find that, because a carriage would have been too conspicuous, it was an open cart waiting for us, with rough wooden seats, the sort that carried servants. I chaffed him for this, for his origins were as poor as mine, and suddenly things were more cordial between us and we talked of old times as the cart rattled through the Kentish Downs. At an inn we had pease and pork and strong beer, brewed with the innkeeper's own hops.

'On your way to see the King?' the innkeeper asked.

'Why? Is he arriving today?' I said innocently.

There was much laughter at this and I was told I must be the only person in Kent who did not know it. People spoke with awe about the gentry who had gone to Dover to meet him, a place which seemed the end of the world to them. Some had never seen the sea. Unlike London, where you might find radicals wherever you scratched the surface, Kent had always been lukewarm about Cromwell, at best. The fervour at the King's return was genuine. There was a maypole on the green and strong beer was being sold for the price of small. We were almost as merry as they were when we heaved ourselves back into the cart, and it took very little jolting for me to fall asleep.

When I awoke I thought for a moment we were back in London. There was a carriage in front of us, a farm cart behind, and a whole army of riders cutting across fields to force their way on to the road. All were waving oak branches. In London hawkers had been out early, selling oak leaves for a penny, claiming they came from the tree in which Charles Stuart had hidden after the battle of Worcester, before he escaped into his long exile. An empty bottle was thrown from the carriage in front where they were toasting the King. I asked the carter where we were.

'North of Dover,' the carter said.

'Dover! I told you to keep to the side roads.'

'Gentleman said it would be quicker.'

'You don't know where we're going,' I said to Clarke.

'Presumably the coast,' he said tartly. 'This is normally much quicker, whichever way you're going.'

'You know the road, do you?'

'I was on it a month ago. Returning from Holland.'

His mood had changed. He sat on the edge of his seat, gripping the side of the cart as the carriage in front of us braked and the carter yanked back his horses. Hemmed in by crowds and other traffic, the heat was oppressive, the air heavy with the smell of horse dung. Clarke took off his cravat and mopped his forehead with it.

'Why were you in Holland?'

'Seeking a position. Like everyone else.'

A young man in petticoat breeches and ruffled shirt jumped out of the carriage in front, declaring it was quicker to walk. He gave three cheers for his monarch, flinging his wig in the air. The carriage lurched forward to cries of alarm from the other occupants. His shaven head bobbed as he retrieved his wig from the hedgerow, and was dragged back into the carriage with shouts of laughter.

'That fool has a position, or don't need one,' Clarke said. 'Whereas with my experience ...' He folded the cravat meticulously and put it into his pocket, staring out across the fields. The horse riders had found another route and we were moving more freely again.

'What happened in Holland?'

'Cant, sir, that's what happened. Fine words took me there but they turned out to be cant, gabble, gammon – in short, I was deceived, sir, by that smooth-talking hypocrite Samuel Pepys.'

'Sam! He is a good man.'

'Aye. Good at saying one thing and meaning another. Your trouble, Tom, if you don't mind me saying so, is that you are always determined to see people in a good light.' He mopped his brow again.

The carter climbed a hill, from which we caught glimpses of the sea. Clarke told me that Pepys had promised an introduction to his patron, Lord Montague, now formally announced as head of the navy. Pepys himself, since he was organising the refurbishing of the ship in Holland for the King, was close to the court.

It was a tenuous thread to draw Clarke to Holland, but careers had been built on less. I only half-followed the all too familiar story of meetings arranged, then cancelled at the last minute, for we were getting near Dover and the road was choked with traffic again. While the carter tried to find the road to Deal that would take us away from Dover, Clarke obsessively went on with his story. Apparently I was involved, because I had promised to write to Montague. I had no recollection of it, then remembered. It was the night of the burning of the rump, when we had found Luke. It had flown from my mind.

Clarke took my apology in silence. The carter found a country lane, a narrow green tunnel running between hedgerows white with hawthorn, which would take us to the main road to Deal. Clarke seemed to have exhausted the subject and I had no wish to return to it. He slumped low in his seat, wiping his forehead, although it was cooler in the shade of the hedgerows.

As we emerged into open fields, with a distant view of the sea, there was the boom of a cannon, followed by others, echoing and re-echoing.

'The King,' the carter said, pointing his whip towards the sails of a ship on the horizon.

'In Holland ...' Clarke was like a dog who drops a bone, only to return to worry it again, 'the worst moment was when I saw Pepys talking to Montague and was determined to interrupt. I had nothing to lose. I was at the very point of approaching them when the King's son, the Duke of York, came by. Well, of course, they were all bows and scrapes and I bowed and half-retreated as I should, but hovered and looked at Pepys and Montague directly. I wanted but a smile, half a smile, a mere nod, any acknowledgement before I withdrew. They cut me. They turned their backs on me and cut me. Later they did the same. Pepys never intended to help me. He deceived me, sir. Well ... You know how it feels. Your wife was there.'

By this time I was beginning to doze again and came to with a jolt, not sure I had heard him correctly. 'What did you say?'

'Your wife was there.'

'In Holland?'

'She was accepted. She was accepted all right.'

'Stop!' I yelled at the carter. 'Stop!'

The lane had taken us in a long detour, avoiding Dover, bringing us to the outskirts of it and the road to Deal. In a bay beyond Deal was the brig that would take us to the ship. For a moment I was sure Clarke was part of a trap. I had fallen asleep and he had told the carter to take the road bringing us much nearer to Dover than I intended. But no one had followed us. We were in this remote spot and he was staring at me with puzzled incomprehension. And the suspicion was displaced by anger at his remarks about Anne, which brought to a head the looks and innuendos I had been forced to bear in silence.

'You said my wife has deceived me.'

The carter stared round, then looked away, clicking at his horses as they dipped to crop grass. Clarke gave me a blank, bewildered look.

'Implied it. You said she was there. I knew how it felt.'

He looked bemused. 'I … I simply meant anyone knows that feeling …'

I felt foolish. I had identified too much with his own sense of betrayal. But, now it was released, I could not keep the bitterness out of my own voice.

'My wife and I are separated by circumstances. For the moment. That is all. I have every trust in her and she in me. Do you understand?'

Up to that moment I had kept a shred of belief. Or hope. Why else had I reserved a place for her on the ship until that day? But putting it into words, having to say it, reduced it, hollowed it.

He bowed his head. 'Of course I understand, Tom, and apologise if I have given any offence. I certainly did not mean it.'

We went off in silence for a short space but, just as he could not leave his obsession alone, neither could I. It was like a sore to which my fingers kept returning. 'What do you mean – accepted?' I thought he knew exactly what I meant, but he gave me another puzzled look. 'You said my wife was accepted. What do you mean?'

He prevaricated, saying he should have realised how sensitive the subject was. When I persisted he told me she had gone to Holland with Lucy. For days, he said, Lady Stonehouse looked as lost as he was, milling about amongst the people looking for favours and positions. Then Richard Stonehouse presented her to the King. She made – he chose his words carefully – an immediate impression. So much so that Barbara Villiers, the King's mistress, was quite put out.

'What nonsense! It's difficult enough to believe my wife and father could be reconciled. Impossible that Richard would ever present the wife of a regicide to the King.'

He brought out his cravat again. 'She is among the party greeting the King today. Part of a special presentation to him.'

'Special presentation? Who on earth told you that?'

'It is all round the Exchange.'

I stared at him with renewed suspicion. Anne part of a special presentation! But I drew back from another clumsy accusation.

'What nonsense. Six months ago it was all round the Exchange the King would never return.'

'True, very true,' he said, in heartfelt tones. He slumped down in a corner of the cart, cutting such a pathetic figure I felt a tinge of guilt at suspecting him.

The carter stopped at the junction with the main road. There were so many people on the cliffs cheering and shouting and struggling for places, and craning and peering, they threatened to tumble into the sea. Maypoles had been erected. From every building fluttered yellow flags emblazoned with *CR*. I put my glass to my eye. Standing out at sea, a short distance away, furled sails fluttering, was a vessel I knew as Cromwell's flagship, *The Naseby*, in recognition of the decisive conflict that had won the war. It had been painted over and renamed *Royal Charles*.

'Go right,' I said.

'Deal is left, sir,' the carter said.

'A little way. Do not get tangled up with the crowds.'

In a narrow space between the buildings, through the glass, I could see a tent on the beach, flying a royal standard. From it scurried Mr Pepys, puffing with exertion, ordering a naval guard to one side, talking urgently to the Mayor, who had a white staff in one hand and a large Bible in the other. They vanished from my view. A fusillade of cannon rolled like thunder round the harbour. I spotted a clear space further down the hill, but the crowd was too thick for the cart to approach.

'Wait there.'

I jumped from the cart, pushing my way through the crowd. Taller than the people round him, the young King – he was not yet thirty – stood silently on Dover beach. He could have been a statue, apart from the wind stirring his own dark hair. No appearance in a cathedral could have matched that moment. Nothing he might have said could match what he did. For a moment his lips curled below his pencil-line moustache and, as he viewed the tier upon tier of cheering faces dwindling into silence, a hint of what might have been amusement flickered across his face. Then he dropped to his knees on the beach and pressed his lips into the sand. Impossible even for me not to feel a lump in the throat before the crowd erupted. I swung the glass round. There were the noblemen. There was Richard. My father had fallen to the ground too, tears on his face. He believed the tall figure rising from the beach was divine. I moved the glass. There she was. Anne stood out because, amongst all the colour and pageantry, she was wearing black. Among the ecstatic faces, only hers remained still. Did I imagine it, or was there an amused look on her face, a faint echo of the King's?

There was a cry and the sounds of a struggle from further up the street. The carter was falling to the ground. Clarke was standing up in the cart. I thought he was going to help the carter but he climbed into the driver's seat, seized the whip from its socket and cracked it at the horse, which jerked forward, almost throwing him. The cart careered crazily down the hill. I leapt forward, aiming to catch at the reins. The whip caught me a stinging cut on the cheek. I rolled away from the hooves as people pressed against walls, yelling in alarm.

The cart disappeared round the corner in the direction of the harbour. I went to help up the carter.

'Madman! Just hit me … no reason, no reason!'

I picked up the oiled packet and ripped it open with my knife. The top sheet was one of the Putney papers but the rest was a mixture of old pamphlets and blank sheets. No wonder he had been so anxious I should not open them until we were on board. I had ten, perhaps fifteen minutes to get out of the place. Before I had even reached the road to Deal I knew it was hopeless. There was no farm in sight where I might get a horse. Even if I did, I would risk leading my pursuers to the ship and endangering the whole enterprise. My only hope lay in the crowds.

At the bottom of the hill the cart was skewed over the road, with one man calming the horse and others all shouting at once to a constable. I was tempted to reclaim it but in the darkness of a doorway saw one of Richard's mercenaries.

It was now mid-afternoon. There was no chance of catching the ship and I determined to do the last thing they expected: go towards the beach and then make my way in the opposite direction to Folkestone.

I was carried by the crowd past market stalls that had sold out of food and small beer, but some enterprising hawkers were preparing to sell sand. One tore old pamphlets into strips while the other poured sand into them and twisted them into makeshift paper bags, which he dropped into a tray behind him.

'As kissed by his Royal Highness,' said one. 'Sell a few bags of that, Jake, and you can live comfortable for a year.'

I squeezed between the stalls and, while they were preparing another tray, snatched up the one they had filled, hearing their arguments as I slipped down an alley.

'What did you do with it?'

'I never touched it!'

Coming out of the alley the sun was blinding. There were so many people I could not see the beach. Above the roar of the crowd were the raucous cries of gulls, dipping, wheeling, snatching up discarded bits of food. A bird dived at the tray, rising with a paper bag in its beak. One of Richard's mercenaries was staring at me. I pushed the tray at him, finding the voice of the youth I had been, that London street whine.

'As kissed by the King. Cure anything. One penny.'

He pushed me away in contempt. A sailor with his protesting girl picked up a bag. 'Any good for love?'

'Never fails. Look how successful the King is.'

He dropped a penny in the tray and carried away the shrieking, laughing girl. I sold more. I could have emptied the tray. Then I saw her. She was just one of a group of noblemen and women, on the periphery of it, while I was hemmed in at the rear of the crowd held back by soldiers, all waiting for the King to appear and step on the coach which would take him to Canterbury.

He came out of the tent to tumultuous applause, smiling and lifting his hand. With him was Richard. He was pointing to a carriage I recognised as Lucy's. The King paused. Richard was gazing round searchingly, beckoning, and the nobles made way for Anne. She did not hurry. Among the women in their tight-boned bodices, skirts, frills, laces and jewellery, agitating their fans at flushed faces, in her simple black dress, with the barest flicker of embroidered underskirt showing as she walked, she looked as cool as if she was in her own drawing room.

Her curtsey was just a little too long in deference, but not long enough to be mocking. They held their gaze a fraction too much. What Clarke had told me was true. They knew one another, although few would have realised it but me. I supposed the King had had much practice at it. A moment later the thought came: in her long years at Highpoint, so had she.

She signalled to Lucy, who was near her coach, and Lucy gave an order to a footman. He opened the boot. Two servants took from it something wrapped in cloth and brought it to the King. Richard unfurled the cloth, revealing a Van Dyck of the King's father, as he loved to be seen, in black armour. I remembered it from Highpoint. I had never allowed her to hang it. The King, visibly moved, bowed his head. Several noblemen, who saw the executed King as a martyr, fell to their knees, hands clasped in devotion. Another picture was being shown. Fighting to see over the heaving crowd, I glimpsed a Holbein that had been a centrepiece of the long gallery at Highpoint. I squeezed and pushed and elbowed as I struggled to see. The leaden sky, with a copper-coloured sun, seemed to press down on me. The sea sounded like the mutter of thunder.

The third picture was a Titian, *The Naked Venus*. That, too, was one of the prize exhibits at Highpoint, albeit in a secluded room, away from Puritan eyes. Fans stopped fluttering and there were knowing looks as the King turned from the curves of Venus to Anne. Her final gift drew gasps from the crowd. It was a crystal-glass goblet which drew shafts of light from the clouded sun. It was exquisitely engraved with the royal standard and the letters *CR*.

'It might work,' she had said to Sam.

She was returning what she had bought – *I* had bought – from the Royal Collection. It was her redemption. And that of the Stonehouse family. The crowd was like a vice round me. It was impossible to breathe. The muttering sea became a roar. Someone had put a noose round my neck. No. It was some kind of tray. With it I began to batter my way through the crowd. There was a knife in my hand. Was it my scream, or the ear-splitting screech of the gulls?

Later, I was told, I managed to get within two feet of her. It took four men to hold me down. By the time they took me away she had gone, part of the King's party, on their way to Canterbury. The last thing I saw at Dover was Mr Clarke talking earnestly to Richard. At last, it seemed, he had obtained his position.

38

London was itself again, doing what it did best: making money and enjoying itself. The cleverest thing Charles did was the same as when he took over the country: nothing. He let Parliament squabble over whose land had been taken over by whom. He was above all that. Of course it was all happening off-stage. Soon it became clear the King would have control over the army again: it was as if the revolution had never happened. The harvest was in. Bread was cheaper again and, naturally, that was due to the King. What London wanted now were circuses.

It had been starved of theatre for eleven years. The Red Bull, often raided by Puritans, opened with *All's Lost by Lust*, a strange choice for an age in which everything seemed to be gained by it. But the biggest free show in town was anticipated to be the execution of the regicides. There were about ten of us imprisoned in the Tower. It had been so long from the arrest through the tedium of the trials that when I was woken on the day of execution it felt like a blessed relief.

Day after day Richard had questioned me. Partly it was about my soul. He did not believe I was his son. I must have been taken over by the Devil. If I confessed it might save my soul and, crucially for him, go some way to exonerate the Stonehouse name. But partly – mostly – his questioning was on a more secular plane.

By slow degrees, Highpoint was crumbling into ruin. Alone of the great landed seats, there was no settlement or compromise found by Parliament for the lands Richard had lost. It was not only the poor hill farms I had sold; rich arable lands, meadows, forests and villages had been sold or were heavily in debt. The life-blood of Highpoint had been drained from it. I was dizzy as he placed document after legal document before me.

'Is that your signature?'

'No.'

He struck me. 'Is that your signature?'

'It looks very like.'

He thumb-screwed and racked me. 'Is that your signature?'

'Yes, yes!'

But however much he had me beaten I could not tell him where the money was. I had no idea. The treasures of Highpoint were still missing. Lawyers, besieged with similar problems, said it would take years to untangle. I was overawed by what Anne had done. If anyone was in league with the Devil, she was.

'Ask the King's whore,' I said.

He struck me so violently I lost a tooth. She was a saint, he declared. Still in black, she prayed to the martyred King for forgiveness. It beggared belief, but he seemed to believe it.

So, feeling nothing could be much worse than I had already been through, on a chill October morning I was glad to be taken from my bed to Charing Cross, where a special gibbet had been erected. Some took drink beforehand but I would have none of it. I was drunk on the occasion itself. It was as if I had been preparing for it all my life. Had I not sworn, when I had first come to London, that I would end the journey either with great treasure, or at Paddington Fair?

The London mob – that great animal, of which I had once been part when it had brought down the King – met me with a deafening roll of sound, jeers, catcalls, cheers, spiced with a hail of rubbish and stones. Some sensitive souls believe that a man should not be executed like a cock, or a bear in a pit. I am not one of them. You have one last chance in life. How you die. The mob knows it. Among the screaming, distorted faces you glimpse the colder, calculating ones, descendants of the Roman crowd, ready to turn their thumbs up or down. I was a double bill. Not only was I a regicide, I had tried to murder my long-suffering wife, whose Royalist son I had killed.

Major-General Harrison, who told me he was not afraid to meet his Maker, was the first course. Shackled in a cart, I was given a ringside seat. He was drawn to the gibbet in a hurdle, then helped up the steps, dazed and bleeding. He was as stubborn and irascible as he had been when I tried to get him to leave the country. The Ordinary asked if he confessed his sins.

Harrison cuffed at his bad leg to stop it trembling and stared at the Ordinary as if he was a junior officer on a charge. '*My* sins, sir? Soon I will be at the side of Jesus to judge yours.'

They hanged him. His voice croaked, his tongue protruded, blood seeped from his bulging eyeballs. Then, like a miracle, the rope snapped. The nubbing-men cut the noose from Harrison's throat. I prayed he was dead. Mercifully, he made no movement.

But when they pulled him up his eyes jerked open, wide and staring. He tried to speak but that irascible voice, at least, was dead. They put him on a bench and pulled down his britches. The executioner cut off his prick and balls. There was pandemonium as he held them up to the crowd. One wit cried they were too small for a Major-General. Another bet mine would be twice as big. Next the executioner cut out his bowels. A man with his hands locked into prayer yelled in terror that, among the green and yellow slime, he could see snakes, the regicide's familiars, writhing to get away. The executioner hastily dumped the guts in a brazier on the scaffold, put there for that purpose.

'Can you not hear them hissing?' the man screamed.

At this point, God took mercy on Harrison. His eyes were open, but he saw nothing.

I was scarcely done with praying for Harrison's soul before my cart began to roll forward and I had to take concern for my own. But, to my amazement, and the great disappointment of the crowd, I was taken back to the Tower. I was told the list was full that day but I soon discovered the real reason.

In an age of cruelty my father was a master of it. He had refined his arts in Catholic France, where the Church blessed any form of torture designed to save the victim's soul.

It is an old adage among torturers that it is often just as effective, and certainly less wearisome, to show the irons instead of using them. Richard went one better. He showed their effect. He broke me. It was the dark night of my soul. I confessed the Devil from birth, a stray dog that wandered the Tower as my familiar. They slaughtered the dog and all but slaughtered me. I confessed everything except what he wanted to know. If I had had the answer to that question I would have told him, but it was as if the Devil himself had spirited away everything from Highpoint: land, money, treasures, leaving only the shell to crumble away and rot. I confessed that. That night I was crazy enough to believe it.

At least they let me have visitors. Scogman came, full of his usual plans. There would be a regiment of former colleagues on the occasion. A rescue would be effected. I scarcely listened but when, with some diffidence, he brought out a crumpled piece of paper which he said was a message from Little Dick, I seized it. There was an incomprehensible scribble, followed by a U, then a very shaky D which collapsed into another scribble.

'Why! He is getting along famously,' I said.

'Is he?' said Scogman doubtfully.

'There is a "B",' I hazarded, 'an "L-E-S", then "U", followed by his name.'

'Well, now you point it out, sir, I see 'em.' Scogman's eyes shone with pride. 'You think the little brat will be able to write?'

'No doubt of it,' I said, smoothing out the paper and folding it carefully. 'This is treasure. These are words that will change the world.'

He thought me mad then. So did Sam when he sidled through the doorway, apprehensive of his reception, surprised when I held him and kissed him, but I told him I understood. She was like a candle to a moth. He grew even more uncomfortable when I congratulated him on the goblet, mumbling that she had come to him with another commission from the King. It was she who told him he must go to see me.

'She said that? Did she say anything about me?' He shook his head. 'Nothing? Nothing again?'

His stammer, which success had controlled, came back in full force. 'She was very ... a-a-agitated.'

'Agitated? Was she. Was she indeed. Agitated. Well, Sam, when you see her again, please be good enough to tell her that I share her agitation.'

They picked me up from the hurdle on which I had been drawn to Charing Cross, all the bravura I had shown on my previous visit gone. I struggled to stand up, let alone walk to the scaffold. But I clutched tight hold of a small wad of paper, the first words of Little Dick, or thereabouts, words, I prayed, not that would change the world, but make it a little better. Deafened by the noise, half-blinded by blood trickling from a gash in my forehead, I would have confessed all my sins to the waiting Ordinary, but for a jeer from the crowd.

'Where is your Good Old Cause now?'

I looked at the child's scribble in my hand. 'Here!' I yelled, putting my hand on my heart. 'And here,' putting my hand on my head.

'And here!' shouted Scogman, lifting his hand.

'And here!' John Wildman, who had written *An Agreement of the People*, raised his hand.

'Here!' A shaky stick went up from the old man who had fought street battles with me in the Trained Band.

More hands went up. It was not the regiment Scogman had promised, but it was enough to make the officials nervous that the mob was turning.

'What is that paper he is holding?' screamed one.

The Ordinary snatched the child's scribble and dropped it as if it was hot. 'It is the Devil's writing. Burn it.'

While it was being picked up with tongs and taken to the brazier, I slipped a sovereign I had hidden into the hand of the hangman. 'Be a good fellow and do a proper job.'

The coin was swallowed up in his hand, the rough hemp put round my neck as careful as if it was fitted by a tailor. Below me, the gaping, suddenly silent faces – Mr Pepys, of course, hand twitching as if he was already scribbling his neat shorthand, the Ordinary gabbling, then my stomach heaving, the clouds boiling like a raging sea roaring in my ears and lungs. Then sweet stillness, merciful blackness.

39

Unmerciful light, blinding as the pain. My soiled britches being ripped off. The hangman had cheated me. Just as carefully as he had put the hemp round my throat, he cupped my balls in his hand. They held me down. No need to stop my voice. It had gone. Every breath I took was a searing agony. The crowd erupted as he showed them the knife. I shut my eyes. *Get on with it. Please get on with it.*

As quickly as it had swelled, the crowd's roar died to a questioning, wondering murmur.

'In the King's name!'

I could see nothing except the knife, the hangman still gripping me, until there was the rattle of boots on the scaffold. Richard stood above me, holding a piece of paper. Even at that moment my printer's eye noted it as the best Dutch weave, with a seal swinging from it. With Richard were two men in the King's livery. One of them was saying that release was to be effected immediately. When Richard demanded to see the King he was told he was in the country: at Greenwich, or Oatlands or Hampton Court.

It was a trick, of course. Another of Richard's tricks to get out of me what I could not tell him. I pleaded with them to finish it, but no sound came out of my throat. They put a sheet over me and carried me on a litter through the crowd. I struggled, hoping that the mob would put an end to me, but they watched in bewildered silence as I was put on the floor of a coach, thrown this way and that before I was pulled out. I was at the back of Whitehall, that great labyrinth of buildings where John Thurloe had ruled for ten years and which the King was using as his palace.

She was standing there. Still in black. A half-mask and hood covered her face. It began to dawn on me then, but before I could open my mouth I caught the sickly sweet smell of laudanum as a rag was clamped over my face.

The world came back gradually, in fits and starts, bits and pieces, the jogging of the coach, the creak of leather, a clean shirt, buttons in the wrong holes, the smell of rosemary.

'How ...' It was meant to be 'how did you get the pardon?' but it came out as a strangulated croak. Still she understood it. I could see from the look in her face. We never needed words.

'Not now. I thought the laudanum would let you sleep until ...'

She pointed out of the window. We were in the flat marsh country of the Thames, with dykes and, here and there, a few sheep lifting their heads, their bells ringing eerily in the evening mist. In the distance, where the widening mouth of the river met the sea, was the ghostly line of the masts and sails of Gravesend. She told me the pardon was conditional on me leaving the country immediately. She was horribly nervous. She kept glancing back down the road, as if the King might already have changed his mind.

I had forgotten how vulnerable she could appear, the brittleness of her voice, the tiny shiver of her lips before she spoke. It was an act, of course. Designed to stop me asking any further questions.

I tried again. 'Why ...'

She stared out of the window as if she had not heard the word, or the noise from my throat. I leaned over to touch her. She shrank back with a shudder. I saw it then. She was getting rid of me. It was because of her I had signed the death warrant. This was to ease her conscience, salve her soul so she could go back to her King. I managed a word then. It tore at my raw throat.

'Whore.'

She hammered at the front of the coach. I only just managed to catch the strap to avoid being flung forward. 'Use that word again and you can get out of the coach.'

She was shaking, constantly twisting the ringlets framing her face, so agitated I could feel her breath. I opened the door. A startled sheep scuttered across the marsh. I would take a chance. I had always taken my chances. But my legs would not obey me, the marsh mist had an October clamminess and I could feel that hand on my balls. I shut the door.

'I am sorry, Martin,' she called to the coachman. 'But please hurry. You must catch the tide.'

Her voice became warm and considerate. The servants would do anything for her. She treated them like human beings. Richard had had no chance: I almost felt sorry for him. Martin lashed at the horses and for a while she was silent, holding on to the strap, staring out at the marsh and the leaden line of the river as it gradually fused into the lowering clouds. When she did speak she did not look at me. At first I thought she was speaking to herself.

'Do you know what it has been like? Do you? Have you *any* idea? When I went to see Samuel and he told me that you had gone to exchange yourself for Luke, I knew it was true. Only a fool like you would do that.'

Her voice choked in her throat. I put my arm out to her but she shook her head violently. The words, dammed up for months, poured out of her. Did I think she believed Richard's lies? She did not need Samuel to tell her Richard killed Luke. She determined to continue what my mother had begun before I was born. Destroy the Stonehouses. The story had always fascinated her. How, after Lord Stonehouse had caused her father's death by ruining his estate, my mother was determined to ruin him. It haunted her. She wore black, just like my mother did. Nothing attracted men more than black. And grief. For the first time she smiled. It was edged with bitterness, but it was a smile.

'In Holland your father could scarcely keep his hands off me.'

The coach clattered over cobbles, down Gravesend High Street. She had been so deep in her story she came to with a start, her agitation returning. She glanced up and down the street, at every cart and carriage, as the coach made its way to the quay.

'My father –'

'He was too late.'

'Too –'

'The King saw me.'

She still had not answered my first question about how she had got the pardon, but we were suddenly caught up in a rush of last-minute boarders, officials, papers being scrutinised, sailors shouting. Among the chaos her agitation vanished. She was an oasis of calm. As always, she had organised everything perfectly, from booking our passage to obtaining papers. We were Thomas Black, Esq., and his wife once more. Our papers were in order. It would not have mattered if they were not. She was charm itself, full of apologies at being so late, but Mr Black was ill and needed help. The fact that it was true only increased my bitterness about her evasions.

As soon as we were on board her smiles went out like a snuffed candle. Her anxiety returned when there was a delay. Nobody knew the reason. It was the tide or the weather. Or they were waiting for someone. She moved restlessly among passengers waving goodbye to people standing on the quay. Her eyes kept returning to the entrance of the quay. By now my voice, or at least a hoarse ghost of it, was returning.

'What is it? I am free to leave. What are you frightened of?'

She turned on me with a sudden violence. 'The King was easy. Much easier than I expected. I could look at him like this.' She gave me a glance: a woman secretly observing a man, then, surprised, jerking away in confusion. 'Or this.' A longer, lingering look that made my heart beat faster. 'Or this.' She lifted her lowered face with a look of such intense suffering it would have pierced any man's heart. 'How can I when my husband is about to –'

She blindly turned towards me. I put my arms round her. Her breath came in great gulping swallows. 'You signed the death warrant but it was *my* signature. As good as. I could not bear the thought of –'

'If you had told me something …'

'You would have stopped me. I know you. You would have –'

She pulled away, spent. People were staring and we moved further down the deck. Sailors were shouting, unfurling the top sails. She began to breathe more easily, spoke almost matter-of-factly, watching sailors scramble up the rigging. The King promised her the pardon if they became lovers. She wanted the pardon first. He wanted the proof of her feelings for him first. The more she refused, the more he wanted her. It was a game he was good at. He had the pardon prepared, with the seal. But he did not sign it. So still she refused. He left the pardon with her to reflect on it.

The ship was cast off, tilting, juddering uncertainly for a moment before the wind caught the sails. A small smile played round her lips. 'Barbara Villiers, the King's mistress, hated me. She wanted to get rid of me. I wanted to leave him. We were the perfect combination. I feared she would never entice him away to the country before it was too late, but …'

There was a sudden swirl of activity at the gate and distant shouting. The tide was quickening, spray flying as we pulled out into the mouth of the estuary, and it was difficult to see but I thought I glimpsed Richard dismounting and arguing with officials.

She remained motionless, gripping the rail, watching the sketchy grey lines of the land disappear until the wind freshened, the rigging sang, and the sails snapped and tautened, and we were out in the open sea.

'I forged the King's signature,' she said.

Epilogue

Boston, Mass., April 1775

That was the story she told, and Tom never contradicted it. The truth, however, was rather different – but first things first.

My name is Joseph Thomas Black, although in these tumultuous times, when another name is handy, people know me as Joe Neave. I am the great-grandson of Anne and Thomas Black, as they were first registered when they landed in Boston in late November 1660. Not a good month to land in Boston, with the worst of the winter storms to come, particularly when you are sick. I know how ill she was because it was one thing they both agreed on.

I take my information from a jumbled mass of papers in an old tin chest which had remained untouched for years, but which, when it did not reduce me to despair, turned out to be the treasure trove Tom talked about as a boy.

The winter of 1660 was a cruel one and she was sick for most of it. All his doubts and recriminations vanished. He rarely left her side. He even lost his doubts in God and prayed for her. He willed her to live. In despair he wrote: *It is as if she wants to die.*

It was not until he realised that the prolongation of her illness was because she was pregnant that their normal relationship – if I may

337

put it that way – was resumed. In the tin chest, together with the manuscript were daily notes, scribbles that he might put in the story later, a habit that he may have caught from Pepys. A page of calculations suggested that if the baby was very early it might be his. The boy was early, but not that early. She was adamant it was his. Nevertheless, when he saw the child he left her.

He set up a business, Thos. Black Printer, which is the firm I now own. A year or two later, how I do not know – one of the curses of that chaotic tin box lies in the gaps you can never hope to fill – he met the child. Tom loved children. Perhaps the best evidence of this is that in his hand on the scaffold he had not a prayer but a child's first attempt at forming words. It is my guess that the child brought them back together, whether or not he believed Joseph – my grandfather – was his child.

Anne built a large manor house near Boston. She called it Pearce Hall, after Tom's mother, whom he never saw, and with whom the whole story began. Gradually, over the years, apart from the pictures, she reassembled nearly all the treasures from Highpoint that she had sold or stored. He spent most of his time in Boston, helping other regicides, or building up the business as a radical printer and publisher: it was almost as before – almost – because they now seemed to accept that they could not live together, but could not live without one another.

He died first, in 1675, Anne much later, in 1704. Several times she determined to destroy the papers – what remains of the American section are charred fragments – but in the end could not bear to. Instead she scored through passages or made virulent comments in her increasingly shaky hand – when he described himself as a compulsive writer, she wrote *compulsive lier!* – and in this way continued to argue bitterly with him right up to the end. She did not destroy the papers because she missed him more than she could bear to say, even to herself. But that is my conjecture, and you must take it or leave it.

I have nearly done. The book is set up in type. I will proof it and print it if I see this present business through. I decided to publish it not just as a family history but as the story of Tom's dream of liberty, which was imported here along with the money and treasures of Highpoint – necessary power and influence, if you like.

Never more necessary than this April night. It has bought guns and powder to fight the King's redcoats. I am a member of the Sons of Liberty and one of the minutemen – very like Tom's Trained Bands which drove the King out of the City of London. Just as he ran through the streets with speeches against ship money, he would have been there, dumping tea in the harbour. No taxation without representation!

I can hear the sound of their horse, the tramp of the redcoats' boots as they march to Lexington where – they think – our armoury is.

I must go – but I almost forgot. I said she did not tell the whole truth when they left the country. Nor did she move an iota from her story while Tom was alive. But when she was near the end she confessed the truth to Tom, at least in the sense that she wrote it next to the neat Italianate script of which he was so proud. She dated it 10th November 1704, a few days before she died at the age of seventy-eight. She did not intend to go quietly. Her writing, which had become increasingly shaky and erratic, found a sudden strength. She wrote with a bitterness that almost drove the pen through the paper:

> *The King cheated me. He showed me the pardon and said he would sign it. He would do anything for me. So I laye with him a number of times. I thought you would go free & I would have my place in the land but once he had me he left me to go to that bitche in Hampton Court. He did not even trouble to take that piece of paper away … I lookt at it & lookt at it and I had done it so often with you and so –*

The entry ends with a splatter of ink across the page, as if in writing it she had rekindled the rage that had consumed her then. Perhaps it was rage as much as anything that fuelled her to forge the King's signature on the pardon. The contempt for her he showed: 'He did not even *trouble* …' No wonder she kept on looking behind her on the road to Gravesend and evaded Tom's questions. He wrote that she was anxious. Anxious! She must have been appalled as it gradually sank in what she had done. They would have been hanged together if they had been caught.

They were never hunted, unlike other regicides. Two colonels, Goffe and Whalley, were forced to hide in caves for three years in Connecticut, supported by republican well-wishers. But Tom and Anne were never pursued or even identified. As the King reflected on it, he must have thought that the last thing he wanted was the truth to come out.

Whatever Tom felt about it, he would have appreciated the irony that, as I pick up my gun to combat the King's redcoats, I have royal blood in my veins.

Historical Note

The Restoration was set in motion when General Monck marched over the Scottish border. 'Honest George' – as his soldiers called him – kept his cards close to his chest. Probably he himself was far from certain how he was going to play them. He wrote to the Rump Parliament in Westminster on 29th December 1659 that he 'awaited their further commands', but three days later, without any such commands or warning, he marched.

His trump card was that he had the only fully functioning army in the country. His soldiers were well equipped and paid. He purged his officers so he could rely on their loyalty. His march turned into a coup, but that may not have been his intention when he crossed the border. On his way to London he consulted both the Rump Parliament and the King (through an obscure cousin of his, Sir Richard Grenville).

When Monck arrived in London on 3rd February, civil government was in total confusion – there had been seven changes of government in the previous year. The leader of the Rump, Sir Arthur Haselrig, had a single-chamber Parliament of only forty-seven members and threadbare legitimacy. The City was threatening not to pay taxes. Monck knew that if he supported Haselrig his soldiers would not be paid. If he backed the City they would insist on a 'free Parliament' – elections that would mean a majority of Royalists and bring back the King. On 11th February, after much agonising, he threw in his lot with the City.

One of Haselrig's many self-inflicted wounds was getting rid of John Thurloe as Secretary of State. Monck had him reinstated. Like Monck, Thurloe was a pragmatist. Both men knew that the key obstacle to a successful return of the King was a violent, unbridled Royalist reaction. On the night when Monck made his decision, London's actual response was a celebration – 'the burning of the rump'. Pepys, who began writing his diary the previous month, thought it spontaneous 'past imagination, both the greatness and the suddenness of it'. From one view, at Strand Bridge, he counted thirty-one fires alone. It is difficult to believe it was not orchestrated and that is how I have portrayed it – Londoners had their fill of rump steaks (the fireworks were my dramatic addition).

When the King returned, Thurloe was accused of high treason and imprisoned in the Tower. However, his knowledge of foreign affairs was too valuable to lose and many Royalists were apprehensive of accusations he might make against them. A deal was struck and he was released. He never held office again but was consulted (in secret) by the new administration.

I have sadly maligned William Clarke who, in reality, was secretary to the Army Council and who recorded the Putney debates. Three books is a long journey and during it he was transformed from a fictional Mr Ink to the real-life Clarke. In the writing, as some characters do, he went his own way, became Mr Ink again and betrayed Tom, but I have no evidence that the solid, worthy Mr Clarke would do this. That being said, Clarke (described as a 'mysterious figure' by one historian) was one of nature's survivors, a bureaucrat who slipped from one regime to another. He worked under General Monck, became Charles II's Secretary at War and was knighted. He was killed on Monck's flagship in 1666 during war with the Dutch.

Lead crystal glass was first successfully produced in England in the 1670s by George Ravenscroft. It would have been perfectly possible for Sam to produce a form of it using Christopher Merrett's translation of the Italian book. In fact Merrett commented wistfully in 1662: 'glass of lead, 'tis a thing unpractised in our furnaces … because of the exceeding brittleness … could this glass be made as tough as that of crystalline, 'twould far surpass it in the glory and beauty of its colours'.

Tom's vision of transplanting the seeds of republicanism with a written Constitution was no pipe dream. New England was not only a safer place for regicides because of its distance from London. Such regicides were more likely to be welcomed and sheltered by exiles of similar views. In 1660, when Tom and Anne landed, Boston was a thriving city, the key trading centre in Britain's Atlantic Empire. Cromwell, who had once thought of emigrating to Massachusetts, had a particular sympathy for it during his Protectorate, allowing it to produce its own currency. Three regicides, Whalley, Goffe and Dixwell, were hidden and helped by New Englanders in Massachusetts and Connecticut for almost thirty years.

The Civil War not only shaped the country that Britain became, a state without a written Constitution, headed by a monarch without power, but it seeded more permanent revolutions. Like Tom's grandson, many of the soldiers who fought in the American War of Independence would have been descended from men who fought with Cromwell.

Acknowledgements

Many thanks to Katy Whitehead who, with her perceptive editorial comments helped steer the trilogy to its conclusion; to Georgia Mason and Morwenna Loughman for producing it so smoothly and efficently; to my copy editor, Helen Gray for picking up my inconsistencies; my researcher, Deborah Rosario, for answering so many questions; and, not least, my wife Cynthia for keeping me (more or less) sane and reminding me, from time to time, that I was living in the twenty-first century, not the seventeenth. Finally, it might seem odd to thank my main characters, but without them where would I be? A very long story, however one may plan it, will always go its own way and Tom and Anne kept surprising me, right up to the very end.